A burned-out pop diva runs away from fame and falls for a handsome Roman Catholic priest, who allows her to hide inside a Church rectory in an idyllic small town known as the *real-life Mayberry*.

Grace Stevens has it all. Beauty. Fame. Money. But, at only twenty-seven, *all* has become too much. Grace has become a prisoner to her own fame. She's tired of the crazy tour schedule, the intrusive fans, the paparazzi hounding her, and her sleazy business manager controlling her. She yearns for a normal life. And she wants to find love, true love.

Danny O'Connor is a thirty-one-year-old Roman Catholic priest and a combat veteran of the Afghan War. He suffers from severe PTSD. Danny made a battlefield promise to God that if He got him safely home from war, he'd become a priest.

Reluctantly, Danny agrees to allow Grace to hide inside the St. Mary's Church rectory, where she takes up residence with him. What he didn't count on, though, was falling in love with her. Now, he's confronted with the ultimate choice — will he choose God or the girl? Will he break his vow of celibacy in the heat of passion or abide by his commitment to the Church?

Just Grace and Danny is a slow burn but steamy romance about the power of love to mend brokenness. It's a triumph of small-town values over the bright lights of the big city. It will get into your laughter, your heart, your soul. And maybe even a little into your tears. And leave you craving penny candy from a small town five and dime store, and *bubble gum kisses* in the rain.

Just Grace and Danny
Copyright © 2021 Arthur Archambeau
ISBN: 978-1-4874-3213-3
Cover art by Martine Jardin

Published by eXtasy Books Inc

Look for us online at:
www.eXtasybooks.com

JUST GRACE AND DANNY

BY

ARTHUR ARCHAMBEAU

DEDICATION

For the heroes. The real heroes. The ones who lived up to it. You know who you are. I hope this book helps others know you.

CHAPTER ONE: THE RUNAWAY

Grace Stevens was literally sick and tired. And the rain was coming down so hard that she could barely see through the windshield of her silver *Mitsubishi Mirage* rental car. The GPS in her vehicle was malfunctioning. And she hadn't been able to find her phone, so she had no access to any information or directions. All she knew was that she was headed northbound on Interstate 95, somewhere in Maryland. She had no particular destination in mind.

Grace was one of the most popular and successful female entertainers in the world, and, now, at only twenty-seven, she was burned-out. She had it all—beauty, money, fame. But *all* had become too much.

The final straw was her manager, Kip Darby, telling her she had to perform that night's show at the Baltimore Arena, despite the fact that she felt lousy and was running a temperature of 101. "I'm not going to tell twelve thousand people that we have to cancel the goddamn show," he'd warned her. So, she signed for a rental car at the hotel and took off. She ran away without telling anyone where she was going, just wanting to disappear from the face of the earth.

Her throat was sore, and her head was pounding. She had the chills. And now she was driving through a torrential downpour. A good old-fashioned April thunderstorm.

The guy behind her was driving a tractor-trailer and kept flashing his lights because she was only going forty miles per hour. "Screw you, asshole. I can't see shit and I'm already in the slow lane," she muttered. He kept riding her bumper, so she looked for a place to get off the highway.

Finally, through the sheets of rain, she saw an exit ahead. It was raining hard enough that she couldn't read the town's name off the sign, but she took the exit anyway. *This is only going to get me more lost — but what the hell? Maybe getting lost is what I need.*

Once off the interstate, she took a series of random roads that led her through a small town. She could make out some of the landmarks. A country store, some antique shops, a small pharmacy. *Such a tiny little town. Where am I?*

She looked for a place to pull over, somewhere to ride out the storm. Somewhere to collect her thoughts. As she drove through Main Street, she squinted through the windshield to identify possible candidates.

Then, at the south end of town, she saw it. A Civil War-era church. A large white sign with black lettering out front read — *St. Mary's Catholic Church, Established 1863. Church Open 24/7 For Prayer and Meditation. All Welcome.* She talked to herself. "Well, I guess I'm part of the *all*." She made a right turn into the church's lot and parked. Tilting her head back, she closed her eyes and rubbed her temples. It was good to be off the road. She wasn't accustomed to driving. It stressed her out. A chauffeur generally drove her.

She rummaged through her purse, frantically looking for her phone. Like everyone, she felt naked without it. *It has to be in here somewhere.* But she couldn't find it. Finally, she dumped the contents of her *Louis Vuitton* handbag on the passenger's side front seat and sifted through everything. Some bubble gum, a small pack of tissues, a taser, a tube of coconut scented moisturizer, a pack of *Virginia Slims*, a couple of tampons, her wallet. But no cellphone. *Shit. I must have left it in the hotel room. Aw, who cares? It's probably blowing up with missed calls and messages by now. And I don't want to deal with that stuff anyway. No biggie. Come to think of it — it's actually better that I don't have it. If I don't have it, I can't obsess over it. It's actually kind of liberating.* She opened the cigarette box and pulled out a smoke. After she cracked the front driver's side window, she lit up. *I know I shouldn't be smoking while I'm sick, but I so need a cigarette right now.* She took deep drags and held them in her lungs before blowing them out through her nose.

After she finished her smoke, she tossed the butt out the window, grabbed her purse, and exited the car. It was still raining hard, though not as hard as it had been when she was on the highway. She had no umbrella, so she ran from the parking lot to the church's front door. Turning the handle of the large white door, she peeked inside. On this Friday afternoon, it was vacant. Tentatively, she walked in and looked around. The ceiling was high and arched. Down the center aisle, a ruby red carpet led up to an altar that featured a life-sized crucifix and a Virgin Mary statue. The place smelled of incense and was quiet except for the building's HVAC system's constant humming. *It's been a long time since I've been in one of these.*

She hacked and sneezed as she walked up the red carpet towards the front of the church. When she reached the first row of wooden pews, she stopped, set down her purse, and moved a stack of Bibles. She sprawled out, closed her eyes, and put her right hand on her forehead to check for fever. The wet jeans and t-shirt she was wearing made her feel cold. She even shivered a little. But after ten minutes or so, she drifted off to sleep to the sound of the rain hitting the stained glass windows.

She woke up when she felt someone jostle her arm. A deep male voice asked, "Miss, are you all right?"

Grace opened one eye, looked up, and saw him. He had black hair, blue eyes, and was tall. She guessed about six-feet-four inches. And he looked to be about thirty. He had an athletic build and was handsome. *Damn. He looks like JFK Jr.*

He wore a black clerical shirt with a white Roman collar, along with black pants and shoes. With a hoarse voice, Grace asked, "Who are you?" She quickly glanced down at her *TAG Heuer* watch. She'd only been asleep for a little over an hour.

He smiled at her, revealing white teeth. "I'm Father O'Connor, Daniel O'Connor. I'm the priest here at Saint Mary's. I was just checking the wine supply for Communion when I saw you lying on the pew. I wanted to make sure you're okay." She caught a whiff of his cologne. *Green Irish Tweed.* She'd recognize it anywhere. It was the cologne her father wore, and it never failed to conjure up the warm and fuzzies. She looked him up and down. *He's much too good-looking to be a Catholic priest. What a waste.*

She sat up. "I was just resting. See, I was on the highway, and between the storm and the fact that I'm not feeling too hot, I decided to take a break." She sneezed and coughed.

He nodded, smiled again, and wagged his index finger at her. "You know, I don't know if anyone's ever told you this, but you're a dead ringer for Grace Stevens—you know, the singer."

She nodded. "That's because I *am* Grace Stevens—you know, the singer." Picking up her purse, she pulled out her driver's license and handed it to him, telling him, "It has my Malibu address on it."

He looked down at it and stared at her with big eyes. He shook his head, smiled, and looked around. "Am I on some type of hidden camera show?"

She swallowed hard. *God, my throat is so sore.* "No."

A perplexed look crossed his face. "What the heck is Grace Stevens doing here?"

She shrugged. "I have to be somewhere, don't I?"

He chuckled. "Yeah, I guess you do. But here? Here in little old North East?"

"Is that the actual name of the town? *North East?*"

He nodded. "Yes. North East, Maryland. Our motto is— *North East: It's Not Just A Direction, It's A Destination.* Didn't you know where you were?"

She shook her head and coughed some more. "No."

"That's a little hard to believe. I mean—unless you're driving a seventy-eight *Gremlin,* every vehicle has GPS nowadays."

"Well, I'm driving a newer *Mirage.* But it's a rental, see? And the GPS is screwed-up. It kept saying, *recalculating, recalculating.* It never did recalculate. It froze up, I guess. I smacked it to, you know, try to get it unclogged or whatever. I was trying to get it thinking again. But then the screen just went black. I even tried screaming at it. I was all like, *come on, you son of a bitch. Work. Work, I said.* But the bastard totally ignored me. It wouldn't listen."

He again chuckled. "Yeah, well, inanimate objects can be very stubborn when it comes to listening. Even when you curse at them."

She sneezed four times in a row. When she finally stopped, she pulled a tissue from her purse, loudly blew her nose, and told him, "I know, right? I swear—it's ignorant. Just plain ignorant. I hate being ignored."

"What about your phone? Don't you have a GPS app on your phone?"

"Yeah, but I left my phone at the hotel in Baltimore—at least I think I did. So, all I really knew was that I was in Maryland and headed northbound on the interstate. That's it. And it was impossible to read any of the highway signs with the rain coming down so hard."

"Yeah, well, that's too bad, about the GPS in the car and your lost phone and all. It sounds like you had a perfect storm of bad luck. A word of advice, though—when you turn the car in, let them know that the GPS was messed-up right from the get-go, when you picked up the vehicle. Otherwise, they may try to bill you for it. And it might be a good idea to just leave out the part about smacking it."

"Look, padre, the busted GPS is the least of my concerns

right now. I could buy that whole freaking rental company if I wanted to. I don't give a damn about that. I'm just glad I got away."

He put his hands on his hips and shook his head as if to clear the cobwebs. "I'm afraid I'm very confused."

She took a deep breath and exhaled loudly. "I ran away, Father. *I. Ran. Away.* Okay?"

"You ran away? Ran away from what?"

"From everything." She patted the wooden seat of the pew and motioned for him to sit. "Sit down, and I'll tell you all about it, but don't get too close because I'm sick as hell." She looked up and added, "Sorry for using that kind of language in Your house, Lord. I know I curse like a teamster. But I am working on it. I am."

He sat down next to her, and she explained. "I can't take any more of it. It's driving me batshit crazy. I'm tired. I'm tired of being Grace Stevens. I'm tired of fame. I'm tired of the insane tour schedule. I'm tired of people liking me because of my name instead of the kind of person I am. I'm tired of the phoniness of show business. I'm tired of dealing with my asshole manager. I'm tired of not being able to go out in public without being mobbed. I'm tired of signing autographs. I'm tired of being told that I have to *cultivate my brand*. Brands are for bread and potato chips, not people. And I am, after all, a person." She looked him in the eye. "I'm just *tired*, Father. Tonight, I'm supposed to be performing in Baltimore. But I got sick, and they were still going to make me do the show. That's when I decided to just take off. I just wanted to get away. Anywhere. So, here I am." She smiled a big, cheesy, exaggerated smile, showing both her top and bottom set of teeth, and waited for him to respond.

He nodded. "I see. And what made you stop at Saint Mary's of all places?"

She shrugged. "I'm Catholic. I'm not a very good Catholic,

mind you. I haven't been to Mass or Confession in years. But I am Catholic. I don't know—I guess I just saw that sign saying *all welcome* and figured that this was as good a landing spot as any. I was desperate."

"Uh-huh. And what's your plan?"

"I don't have one. I guess I need some time to think and get better."

He nodded approvingly. "I can understand that. Is there anything that I can do for you?"

"Yes. For starters, you can keep our meeting confidential. Right now, you're the only person on earth who knows where I am. And I want to keep it that way."

"I won't say anything. But it still might be tough remaining undetected. For example, with that rental you're driving—does it have an internal tracking system that lets them see where the car is? Some rental companies install those nowadays, you know."

"Nope. I thought of that. I tried to think of everything. That's why I'm driving a *Mirage*, an economy car, instead of a *Mercedes* or *BMW*. They'll spend the money to put those in on the luxury models, but not on the economy deals. I specifically asked for one that didn't have an internal GPS. I just told them that a big star like me needs her privacy and doesn't want to be tracked. That simple. It didn't arouse an ounce of suspicion. And it wasn't even a lie. I didn't want to be tracked. Of course, they had no idea I was planning on disappearing. But that's none of their damn business anyhow."

"Wow. Impressive. You thought of everything, huh? It was a well-planned and perfectly executed operation. Seal Team Six couldn't have done it any better."

"Oh, I'm a good little schemer," she assured him.

"Indeed. But even if the world can't locate you, it'll still notice that you're missing."

She looked down at her watch. It was four o'clock. "I'm

sure it already has. I was supposed to be at the afternoon sound check a half-hour ago. I'm sure my people are already looking for me. But I don't care if the world frets over my disappearance, so long as it can't find me. At least not until I decide that I want to be found again." She looked down and fiddled with her nails. An idea crossed her mind. Tentatively, she began to make her pitch, "Father—" She had to stop because of another coughing fit. After she regained her composure, she continued. "Father, I need a place to stay for a while. Someplace quiet and private. A place where no one would ever think to look for me."

He scratched his cheek and laughed. "Well, North East is definitely a place where no one would look for a big celebrity like yourself. But it's going to be tough finding somewhere to stay within the town while maintaining your anonymity, too." He paused, then added, "And you really should see a doctor for that cold."

"No. No doctors. I don't want anyone else to know where I am. And I was kind of, sort of, thinking that maybe I could stay . . . here."

He raised his eyebrows. "Here? In the church?"

"Not in the church *per se*. Just on the property. I mean — where do you live?"

"I live in the rectory, the big brick Colonial right next to the church."

"You live alone?"

He nodded. "Of course, I live alone. Well, I do have a dog. A little Sheltie. Her name's Tippy."

"Can I stay with you? Just for a little while."

He shook his head. "Miss Stevens, I'm sorry, but that's not possible."

"Doesn't the Bible say that *with God all things are possible?*" *Oh, that was such a good point. He has to give you that one. You go, girl.*

He nervously smiled. "Yes, it does. But it's not that simple.

There are rules governing who's allowed to stay at the rectory. Besides, we don't know one another. How do you know I'm not some creep?"

She looked him in the eyes, his powder blue eyes. *Those eyes. There's passion and compassion in them. They're haunting and haunted. Yes. This surely must have been what the eyes of The Carpenter Himself would have looked like.* After a long pause, she finally answered, "Because I have faith. And isn't faith a good thing? Like I said, I'm not the best Catholic in the world, but I do believe in God. Maybe He's the one who guided me here."

He looked up at the ceiling and muttered, "Jesus, Mary, and Joseph. There's nothing in the priest handbook that covers what you do when a pop superstar wanders into your church and essentially asks for asylum."

He's softening but I still need a clincher. She bit her lower lip and again locked eyes with him. Flashing *puppy dog eyes*, she added, "All I'm asking of you is to stop looking at me as Grace Stevens — the big celebrity — and start seeing me as Grace Stevens, the human being who needs your help. Do you really think that Jesus would turn me away?" *I know what buttons to push.*

He loudly exhaled, looked at her, and shook his head. "No. Jesus wouldn't turn you away. And . . . neither will I. You can stay at the rectory. There's plenty of room. I have two spare bedrooms. You can have one."

She smiled and felt relieved. "And you won't tell anyone that I'm here, no matter what, right?"

He nodded. "I promise you confidentiality." He wagged his finger at her. "And I expect the same, by the way. You can never tell anyone that I let you stay here. I could lose my job."

"It's a deal," she promised.

He laughed, shook his head, and looked upwards. "I sure hope I'm doing the right thing, Boss."

"You are," she assured him.

He checked to make sure the coast was clear, and they

walked out of the church together. By now, it had stopped raining. She moved her car into the rectory's garage so no one would see it. He opened the house's front door, and a tan and white Sheltie immediately greeted them. The dog wagged her tail and barked excitedly. "Well, hello there, sweetie. Yes, Daddy's home."

He picked the little dog up and rubbed her belly, telling Grace, "Miss Stevens, I'd like you to meet Tippy." Grace sneezed, walked over to the dog, and shook her paw. "Pleased to meet you, Tippy."

He put the dog down and said, "And welcome to my home."

She looked around. It was a big house for only one person. The ceilings were high. There were a foyer and a staircase. On the walls hung paintings, old paintings, of important-looking men decked out in clothing from the nineteenth century. There were chairs upholstered in red and yellow velvet in the living room. Grace nodded her approval. "Not bad, Father."

"Thanks. It's not a Malibu mansion, but I'm comfortable here. The thing I enjoy the most is that we're right on the North East River. There's a little beach on the property, in the backyard." He smiled at her. They locked eyes, and she smiled back. Then she started hacking again.

"Boy, you really feel miserable, don't you?"

She nodded. "Uh-huh." She massaged her temples. "My head feels like it's going to explode."

"The first thing we need to do is get you into some dry clothes."

"I didn't bring a change of clothing with me. I have nothing except the clothes on my back and my purse."

"Okay. Well, I don't think we've had any women's clothes donated to the Outreach Office lately. But you'd be welcome to a pair of my sweatpants and a sweatshirt. Why don't you follow me upstairs, and I'll show you to your room?"

They walked up the stairs, down a long hallway, stopping at the second door on the right. He opened the door, and they walked in. The room was painted light blue, and the furnishings were sparse. There was a small desk with a mirror on it and a bed. On the wall hung a crucifix and a picture of St. Francis of Assisi that had gathered some dust. That was it. "You'll be the first person to stay in this room since I've been the priest here."

She patted the bed and sat on it. "I'll be right back with your clothes," he promised. She lay down on the bed, closed her eyes, and thought about the absolute panic that surely must have set in by now amongst the members of her entourage. *Am I being selfish for just taking off?* She wondered what the world would say about her, about her disappearance. What would the narrative be? Did it even matter to her? *Hell, no. I don't give a damn.*

After a few minutes, he returned with the clothing. An old, gray sweatshirt with a Snoopy picture on it and a pair of gray sweatpants. He excused himself, and she changed. She undressed and looked at herself in the mirror. She was short, too short, she thought. At only five-feet-two inches, she'd been turned down for jobs as a model because of her diminutive stature. They all said she looked like a young Audrey Hepburn. She had shoulder-length brown hair and big, honey-brown doe eyes. As she peeled off her wet t-shirt and white sports bra, she looked closely at her breasts. They were 34DD and looked even larger because of her small frame. She always considered them too big and once even considered having a reduction done. But her manager had told her, "There's no such thing as tits being too big, honey." Her legs were short but silky and shiny. They'd just been waxed. She knew that she was a good-looking woman, even beautiful. But where had her beauty, fame, and money gotten her? *Sick as hell and alone, that's where.* She had no husband, no boyfriend. A relationship was tough with her schedule. Besides, she'd been burned way too many times. She shrugged it off and finished dressing. The outfit was way too big for her.

She walked out of the bedroom, and he saw her. He smiled that gorgeous smile again and said, "A little too big, huh?"

"Just a little," she said as she flailed the sleeves of the sweatshirt around.

He shrugged. "It'll have to do, for now, I guess."

He paused, then asked, "How do you feel?"

She moaned. "Like someone put my head in a vice. My throat feels raw, and I think there's some cold on my chest."

"Here. Let me see if you have a fever." He walked over to her and put his hand on her forehead. His hand was large but soft and warm. She closed her eyes and absorbed his touch. Even though she was sick, his touch felt good. So good that it put butterflies in her stomach. A soft sigh escaped her lips.

"Oh, yes," he told her, "You're warm. Let me go get my digital thermometer so we can see exactly how high that temperature is. In the meantime, why don't you get in bed?"

Again, she looked at him with sad, puppy dog eyes and softly said, "Kay."

He smiled at her. "I'll be right back, Miss Stevens."

"Grace. Call me Grace. Please."

He smiled and nodded. "Okay. Grace, it is. And you may as well call me Danny. That's what my friends call me."

"So, we're just Grace and Danny?" she asked.

He laughed. "That's right. Just Grace and Danny."

He walked downstairs, and she crawled into bed. He came back with a thermometer, some over-the-counter cold medications, and a glass of water.

Her fever was 100.7.

"That's actually down a bit. It was a hundred and one," she told him.

"Yeah? Well, one-hundred-point-seven is still nothing to

sneeze at, no pun intended." He opened the bottle of *Mucinex DM*, shook out a pill, and handed it to her, along with the glass of water. "Here. I want you to take this. It's good for congestion."

She took the pill and a sip of water, then handed the glass back to him. Looking at him thoughtfully, she tilted her head and asked, "Are you going to, like, take care of me?"

He smiled and nodded. "Yes. I am. What else can I do?"

"So, I'm pretty much your responsibility right now, aren't I?"

He chuckled. "In terms of your health and safety, yes, I guess you could say that."

She reached out and grabbed his left hand. On the finger where a wedding ring would be worn, he wore a gold ring with the face of Jesus on it. She caressed his hand for a moment, and they looked at one another. There was silence as they just stared into each other's eyes. Finally, she squeezed his hand and said, "Thank you, Danny."

He nodded and winked at her. "You bet."

He left the room, and she slowly drifted off to sleep, still feeling sick. But, also, for the first time in a long, long time, feeling safe and protected.

CHAPTER TWO: TWENTY QUESTIONS

Danny sat in a recliner in the living room with his laptop out. He looked up from the keyboard and rubbed his eyes. Looking back down, he saw by the computer's time display that it was nearly midnight. He yawned and stretched out his arms. Tippy sat in her doggie bed in the corner of the room. He turned around, looked at her, and said, "Okay, girl, I think it's time to call it a night. I'll finish up this sermon tomorrow."

He sat there and thought about the events of the day. The incongruity of it all. *Life is so unpredictable. If someone would have told me twenty-four hours ago that Grace Stevens would be living here in the rectory, I'd have called them crazy.* He shook his head and laughed to himself. He walked up the stairs to Grace's room.

"Grace," he called out as he knocked. "May I come in?"

Through the door, he heard her say, "Sure. Come on in."

He walked in and saw her still in bed. "Hope I didn't wake you."

"Oh, no. I've been awake for about a half-hour."

"How are you feeling?" He sat down on the edge of the bed.

She sniffled. "About the same. What time is it anyway?"

"Zero dark thirty."

"Huh?"

"Late. Close to midnight."

She frowned. "That means I've officially missed the Baltimore show."

He nodded but told her, "Let the world turn without you tonight, okay?"

She nodded and smiled at him. "Kay."

"Are you hungry?"

She shook her head. "No. Not right now. Maybe in the morning I'll have something to eat."

"Do you need anything else? Anything at all?"

"Maybe an extra blanket if you have one. I'm cold."

"I think I should have one. Just give me a sec to find it." He left the room, retrieved a baby blue blanket from the linen closet down the hall, and returned. Again, sitting on the edge of the bed, he unfolded the blanket and spread it out over her, essentially tucking her in.

"There. How's that?" he asked.

"Much better. Thank you."

He smiled. "Well, goodnight." He started to get up off the bed when she grabbed his hand and pulled him back towards her.

"No. Don't go just yet. I'm lonely. Please stay and talk to me for a while," she begged.

He sat back down. "What would you like to talk about?"

"*You.* I'm staying in your house, and I know virtually nothing about you. I want to know who you are, Danny O'Connor."

"What would you like to know?"

"For starters, why'd you become a priest?"

Should I give her the yearbook answer about being called by God, or should I tell her the truth?

He paused and took a deep breath. Finally, he spoke. "Before I became a priest, I was a soldier. I was in the Army. A combat radio operator with the One-hundred-seventy-third Airborne Brigade Combat Team. I was in Afghanistan, in a little acre of Hell known as the Korengal Valley. It was a pretty hot area, a lot of action. The fighting was tough up there, Grace. Very tough. We were the *tip of the spear*, as they say — the real-life *Generation Kill*. One night, my platoon walked into an ambush. It was what they call an L-shaped ambush. And we walked right into their kill box. We were taking fire from several directions. I thought for sure we were all going to die — the entire platoon. So, I made a bargain with God that night. I promised that if He got me out alive, I'd become a priest and serve Him for the rest of my days."

"And you kept your promise."

He nodded. "I kept my promise. I take promises seriously."

"You live in this big house all by yourself. Don't you ever get lonely?"

"There are a lot of lonely people in the world. My own loneliness helps me to better serve those who are most in need of help. And I do have Tippy. She's a blessing. A big source of comfort."

"I don't think God wants any of us to be lonely," she countered. There was a period of silence, and they looked at one another.

She's gorgeous, even more gorgeous in person than she is on TV.

Finally, she said, "So, tell me more. Where are you from?"

"Right here in Maryland. A little town on the Eastern Shore called Warwick."

"Why'd you join the Army?"

"To be all that I could be."

"Aw, come on now. No recruiting slogans allowed. Seriously, why'd you join?"

"Well, my dad was a soldier. He was in the Gulf War. And my granddad was a Marine. He was in Vietnam. He was there for the Fall of Saigon. And before that, my great-granddad was in Korea, at a place called Heartbreak Ridge. It just seemed like I was carrying on a family tradition. And I certainly didn't want to be a yuppie. I didn't want to be one of those people who have great lives but nonetheless love to sit around and complain because they didn't get an invite to so-and-sos cocktail party. Didn't want to be one of those types.

16

When I joined, my recruiter told me that I'd be stationed in Italy for my entire enlistment. Vicenza, Italy. He said I'd be doing desk work by day and chasing Italian women by night. Yeah. Well. Recruiters lie. Or at least have a knack for making manure smell like roses. But I digress. I was stationed in Italy. For, like, two months. Then, one day, they said, *okay, boys, we're going to send you all to a beautiful and exotic land. You'll learn about a foreign culture. You'll meet new and interesting people . . . and you'll kill them.*"

"Wow. And, ah . . . wow. Just wow. I . . . I don't know what else to say." She shook her head as if to clear her mind.

"You don't have to say anything," he assured her. "It is what it is." He paused, cleared his voice, and added, "I was actually okay with going overseas. I kind of liked the idea. War. The ultimate *reality show.* That type of mentality, you know? I know better now."

They stared at each other in silence for a few seconds.

Finally, she started asking questions again. "Anyway, what do you like to do in your spare time?"

"Golf. I love to play golf."

She laughed and wheezed. "You mean you chase that little white ball around that huge course?"

He nodded and laughed, too. "Yes. It teaches patience and humility, two qualities that are virtues in the eyes of God."

She shrugged. "I guess . . . what's your favorite color?"

"Baby blue."

"Is it okay to drink soda straight from the can?"

"Of course. Why waste time pouring it into a glass when you have a perfectly good can to drink out of?"

"Hey — that's what I say, too. You're one of the few people who agree with me on this. I always drink mine right from the can. I read an article once that said the average person spends the equivalent of a week's time pouring soda from can to glass over the course of their life. I have much better things to do with my time. I mean — a whole week? I could watch the best episodes of *The Jerry Springer Show* in that time. My favorite was the one called *Redneck Rumble*. That was the one that showed the two women from the same trailer park who were fighting over the hillbilly dude who was missing all of his teeth. They actually got into a fistfight over him. A fistfight right there on the show. Can you believe that?"

"I think you're pretty much describing every episode of that show."

She laughed. "I know, right?"

"My favorite episode was the one called *Stripping For Jesus*. It was about a female exotic dancer who passed out bible tracts and preached while she took her clothes off. She wasn't a bad-looking woman, either. I think she had better attendance at her little strip club *church* than we have here at Saint Mary's. Instead of putting money in the collection plate, you were expected to put dollar bills down her G-string."

"Oh my God. For real?"

He laughed. "No. Not for real. I just made it up. I had to try to one-up you. I might actually send them that as an idea for a storyline, though. I mean, it sounds like the type of thing they'd really have on the show, you know?"

"You should be a producer for one of those shows."

"Hey, I have my finger on the pulse of America. I know what garners ratings, what entertains people."

"And speaking of entertainment — who's your favorite entertainer?"

"I think this one's a setup. Me thinks the only right answer is to say that my favorite entertainer is the one who just asked me who my favorite entertainer is. There. How's that?"

"*Aw.* Good answer. Yes, that was the response we were looking for."

He added, "But I've always admired Bob Hope, too. Consider all the hundreds and hundreds of shows that man put on for the troops throughout his life. And he never got paid for any of them. Just think, Grace—for some of those guys, the last time they ever laughed was when they saw Bob Hope. That's some pretty heavy stuff, you know?" He had to fight back the tears.

It got quiet for a moment. She looked down. "That's an interesting perspective," she said softly.

"Yeah. Anyway, I don't mean to be Danny Downer. So, ah, on to the next question."

She perked up and sneezed. "What's the geekiest thing about you?"

"I collect coins."

"Couples who use pet names for one another—sweet or sickening?"

"Truth be told, it's sickening. It's like nails on a chalkboard."

"*Yes*. Thank you. I mean—*honey, sweetheart, babe, darling*. All fine. But I draw the line at *pooh bear*."

"Amen. Glad we're in agreement on that issue."

"Okay. Next thing I want to know—tell me three things that you admire." She hacked.

He thought for a moment. "Purple sunsets, Special Olympians, and boxers who don't quit, even when they're hurt. No, wait. Check that. I'm going to slightly modify that last one—boxers who don't quit, *especially* when they're hurt."

"Ever buy anything from an infomercial?"

"Yes."

"What?"

"A food dehydrator, among many other items."

"How'd that work out for you?"

"Good. Five easy payments of nineteen ninety-nine and I can make banana chips anytime I want."

"Ah, let's see . . . what else do I want to know? What else? What else? Oh, I know—ever been in a fistfight?"

"Yes."

"Tell me about it."

"I was seventeen years old. It was right before I joined the Army. Me and my buddy, Mark Millard, went to a bar on Russell Street in Baltimore called *Garfield's*. We were playing Beyonce on the jukebox and a couple of redneck boys didn't appreciate that too much. So, we got into it with them."

"Did you win?"

"No. We got our butts kicked. Those redneck boys really know how to mix it up."

"How'd you manage to get into a bar when you were only seventeen?"

"It's called a fake ID."

"What photo and name did you use?"

"The photo was a picture of me with a fake mustache glued on. The name I used was *Phil Packer.*"

"Sounds like a porn name."

He laughed. "It kind of does, doesn't it? Not that I would know anything about porn."

She giggled. "I'm going to look at the browsing history on your computer to verify that."

"I always delete it as I go along," he joked.

"Oh, good Gawd. Okay, enough talk about porn. On to the next question. What's your pet peeve?"

"Getting behind someone at a convenience store who's buying two-hundred dollars in lottery tickets and doesn't even know what numbers they want to play."

"Yes, that would piss me off, too. Okay, moving forward— favorite TV show?"

"*Gunsmoke*. I like old Westerns. I like to imagine myself as Marshall Dillon or somebody like that. I'd have a trusty horse and a sidekick with a funny name. Maybe have a shootout in the town square with the bad guys. It'd have to be at high noon, of course. I guess I have a cowboy fantasy."

"So even priests have their fantasies, huh?"

"We do."

"Speaking of fantasies, what's your biggest turn-on when it comes to women?"

"Let's not go there."

"Aw, you're no fun. Come on. You must have things that you like to see in the fairer sex." She coughed.

"Okay. Fine. Sneakers."

"Excuse me?"

"Sneakers. I like women in sneakers."

"Have a foot fetish, do you, padre?"

"Hardly. I just think they're cute on a woman, that's all."

"Okay. Sure. Whatever. Now, tell me something that makes you laugh."

"The bathroom scene in *Dumb and Dumber*."

She shook her head in disgust. "Juvenile. So juvenile."

"I'm sorry, but it's funny."

"Okay. If you say so." She paused to blow her nose before continuing. "Tell me something that makes you cry."

"Those *ASPCA* commercials. The ones that show the abused and neglected animals."

"Oh my God. *Yes*. Those get to me, too. Whenever I see one, I send them money."

"Me, too."

"Best advice anyone's ever given you?"

"Always split aces and eights."

"Say what?"

"Blackjack. It's a reference to blackjack."

"Sorry, but I don't gamble. It's a waste of money."

"I don't either, actually. I just heard it in a Kenny Rogers song once and thought it sounded cool."

She raised her eyebrows. "Ever been to jail?"

He chuckled. "No. Certainly not."

"I have."

"Oh, yeah? Do tell."

"When I was eighteen, me and my friends got caught walking around the mall smoking a little weed, went to jail for, like, two hours, got community service, had to clean bathrooms at the courthouse for a month. Public bathrooms are the worst."

He dismissively waved his hand at her. "Aw. That's nothing."

"I know. And I don't do that shit anymore. But, technically, I do have a criminal record."

"You're a regular Bonnie Parker."

She giggled, then sneezed. "All right. Enough about my seedy past. Next question—favorite song?"

"It varies, depending on my mood. Right now, I'm kind of digging *Atomic Kitten's* version of *Eternal Flame*."

She laughed. "Oh. My. God. *Atomic Kitten*? That is *so* nineteen ninety-nine. Do you still have dial-up internet and an *AOL* account, too?"

"I used to have a crush on Tash, okay? I thought she was, you know, sexy. But sweet, too. Sexy and sweet."

"Oh, so, you like your women sexy and sweet, huh?"

He smiled a big smile. "Oh, *yeah* . . . I mean no. I mean, back before I became a . . . aw, skip it, will you?"

"There's nothing wrong with being attracted to a woman, especially if she's both sexy and sweet. I mean, it would be tough for a man, any man, to resist a woman like that, right?" She wheezed a bit.

"Let's just move forward. Okay?"

"Fine. You're not comfortable talking about relationships and sex. Even though they make up the foundation of life."

"Let's move on, Grace. Please. Move it on."

"Say no more. Won't mention it again. Okay—favorite comedian?"

"John Candy, God rest his soul."

"Aw. He seemed like such a sweet man. I loved him in

Uncle Buck. Uncle Buck was a total sweetheart."

"He left this world way too soon, that's for sure."

"Yep, way too soon. Anyway, what's your guilty pleasure?"

"Pro rasslin'. My favorite rassler is Captain Patriot. He leads the fans in the *Pledge of Allegiance* before each of his matches. But I can't stand Boris Bolshevic. He's a leftover communist from the nineteen-eighties. And he hates America. I don't know how I'll cope if he wins the title. I really don't."

"You know that shit's fake, don't you?"

He shook his head and corrected her. "We fans prefer the term *choreographed.*"

She rolled her eyes. "Oh, Jesus. Seriously?"

"I've been watching it since I was a kid."

"Okay. I'll give you a pass on that one. But that's your *one* pass."

"That's awfully big of you."

"You're welcome. So . . . any siblings?"

"Only child."

"Hey, so am I. How about politics? Democrat or Republican?"

"I never discuss politics."

"Me neither. I was just testing you. I hate politics. I'm not even registered to vote."

He chastised her. "Well, you really should vote. I don't care who you vote *for* as long as you vote."

"Why? It's a waste. It's meaningless. Totally worthless."

He turned serious and spoke sharply. "*Why?* Because several of my friends died half a world away to guarantee you that right. *That's why.* And *do not* sit there and say *it's meaningless.* You don't have the right to say that. Their lives were not *meaningless.* Just because most of them died before their twentieth birthday, it does not make their lives *meaningless.*

You dishonor those men when you say that. And I won't stand for it. Those kids gave up all of their tomorrows for your today. I mean—I hate to sound like a damn bumper sticker, but it's true, Grace—freedom isn't free. And those kids paid for *yours*, Little Miss Pop Princess. Now, don't you give them anything less. Don't you dare give them anything less." He immediately regretted having said it. *That wasn't right. I over-reacted. God. I feel like such a heel.*

She looked down and fiddled with the bedsheets. Then she looked up to the ceiling. Her lower lip quivered. A tear raced down her cheek. "God, I'm sorry. I'm so sorry, Danny. I didn't mean any disrespect. I guess I've never thought of it that way. Forgive me. Please. Please forgive me. I am so, so sorry."

He broke the tension by smiling and telling her, "You're forgiven. In fact, there's really nothing that you need to be forgiven for. And don't . . . don't cry, okay? It's not worth crying over. It was just a misunderstanding. That's all. I didn't mean to snap at you. I shouldn't have done that. I overreacted. I did. I'm the one who was in the wrong, not you. I know you didn't mean any disrespect. So, I'm sorry. It's just a touchy subject for me. Let's . . . let's just move along and forget all about it, okay? Ask . . . ask me another question. Go ahead."

She wiped the tears from her eyes and sniffled. "Um, okay . . . okay . . . do you ah, do you believe in ghosts?"

He threw up his hands. "Ghosts. UFOs. Bigfoot. The Bermuda Triangle. I think anything's possible."

"How about love at first sight? Do you believe in that?"

He chuckled. "The priest in me says that love is something that takes time to grow. But another side of me, the sentimental side, says that it can happen. For example, did you know that Lyndon Johnson asked Lady Bird to marry him after their first date? They married in nineteen thirty-four and it lasted until he died, in nineteen seventy-three."

"Lyndon Johnson . . . *Lyndon Johnson*. I think I might have heard that name before. Who was he?"

"Lyndon Baines Johnson, the thirty-sixth president of the United States."

She shook her head. "I don't remember him."

"You wouldn't. He was in office in the sixties. He took over after Kennedy was assassinated. He's the one who got us all deep into Vietnam."

"That was an eternity ago. Like, during my grandparents' time."

"That's why they call it *history*. Anyway, my point is that maybe some things are just meant to be."

"Yeah. That's what I say, too. Somethings are just meant to be."

"Okay. Enough about me. It's my turn to ask *you* some questions. All I know about you is based on the covers of supermarket tabloids."

She stuck her tongue out and said, "Oh, phooey. Don't get me started on those damn tabloids. And pardon my language. I know I cuss a lot. I don't want to offend you."

"No offense taken. Remember, I was in the Army. I've heard plenty of cursing in my day. I've even done some." He winked at her and asked, "So, where are you originally from?"

She pulled out a tissue from a box sitting on her bed and sneezed into it. "Long Island. Oyster Bay, to be exact."

"How'd you get from Long Island to Hollywood?"

"I've always been a singer. When I was a little girl, five and six years old, I'd be singing along to the radio. After high school, I went to cosmetology school for a year. But I dropped out to pursue my music. Then, when I turned nineteen, I started playing clubs around New York state. One night, I was playing this little club, a real hole in the wall, in Schenectady called *Ringo's Star Lounge*. Well, in walks Kip Darby. He sat down and listened to me. After my set, he came up to the stage, wagged his finger at me, and said, *I'm going to make you a star, kid.* And he did. That's one promise that he kept."

"Sounds like a real fairytale. A dream come true."

"It was. Until the dream turned into a nightmare. Yeah, I followed the Yellow Brick Road, all right. I followed it all the way to the Emerald City. And when I got there, I eventually found out that the emeralds were as fake as those cubic zirconias that they hawk on the home shopping networks."

"Yeah. I guess that can sometimes happen in the entertainment business." He changed the topic. "Anyway, what's the most interesting item currently in your purse?"

"A taser."

He laughed. "Beg your pardon?"

"A taser. I carry a taser."

"Is that even legal?"

"In all but thirty-four states and the District of Columbia."

"Ever had to use it?"

"No, but it's nice to know that it's there. The world's full of creeps and perverts. A girl can't be too careful. Anybody messes with me, and I'll go all medieval on them in a heartbeat. I might be tiny, but I'm not one to be messed with."

"I'd feel sorry for anyone who tried."

She nodded emphatically. "Damn straight."

"Do you believe in any conspiracy theories?"

"Yes. Princess Diana. That was no accident. She was murdered."

"As long as you don't think the moon landings were fake. Ah . . . favorite flower?"

"Roses. I'm a traditionalist."

"Name one type of person whom you wouldn't want to be stuck in an elevator with."

"A hippie. They stink."

"I always thought that was just kind of a myth."

"Nope. It's true. They smell like a combination of dope, patchouli, and BO."

"Okay. Fair enough. I'll take your word for it since I've never been around any of them. I mean, you really don't see too many of them in this area. But I can understand — nobody wants to be close to someone who reeks."

"Well, you don't see them around here because they already found their own little paradise in LA. But I do appreciate your being understanding. I was afraid you were going to be all like — *oh, but, Grace, Jesus was a hippie.*"

"I don't think he was a hippie so much as he just lived at a time when there really weren't many barbershops."

She laughed. "*Many*, huh?"

"Seriously, though, we so take things for granted today. Barbershops. Indoor plumbing. Toilet paper. Chia Pets. The comedy of Carrot Top. The world wasn't always so fortunate. We should really count our blessings."

"Thank you for reminding me of that. That's beautiful," she said with mock sincerity.

"What's your secret talent?"

"I can name the capitals of all fifty states," she said with pride.

"Huh. That's cool."

"I think so."

He stared at her. "And . . . go. New York."

"Albany."

He nodded. "That was too easy. That's your home state. Okay, how about . . . Wyoming?"

"Cheyenne."

"The state you're currently in — the great state of Maryland. The birthplace of yours truly, Babe Ruth, and David Hasselhoff."

"Annapolis. The capital's Annapolis, but ah . . . David Hasselhoff? David Hasselhoff was born in Maryland?"

"Yep. Baltimore."

"And you all tout that as one of your state's crowning

glories?"

"Hey, come on now—don't Hassle The Hoff. We're proud of him. And, by the way, he's still huge in Germany. Huge."

She laughed and shook her head. "You're funny. You are. And women like men who make them laugh. You know that, don't you? That's not a myth. It's true. Funny men are sexy."

"Now, if that were true, *The Three Stooges* would have each had their own harem."

"They were not funny, my dear. Moe plucking hairs from Larry's nose isn't funny. It's disgusting."

"I guess it's a guy thing. I think you must have to be a guy to *get The Stooges.*"

"Yeah, I guess . . . okay, come on, padre—give me some more states. I'm on a roll here." She coughed.

"Minnesota."

"Oh, um . . . give me just a second—I always have to think about this one a little . . . just a second here . . . don't tell me . . . Oh—I remember now. It's Saint Paul. Definitely Saint Paul."

"Kansas."

"Topeka."

"Delaware."

"Dover."

"Oregon."

"Salem."

"North Dakota."

"Bismarck."

"All right. Let's take a little trip down south. Mississippi."

"Jackson. Impressive, aren't I?"

"I can't say whether you're impressive or not because, other than Maryland, I don't know any of them myself." He laughed heartily.

She playfully smacked him. "Jerk."

"Do you know how to drive a stick shift?"

She made a face. "Ah, *no*. It's not nineteen eighty-two, for God's sake. I mean—who knows how to drive a stick these days?"

"I do."

"Well, aren't you special? Do you know how to program your VCR, too?"

"What's your favorite movie?"

"*Forrest Gump*. It never fails to get me blubbering. Oh, Jesus—Forrest was nothing less than the kindest, sweetest, most decent man ever to walk the face of the earth. And—"

He interrupted. Chuckling, he told her, "Well, he was a fictional character, so he never actually *walked the face of the earth*."

"I am trying to have a moment here. Please do not ruin it with facts."

"Sorry. Continue. Please."

"Okay. Now, as I was saying before I was interrupted—Forrest was a beautiful soul. But Jenny? Oh, that bitch, Jenny. He was way too good for her. Way too good. She actually had the balls to tell that man—right before he went to Vietnam, no less—that he didn't know what love was? Ha. He loved with the purest of hearts. And if a man like Forrest Gump loved me, I'd marry him in a New York minute and have his babies. Yes, I would. And Jenny was a damn hippie, too. She probably smelled."

"You're not being fair to Jenny. You don't understand her. Not in the least. She had self-esteem issues going back to her childhood. She did love Forrest. She kept pushing him away because she, herself, didn't think she was good enough for him. How sad is that? It's the most poignant aspect of the story."

"Whatever." She paused and then went on a rant about her distaste for hippies. "Why do the hippies always have to be protesting something? Huh? If it's not the high price of recreational marijuana, it's toilet paper that isn't biodegradable. Most of them are communists, you know. They love nothing better than giving the red, white, and blue a black eye. Oh, and they push that *free love* of theirs. Sure, go ahead and screw anybody you want. You don't have to be in love. Hell, have a damn orgy if you want. It doesn't matter. Sorry, but I don't believe in that shit. You should love someone before you screw them. I'm not the best Catholic in the world, but this Long Island girl has her values. Free love? It's shit like that that brought down the Roman Empire. And it can bring down America, too."

"Well, that might be a little hyperbolic—to say that sexual immorality caused the fall of Rome. But be that as it may—I think you should cut the hippies some slack. You seem to really have an ax to grind against them. Now, I certainly don't subscribe to a lot of their values. They're not exactly my cup of tea, either. And I agree with you about the whole free love thing. I don't approve of that. You and me—we're old-fashioned that way, I guess. But part of what I fought for in Afghanistan was the hippies' right to protest as they see fit. That's freedom, Grace. It's what makes us different from the Taliban, or Russia, or North Korea. Try going over to North Korea and protesting Dear Leader's lavish lifestyle. You'll never be heard from again. So, if the hair heads—that's what we called them in the Army—*hair heads*—want to protest war, or strip mining, or the fact that they think Trump is polluting the environment with all that hair spray he uses, let them be. Okay? Plus, some of the things that they protest are good causes. For example, they protest the clubbing of baby seals in Canada. Did you know that?"

"No . . . ah, I didn't. I didn't know that. I . . . I don't want baby seals to be clubbed to death."

"Neither do I. So, let's just let them do their thing, shall we? Live and let live. Fair enough? I mean, we don't have to attend their orgies, right? But wouldn't it be great if everyone tried to understand everyone else just a little? Huh?" He started singing The Youngbloods' *Get Together.*

She laughed. "Oh, good Gawd. That's hippie music."

He stopped singing and told her, "Yeah, it is. But it's still a beautiful song. And it cryptically alludes to The Second Coming, did you know that?"

"No, I didn't. Really?"

"Yes, listen to the lyrics — the whole song, not just the chorus. Everyone just listens to the chorus. The message is in the whole song."

"If He came back, what do you think would happen?" she asked.

"The same thing that happened before," he matter-of-factly told her.

"Really?"

"Really."

"Do you think He would have a message for people? Do you think He'd have a message for *you*?"

He chuckled. "I don't know if He would have a message for little old me."

"Didn't He specialize in *Little Old Mes*?"

He smiled and chuckled. *Out of the mouths of babes. Bless her heart.* "Yeah, He did. He did, Grace. You're exactly right. So, if He ever comes back, I'll wait for His message. Okay?"

"Okay."

"Now, Grace Stevens, tell me something that you can't resist. Inquiring minds want to know."

"Jelly donuts. Every once in a while, I just have to have one. I end up paying for it at the gym, but, oh golly, is it ever worth it."

He laughed. "You and Elvis. Elvis liked jelly donuts, too. Only he didn't pay for his at the gym."

She laughed and did her best Elvis impression. "Ah, thank

ya, thankyaverymuch."

"Speaking of Elvis—what's it like being famous?"

She frowned. "At first it was great. I loved all the attention. But one thing you learn very quickly is that you can't turn it on and off. It becomes a way of life. Everywhere you go, you have fans who hound you for a picture or autograph. You've got the paparazzi who won't leave you alone. Constantly on the road. People are speculating about all aspects of your life, including very personal ones."

He nodded his understanding.

"It's lonely, Danny. You perform in front of a crowd of fifteen or twenty thousand people every night. And then go back to a hotel room and you're all by yourself. You know, I love Ferris wheels. And there's this amusement park near Malibu called *Marty's Fun Land*. They have a huge Ferris wheel, one of the biggest on the West Coast. Well, sometimes, on those super rare occasions when I actually get a day off, I rent the whole park out. And I just ride the Ferris wheel. All by myself."

A tear raced down her cheek. "I'm tired of it all. I'm burned-the-hell out. I've been on and through stages. And I've come to the conclusion that you can either be famous or normal. But not both. Well, I want to be normal. Is that too much to ask?"

"No. Not too much."

She looked down, fidgeted with her nails, and told him, "You know, I don't even have a boyfriend."

"Is that right? I thought you were dating that one fellow . . . oh, what's his name? The actor."

She interjected. "You mean Orion Taylor?"

He snapped his fingers and pointed at her. "Right. That's the one."

"That's not his real name, by the way. He uses the stage name *Orion Taylor* because his real name's Brad. Brad *Douche.*

Oh, he tries to say it's all fancy-schmancy and is pronounced *Do-shay*. But it's not. It's Douche. See, I went home with him once, to meet his folks. It was around Easter time, and they have this really weird tradition where every member of the family gets a bag of black jellybeans as an Easter present. His mom handed him his and said, *here you go, Bradley. Big star or not – every Douche gets a bag."*

"Wow. That's quite a story. I didn't realize anyone likes the black jellybeans. I thought they only make them to elevate the other jellybeans' self-esteem. Anyway, sorry it didn't work out for you all."

"It's okay. He just wasn't the person that I had hoped he was."

"It's important to make sure that the person with whom you're romantically involved meets all of your expectations. When I counsel couples, that's one of the things that I stress."

She tilted her head and squinted her eyes. "But you don't know what it's like to be in love. That's one of the bones I have to pick with the Catholic Church. How can a priest – who's celibate – counsel people on romantic love and marriage?"

She has a point. But I don't feel like getting into that whole issue right now. He looked at his watch and announced, "It's twenty after twelve. I really have to hit the sack. I'm getting up early tomorrow. Saturday is one of my days off, and I'm playing a round of golf."

She was indignant. "You mean you're going to leave me here all by myself?"

"I wouldn't be gone that long, a few hours. Besides, Tippy can keep you company."

"Well, I was hoping that you could do some shopping for me tomorrow."

"Shopping?"

"Yes, I need clothes. Wearing your old sweatshirts and sweatpants isn't going to cut it. I need other stuff, too."

"What kind of clothes do you want?"

"Lots of stuff. Jeans, t-shirts, shoes, socks, bras, panties, teddies, shorts, tank tops, sweatpants, a couple of hoodies, among other things."

"Wait a second. Did you say *bras* and *panties*?"

"Uh-huh."

He pointed to himself. "You expect me to go into a store and buy your bras and panties for you?"

She nodded. "Yeah. Sure." Then added, "Now, for my bras, I'm 34DD. I have big boobs, in case you haven't noticed. I call them my *personal floatation devices*. I'll never drown with these puppies." She briefly looked down at them and giggled.

He blushed.

She reached out and squeezed his hand. "Aw. How cute. You're embarrassed. The mere mention of breasts caused you to blush. That's sweet."

He shook his head. "You don't understand. This is a small, rural area. Here in this county, everyone knows everyone else. In other words, everyone knows that I'm a Catholic priest. If I go into a store and buy a bunch of women's clothing, it'll arouse suspicion."

She shrugged her shoulders. "If anyone asks, tell them you're buying for your sister. Your sister who's visiting from out of town."

"So, I'm buying lingerie for *my sister*?"

Without missing a beat, she built on the lie. "Sure. You're buying lingerie for your sister because when she flew in, the airline lost all of her baggage."

"In other words, you want me to lie."

"Just a little white lie." She held her thumb and forefinger close to one another.

"Yeah, well, priests aren't supposed to lie. It's kind of against the rules, you know?"

She shook her head. "I don't think telling the truth is always an absolute moral imperative."

"Really?" He raised his eyebrows.

She nodded. "Really. I mean, it's a complex world, and sometimes you have to lie in order to serve the greater good. Think about it. Think about those people who lied to the Gestapo about hiding Jews in their attics or basements. I believe that God understands such things."

"Good point. You're a good debater." He chuckled and added, "You know, twenty-four hours ago, if someone would have told me that I'd be sitting here in the wee hours of the morning discussing moral imperatives with Grace Stevens, I would have said there's a better chance of me winning the lottery *and* being abducted by aliens. Literally."

She again reached out, squeezed his hand, and smiled at him. "I know, right? Life is crazy that way. But sometimes things have a way of working out for the best."

He looked down at their two hands. Finally, she let go.

"I guess I could do a little shopping for you tomorrow." He got up off the bed and started to walk out of the room. When he got to the doorway, he stopped, turned around and asked, "Would you like me to say a prayer of healing for you?"

She nodded. "Sure. Okay. I guess it couldn't hurt."

He sat back down on the bed and gently put his large hands on her forehead. "Heavenly Father, we ask that you heal your servant, Grace. Free her body of disease and illness. In Jesus's name, we pray. Amen."

He made the sign of the cross on her forehead. "Now, try to get some rest." He got up, walked to the door, and turned out the light.

"Goodnight, Grace."

"Goodnight, Danny."

Chapter Three: The Tampon Terrors

Danny walked into his room with Tippy in tow. She slept on his bed at night. He undressed, stripped down to a pair of light blue boxer shorts. A gold crucifix hung from a chain around his neck. His chest was cut and hairless. There was a scar just below his left shoulder blade. While serving in Afghanistan, he had been hit with shrapnel from a rocket-propelled grenade.

He kneeled down along the side of the bed and prayed, as he did every night. As much as he tried to focus and concentrate, his mind kept wandering. The utter insanity of the day's events was distracting. His adrenalin was still pumping. And he thought about Grace. He couldn't help but dwell on how beautiful she was. Even sick, she was ravishing. The fact that he was thinking about it made him feel guilty. *I'm not supposed to notice these kinds of things, not supposed to think these thoughts.* To top it all off, she seemed like a genuinely nice person, too. Then his mind focused on how she'd grabbed and squeezed his hand. *Was that a sign? Or maybe she's just a touchy-feely kind of person.* Did he *want* it to be a sign? Had he made the right decision by allowing her to stay at the rectory?

The only thing he could decide was that he'd done enough pondering for one day. He finished his prayers, got off his knees, and climbed into bed. Tippy jumped up on the bed and crawled up next to him. She placed her head on his pillow. Yawning, he rubbed his eyes and deeply exhaled. He closed his eyes and tried to sleep, but his mind kept racing. It was a fitful night of tossing and turning.

He got up at seven the following morning. After showering and shaving, he splashed some *Green Irish Tweed* on his cheeks and put on a pair of black gabardine slacks and a yellow cardigan over top of a white polo shirt.

Tippy raced ahead of him down the stairs. He fed her and prepared a tray for Grace's breakfast. Chicken broth, a slice of toast, orange juice, and coffee. He carried it up the stairs and held the tray in one hand as he knocked on her door.

"Grace," he called out. "Are you awake yet?"

"Yeah. Come on in," she replied through the door. Her voice was hoarse.

He brought in the tray and set it at the foot of the bed.

"How did you sleep?" he asked.

"Okay, all things considered." She coughed.

"How about you? How did you sleep?"

"Not that great, to be honest with you. I guess I had a lot of things on my mind."

She nodded, then pointed to the tray. "I guess that's for me, huh?"

"Oh, yeah. Yeah. I fixed you a little something for breakfast."

She smiled. "That was very sweet of you." She stuck her forehead out. "Do me a favor and see if I feel as warm as I did yesterday."

He placed his right hand on her forehead. "About the same. How do you feel?"

"Still pretty lousy. I sure hope you don't get sick from being around me."

He laughed. "Well, Jesus walked among the lepers."

"Oh, so I'm a leper, am I?" She took one of her pillows, playfully threw it at him, and giggled.

"I didn't mean it like that."

"I know you didn't. I'm just teasing."

She looked at his outfit and nodded. "You look very nice. You smell good, too. I haven't lost my sense of smell yet. You wear *Green Irish Tweed,* don't you?"

He smiled and nodded.

"My dad wears that cologne. It's a classic," she told him. She paused and then added, "I must look like hell. I'm sick and not wearing any makeup, wearing these men's clothes."

Before he could think about the wisdom of it, he blurted out, "You look lovely. Beautiful, actually." *Oh, God. I shouldn't have said that.*

She smiled. "You really think I look beautiful?"

He hesitated but nodded. *You can't take a compliment back once it's been issued. Besides, it's the truth."*

"You're a nice guy, Danny."

He shrugged. "Oh, by the way, I decided to pass on golf. I don't think it's a good idea to leave you here by yourself all afternoon when you're not feeling well. I thought what I'd do is go shopping for you and come straight home."

"Maybe we can watch a movie or something when you get back."

"Sure. We could do that."

"I wonder what they're saying about me?"

"Let's find out. Give me one sec." He left the room and returned with his phone. He went to a news website and read her the headline. *"Pop Star Grace Stevens Missing."* Then he handed her the phone and allowed her to read the rest of the article.

She shook her head as she read. "Says here that I disappeared yesterday afternoon at four o'clock. Wrong. I was gone by two o'clock." She continued to scan the article. "It also says that *foul play has not been ruled out . . .* that the police are investigating . . . that I was last seen renting a car in downtown Baltimore . . . all remaining shows on my *Amazing Grace* tour have been canceled. Oh, and get a load of this quote from my manager, Kip Darby —*while we regret the cancellation of the remaining shows on the tour, our main concern has always been and continues to be for the safety of Ms. Stevens.* Bull. Shit. I'm nothing more than a meal ticket to that man—a cash cow. All he cares about is making the register ring. He's a phony. He's scum. A really, really bad dude. I'm sorry I ever got mixed up with him." She paused and added, "But, you know, I feel guilty about all those people, twelve thousand or so, who had tickets to the show. And what about all the other people in the other cities who were counting on me to perform?" A pained look came over her face. "I feel like I'm letting those people down, Danny. Did I do the right thing by leaving? Tell me I did the right thing. Please tell me I did the right thing."

He sat on the edge of the bed and took her hand. In a quiet, low voice, he told her, "Nobody owns you. Not your manager, not the fans, not even God Himself. No one. You're sick and exhausted. You need this rest."

She smiled at him. "Aw. You say all the right things." She interlocked their fingers and squeezed. "Thank you," she said in a near whisper. He looked at their two hands, now intertwined. Her hand felt so warm and dainty. So feminine. For a moment, he closed his eyes and drank it all in. There was silence in the room.

A few seconds later, Tippy came running in. She had her rubber ducky toy in her mouth and leaped up on the bed, knocking over Grace's breakfast tray. She shook the toy with her mouth, threw it up in the air, and caught it. It snapped Danny out of his trance, and he quickly let go of Grace's hand and withdrew his own.

Tippy climbed up on Grace's chest and dropped her toy. Danny laughed. "She must like you. She wants to share her rubber ducky with you."

Grace chuckled. She picked up the slobber-covered toy and threw it across the room. Tippy ran after it, retrieved it, and jumped back up on the bed. Danny looked at the mess she'd made. The broth, coffee, and orange juice had all spilled. "Sorry about your breakfast. I can fix you another tray."

She shook her head. "That's okay. Really it is. I'm not that hungry anyway." She grabbed another tissue and blew her nose again. It was now red and chapped from tissue burn.

He rubbed his hands together. "Okay. So, you need some clothes."

She nodded. "Uh-huh. I need a bunch of stuff, actually."

"Well, there's a *Walmart* in Aberdeen that's about fifteen miles from here."

She made a face. "*Walmart?*"

He nodded. "Yes. *Walmart.* This isn't Beverly Hills. We don't have any fancy boutiques around here."

She sighed. "Okay, I guess *Walmart* it is. Do me a favor and get me a sheet of paper and a pen so I can make out a list of what I want and my sizes."

He left the room and returned with a yellow legal pad and pen. "Here you go."

She coughed as she wrote down her needs. When she was done, she tore off the sheet of paper from the pad and handed it to him.

He studied it carefully. *Oh, she has that lovely, girly handwriting. So very feminine. So cute. Even kind of sexy.* He cleared his throat and read it back to her. "Let's see here . . . jeans, t-shirts, sweaters, socks, sneakers, bras, panties, hoodies, teddies, shorts, tank tops, halter tops. This, ah, this is quite a list. Exactly how long were you planning on staying here?"

She ignored his question, instead telling him, "Look, everything on that list is something that I really need. Oh, and I have to have some makeup, too — eyeliner, eyeshadow, blush, lipstick, Peaches and Cream nail polish, and polish remover. Plus, some hair dye. I want to change the color of my hair. I'm going blonde. And some bubble gum. I like bubble gum. Get *Hubba Bubba.* Watermelon flavor if they have it. If not, grape will do. Oh, yeah—some bikini waxing strips, too. Because I, ah, you know, wax *down there*." She paused for a moment, giggled, and continued. "That reminds me of a story. True story. I was on a date with this dude. First date, mind you. His name was Jerry Rogers. Creep. He asked me, right out of the blue—*does the carpeting match the drapes?* I guess he thought I dyed my hair or something. So, I told him—*you'll never find out, jerkoff.* Then I slapped him in the face and walked the hell out. Totally inappropriate question, especially on a first date. But the reality is that it's a hardwood floor."

"Okay. Uh-huh. And, um, what styles do you like when it comes to clothing?"

"I like stuff that's cute." She pointed to his outfit. "Look, you seem to have a good fashion sense. Use your judgment. I'm sure you'll do fine."

"I'll do my best."

"Oh, and before I forget, there's one more thing that I didn't put on the list."

He bowed to her the way a peasant would bow to royalty. "Yes, milady. Your wish is my command."

"Tampons," she said casually.

Dun, dun, dun.

"Excuse me? Say again?"

"Tampons."

"Tampons. *Huh.* You don't say?"

"Is there a problem?" she asked.

"Oh, no—no. Of course not. No problem. Don't be silly. Why would there be a problem? Well . . . I mean . . . it's just that I'm a guy and all."

"And I'm a girl and all, which means that I have a menstrual cycle," she matter-of-factly told him.

"I understand the biology of it, but it's something that most guys don't want to get involved with. The reality is that most of us fellas don't even want to talk about your periods. *Period.* Truth be told, if you took a poll, most men would say that it

would be better if, you know, you all didn't even *have* them."
He laughed a nervous laugh.

"Yeah? Well, maybe if the men of the world get together and pray *real* hard, you all can get God to just miracle them away." She snapped her fingers. "Just like that. Maybe He'll miracle them right out of existence."

"Look, it's just a little embarrassing, that's all."

"Embarrassing?"

"For a guy, it is. Yes."

"So, you're telling me that you've never bought tampons for a girl before?"

"Never. The only experience I have with them was in Afghanistan. Our platoon medic, Doc Meadows, used to carry them. He swore that they worked better to plug sucking chest wounds than anything else."

"Are you telling me that you've never had a real girlfriend before? Because making a tampon run is a pretty common boyfriend chore. And if you've never done that, to me, that means you've never had a serious relationship. Have you ever had a serious girlfriend? I mean before you became a priest and all?"

"Aw, let's just skip it."

She looked at him with suspicion. "You sure you're not gay?"

"No. I'm not gay. I mean, yeah—I use moisturizer. Religiously. Also, I might have a couple of Liza Minnelli CDs lying around here somewhere. But, come on, I'm not gay. *Not* that there would be anything wrong with that, mind you. But it's not my bag. I might be metro, though. Yeah, I'll say I'm somewhat metro. That's a fair appraisal. Anyhow, it's just that between being overseas and then going to seminary, I never got around to having a significant girlfriend, that's all."

"That's a shame. You've missed out on one of the joys of life. I mean—I guess I have, too. I've had plenty of boyfriends, but I've never found a really decent guy. I've often wondered what it would be like to have a really, really good guy, you know?"

"Let's just drop this whole topic. I'll get the darn tampons for you."

"It's really not a big deal. Come on. Get over your Tampon Terrors. Put on your big boy pants. All you have to do is put the box in your shopping cart and pay for them. After that, they'll put them in a bag for you, and nobody will even see them anymore."

"Right. I'm sure it'll be fine. It doesn't have to be a big deal. Mind over matter. If I don't mind, it don't matter."

She snapped her fingers. "Oh, yeah — one more thing. Last item — I promise. I want some overalls. I was watching reruns of *Hee Haw* the other day, and the girls on the show were wearing them, and they looked really cute. I want two pairs."

"Hand me the pen, will you?"

She handed him the pen.

He wrote the overalls down on the list. He spoke the words he was writing. "Two . . . pairs . . . of . . . overalls." He stopped writing and looked at her closely before he continued making his notation. "*Extra-small.*"

"Shouldn't you put the tampons on the list, too?"

"No. I won't forget those. Trust me."

"Oh, and I'll have to owe you for all this. I don't have any cash on me, only a credit card. Do you, by chance, take *Visa*?"

"This is a church, Grace. It's cash and carry. We don't even take checks anymore. Too many of the donation checks bounced."

"Well, in that case, I'll have to owe you. But I'm good for it. I'm worth something like three-hundred million dollars. When this is all over, I promise, I'll make it up to you and then some. Just keep a running total of what I owe you."

He smiled an easy smile. "Don't sweat it. And I don't want

your money."

She tilted her head, softly bit her lower lip, and said, "I do believe you mean that, too. And that would make you about the only person who doesn't want my money."

They stared at one another in silence for a few seconds. Finally, he took her list, folded it, and placed it in his pocket. "Well, I guess I'll head out after I clean this mess up."

He retrieved some paper towels from the kitchen and soaked up the combination of coffee, juice, and chicken broth. He got her a fresh comforter from the linen closet. "Now, listen, if anyone comes to the door while I'm gone, just let them knock. Don't answer the phone. Don't even look out the windows, okay?"

She nodded. "Right. Got it."

"Okay then. I'll be back as soon as I can. In the meantime, Tippy will be your gracious host."

He went to his room and retrieved a navy blue windbreaker from his closet. After he walked out the front door, he pulled the collar of the jacket up. It was raw outside. Raw and windy. Typical April in Maryland. The storm had ushered in a cold front.

The plan was to drive to the *Walmart* in Fallston. That was farther than the one in Aberdeen that he normally used, but he wasn't comfortable shopping for women's clothing in Aberdeen. Too many familiar faces. Too many potential questions. It would be worth his while to drive the extra twenty miles where he'd be less likely to run into people he knew.

He turned on the radio and tuned in to the local pop music station. The disk jockey was playing Grace Stevens songs and talking about her disappearance. They played one of her more famous songs—*I Think I'm In Love*. He thought that her voice had a sweetness, almost an innocence, to it. Classic and classy. It was a beautiful song, sung by a talented artist. But there was a longing that he detected in her voice. It was as if she was singing about something she wanted rather than something she'd experienced. And it was so soulful that it brought a tear to his eye as he drove.

CHAPTER FOUR: THE PEOPLE OF WALMART

When he got to *Walmart*, as he walked in from the parking lot, there was a gaggle of teenage girls milling about. One of them whistled a catcall as he walked by. His looks always garnered attention and it embarrassed him. Quickly, he walked through the front door and grabbed a shopping cart, hoping to get away before the girls said anything to him.

He meandered through the store. On his way to the women's department, he saw some patio furniture that was on sale. He stopped, looked at it, and examined the price tag. *Too bad I don't have a patio because this is a really good sale.*

As he passed the music department, he noticed they had a display of Grace's albums set up. He flipped through them. *Amazing Grace, Grace Stevens: Live in Las Vegas, From Grace With Love, Long Island Girl.* He nodded approvingly and focused on the cover of the Las Vegas album. It showed her in a black sequined two-piece outfit. The top was kind of low-cut and exposed a little cleavage. The pants were tight-fitting and showed off the perfect bubble butt. There could be no denying that she was a woman who oozed sex. He put the records away and pushed his cart towards his destination.

The paths around the clothing racks in the women's department were narrow. It was a tight squeeze, too tight to venture into with a shopping cart. As he tried to push his cart around, he knocked over an entire display of bras. Everyone looked at him. He felt the heat of his face blushing. Quickly, he began to pick up the displaced brasiers. An older lady with gray-blue hair and strong-smelling cheap perfume came over and helped him pick up the mess. In a southern accent, she told him, "Can't fit a cart in this maze, darlin'. You gotta park it in the main aisle and then carry the stuff over, okay? I know it's a pain in the ass, but it's the only way to do it."

He nodded, thanked her, and pushed his cart into the main aisle. Walking back over, he started looking at the clothes. He pulled out the list she'd written for him. *Let's start with something simple. T-shirts.* There was a pink shirt with a picture of *Bob the Minion* holding his teddy bear on it. *That's cute. This one's a no-brainer.* He took it over and placed it in his cart. Quickly, he picked other shirts for her — one with a unicorn on it, another with a kitten floating through space in an astronaut suit, some that were plain, without any design. He even found one with her name on it — a pink one with the name *Grace* in white script lettering. *Have to get that.* He placed it in the cart. The jeans were right next to the shirts. Easily, he found her size and picked out five pairs in various colors. He found some adorable pink and white ankle socks, along with two pairs of sweatpants, a few sweatshirts, and two pairs of white canvass sneakers. Into the cart, they went. Next, he selected four tank tops, two hoodies, and three pairs of shorts. He was proud of himself. *So far, this has been easier than I imagined.*

But now, things were starting to get more difficult. The *unmentionables.* Bras, panties, and teddies. He had to be careful with these. *I don't want to get something too sexy and have her think it inappropriate. On the other hand, I don't want to offend her by getting something that's dowdy.* After looking at the lingerie for about ten minutes, he picked out several matching lace bra-panty sets in different colors. Finally, he chose four satin teddies — one black, one powder blue, one royal blue, and one off-white. *I'm getting there. Not much left on the list.*

And then it happened. As he placed the last teddy in the

cart, he heard a booming voice from behind.

"Hey, how ya doin' there, chief?"

He turned around and saw a heavy-set man in his 40s. The man was balding and wore a shirt that proudly proclaimed himself a—*Degenerate Gambler*. On his feet were shabby flip-flops that showcased long, razor-sharp toenails tinged with yellow. Danny sized him up. *He needs a good bath.*

Danny didn't want to make eye contact. *This is no place to get sucked into a conversation. Keep your answer simple.* "Oh-kay."

The man pointed at the underwear in Danny's cart and asked, "What? Your old lady got you here shopping for her?"

Danny squinted. "Beg your pardon? My what?"

"Your old lady—you know, your *woman*."

He decided to play along. "Oh, yeah. My old lady. Yeah—she's been nagging me all week to pick up this stuff for her. Yep. Nag, nag, nag. You know how it is."

He hoped that this would conclude the conversation, but it wasn't going to be that easy.

The man extended his hand. "Name's Jimmy, by the way."

They shook.

"Pleased to meet you."

Jimmy smiled and nodded. "Just got out of prison," he volunteered.

Danny forced a smile. "Marvelous."

"I know you're curious about what I was in for."

"Well, to be honest, Jimmy, I'm kind of in a hurr—"

Jimmy cut him off. "I highjacked a tractor-trailer full of *Viagra*. Yeah, I tried to go on the lamb, but I was pretty easy to catch. See, the cops knew they were dealing with a *hardened* criminal." He grinned a shit-eating grin and heartily laughed at his own joke.

Danny nodded and replied, "Yeah, I'll bet you did some *hard* time for that, too, huh?" *Oh, Good Lord, why did I say that? It's a mistake to engage with this guy. But I just couldn't resist that line. It was the perfect line.*

Jimmy nodded. "Damn straight, fella. Prison ain't nearly as glamorous as they make it out to be on TV."

"Yeah, I've often wondered about that aspect of it." Danny put his hands in his pockets and nervously whistled *Camptown Races.* When he finished, he told Jimmy, "Any-who, I really have to be go—"

Jimmy again cut him off. "Hold on one second there, cuz."

Oh, God, he's one of those types who doesn't know when to end the conversation.

He peered into Danny's cart and looked at the underwear. Reaching in, he picked up a black bra, examined it, and whistled. "Damn, Homer! Your old lady's got some big-ass knockers, don't she? Thirty-four double D. That's what I'm talkin' about. Bet you have fun playin' with those milk monsters, huh?" He winked at Danny.

He snatched the bra back. "Look, Jimmy, I really have to be going. My old lady's at home waiting, and I'm planning on gettin' some this afternoon. So . . . best of luck to you."

He beat a hasty retreat. As he made his getaway, he shook his head. *The people you run into in Walmart.*

Now came the hardest part of the whole trip. The tampons. Operation Tampon. He wandered the store looking for them. *No way I'm going to ask anyone. I don't care if it takes an hour. I'll aimlessly meander through this place until I happen upon them.* After fifteen minutes, he finally found a department marked— *Lifestyles. Yeah. That has to be it.* As he walked down the aisle, he surveyed the various products that fell into the *Lifestyles* category—condoms, *KY Jelly,* vibrators, medicines that treated yeast infections and head lice, and, yes, tampons. *I guess they put all the embarrassing stuff in one place.* He perused the various brands. *Oh, shoot. I didn't know there would be so many different kinds. And she didn't tell me what brand she uses.*

He just stood there. For five minutes, he just stood there. *I've got to get this right because if it's not, I'm just going to have to come back and do it all over again.*

Finally, an attractive, busty redhead approached him. She was tall. Her hair was shoulder-length and shiny. She sported trendy, designer glasses. The pair of expensive jeans she wore were tight-fitting, as was her pink polo shirt. Her brown leather boots went up to her knees. She looked to be in her late 20s.

She greeted him with a smile and an enthusiastic, "Hi there!" She had a high-pitched, *little girl* voice. *Oh, goodness. She sounds like Kristin Chenoweth.*

"Hi yourself." *And she looks like Jessica Rabbit. A real-life Jessica Rabbit.*

"So, how's your life?"

He shrugged. "Oh, can't complain. Not that anyone would listen if I did, right?"

She laughed. Loudly. "You're funny." She reached out and playfully tapped his arm.

She laughed at that lame line? Is she selling Amway or recruiting for a cult or something? "How's *your* life, ma'am?"

She purred to him. "Oh, mine's outstanding, *most outstanding.* And it just got better within the last ten seconds or so. And don't call me *ma'am*—my name's Dawn. And I'm here getting batteries, of all things. Can you believe that? *Batteries.* I mean—seriously—I'm, like, such a weirdo. Who else would go out just for batteries?"

"*The Energizer Bunny.* For him, it's a matter of life and death."

Dawn again laughed and touched his arm. "Don't you ever stop? Oh, Gawd. You're funnier than Mel Gibson when he's drunk—that's what you are, mister. Any-who . . . that's what I'm here for. Batteries."

"Uh-huh. Um, in terms of batteries, they have them here. There's a big display over by the area where they have all the gift cards. A whole wall of batteries. Any size you'd want."

"Oh, I'm into big. I like things that are big. Really big.

Because no matter how big it is, I can always make it fit. It might be a tight squeeze, but then — hey, all the better, right?" She giggled and winked at him.

He nervously chuckled. "Go big or go home, huh?"

"Yes. Oh my God — *yes*! Thank you. I was just getting ready to use that line. *Go big or go home.* Seriously, I was just getting ready to say that. Do we have, like, this telepathy thing going on between us? Because I think we do."

"I think it's probably just a coincidence. It's a popular saying."

"Maybe. But irregardless — I like things that are big." She pointed to his hands. "For example, you have really big hands. Can you, like, palm a basketball? I think you could. Easily."

"Never tried. Basketball's not my game. I'm a golfer."

"Oh, golf. That's cool, too. That's the game where the men swing those big, long, hard clubs. And they try for a hole in one, right?"

"Yeah, a hole in one is what every golfer dreams of. It's the Holy Grail of golf."

"Yeah, you can have a lot of fun with holes, inside of holes and whatnot."

"My dog, Tippy — she's a little Sheltie. I got her from an animal shelter. Anyhow, she likes holes. She digs them in the backyard and buries bones in them."

She emphatically pointed at him. "Exactly. That's such a good use for a hole, too. Yeah. Burying a bone in a hole is, like, ideal. It's perfection." She smiled a naughty smile.

"Uh-huh." *Could she perhaps be a porn star?*

She looked him up and down. "You know, I can't help but notice — you have a terrific body."

"Well, gee, thanks, Dawn. I try to take care of myself. I eat right, workout a little. Try to lay off the ice cream and the *McDonald's*." He chuckled. "It's tough to resist that ice cream, though." He briefly paused. "Come to think of it, it's tough to resist *McDonald's*, too. And it's downright impossible to resist the ice cream *at McDonald's*."

She shook her finger at him. "I really think you could, like, be a *Chippendale*. Yeah, you could totally be a *Chippendale*."

He shrugged. "I don't know about *that*. I'm not crazy about the idea of living in a tree. And I don't really like nuts, either."

She raised her eyebrows. "*I do*."

"Well, that's wonderful. They're good for you. High in protein, so they say."

"Oh, *yes*—and I like stuff that's high in protein. Love it, in fact. I just slurp it right up." She made a slurping sound.

"Uh-huh."

She loudly exhaled. "So, anyway, I'm single. Yeppers. Single. Single and ready to mingle," she told him with a big smile.

And desperate enough to do Kris Kringle. God forgive me. That was unkind. She's a child of God, too. Bless her heart. "Lovely."

There was a long, awkward pause. Finally, she observed, "You just look kind of lost. *Lost in the Walmart Lifestyles Department*. That could be, like, a documentary at Sundance. Seriously, do you need help with something, Arnold Palmer? I'm going to call you *Arnold Palmer* because that's the only golfer that I know of, but you are so much cuter than he ever was. Seriously."

"Yeah, well . . . it's just that. Well, it's just that I don't really know . . ."

She pointed to the display of tampons. "What brand she uses. You don't know what brand she uses."

He snapped his fingers and pointed at her. "Exactly. That's it exactly."

"But you're still doing your best."

He threw up his hands. "Hey, I'm tryin'."

"*Aw*. What a good boyfriend you are. She's lucky to have

you. Hope she realizes that."

"Right. That's ah, that's very kind of you to say, but I'm actually just a friend."

"Really? Wow. Because unless you all are *friends with benefits*, you're getting ripped off. The reason I say that is because if — as a guy — you're doing this kind of dirty field work, you should at least be getting some sex out of it, you know?" She cooed to him. "I mean — you're a good-looking guy. If she's not putting out for you, maybe it's time to find someone who will . . . say, babe, have you ever been with a Red? What they say about redheads — well, I can tell you, it's true. Oh, yeah. It's true." She giggled. "So, what do you say? My roommate's going to be gone all day — has to work. She's a lawyer, and she's getting ready for this huge case. Multimillion-dollar case. She was telling me about it this morning. Want to hear about it?"

"Um, well, I really have to find these tamp —"

She cut him off and launched into the details of the litigation. "Okay, so her clients are suing this dude because he hires himself out as a *Minion* for children's parties. Calls himself *Matt the Minion*. Okay? So, my roommate's clients hired him for their little boy's birthday party. The kid was turning five. So, the guy shows up, and the first thing that's fucked-up is that he has a bottle of *Mad Dog Twenty-Twenty* in his back pocket. Okay? You following me here?"

Danny nodded. "Oh, goodness. The *Mad Dog*? Dang. My man was serious." He shook his head in disgust.

"Right. *Mad Dog*. So, he's drunk off the *Mad Dog*, but he's also, like, six-eight. He's a six-foot-eight-inch *Minion*. And he's ripped. I mean, he looked like Chyna or Rich Piana or whatever." She wrinkled her nose and added, "Isn't that fucked-up?" He laughed to himself. *Curse words sound silly coming from that high voice. It's like listening to Punky Brewster cuss.*

He tried to use his mind's eye to conjure up an image of

what Dawn was describing. *Hmm. Let me try to visualize a Minion that's a combination of Andre The Giant, Arnold Schwarzenegger in his prime, and Ulysses S. Grant. Got to have Grant in there, too, to cover the whole drinking thing. Wow. That's tough to even imagine.* "Yeah. There's no doggone excuse for a *Minion* being six-eight. And there's even less of an excuse for a *Minion* looking like Rich Piana? Come on, now. He can control that. You have to live in a gym to look like Rich Piana. Well, that and take plenty of what I believe they call *gym candy*. I mean—I just picked up a *Minion* shirt for my friend over in the women's department, and that *Minion* is tiny. Not all big and hulked-up. Because that's the way *Minions* should be. Tiny."

"I know, right? So, yeah, my roommate's suing his ass. I think they're asking for two mil because all the kids at that party were traumatized. It's a class-action lawsuit. Poor things. It's had a cross-over effect, too. Now, none of those kids will even watch *The Smurfs* because they have flashbacks every time they try. That's sad."

"Indeed. Quite a story. I'd like to be on the jury for that one," he confessed.

"Seriously. Anyway, my roommate's going to be at the office all day. All. Freaking. Day."

"Uh-huh. Uh-huh. And are you a lawyer, too? Those glasses kind of make you look lawyer-ish." *Oh, why did I ask that question? I definitely have issues in terms of engaging with people with whom I shouldn't. But those glasses do make her look like a lawyer.*

"Me? No. But I make real good money. I'm a day trader. And, honey, your stock just went up. Way up. Now, the only question is—are you good at *keeping it up*? Can you *keep it up* all afternoon? Hmm?" She licked her lips. "You know, babe, there's three things in life you should experience before you die. One. The Grand Canyon. Two. Getting your hands on some excellent *Trainwreck*. And three. Go to *Bed with a Red*.

Now, I can't help you with the first one, but I could start taking care of numbers two and three for you within, oh, I don't know, the next half hour or so. That's two out of three. And as Meatloaf once said, *Two Out Of Three Ain't Bad*. Oh, and by the way, number two makes number three even better. What do you say, cutie?" She winked at him, kissed the air, and made pouty lips.

He got nervous. It was always the same when women hit on him. Sweat ran down his forehead. He trembled a bit. He got cottonmouth. Sometimes, he even stuttered. On this day, a fib came out. "Well, with my friend — we are kind of *friends with benefits*. We do it all the dang time, you know? And she's psychic. So, if I took you up on your offer, she'd know, and she might cut off my *you know what* when I get home. Because even though we're just *friends with benefits*, she, like, doesn't want me to see other women. She's funny that way. And she has some really good, excellent *Trainwreck*, in her own right. Yeah, I dig her *Trainwreck*. I love getting jiggy with her *Trainwreck*." *What the hell's Trainwreck? Google it when you get home.* "So, unfortunately, as flattering as your invitation is, I have to pass."

She shrugged her shoulders. "Okay. Fine. No prob. I'm going to ask the guy who corrals the carts if he wants to. He looks like one of the Jonas Brothers." She smiled, raised her eyebrows, and started to walk away.

He called her back. "Oh, Dawn — before you leave, I was just wondering." He pointed to the display of tampons. "Do you, by chance, use any of this stuff?"

She flashed him a scowl. "I'm a *woman*."

"Right. Righto. You are definitely a woman. The only reason I ask is I was wondering if you had any recommendations."

She pulled a box from the shelf and handed it to him. "Here. These are good. They're a little pricey, but they're good."

He looked at the box and read the name of the brand aloud. *"Tampax Radiant." Tampons can be radiant?* "So, you're sure these ones are good?"

"Yeah."

"I just want to make sure I get the right ones."

"They're good. They're the *Lamborghini* of tampons," she assured him. "Look, if you don't believe me, go look it up in *Consumer Reports*, okay?"

"No. That won't be necessary. I'll take your word. *Tampax Radiant* it is. Thank you for your help, Dawn." He put the box in his cart, picked up a second one, and put that in his cart, too. *May as well get two boxes while I'm here.* He strategically arranged the cart so that the clothing covered the tampons.

Dawn started to walk away, abruptly stopped, turned around, and walked back over to him. She shook her finger at him. "Just so you know — if your *friend with benefits* is really as possessive and jealous as you say — she's not a *friend* with *benefits*. She's a freaking girlfriend. Just thought you should know. And do you even know what *Trainwreck* is?"

"Sure, I do. Of course, I do. I'm a . . . I'm a hipster."

"Then what is it?"

Confidently, he told her. "It's that new form of music that the whole world's going gaga over. It's a combination of murder rap, classical, and the boyband sound. With a touch of disco thrown in just for good measure." *Okay, if it's true that if you put enough monkeys in a room with typewriters that they'll eventually produce, verbatim, The Complete Works of William Shakespeare, then I theoretically have a chance at being right with my guess.*

She looked at him and shook her head. "I am *so* glad I didn't take you home. Don't get me wrong — you're cute and all, but I'll bet anything that you'd want to cuddle afterward. And that's just gross. Geek."

She walked away.

He shook it off and went on his way, picking up the makeup, the bikini wax, nail polish, and a box of *Glamor Gal Sunkissed Blonde* hair dye. And he picked up two pairs of overalls. The entire excursion had taken about an hour and a half. But he was finally done and headed for the checkout line. It was a long line on that Saturday morning. *They never have enough cashiers on duty. Too cheap to hire more, that's what it is. Let the customers be inconvenienced.*

While waiting, he looked at the magazines on display. There was a tabloid called *Tattle Tales* that had a picture of Grace on the cover. The headline proclaimed — *Why Pop Diva Grace Stevens Can't Keep A Boyfriend*. He picked it up and briefly thumbed through it. An older man behind him, who reeked of cigar smoke, pointed to the photo and told Danny, "Grace Stevens. She went missing. They have no idea what happened to her."

Danny nodded. "Yeah. I heard something about that on the news."

The man continued. "Bet you anything she's dead. Probably lying dead somewhere. And I'll bet you it was dope that did it. These celebrities like their dope, you know? Oh, they just have to have that dope. Can't live without it, just like that Whitney Houston. She was on dope. So was Marilyn Monroe, Michael Jackson, and Janis Joplin. Oh, and Jim Morrison. Him, too. They were all on dope — all of them. And I'll tell you something else about these goddamn celebrities. They think they're really something, and they also — "

The man was starting to get on his nerves. Danny cut him off in mid-sentence. "Not all famous people fall into that trap. And I've never heard anything about Grace Stevens using drugs," he said pointedly. He felt compelled to defend Grace's honor. He put the magazine back and turned around, ignoring the rest of the man's rant about celebrities. *What is it about the People of Walmart today?* He looked at the *impulse buy* display and saw boxes of *Krispy Kreme* jelly donuts. He picked up a box for her and placed it in the cart. Once he got towards the front of the line, he found the bubble gum, too, right next to the candy bars. He'd almost forgot. He placed nine packs of *Hubba Bubba* watermelon in his cart.

When he finally got to the front of the checkout line, he started to unload. *The worst of this little excursion is over. I'm basically home free.* He looked up to greet the cashier. And then he saw her. He saw that his cashier was going to be Donna Marshall. She was active at St. Mary's, a member of the Church Finance Committee, in fact. And she was a gossip — the gossip of all gossips. The running joke that circulated throughout the parish was — *Donna doesn't repeat gossip . . . so you'd better listen close the* first *time.* The truth was, she loved to get into everyone's business. Her hair was bleached blonde, she wore too much makeup, and she had a deep, tanning salon tan that produced that hideous artificial orange skin tone.

He thought about switching to another line, but it was too late. The conveyer belt was already moving his items forward. She had even scanned the first product.

They looked at each other. There was an awkward pause. She surveyed the totality of what he intended to purchase.

He finally raised his hand and meekly said, "Hello, Donna. How are you doing?"

"Fine, Father O'Connor." She was just starting to scan some of the bras.

After another pause, Danny said, "I thought you worked at the Aberdeen *Walmart.*"

"Not anymore. Had to transfer down here a couple of weeks ago because they were cutting hours in Aberdeen."

He nodded. *Okay, just play it cool. Act like there's nothing unusual about what you're buying.* He started to sweat. *God, just get me out of this store. Maybe she won't make any comments.*

No such luck. Donna giggled, held one of the bras up high for the entire line to see, and said, "There are certainly some interesting items on your shopping list today, Father

O'Connor."

"Yeah, well, they're not for me."

"Well, I should hope not."

Should I just leave it at that or offer an explanation? He thought about it for a few seconds and finally decided he had to come up with some acceptable reason for a Catholic priest buying a whole cart full of women's products.

He took a deep breath. "If you're wondering about this stuff, it's, ah, it's all for my sister."

She looked at him with suspicion. "Your sister? I didn't know you have a sister."

He smiled a nervous smile. "Oh, yes. I have a sister. She's visiting from out of town. Staying with me at the rectory, in fact."

Donna nodded but asked, "Didn't she bring her own clothes?"

"Well . . . sure she did, but that darn airline lost all of her luggage. Boy, she was really upset when that happened. Oh, yessiree, Bob. She called that airline and gave them a piece of her mind, don't you think she didn't."

"I see. Will we be seeing her at Mass on Sunday?"

"At Mass? No. No. She's, uh, she's allergic to incense. Poor thing sneezes her head off every time she's around the stuff. Eyes all watery. The whole nine yards. It's an ugly scene. She'd be much better off being Baptist, actually."

"Well, that's too bad, Father. Please send her my regards."

He smiled and nodded. "Righto."

She tried scanning the tampons. Both boxes. Neither would scan.

"Huh. They're not coming up," she told him. *Of course, they're not. Just my luck.*

She held one of the boxes up high and yelled to a young man sweeping the floor fifty feet away. "Hey, Bubba! I need a price check. Lifestyles Department. *Tampax Radiant* tampons." Danny looked down and again felt the heat on his cheeks. Bubba walked up to the register, grabbed the box from Donna, and snickered.

A few minutes later, he came back and called out, "Six ninety-nine. The tampons are six ninety-nine. Per box."

"Thank you, Bubba," she called out.

She finished ringing him up, and he paid with his credit card. Six-hundred-ninety-six-dollars-seventy-six cents.

He exhaled as he finally pushed his cart out the door. And he wondered if Donna had bought his story. Then it dawned on him that he'd lied, and a profound sense of shame briefly overcame him. He quickly dismissed it, though. *It's all for the greater good. I have an obligation to protect Grace, and if I have to lie to do it, oh well, so be it. I can only hope that God understands that, in an imperfect world, lying is sometimes the lesser of two evils.*

On his way out, he saw that the local animal shelter, *Precious Paws Animal Rescue League,* had set up a table where they were selling dog and cat toys to benefit the shelter animals. He bought Tippy a rubber teddy bear squeak toy. It was only five dollars, but he gave the lady a twenty and told her to keep the change.

"God bless you," she said.

"God bless you, ma'am," he replied with a warm smile.

Chapter Five: Catch a Falling Star

When he got home, he sat in his car for a few moments, tilting his head back, feeling like he had been through the wringer. He loudly exhaled, grabbed the shopping bags, and walked into the house.

All was quiet. Tippy didn't even come to the door to greet him, which was unusual. He walked up to the guest room to let Grace know that he was back. The room was empty.

Then he heard her call out, "I'm in here." He followed her voice to the master bedroom, his room. She was lying in his bed. Tippy was curled up next to her with her head on Grace's shoulder. The TV was on, and she was watching an episode of *The Brady Bunch* on the *TV Classics Network*.

She looked up at him, sniffled, and said, "Hi-ya."

"Hey," he called out. "Watching *The Brady Bunch*, huh?"

She looked back at the TV and nodded. "Uh-huh. This is the one where Marcia gets hit in the nose with a football right before her big date with Doug Simpson."

"Oh, that's a good one."

She giggled. "I know, right?" A thoughtful look crossed her face. "You know what I've always wondered about *The Brady Bunch*?"

"What's that?"

"I've always wondered if Sam and Alice were having sex? Or was Sam just using her for a bowling partner?"

He shook his head. "Oh, no, no. Sam wasn't using her. He wouldn't do that. Sam was a stand-up guy. They were definitely boyfriend and girlfriend, but I like to believe that they weren't having sex. You see, I don't even want to think about Alice having sex. Or Sam, for that matter. Alice was a good, sturdy, dependable woman. Thinking about her having sex is like thinking about your grandmother having sex. You just don't want to go there."

"Yeah, I suppose you're right. It is kind of gross. But, still, I can't help but wonder if they were doing it, you know?" She tee-heed.

He looked closely at her, took her beauty in. She'd taken off the sweatpants and sweatshirt he'd given her and put on one of his *Ralph Lauren* polo shirts. She was wearing it like a nightshirt and had nothing else on. It was big on her and would have extended down past her knees, but she had it hiked up so that it showcased her silky, smooth legs to good advantage.

He couldn't help but feel aroused. Priest or not, he was, after all, a heterosexual male. And one of the most beautiful women in the world was lying in *his* bed, wearing only one of *his* shirts. He stared at her legs.

She looked at him and tittered. "I hate my legs. They're too damn short. That's why I got rejected as a fashion model. They told me that my legs were too short and my boobs were too big. In the fashion industry, they like long legs and little boobs." She frowned.

He swallowed hard. "I see."

"Oh, hey, I hope you don't mind me coming in your room and borrowing your shirt. I just got hot, and those sweatpants and shirt were making things worse. And I wanted to watch TV. There's no TV in the guest room. I thought coming in here was better than going down to the living room, where someone might see me through a window or something. You don't mind, do you?"

He shook his head. "No. Of course not. In fact, why don't we switch rooms? I'll take the guest room, and you can have my room. I should have offered you the master bedroom right from the start."

"I'd hate to kick you out of your own room."

"It's perfectly fine. I insist."

She looked up at him and smiled. "You're a gentleman. And the world needs more gentlemen. I should know. I've dated plenty of jerks."

He smiled back and winked.

Grace coughed, then rubbed her hands together. "Now, show me what you bought for me."

He brought in the bags, and she went through them while still in bed. She liked the *Minion* shirt. Holding it up, she declared, "Oh, that's cute. I love the *Minions.*"

He shrugged. "I know. Seriously. Who doesn't love the *Minions?*"

"Did you have any problems?" she casually asked.

"You could say that I met some rather interesting people . . . say, could you tell me what *Trainwreck* is?"

"*Trainwreck? Trainwreck* was a really cute little Amy Schumer flick from a while back, like twenty-fifteen or so. Bill Hader was in it, too. So was Colin Quinn. And I'm not an Amy Schumer fan, but she was adorable in that movie. I didn't expect much from it, but it was surprisingly good. Why? Did you see it in the movie section?"

"No. I . . . I don't think she was talking about some movie."

"Who's *she?*"

"A lady — her name was Dawn — came up to me in the Lifestyles Department when I was looking for the tampons. She started talking to me. She said that she had some *Trainwreck* at home. She invited me to go back to her place. I think she wanted me to have sex with her, to be perfectly honest with you."

"That's exactly what she wanted. That's what they use *Trainwreck* for. It's the strain of dope that's supposed to enhance sex. And before you ask — the only way that I know that is because it's pretty common in Hollywood. A lot of big stars use it. Not me, though. I don't do that shit. I haven't smoked dope since I was eighteen. Anyway — you didn't go anywhere with her, did you?"

"Of course not. No. I wouldn't do that. No way." *Why would you think I'd go somewhere with her? That's a little insulting.*

"Good. You don't want to get mixed up with some cheap floozy pothead. It makes me angry that she was bold enough to even approach you. People have no values anymore. Now, was this *Dawn* a hippie? Because *Dawn* kind of sounds like a hippie name. And, by the way, you *do not* want to get on a first-name basis with these women."

Geez, again with the hippies. What did they ever do to you, woman? "Nah. She wasn't a hippie. Not at all. A yuppie, not a hippie. And Dawn's *not* a hippie name. You want a good hippie name? Here. *Moonbeam.* Now *that's* a good hippie name. Gender-neutral, too. Can fit either a male or female hair head . . . but anyway, she had red hair and said that *all the stuff that they say about redheads is true* — whatever that means — and that I should have the experience of going to *bed with a red* at least once."

"What she meant was that redheads, female redheads specifically, are supposedly known for being really wild and kinky in bed. She was telling you that she was basically down for anything."

"Dang. Really?"

"Really."

"Wow. Didn't know any of that."

"Well, you do now. Live and learn. Next time, just walk away, okay? As soon as they start talking their shit, walk away. It's not rude to walk away when someone sexually harasses you."

"Well, I don't know that — technically speaking — what she did satisfied the legal requirements for *sexual harassment.*

When I told her *no,* she seemed to respect that."

"It *was* sexual harassment. And don't defend her. When you defend them, you empower them. You legitimize them. Okay?"

He rolled his eyes. "Yeah. Okay."

"Was she pretty?"

This could be a trap. Be very careful. More careful than when you walked through minefields in Afghanistan. "I mean — she didn't look like Marge Simpson or Cha-Ka from *Land of the Lost* or what have you. Didn't look like Howard Cosell."

"She *was* pretty."

"No. Listen — you want to know the truth? The woman was a dead ringer for Jessica Rabbit."

"Ah, *yeah,* and Jessica Rabbit was freaking gorgeous."

"Okay, well then, she didn't look like Jessica Rabbit. She looked like Peppermint Patty. There. Happy now?"

"Your first response is the official one."

"Oh — and she had this crazy, high-pitched, little girl voice. I thought she was going to shatter the glassware, and that was all the way on the other end of the store."

"Yeah, and you know what they say about women who have those super high voices, don't you?"

"No. What?"

"That they're good in bed. That's what they say — they're good in bed. I read it in *Vogue,* so I know it's true."

"Yeah? Then I guess the actress who voiced Smurfette must be a real tigress, huh?"

She sneezed, coughed, and then informed him, "Oh, you're impossible."

"Look — what difference does it make? I didn't go home with her. I didn't smoke dope with her. I didn't join a damn hippie drum circle. And I didn't burn my *BJ's* card. It's all good, Grace. She was just a very forward, sexually aggressive woman. It's not all that uncommon in the modern world." He threw up his hands. "It is what it is."

"*God.* What's the world coming to? You've got skanks trying to pick up priests in freaking *Walmart,* so they can take them home, get them high, and screw them. *Disgusting.* I'll tell you something—I was watching that Catholic TV evangelist, Father Fabian, this afternoon. He has that show called—*Liturgy For The Last Days.* And he said that we're in the End Times. The End of freaking Days, all right? And shit like this makes me agree with him. Yes, it does. This world is full of depravity." She threw her hands in the air in praise. "Come on, people. Y'all need Jesus."

Oh, Good Lord. That's a full-scale diatribe. Hurricane Grace is making landfall. And she's a Cat 5 storm. "Now, in all fairness to her, she had no way of knowing that I'm a priest. I didn't mention it, either. And as far as being in the End Times, I don't know how Father Fabian's privy to that information, since the Bible says that only God Himself knows when Time will End."

"Listen here—Father Fabian's the real deal. I read somewhere that he predicted the success of *Vanilla Ice* and the failure of *Vanilla Coke.*"

"He also predicted that Andy Dick would win the last presidential election as a spur-of-the-moment write-in candidate. The guy's a nut case."

"Look, all I'm saying is that you shouldn't make excuses for this woman."

"I was just stating the facts, that's all."

"Well, the *facts* are that she's a dirty, filthy whore who's also a stoner."

You can't win this argument. Dad always said it's easier to just let them win. Let them win and be done with it. "Right. You're totally right. I'm sorry. After reflecting on it, I can see that you're totally on point with your analysis. You were right. I was wrong. Sorry."

"Thank you. I like the fact that you can admit when you're wrong. So . . . anything else noteworthy happen?"

"Yeah. I got checked out by one of my parishioners."

"One of your parishioners was checking you out, too? *God.* This world is so fucked-up. I swear."

"No—no—no. Not *checking me out*, ringing me up. She's a cashier. Donna Marshall. She's a busybody, too. She commented on the fact that I had a cart full of women's clothing and so forth."

"Did you tell her you were buying for your sister?"

"Yeah. I went with the whole sister thing. I feel really guilty, too. Not only did I lie, but I lied to a member of my congregation."

"You did the right thing. Thank you."

"Yeah, well, I hope it was the right thing. I guess it was. I just hope Donna doesn't decide to stir the pot."

"Do you think she bought the story?"

"I suppose. I mean—she can't prove that I *don't* have a sister who's visiting from out of town."

"I know you're taking a risk by helping me out like this. I truly do appreciate it. More than you'll ever know."

"Sure. My pleasure."

She examined each article of clothing and nodded her approval. "You did good, Danny. Real good. And I love those pink and white ankle socks. They're absolutely darling. And those teddies look cute, too. I'm glad you didn't get a bunch of stuff that's frumpy. And I love the overalls. They're totally adorable. I'm going to be cuter than a *Hee Haw* Honey."

You already are. Way cuter. "Glad you're happy with it. Anything else you need I can order online. But at least this gives you a basic wardrobe to start with."

As she folded the overalls, she glanced down at the tag. She held it close to her face and examined it. "Junior Miss?"

He shrugged his shoulders. "So?"

"Where'd you find these?"

"In the store." He grinned a shit-eating grin.

"Do not be a smartass. You'd better wipe that Mister Roper smile off your face, pal. Where in the store?" *Dang. She turned on me real fast. I went from a hero to a zero in a split second. Doesn't take much to set her off. The spicy little thing speaks her mind without any filters. I guess nobody puts Baby in the corner. Kind of turns me on.*

He pointed to the tag. "What the tag says. That's where I got them. The, ah, the Junior Miss Department."

She flashed him a scowl.

"Look—I'm sorry, but the ones in the Women's Department would not have fit you. They'd have been way too big. For some reason, with the overalls, they don't make them in petite sizes. Everything else they had in the smaller sizes. But not the overalls. Listen—I'll bet you anything they fit perfect."

"My boobs, Danny. My boobs. These are made for little teenaged girls who are freaking A cups. I am double D. Thirty-four double D."

He threw up his hands. "Well then, I guess I screwed up, didn't I? Because I forgot all about your boobs."

"*Uh-huh. Uh-huh.* And the reason you forgot about them was that you were too busy thinking about that *Dawn* character. You were probably thinking about *her* boobs."

"I said I'm sorry. And I wasn't thinking about Dawn."

She raised her voice and talked through gritted teeth. "*Stop* calling her by her first name. Please. You are getting on my nerves with that shit. I think you're doing it just to be ornery. And if you *must* invoke her name, she is to be referred to as *That Weedhead Whore.* Woman tried to drug and molest you, and you're all like, *Gee, Dawn, you sure are groovy. Want to come over to my house and watch Sex in the City and listen to my new Wayne Newton album? Maybe we can even grab a Happy Meal afterward.*"

"I do listen to Wayne. That's true. He's Mister Las Vegas and a great showman. He sings beautiful, lovely songs. A real class act, too. Unlike *some* entertainers, he never let success go to his head. And listening to the man sing *Danke Schoen* is like experiencing a little piece of Heaven on earth. But I *do not* watch *Sex in the City.*" He laughed a nervous laugh. "That's a total chick show."

She crossed her arms and confidently announced, "You *do* watch it. I found it on your DVR. You had the whole damn series recorded. Plus, both of the movies, to boot. Or maybe it was just the Fairy *Freaking* Godmother who did that, huh?"

I don't know why I ever wasted my time with that show. So frustrating. Carrie was such a glutton for punishment. Mister Big was all wrong for her, but no matter how many times he broke her heart, she just kept going back for more. "Listen up, lady—I don't have to justify my viewing habits to you. You are, after all, the *houseguest.* And in this household, the houseguest does not run the show. And I don't care if that houseguest is Grace Stevens, or Kato Kaelin or the damn Pope himself. Now, see that? You made me say a bad word. Happy now? You drove a priest to curse." *Got to stand up for myself a little here.*

She coughed and shook her finger at him. "I'll tell you something right now, buddy—if this Dawn girl shows up here at our house, you and me are going to have a major problem. I am freaking serious, dude."

"Our house? *Our* house? What? Is there a new law that gives vagrants squatter's rights after only twenty-four hours? Must be. Because last I checked, your name wasn't on the deed."

"Neither is yours, honey. This damn house belongs to the Roman Catholic Church, of which I am a member. Okay, so I don't attend Mass or go to Confession. But I give *boo koo* money to the church. Yes, I do. Make regular and significant donations to the *Little Sisters of the Poor.* Oh, golly—those nuns make the best fruitcakes. Anyway, given all those facts, that makes this as much *my* house as it is yours, babe."

"Fine. Dawn's not coming over. I'll cancel our slumber party and let her know that one of the *homeowners* has banned her. Okay? And I honestly did the best I could with the shopping. And the overalls thing? Well, it just is what it is. So live with it. *Babe.*"

"Fine. I'll wear the darn Junior Miss overalls. And my boobs will just pop right out. And I don't want to hear you complaining when that happens. Be all like—*oh, Grace. You traumatized me because I saw your big boobies.* I don't want to hear that shit."

"I don't see how your boobs would pop out—unless you weren't planning on wearing anything underneath. I mean—most women who wear overalls wear a t-shirt or something underneath."

"Well, maybe I won't just to prove my point. And I don't want to hear you complain when my girls peek out to say *hello.* You read me, boy?" She sneezed.

"*Lima Charlie.* I read you Lima Charlie. And for you civilian types, that's—Loud and Clear." *And you definitely won't hear me complaining about it.*

"Just remember you said that."

"Let's move beyond the whole overalls fiasco, shall we? I'm not used to buying women's clothing, I did the best I could, and I put up with a lot of grief to get this stuff. I think I did a pretty good job, too. And if it makes you feel any better, you don't have to pay me for the overalls. Okay? I did not mean to insult you by buying you the Junior Miss size. It's just that you're a very petite woman and I was trying to get you something that would fit. Fair enough?" *God. This woman is a piece of work. She's rude, profane, bossy, intrusive. Thinks it's her house and that I'm the guest. And . . . and . . . and God. I want to kiss her. I just want to hug her and kiss her and hold her. I do. God help me, but I do.*

She sneezed again and nodded. "Yeah. Fair enough. It's just that I'm sensitive about my size, or lack thereof. Before I developed, the boys in school all made fun of me, called me a Munchkin, and such. Of course, once I developed, they couldn't have cared less about how short I was. At that point, they only cared that I was growing out, not up."

"Right. Well, case closed. I'm sorry if I offended you. I'd never set out to hurt your feelings. Never."

"*Aw.* We just had our first fight, didn't we?"

He chuckled. "Yeah. I guess we did. It was just a little tiff, though. It happens when people live together. Me and my Army buddies argued all the time in the barracks. It's perfectly natural, Grace."

"And you didn't even hit me. How cool is that?"

"Hit you? God, Grace. I'd never strike a woman. Never. Did a guy hit you?"

"Uh-huh. I've had boyfriends who've hit me before. More than one, actually. Called me *a bitch, a cunt*, and smacked me around. Had one who beat me once because I wouldn't do anal."

A tear ran down her cheek. He reached over and wiped it away with his thumb.

"Listen, Grace—nobody will ever do that to you here. Do you believe me when I say that? I will never hurt you. Never. And I would never let anyone else hurt you. Please believe that. It's really important to me that you believe that. I don't want you to be fearful."

She nodded. "I believe you." She looked at him, stared into his eyes. "I trust those eyes. I know I can trust those eyes."

The room got quiet and stayed that way for a few seconds.

Finally, she picked up one of the boxes of tampons and examined it.

"Is that the right brand? They had a million different brands. I wasn't sure which one you liked."

"*Tampax Radiant.* Wow. That's actually the brand that I use. I totally forgot to mention that to you. Good job. Thank you. I know that was a tough assignment. I appreciate your biting the bullet on it. I'm glad you got two boxes, too. That was good thinking. That way, you won't have to buy them again anytime soon."

"Yeah. That was my thinking, as well."

"How much did all this cost?"

"Six-hundred-ninety-some dollars. But that was for everything."

"I'll pay it back. I promise."

"How many times do I have to tell you—I don't want your money. That's not why I'm doing this."

"Why *are* you doing this? Why are you helping me out like this?"

"Because it's the right thing to do."

She sat up in the bed. "I believe you mean that, too."

"I do," he assured her.

She wagged her index finger at him. "You're different. Different from any other man I've ever met. Why, I bet you even put the toilet seat down when you're done?"

He laughed. "As a matter of fact, I do." He thought for a moment and then got serious. "But I'm not perfect."

"You're a lot more perfect than I am. You've got your life together. And me—well, my life's a mess."

I may not have my life as together as you think. "We're all a work in progress, Grace. At least that's how I think God sees us."

She nodded agreement. "That's a good way to think of it. A work in progress."

"I think so."

The room fell silent. She was gazing up at him. Softly, she bit her lower lip. There was a look of expectancy in her eyes. *What does she want me to do? What do I want to do?* He wondered if God was testing him but quickly dismissed the notion. *God wouldn't use Grace as a pawn to test my will. God doesn't use any of his Creatures as a means to an end.*

He was tired. Too tired to think on heavy matters. For now, he wanted to escape all that. He ran his hand through his thick, black hair and let out a sigh. "What do you say we put in a movie?"

She clapped her dainty hands. "Yay. A movie. Sounds good. Can I pick it?"

"Sure. Lady's choice."

She got up and walked over to a bookcase that was setup along the wall in his bedroom. She read the titles out loud as she perused his DVD collection. "Let's see here. You've got *My Fair Lady, Roman Holiday, Paris When It Sizzles*. Boy, you like Audrey Hepburn, huh?"

"She was a fine actress."

"A lot of people think that I look like Audrey."

He nodded. "I can see the resemblance." *But you have a much, much better body than she ever did.*

She continued to browse. Finally, she picked one. "Here you go. This one. Let's watch this one. I've seen it, like, a zillion times, but I never get tired of it." She held it up.

He read the title aloud. "*Rocky*. The original *Rocky*, no less." He nodded. "Yeah. One of the best films ever made, in my humble opinion."

"I know it's about boxing, but it's actually a great love story, too," she said.

"Indeed. It's my favorite Stallone film. It was brilliant. It never needed any of those silly sequels. None of them could recapture the magic of the original."

"First rule of the entertainment business—always push to capitalize when there's money to be made off something. Even if what you're pushing is a human being. And even if you're pushing that human being beyond her limits."

"It's sad that it's that way. I'm sorry. Money should never come before people."

"Thank you. You're kind." She smiled at him.

He cleared his voice. "Ah, getting back to the film—you're right. It is, in its own way, a great romance."

"I think you're a closet romantic," she told him.

He laughed. "Guilty as charged. In fact, I'm not even in the closet. Truth be told, I love a good romance."

She started to walk back over to the bed when she tripped over a rawhide that Tippy had been playing with.

She teetered and then started to fall forward. "Whoa!"

Quickly, he positioned himself to make the save. He caught her right before she fell flat on her face.

Gently, he lifted her up. Holding her close, he could feel her breasts mashing against his chest. It felt warm and cozy. *God. Holding her feels good. So good. So right.*

"Are you okay?" he asked.

She nodded. "Uh-huh." Then she put one arm around his neck and pulled him even closer to her. She looked up at him, and with her free hand, she brushed the tip of his nose with her index finger. In a whisper, she said, "You caught a falling star." They both laughed. He quickly let go of her. And a look of disappointment crossed her face.

CHAPTER SIX: THE HALL OF HEROES

Sunday morning. Grace awoke to the sound of Tippy barking downstairs. She looked at the clock on the nightstand. It was 5:30. She got up and looked at herself in a small, antique mirror which hung on the wall. She was wearing a black lace bra with matching panties. A white, terrycloth bathrobe hung in Danny's closet. She put it on. As she walked downstairs, she used a rubber band to put her hair into a ponytail.

There was an aroma of pancakes and sausage coming from the kitchen. There, she found Danny taking some sausage links out of the microwave. There was a stack of pancakes already on the kitchen counter.

He was dressed for work, wearing his Roman collar, a black clerical shirt, black pants, and black oxfords. The smell of his cologne mixed with the scent of the food cooking. *Oh, golly. Smells so good. Kind of arouses me.*

She yawned and casually called out to him, "Hey."

He turned around and smiled. "Hey there. How are you today?"

She sat at the kitchen table. "Good, actually."

"Feeling better?"

She nodded. "Yeah. I am. I'm not sneezing or coughing as much. And my throat doesn't hurt anymore. Neither does my head." She got up, walked over to the microwave, and stuck her forehead out. "Here. Feel me. See if I still have a temperature."

He placed his hand on her forehead. She closed her eyes and took a deep breath.

"You don't feel warm. I think your fever broke overnight."

"You've taken good care of me. Thank you."

"My pleasure. Would you care for some breakfast? I took the liberty of setting two places at the table. I made some microwavable pancakes and sausage. Nothing fancy, but it'll fill you up."

"Yeah, sure. I'll try some. I think I could eat a little today."

"How about some coffee? Are you a coffee drinker?"

"I love coffee. And I take mine black. No cream or sugar."

He turned around, grabbed two mugs from the cupboard, and poured them both a cup. "I take mine black, too. I learned to drink it that way in Afghanistan. We didn't have the luxury of cream or sugar over there. I eventually learned to prefer it black."

He handed the coffee to her, then brought all of the food to the table on a large serving tray.

He pointed to the robe. "I see you found my housecoat."

She looked down at it. "Oh, yeah. I'm only wearing a bra and panties, so I figured I'd make myself decent by throwing this on. I hope you don't mind."

He shook his head. "No. Not at all. It's really big on you, though. Just be careful not to trip yourself."

She rolled the sleeves up. "I know, right?"

They both sat at the table.

She stabbed a pancake and a sausage link from the serving tray with her fork and set it on her plate. She took a sip of her coffee. "So, I guess Sunday's kind of your big day, huh?"

He took a drink of his coffee, too, and nodded. "I guess you could say that." He smiled at her.

God. His smile is so amazing. He's got white teeth, but it's a natural white, not that hideous, artificial white that you see with people who bleach their teeth.

He cleared his voice and tentatively asked, "So, what are your plans? What are you going to do?"

"About what?"

He shot her a look of disbelief. "About what? About this situation. You're hiding from the world. You can't do that forever."

The question hurt her. "Trying to get rid of me already?" she asked indignantly. "I haven't even been here forty-eight hours, and you're trying to get rid of me?"

He shook his head. "I'm not trying to get rid of you. Not at all. I'm just trying to find out if you have a game plan."

"Well, I don't," she shot back. "Not yet anyway."

He looked her in the eyes. "What about your family? Your folks? They probably think that something terrible has happened to their daughter. Don't you think you should at least call them to let them know that you're okay? Don't you owe them that?"

She started to cry. "Don't lay that guilt trip on me. I feel bad enough."

He reached across the table and patted her hand. "I'm sorry. I didn't mean to come across that way."

She took a napkin and dabbed her eyes. "I know you didn't. It's just that I think that if I tell anyone where I am, it'll somehow get out. The press will find out. The paparazzi will find out. Maybe I'm just being paranoid, but that's how I feel." She paused, looked down, and then looked back up at him. "I've found peace here. I had so much fun last night watching that movie with you. It was just the two of us — no fans, no photographers, no members of an entourage. It was just me and you — just Grace and Danny. I'm tired of living up to an image. Do you realize how hard that is?"

He nodded. "Yes. I do, as a matter of fact. People expect me to be perfect. Because I'm a priest, I'm not allowed to ever have a bad day or be in a rotten mood. People expect perfection. So, yes, I know what that's like."

"I guess we're kind of kindred spirits," she said with a smile.

"I guess so." Tippy sat at his feet and begged for some food. She whined and wagged her tail. He hand-fed her a sausage link, which she devoured in one gulp.

Grace walked over to Tippy, kneeled, and patted her on the head. "Now, see, I love animals. I'd love to have a dog." She looked at Danny as Tippy licked her face. "But it wouldn't be fair to the animal. I'm always on tour."

After they finished breakfast, he cleared the table and washed the dishes. Grace dried them.

As she dried a porcelain plate, she asked, "So, when you get home from church this morning, how about we watch another movie? Maybe *Paris When It Sizzles?* That's a good one."

"I'll be gone for most of the day. After Mass, I have to take Communion to members of the parish who are homebound. Then, it's off to the nursing homes and hospitals to see various people." He paused before continuing. "And finally, I have to stop off for a meeting. A meeting for vets who suffer from . . . from . . . PTSD."

"That's awfully nice of you to facilitate their meeting for them."

He looked down. "I'm not going to *facilitate* the meeting. I'm going there *for* the meeting. To participate, that is."

It took a moment for it to sink in. Finally, she tentatively asked, "Oh. So . . . you have PTSD?"

Still looking down, he nodded. "I do."

She spoke in a soft, gentle tone. "It's nothing to be ashamed of, you know."

"I feel like it is. I haven't talked to many people about it. Members of the parish don't even know. I've talked to Father Larkin, the priest over at Saint Jude's, a little. He's sort of my one confidant within the Church. But I've never told anyone here at Saint Mary's about my time in Afghanistan. And I certainly don't tell them that I go to meetings for PTSD."

"Why not?"

"Because they might judge it to be a sign of weakness."

"But it's not."

"That's not how the world works. You know that."

"Would you like to talk to me about it? Maybe? Sometime?"

He shook his head. "No. I'm sorry. I think it would be hard for you to understand."

"But I could try to understand. I could try."

He pointed out the window. "You see the churchyard out there? All those tombstones?"

She looked at the window and nodded. "Yeah. What about them?"

"Here at Saint Mary's, we have Civil War soldiers buried in our cemetery. Some Union. Some Confederate. Maryland was a border state during the War. It had divided loyalties, you see. Both the North and South fielded Maryland units in their armies. At Gettysburg, Marylanders fought one another at a place called Culp's Hill. At the beginning of the War, all those boys got dressed up in their fanciest uniforms and marched off for what they thought was the ultimate adventure. They sang patriotic songs about how they were going to whup the other side and worried that the War might be over before they got a chance to fight and earn their glory. Well, that's kind of what happened with me. I thought going to war was romantic. That notion lasts as long as it takes for you to see what modern technology can do to the human body. Don't get me wrong — I'm proud that I served. I served with the best of my generation. The finest group of men I've ever been around. Still, I can't help but think of the words of Robert E. Lee when he said, *it is well that war is so terrible — otherwise we should grow too fond of it*. Now, that's the Lord's Truth. And don't let anyone tell you different."

She didn't know what to say. Slowly, she raised her hand to put it on his shoulder, but he turned and walked away.

79

With a deep sigh, he said, "Anyhow, I have to get going." He neatly folded the dishcloth and set it on the counter. "I'll stop on my way home and pick up a pizza from *Frank's* for dinner tonight. How does that sound?"

She nodded. "Sure. Sounds good."

"So, what do pop divas like on their pizzas?"

"Sausage and anchovies."

He made a face. "Anchovies? Really?"

"Yeah. Really."

He warmly smiled and nodded. "Okay. Sausage and anchovies, it is."

They walked to the living room. A black fedora hung on a hat rack near the front door. He put it on and pulled down the brim. "I'll see you later, lassie. And as we used to say in Afghanistan—keep your head down." He winked at her.

"I will. See ya, Danny." She waved goodbye.

From the living room, she watched him walk out the door, down a cobblestone walkway that led to the church. When he disappeared from view, she walked upstairs and plopped herself down on his bed. A few minutes later, Tippy entered and jumped up with her. The dog lay by Grace's side. She turned on the TV and watched the latest reports of her disappearance. There was a lot of speculation. Drugs. Foul play. Even rumors of suicide had surfaced. *Maybe it would be better if the world thought I was dead.*

She turned off the TV, got out of bed, and looked around the room. On his desk sat a fairly large ceramic statue of the Virgin Mary. Propped up against the statue was a photo that caught her eye. It was a picture of him in a pair of Army camouflaged trousers. He didn't have a shirt on. His chest was hairless and well developed—his hair was cut high and tight. A lit cigarette dangled from his mouth. *He can't be any older than eighteen in this picture.* And he was holding a tiny black kitten, whom he was bottle feeding. Over his shoulder was slung an *M16* assault rifle. She turned the picture over. On the back, someone had written, *Korengal Valley 2007*. She looked over at Tippy, who was still lying on the bed, and said, "See? This is your daddy when he was a soldier." She held the photo up for the dog to look at.

There was something about the picture that moved her. She couldn't help but feel a wave of emotion overcome her. *He's holding that little kitten so tenderly. There is just something so poignant about that.* She wondered whatever happened to that kitten, wondered if he was, by chance, still alive.

There was a photo album on a bookshelf. The album was labeled *Tippy*. She pulled it off the shelf and flipped through it. It was a memory book, and it had photos of the dog from the time she was a puppy right up to the present. One photo showed her in a pet store, at Christmas time, sitting on Santa's lap. Grace smiled and told the little Sheltie, "Your daddy must be a good guy if he took you to see Santa."

She looked at the other books on the shelf. There was a copy of the *Greek New Testament*. She opened it up and briefly paged through it. *It's Greek to me.* He had a book on the philosophy of Emmanuel Kant. *Bor-ring.* There was a coffee table book called *The Pictorial History of The Masters Golf Tournament. How does anyone get pleasure from chasing a little white ball around all day? Hmm. Wonder if I could learn how to play? Do couples do that kind of thing together?* Next, she found a publication called *Magic For Dummies. He's into magic. Well, now — that's kind of interesting.* She picked up a book called *Brother Against Brother: An Anecdotal History of the American Civil War. Why do they call it The* Civil *War? There was nothing civil about it.* Finally, she leafed through a title called, *The Kennedy Half Dollar: America's Love Affair With A Legendary Coin. Oh, yeah. He said he was a coin nerd.* The rest of the books were mostly on religion. *Overall, pretty dull, but at least I didn't stumble onto a stash of porn. I'd rather have dull than a porn addict.*

She looked over at Danny's desktop computer. *Would it be wrong to search his name?* She pondered it for a moment but decided a little background check wouldn't be unfair. *I'm living in his house with him, after all. I have a right to objective, unbiased information about the man. And everyone leaves an online footprint nowadays.* She did a google search, typing in *Daniel O'Connor, Maryland.* A newspaper article from *The Howard County Times* popped up. The headline read *Daniel O'Connor Sets Maryland Scofflaw Record, Owes County More Than 43K In Unpaid Parking Tickets.* She clicked the link and looked at the photo that accompanied the article. The Daniel O'Connor in question appeared to be in his fifties, was balding, and looked to weigh nearly four-hundred pounds. She was relieved.

Eventually, she waded through all the extraneous hits and zeroed in on the relevant results. She discovered that he'd graduated from the University of Baltimore with a BA in history and Moreau Seminary in Indiana with a master of divinity degree. The *Pets With Disabilities* website listed him as a Sustaining Sponsor. *Aw. I love that.*

She found his *Facebook* page. Mostly, it was a bunch of pictures of Tippy mixed in with inspirational quotes from the Bible. Then, an article about him appeared in *The Maryland Catholic* that talked about a tour that he'd led a few years earlier to the Holy Land.

Finally, she found his name associated with a website called *The Hall Of Heroes.* She went to the site and found him listed as a Silver Star recipient. *Oh, Jesus. The Silver Star's a big deal. I don't know shit about the military, but I do know that much.* She clicked on his name. It took her to a page that displayed a photo of him in his dress uniform and the text of the citation, which read —

The President of the United States of America, authorized by Act of Congress July 9th, 1918, takes great pride in presenting the Silver Star for valor to Private First Class Daniel Owen O'Connor, United States Army, for gallantry in connection with military operations against an armed enemy force while serving with D Company, 2nd

Battalion, 503 Infantry Regiment (Airborne) of the 173rd Airborne Brigade Combat Team. On the afternoon of 20 October 2007, in support of Operation Enduring Freedom, in the Korengal Valley, Afghanistan, Private First Class O'Connor exposed himself to enemy fire while rescuing his wounded squad leader. Private First Class O'Connor was struck with shrapnel from a rocket-propelled grenade. Despite his wound, he pressed on in his efforts to recover his fallen comrade, eventually dragging him to safety. Private First Class O'Connor's gallant actions and devotion to duty, without regard for his own life, were in keeping with the highest traditions of military service and reflect great credit upon himself, the 173rd Airborne Brigade Combat Team, and the United States Army. Hometown: Warwick, Maryland

It gave her chills, almost made her cry. And it made him all the more attractive to her. But there was a part of her that wished that her research had uncovered that he had feet of clay, that he was a jerk. *It would be so much simpler if he were just another asshole. The world's full of assholes. Why can't he be just one more?* She sneezed, sighed, and got up from the computer.

The bottle of *Glamor Gal* hair dye that he'd bought for her was still sitting on the nightstand. She picked it up and looked at it. *Should I? Yes, I think I need a fresh look. Wonder if he likes blondes?* She took the bottle into the bathroom. When she finished dyeing her hair, she took a shower and put on a pair of jeans and her *Minion* t-shirt. Looking in the bathroom mirror, she inspected the dye job and nodded approvingly. *Not bad if I do say so myself. I mean — I'm sure Mister Maurice could have done it better, but he's nearly three-thousand miles away, back in the Hills. So, this will have to do. And as home dye jobs go, it really is pretty decent.* She completed her look by applying a little makeup.

Her cold was quickly getting better, but her legs started to ache. She walked downstairs and found a bottle of *Tylenol* sitting on the kitchen table. She took two and wandered around the first floor — she still hadn't had a chance to see the entire rectory. When she entered the parlor, she saw a vintage *Baldwin* piano sitting in the middle of the room. She sat at the keyboard and played *I Don't Know How To Love Him*. It was from the rock opera *Jesus Christ Superstar*. She'd played Mary Magdalene in the show, toured the country during the *AD 2019 Tour*. She'd had to sing the song every night. It was always a struggle to hold back the tears. On this day, she didn't even try. Her tears made her mascara run, giving her the appearance of a ballplayer wearing a thin layer of eye black for an afternoon baseball game. *Now, I know how she felt. I know how Mary felt.* Once she composed herself, she went to the upstairs bathroom. She wiped all the makeup off her face and reapplied it.

She returned to Danny's room and turned the TV back on, this time tuning into *The Romance Channel*. They were running a Jimmy Stewart marathon. She watched the first half of *The Shop Around the Corner* before drifting off to sleep.

Chapter Seven: The Blonde and the Barracuda

The sound of Tippy barking downstairs woke her up. She looked at the clock on the nightstand. It was five-thirty. She'd been asleep for several hours. Downstairs, she could hear Danny's voice, talking to Tippy. She walked down and found him in the kitchen, holding a pizza box.

He looked at her, smiled, and pointed. "Hey, I see you dyed your hair."

"Yeah. You like it? They say *gentlemen prefer blondes.*"

He nodded. "I think it looks nice. Very cute, in fact."

"Thank you."

"And how was your day?" he asked.

"I watched the news and part of an old Jimmy Stewart picture. A lovely little romantic comedy, but I fell asleep halfway through. Oh, and, before that, I got into a fight."

"*A fight?*"

"A virtual fight. An online catfight. Yup."

"Do tell."

"Not much to tell, really. I was surfing *YouTube* on your desktop, looking at a clip from *Friends*. I love that show. Golly, I wish I had friends like that. Anyway, this *bitch*—calls herself *ScottBaioLover1968*—posted in the comments that Ross and Rachel *were* on a break. So, I replied that they most certainly were not and that Ross was a no-good cheater. It took off from there. Got real nasty and personal, too. Expletives flew. But thirty-seven comments later, I won. She who posts last wins.

That's how the internet works."

"Congrats. What'd you do? Make up a fake account?"

"No, I used yours. You were already logged in. Oh . . . you *might* get an email from *YouTube* saying you're *suspended* for thirty days for violating their stupid *Community Standards*. I don't know if they're really serious about that or not."

"*Uh. Huh.* Now I feel compelled to ask—what else did you do while I was gone? You didn't sign me up for the *Columbia Record and Tape Club*, did you?"

"No. Of course not. That went bankrupt a few years ago. No, I took a shower. Then, I played that old *Baldwin.* You know, I didn't even realize you had a piano."

He laughed. "It's not mine. It belongs to the church. It's an antique and more of a decorative piece than anything. I don't play. I don't have too much musical talent." He paused, chuckled, and added, "Of course, in Junior High, I was in a *KISS* tribute band called *Shout It Out Loud.* We were the hottest thing going at Immaculate Conception School for a while."

She giggled. "Seriously? Oh my God. That's adorable. So, you guys wore the makeup and everything?"

"Yep. The makeup and everything."

"Which one were you? No—wait. Let me guess . . . Peter. You were Peter."

"Very good. I was Peter Criss. *The Catman.* I got to sing *Beth* at every gig. Now, how'd you figure that out?"

"It wasn't too hard. Peter was always the quiet, cute, sweet, sensitive one. Plus, I had a one-in-four chance at being right anyway." They both laughed.

"Right. Well, that was a long time ago. But getting back to the piano, I think it's an antique. Goes back to the nineteen-thirties."

"I'd like to play it for you. It seems to play just fine. Maybe we can go into the parlor after dinner and I'll play some songs."

He nodded. "I'd love to have you play for me. I mean, who wouldn't want their own private Grace Stevens concert? But it'll have to wait until after my meeting is over. We're having some company tonight, in about twenty minutes or so. So, you'll need to make yourself scarce. Understand?"

"Who's coming over?"

"Marie Gianelli."

"Who's Marie Gianelli?"

"She's the head of the Youth Group at Saint Mary's."

"Why's she coming here?"

"She wants my input in planning some outings for the kids."

She wasn't happy about this development. "How come you didn't mention her coming over this morning?"

"Well, it was kind of a spur of the moment thing. This morning, after Mass, she mentioned she was free tonight and that it would be a good time to talk about some possible activities for the children."

She raised her eyebrows. "Oh, so she invited herself over?"

He corrected her. "No. She *volunteered* to come over so we can plan these trips. Volunteers are the lifeblood of the Church. I can't be everywhere, do everything. Without a lay ministry, we wouldn't be able to do even half the things that we do. People like Marie are invaluable to the mission of the Church."

She shrugged and dismissively waved her hand at him. "Yeah, well, whatever." With a sigh, she added, "I guess I'll hang out in your room until after she leaves."

"You'll have to. But once she leaves, we can have our pizza, you can play the piano, and we'll watch a movie. I promise." He looked at his watch. "Look, she'll be here soon." With his head, he motioned towards the stairs. "You better run along. Go on now. Skedaddle, lass."

She made a pouty face. "Okay. Okay." She slinked up the stairs like a child being sent to her room without supper. Tippy followed.

The two of them went into Danny's bedroom, and Grace looked out the window, down into the driveway. Tippy jumped up, placed her paws on the windowsill, and looked out, too.

Grace talked to herself as she watched. "Let's see what this hussy looks like." She thought for a moment before adding, "Of course, how bad will I feel for saying that if this chick turns out to be, like, seventy-five years old, has blue-gray hair, and uses a walker?"

After fifteen minutes, a huge black *Cadillac* pulled into the driveway. Out of the vehicle stepped a tall brunette in her late thirties with long legs — she was pretty by anyone's standards. She was wearing a pair of tight-fitting jeans, a low-cut black top that revealed considerable cleavage, and a pair of black boots. Grace again talked to herself, providing a running commentary. "Ah, excuse me. Those boots went out of style five years ago, honey." She watched her walk up to the front door. "Look at her wiggling that ass of hers. *Skank*. She looks like she should be turning tricks on Sunset Boulevard. And those tits are totally fake. I can tell from all the way up here. I can spot implants a mile away. My boobs are real."

When the woman walked into the house, Grace went to the top of the stairs and lay down on the floor. She could see a bit into the living room, but she couldn't see the entire room. Danny and Marie were in the living room talking, but they were just out of Grace's view. She could, however, hear everything.

They discussed business, but the conversation was peppered with personal talk as well. At one point, she heard Marie tell Danny that she'd just separated from her husband. Then she told him that he had a *nice smile*. Grace gasped and covered her mouth in disbelief. *Oh! She is so trying to get with him.*

After an hour, Marie left. Grace again went to the bedroom window to watch. She looked on as Danny walk out with her. They hugged. *God Almighty. She almost has her hand on his ass. She wants to go all Pepe Le Pew on him!*

When the car pulled out of the driveway, Grace mockingly waved a Miss America wave and said, "Bub-bye." And she tacked on, "Get out of my house, *bitch*. And don't come back. You do not want beef with me, girlfriend. Damn hoe!" She turned, looked at the dog, and told her, "Don't worry, Tippy. That homewrecker's never going to darken our doorstep again with her presence. I'm going to throw a major hissy fit over this. The Mother of All Hissy Fits. Because if there's one thing that Grace Stevens knows how to do, it's throwing a good hissy fit."

Danny called up the stairs. "Okay, Grace, the coast is clear. You can come out now."

She was already bounding down the steps with Tippy right behind her.

"We have to talk. *Now,*" she insisted. "I'm calling a family meeting."

"*Family meeting*? About what?"

"About that barracuda who was just here."

He laughed. "Barracuda?"

She emphatically nodded. "That's right. *Barracuda.*"

He shot her a leery look.

"Danny, *she is.*"

"What makes you say that?"

"The way she was dressed, the way she walked, the way she hugged you, the fact that she told you she had split with her husband."

He crossed his arms. "And how exactly did you come by all of this information? Hmm?"

She shrugged, looked down, and fiddled with her nails. "I

don't know. I might have been eavesdropping. And looking out the window. Maybe . . . possibly . . . probably."

He shook his head in disgust. "You don't have the right to spy on me."

"Well, somebody has to. I'm telling you—that woman wants you. She's trying to seduce you." She paused and sniffed the air. "By the way, you reek of her perfume. Some cheap-ass shit." She again sniffed to get another whiff. "I don't even know what it is. I don't recognize it. Some women's version of bathroom *Polo,* I suppose. And if you think her boobs are real, you've got another thing coming, mister. Those things are about as real as William Shatner's hair. Now, my boobs, on the other hand, are the real deal."

"I can assure you, she's a fine Christian woman," he retorted.

She stuck her tongue out at him and blew raspberries. "Like hell, she is. She has some unholy ideas in her mind. You are so freaking naïve."

"How do you know all this?"

With great confidence, she replied, "Because I'm a *woman,* honey. A woman. *W-o-m-a-n.*" She pointed to her head. "And I know how the female mind works. I'm just trying to warn you, that's all. I mean—I'd hate to see you fall from grace and break your priestly vows."

"Your concerns have been duly noted. And I have no intention of breaking any of my vows. Besides, this meeting was a one-time thing. It's not like she's going to be hanging around here constantly."

Good. She smiled and calmed down. "I don't mean to sound preachy. And I shouldn't have spied on you. But you're a nice guy. A real nice guy. One of the nicest I've ever met. And I don't want to see anyone take advantage of you, that's all. I swear, I'd claw the eyes out of any woman who tried to hurt you."

"I believe you would."

She emphatically nodded one time. "Damn right, I would. And you know why?"

"Why?"

She placed her hands on her hips and wiggled them from side to side. "Because I'm feisty, baby. And I have spunk."

He threw his head back and laughed heartily. "Yes, you do. In spades."

"Just know that my intentions were good, even if my methods weren't. Okay?"

He nodded. "Okay. Fair enough. Let's not talk anymore about Marie Gianelli. Besides, she's not my type anyway."

"Not your type? Really? She's quite beautiful."

He shook his head. "Nah. After all—gentlemen prefer blondes." He smiled and winked at her.

She smiled back and briefly looked down before looking back up. "So, besides Marie Gianelli, how was your day today?"

"Good. Good day. I thought my homily this morning—I titled it *Forgiving Means Forgetting*—was one of my better ones. Good visitations, too. Misses Flanagan, over at *Laurelwood Nursing Home,* is doing a lot better. Might be able to go home soon."

Tentatively, she asked, "How about your veterans' meeting? How was that?"

"Oh, it was okay, I guess."

"You know—for whatever it's worth—I just wanted to say . . . well . . . I just wanted to say thank you for your service. I thought it was important to say that. I've never thanked a veteran before. I guess I kind of took it for granted. I'm not going to do that anymore, though. I promise."

He warmly smiled. "You're quite welcome."

She could tell that the gesture had touched him.

They had the pizza for dinner—Danny took the anchovies

off his—and did the dishes together. He went to his bedroom to change. When he exited, he was wearing a pair of *Calvin Klein* jeans and a t-shirt with the 173rd Airborne Brigade Combat Team logo on it.

She nodded her approval. *Damn. He looks good in a pair of jeans. Nice ass.* "I'm glad you took off your priest's uniform or whatever you call it."

He chuckled. "And why's that?"

"Because I want to talk to Danny, not Father Daniel. Remember what we agreed to—we're just Grace and Danny. Not Grace Stevens, pop superstar. Not Daniel O'Connor, Catholic priest. Just Grace and Danny."

"That's right. We did agree to that."

She took him by the hand and led him into the parlor. She sat down at the *Baldwin*. He leaned on the piano and gazed down at her.

"I'm going to play a special song for you. Ready?"

"Yes, milady."

She poured out a haunting rendition of *Danny Boy*. As she played and sang, she looked up, trying to gauge his reaction.

She saw him dab his eyes with his palm. *Yes! You're getting to him. Keep working it, girl. Keep working it.* When she finished, the dull hum of the last note marked the end of the ephemeral beauty. For a few seconds, there was silence. They just stared at one another.

Finally, he very slowly clapped his hands. He feigned an Irish accent and told her, "Aye, lass, you just made this Irishman a wee bit teary-eyed, you did." He paused for a moment before adding, "Seriously, Grace, that was lovely. *Lovely.* One of the most soulful renditions of that song I've ever heard. And you're not even Irish. You did it justice."

She corrected him. "I'm half Irish on my mom's side. Her maiden name was *Donavan*. So there." She playfully stuck her tongue out at him. They laughed.

They settled in for their movie. She picked *An Officer and a Gentleman*. The ending made her cry. "God, that was beautiful," she told him as she dabbed her eyes. "So freaking beautiful, the way he literally swept her off her feet at the end. I'd love for a guy to do that to me. And did you notice, as he carried her out of the factory, they said something to one another? Ever notice that? You couldn't hear it over the music, but it didn't look like a simple *I love you*. What do you think they said to each other in that moment?"

He thought for a couple of seconds. "I think that was just for them. Always just for them. I don't think we even have a right to know. And if we did know, it would take all the magic, the mystique, out of it. There. How's that for a non-answer?"

She clutched her chest. "*Oh*. Danny. I think that's a beautiful answer, actually."

"So, what do you want to do now? Watch another movie?" he asked.

She looked at him and licked her lips. "Let's make love," she whispered.

He shot her and incredulous look and for a couple of seconds stared at her with his mouth open. Finally, he swallowed hard and asked, "M–m — m — make, make love, you say?" His voice cracked like a teen boy in puberty.

She lost her nerve. "Yeah, um . . . the movie. The Marilyn Monroe movie. *Let's Make Love*. Nineteen sixty. Tony Randall was in it. So was Milton Berle. I'm a huge Marilyn fan. Do you, by chance, have that one in your collection?"

"Oh, the movie. Right, the movie. *Let's Make Love*. Duh. No, I, ah, I don't have that one. Sorry."

They stared at one another for several seconds. *He's shy and he's a gentleman. Not like those Hollywood sleazebags. I'm going to have to up my game, be bold, take the initiative to move things along.*

He turned on the TV to watch a home shopping program called *Cal's Coin Craziness*. The host wore a bad toupee, a goatee, and a bright Hawaiian shirt underneath a navy-blue sports jacket. He hawked various collectible coins at prices that Grace thought to be astronomical.

She watched it with him and provided a running commentary. "Now, see, I don't understand this. He's trying to sell a dime for three-hundred bucks. It's a freaking dime, people. It's worth ten cents. This guy's a scam artist."

He shook his head. "No. You don't understand. This is a nineteen fifty-two Roosevelt dime in proof sixty-nine condition. That means it's nearly perfect. Proof seventy is the highest grade a coin can get."

"So what?"

"So plenty. It's rare, Grace. Super rare."

"So that makes a coin with a ten-cent face value worth three-hundred dollars?"

"Basically, yeah."

"So, rarity equals value?"

"Sure. That's how it works."

"Does that just work for coins or other things, as well?"

"Well, come to think of it, I guess that principle could apply to a lot of stuff."

"How about people? Does it apply to people, too?"

"Elaborate on that thought."

"I mean—let's take guys, for example. Totally hypothetical. Let's say a girl finds a guy. And he's unlike any guy she's ever met. He's unlike the vast majority of guys out there. He's handsome, but he's also sweet and kind, gentle. All that jazz. Would that guy become, like, super valuable?"

"I think that's something that would be in the eye of the beholder."

"Yeah. I suppose."

He turned his attention back to the coin presentation. "Anyhow, I think I might get one."

She smiled, stared at him, and got lost in the daydream.

"Yeah. Get one. You should. I think I might just get one for myself, too."

Chapter Eight: Daniel

Later that night, Grace lay in bed, tossing and turning. She tried to get comfortable, to no avail. Her legs were hurting again. She looked at the clock. Almost two-thirty. She thought for a moment. An idea crossed her mind. *Should I? Nothing ventured, nothing gained.* She got up and put on Danny's terry-cloth bathrobe. Underneath it, she was only wearing a lowcut powder blue satin teddy. She ambled down the hall and stopped at Danny's room. She took a deep breath and started to knock on the door but decided she'd go for broke and just open it. Slowly, she pushed the door open. It creaked. Tippy jumped off the bed and barked. Grace walked in and turned on the overhead light.

Danny sat up in bed. He wasn't wearing a shirt but did have a gold crucifix around his neck. He wiped the sleep out of his eyes.

"It's just me," she called out.

Still half asleep, he asked, "Is everything okay? Are you all right?"

She shook her head. "No. Not all right. Can't sleep."

He yawned. "What time is it anyway?"

"About two-thirty."

"What can I do for you?" he asked.

She shrugged. "I don't know. I just thought I'd come in here to see what you were up to, that's all."

"What did you think that I'd be up to at two in the morning?"

"Oh, I don't know. Whatever priests do at that time, I

guess."

"We try to sleep like everyone else," he said pointedly.

She shook her index finger at him. "Right. Right you are."

Sarcastically, he told her, "Oh, and by the way—don't bother to knock."

"Yeah. *Don't Bother To Knock.* Another Marilyn picture. Guess you're a fan, too, huh?"

He stared her down for a few seconds, but then shook his head and chuckled.

There was awkward silence. *Do it now, before you lose your nerve again.*

She cleared her voice and tentatively said, "Um . . . there *is* kind of something that you can do for me."

"What's that?"

"Would you . . . would you mind if I just, you know . . . climbed in with you for a while?"

"Climb in with me?"

She nodded. "Uh-huh."

"You mean climb in bed with me?"

She again nodded, raised her eyebrows, and smiled. "Uh-huh." Slipping off the robe, she let it drop to the floor. She kicked it out of the way and stood there in just her teddy. Her large breasts were nearly spilling out.

He ran his fingers through his hair and loudly exhaled. But he didn't take his eyes off her. She sensed she had the advantage and walked over to the bed.

He finally spoke. "Grace, I don't think that's such a good—"

She placed her index finger over his mouth to hush him. Pressing her French manicured nail to his lips, she whispered, "Shhh. Okay? Just *shhh.*" He stared at her with big, powder-blue eyes but didn't speak.

She turned down the bed, got under the covers next to him, and told him, "It's okay. Really it is. We're friends, after all. Just friends. And friends sometimes do things like this. It's perfectly all right for us to sleep together. I mean, it's not like we're *sleeping together*. There's no sin in it, nothing to be ashamed of. I'll have my half of the bed, and you'll have yours."

"It's just that I've never had a *friend* crawl into bed with me at two o'clock in the morning."

She turned and lay on her side so that she was facing him. With a giggle, she asked, "Have you had *anyone* crawl into bed with you at two in the morning?"

He turned red.

"Aw, I embarrassed you, didn't I?"

He didn't answer. His gaze seemed to be focused on her chest. She looked down. The dark brown areola of her right breast was peeking out from underneath the top of the teddy. With a laugh, she said, "Oh my God. I didn't even notice that." She talked to her breast. "Miss areola—get back in there. No one invited you to the party." She fixed the garment so that she was fully covered and added, "You know, I think these teddies might be too small up top for me." She smiled a devilish smile. "Did you do that on purpose, Danny? Did you buy me teddies that are too small, knowing that my big boobies would pop out?"

He turned an even deeper shade of red. She propped her head up with her hand, smiled, and said, "You know, you're sweet. You really are. Like the sweetest guy I've ever known."

"Thanks," he said with a nervous laugh. He took a whiff of the air. "Are you wearing my cologne?"

She tittered. "Uh-huh. I'm addicted to it. It smells so good. It's what I imagine Heaven must smell like. Truth be told—it makes me horny."

"Is that so?"

She raised her eyebrows and nodded. "Mm."

Loudly, she exhaled and declared, "Some like it hot."

"Right. *Some Like It Hot*. Another Marilyn movie. Don't

have that one, either."

"Oh, I wasn't talking about a movie." She smiled a naughty smile.

He swallowed hard but said nothing.

She focused on the scar on his left shoulder. With her left hand, she reached across the bed and tenderly touched it.

"I got hit with shrapnel."

"I know."

"How do you know?"

"I found you on *The Hall of Heroes* website. You got the Silver Star."

"And what made you look at *The Hall of Heroes* website?"

"I don't know." She fidgeted with her hair, twisting it around her finger. "I might have been looking you up online or something."

"So, you were snooping?"

"No. Totally not snooping. Just checking you out. There's a difference. I have a right to know what kind of man I'm living with."

"And what kind of man are you living with?"

Quietly, she said, "A hero."

"I'm not a hero."

"You *are*. I read the citation. You saved a man's life by risking your own. Where I come from, that's a hero."

"No, Grace. The heroes are the guys who didn't come home."

She again touched his scar. "Does it still hurt?"

He nodded. "Sometimes. There's still a little bit of shrapnel in there. They couldn't get it all out. I actually set off metal detectors. Look, let's just change the subject, okay?"

She frowned but said nothing.

After a few seconds, she closed her eyes and moaned. "*Aye yai yai*. My legs ache. These tiny little legs of mine really hurt tonight. I have no idea what it is. I'm way too young for arthritis."

"I can run down and get you a *Tylenol*."

"No. That won't help much." She thought for a moment and smiled. An inspired idea entered her mind. "But I know what would."

"What's that?"

She pulled the covers back to reveal her bare legs. She kicked them in the air and squealed with delight. "A leg massage."

He shot her a leery look. "A *leg massage*?"

"Yeah. I get them on Rodeo Drive all the time."

"Is that right?"

"Sure."

"Yeah, well, too bad there's no masseuse on duty here in the bedroom."

She looked at him and smiled. "Ah, but there is."

He pointed to himself. "You want me to do it?"

"Would you?"

"Oh, Grace, that's an even worse idea than allowing you in bed with me."

She grabbed her left calf. "*Ow*. My calf muscle is cramping up on me. It really hurts. Come on. Help a girl out. You don't want me in pain, do you?"

He loudly exhaled and got up. She could see that he was wearing a pair of olive drab Army shorts. He got down on his hands and knees at the bottom of the bed and leaned over her legs. "Okay. Tell me what to do."

"Very slowly, very gently, extend my leg, my left leg to start with. That's the one that really hurts."

Mechanically, he followed her instructions. "Okay. What's next?"

She shook her head. "Oh, God. You look like you're putting together a piece of lawn furniture from the instructions or something. Come on. Put some heart and soul into it." She started singing T'Pau's *Heart and Soul.*

He rolled his eyes.

She bit her lower lip. The feeling of his large, warm hands on her small, silky-smooth legs was amazing. "Just massage it, very gently," she instructed.

He ran his hand along the back of her leg. She closed her eyes, and a faint gasp and sigh escaped her lips. "*Ah.*" She was breathing a bit heavier, too. "Oh, God. *God,*" she said.

"You okay?"

"*Uh. Huh.* You're doing a fine job. Good boy. Good, good boy." She extended her left arm and patted him on the head, adding, "You know, I've always hated my legs. They're too damn short. What do you think?"

He shook his head. "No. That's rubbish. Absolute rubbish. They're not too short."

"So, you like my legs? You think they're sexy?"

He turned red.

"I embarrassed you again. I'm sorry."

"It's okay."

He paused and sniffed the air. "I'm getting a distinct aroma of coconut."

"Oh, yeah. That would be my legs. I have this *amazing* coconut scented moisturizer that I use on them. Is it bothering you?"

"No. Quite the opposite, in fact. It smells wonderful. Reminds me of when I was a kid, and my mom would bake these cakes and put coconut frosting on top. She'd always let me lick the bowl."

"Oh, is that right?"

"Yeah. Sure."

"Well . . . do you . . . want to . . . lick my leg? I just used the moisturizer not more than a couple of hours ago. I'm sure you'd still be able to taste the coconut."

He cleared his voice. "Lick your leg?"

"Yeah. Sure. You can if you want. It'd be fine by me. And it wouldn't be anything sexual. I mean, there'd certainly be nothing erotic about it. It would just be for the sake of . . . nostalgia. Yeah, that's it—nostalgia."

He looked at her chest. "You mean, like a trip down mammary—I mean, *memory*—lane?"

"Yeah. Like that. Just like that. I think you should just go for it. I really do."

He nervously smiled and again gawked at her chest. "Well, I do love coconuts, but, ah, I think I'll pass. I seem to recall that they always gave me hives. I think I was allergic."

She shrugged. "Suit yourself." *I'm wearing him down. Slowly but surely.*

As he continued the massage, she arched her back and again bit her lower lip. "Oh, yeah. Feels so good. God, it feels good. Go up higher on the leg, will you?"

His hand slowly worked its way up from her calf. Eventually, he reached the area near her thigh. He stopped. She looked at him. He trembled. "I think that's high enough," he told her. His voice was shaky. He withdrew his hand.

She let out a deep sigh of frustration and looked him directly in the eye. "Darn it. It was just starting to get interesting, too."

He lay back down in bed and asked her, "Before we go to sleep, is there anything else you need?"

"No. I just want you to lie here with me. Will you do that for me? Just *be here* with me, stay with me. I feel so lonely, like you're the only friend that I have in the whole world."

He patted her hand. "I'll stay with you."

She reached over and briefly brushed his cheek with the back of her hand. "Thank you, my friend." She paused for a moment and then asked, "We are friends, aren't we?"

"We're friends," he assured her. Loudly, he clapped his hands twice, and the main light went out.

She howled. "*The Clapper*. Oh, Jesus. You have *The Clapper*.

Aw, Danny likes infomercial products. Oh, God. You're so freaking cute. Do you have the *George Foreman Grill* and *The Pocket Fisherman*, too?"

"*The Clapper's* a fine product. Manufactured in the good ole US of A, too. A quality item made *by* decent, hard-working Americans *for* decent, hard-working Americans. Not all infomercial products are pieces of junk, you know. It was well worth the forty-nine ninety-nine," he retorted.

"Forty-nine ninety-nine? For *The Clapper*? You got taken, babe. And I just made an executive decision—I'm going to be handling all of our cash. Just so you know. I'm telling you now so we won't fight over it later." She immediately regretted the bold declaration. *Oh, shit. What I just told him is true, but he doesn't need to know all that just yet. I guess I got too cocky by virtue of the fact that I infiltrated the bed with only light resistance.*

"You're going to be handling all of our *what?*"

"I said, ah—I said, ah, I'm going to, ah, handle all of our, ah . . . *hash.* Yeah, that's it. Our hash. Our corned beef and hash. I'm . . . uh . . . making corned beef and hash for breakfast in the morning. I'll handle that. I don't want us to fight over who gets to make it because *I'm* making it. Corned beef and hash is my passion."

"Oh, okay. I thought I heard something else."

"Nope. I said *hash.* I did."

"Okay. Fine. You said *hash.*"

There was silence in the room for a minute or so. Finally, Danny reached across and gently tugged on her teddy.

"Grace—you still awake?"

She didn't open her eyes but said, "Yeah, what is it?"

"I was just thinking—we don't have any corned beef and hash. How are you going to make it if we don't even have any in the house?"

"What's the closest thing you have, babe?"

"An old can of *Spam* that expired six months ago."

She opened her eyes to roll them. "Kay. So, what I want you to do is open that and pray over it, see? Pray over it *real hard*. And God will miracle that *Spam* into the most delicious corned beef and hash you've ever tasted. Kay? Can we go to sleep now?"

"Well, you said that If I prayed about women's menstrual cycles that He'd miracle them away. And He didn't. He definitely didn't. I know that because the janitor — oh, wait, excuse me, the *custodial engineer* — at Saint Mary's, Levi, told me yesterday, before Mass, that the toilet in the women's room at the Parish Hall was clogged up. And that tampons were the culprits. Evidently, parishioners were trying to flush them."

"Look, Levi's an excellent custodial engineer. The man's awesome at what he does. I heard he was up for the Janitor of the Year award. The coveted *Golden Plunger*. I'm sure he took care of it."

"No. He didn't. He didn't take care of it. Levi's Amish and he said it would be against his religion to dig tampons out of a toilet because both tampons and toilets are *modern conveniences*. And he can't have anything to do with modern conveniences. He uses an outhouse, you see. And he doesn't have to worry about tampons because he's single. So, yours truly had to put on the gloves and fish those babies out. Not only that, but Levi demanded that I make an announcement in church next Sunday to the effect that feminine sanitary items are not to be flushed in church toilets. So, again, I'm the one stuck dealing with an embarrassing topic. I'd rather give a sermon on the evils of STDs. *Crabs: The Devil's Itch.*"

"Who's running that church? Huh? You or Levi? Because it sounds like Levi's calling the shots over there. And that's not cool. And if Levi isn't willing to deal with the modern world, he really should not even have the freaking job. That simple. I mean — how does the son of a bitch even know when to show up for work? Because I'm sure a wristwatch or a clock would be considered a *modern convenience*, too, right?"

"He has a sundial."

"What does he do on days when it's cloudy?"

"He's late. Usually only by a few hours, though. He can *ballpark it* pretty well by now."

"You need to fire Levi. Fire his ass."

"I'm not firing Levi. He's been here for twenty-some years, much longer than I have. Saint Mary's wouldn't be the same without him."

"So, you just accept his incompetence?"

"Yup. It makes him all the more endearing. Besides, he brings in the best chicken pot pie for the parish dinners. It's some kind of secret Dutch recipe. If I fired him, he probably wouldn't do that anymore."

"What. Ever. I still say Levi should find himself a nice little farmer's market where he can sell his produce and quilts and birdhouses and pies — oh, golly, the best shoofly pie I ever had was from an Amish farmer's market on Long Island, in Garden City. I kid you not. Oh, and he could pose for pictures with tourists. Charge five bucks a pop. Tourists love that shit. He'd get rich. He could buy himself a thousand black suits that all look the same. With matching hats, no less. Kay, babe?"

She thought for a moment and added, "How the hell did we go from talking about corned beef and hash to discussing Levi?"

"I'm not sure. We were actually originally talking about *The Clapper*. I think things just kind of snowballed and got all out of control. But what about the corned beef and hash? I love that stuff. I do. That's one of the few dishes that I was exposed to in the Army and actually liked. I was all jazzed when you said you were going to make some."

"Fine. Get the corned beef and hash at the market and I'll make it up for you sometime. *Sometime.* I'm not going to commit on exactly when. Won't be today. I have to be in the *corned beef and hash mood*, and right now, I'm not."

"But you just said that you were going to make some for breakfast. You were in the mood, literally two minutes ago. What happened?"

"I'm a woman. A Scottish woman. My moods can change very fast. But I will eventually make it for you. I promise. Happy now?"

"Yeah. I guess that'll have to do. Goodnight, Grace."

"Goodnight, Danny."

Tippy jumped up on the bed and lay between them. Grace closed her eyes and felt secure, even triumphant. *You took a chance and it paid off. Now you have a foothold. He'll have to let you sleep with him every night from now on. The precedent has been set. Well done, girl. And even Levi can't ruin this moment.*

Finally, she was content and drifted off to sleep.

She awoke to the sounds of Tippy barking and Danny's screams. In his sleep, he was shouting, "Incoming! Get down! Get down!" He woke up suddenly and popped straight up in the bed. He was breathing heavily. She got up, turned on the lights, and saw that his face and chest were covered in sweat. He was trembling.

"Danny, what's wrong? Are you okay?"

He looked at her and tried to force a smile. Dismissively, he waved his hand at her. "Yeah. Yeah. It's okay. It'll be all right."

He got up, sat on the edge of the bed, and tried to take deep breaths, but he was hyperventilating. The scene frightened her. *What the hell's happening?* "Danny, do you need an ambulance?" She searched his face for answers.

"No. No ambulance. I just need my medication. Excuse me for a minute." He left the room and quickly returned with a bottle of pills and some water.

She was sitting on the edge of the bed and he sat next to her.

He opened the pill bottle and tapped out one of the little white disks. With a swig of water, he swallowed it. After a few minutes, he started to calm down. His breathing returned to normal. He took another drink of water and held up the pill bottle. "*Ativan,*" he told her. He smiled. "It works pretty well for my panic attacks."

"It sounded like you were having a bad dream."

He nodded. "Yeah. We were getting hit with mortars. It was real bad." He paused and looked directly at her. "And there's nothing worse than getting hit with mortars. You can't fight back."

"How often do you have these dreams?"

"Nearly every night. Almost every night, I go back to Afghanistan, back to the Korengal Valley. *The Valley of Death* as everyone called it."

"Oh, God. I'm sorry. I am *so* sorry. You're way too good to have this happen to you." She placed her hand on his shoulder.

They sat there silent for a couple of minutes. She wiped the remaining sweat from his forehead with her palm.

Finally, she tentatively asked, "What . . . whatever happened to the kitten? The little black kitten. The one in the photo that's on your desk."

He shot her a hard look before answering, "He stepped on a landmine a day after that picture was taken." By the time he got to the word *taken,* tears had filled his eyes. He broke down and cried.

A tear rolled down Grace's cheek. She briefly looked up at the ceiling as her tears flowed. Her lower lip quivered. Then she lay back down on the bed and held her arms open. "Come here, come to me," she said.

"What?"

"I said — come here."

"Why?"

"Because you need to, that's why. I'm going to make it better for you."

He hesitated.

"Danny, come here. Come on now. Get over here. It's chilly in this room. So, get over here so I can pull the covers over us. Now please."

He tentatively lay down next to her. She put her arm around him and pulled his head to her so it was nuzzled against her breast. He resisted at first, tried to pull away. But she was insistent and pulled him back into her. After thirty seconds of the two of them going back and forth, she softly and gently whispered to him, "Come on. Don't fight me. Calm down and stop trying to pull away." He started to settle down and got more comfortable. He stopped trying to pull away. And he buried his head in her chest, getting as close to her as he possibly could. He put his arms around her and held her tight. She pulled the covers over top of them. She stroked his head and whispered, "That's right. Snuggle up as close as you can. It'll all be okay. I've got you, babe. You took care of me. Now, let me take care of you. That's what friends do for one another. I care about you, Danny. You know that, right? I know I can be kind of difficult at times. But that's just because I care."

He'd stopped crying. "I know," he quietly told her. "I care about you, too."

She felt important and fulfilled. *What I'm doing for him right now is more important than anything I've accomplished in show business.*

Kissing the top of his head, she whispered, "We care about each other." She thought for a moment and added, "It feels good to hold someone, doesn't it? It's good to feel that warmth, right?"

"Yeah. It's good." His voice was muffled because his face was pressed to her chest.

She again stroked the top of his head. "It's not wrong to

want that, Danny. We all need it. We need it just like we need air. It's natural. It's human. *I'm* human. And you are, too. Do you understand what I'm saying?"

"Yeah."

She sang him a lullaby. She sang Elton John's *Daniel*. It was a song that she'd performed in concert. She'd researched the cryptic lyrics and found out it was about a traumatized veteran returning home from Vietnam. It took on new meaning for her. *Now, I know Daniel.*

She started out in control, the consummate performer. But by the time she got to the part of the song that talked about scars that wouldn't heal, she couldn't take it anymore. She lost it and started to sob, unable to finish the song. He cried again, too.

She held him close to her and kissed him on the forehead. And they stayed just like that until they had both cried themselves back to sleep.

CHAPTER NINE: WHAT'S YOUR INSPIRATION?

Danny lay in bed on Monday morning, staring at the ceiling. Grace was still next to him. She lay on her side, facing him.

"Penny for your thoughts," she told him.

He turned his head and looked at her. "I want to apologize to you. I'm sorry you had to be subjected to that ugly scene last night. I'm embarrassed, ashamed, in fact."

"What's there to be ashamed of?"

He ignored her question and looked back up at the ceiling.

She brushed his hair with her hand and asked him, "Do you know what I see?"

"What's that?"

"I see a man who went off and fought for his country and was left scarred by it, both literally and figuratively."

"I'm just sorry I broke down like that. I hate for that to happen when someone's around to see."

She shook her head. "No. That's the wrong way to think of it. You let me in a little bit last night, into your world. That's a good thing. And I feel honored that you did. Like I said—you took care of me. Now, let me return the favor."

"You shouldn't have to."

"*I want to.*"

"I should be able to handle it myself."

"No. You shouldn't. I don't think God wants anyone to bear those types of crosses by themselves. That wouldn't be very compassionate, you know?"

"I suppose."

"You can talk to me about anything, Danny. Anything. Anytime. Do you understand?"

"Yes."

Softly, she said, "Okay then."

He rolled over on his side, so he was facing her. "You know, I'm off today. I'm always off Saturdays and Mondays."

"What's on your agenda?"

"This morning, I'm playing golf with Father Larkin. We're going to check out that new course over at *Chesapeake Bay Country Club*. Like I was telling you before—I love golf."

She did her best Mae West impression. "*Oooh*, and I'll bet you have a nice long, hard nine iron, too, fella."

He laughed. "You have a dirty mind, girl."

She giggled. "Seriously, dude. You have no idea how long it's been since I've had sex."

He said nothing.

She continued to press the topic. She propped her head up with her hand. "Do you want to know?"

Still, he said nothing.

"A whole year. So, you see, we have something in common. We're both celibate. How about that? I mean—I broke up with Orion eight months ago, but we didn't have sex for the last four months that we were technically together. By that time, I suspected that he was running around on me. And I will not screw any man who runs around on me—end of story. And it's not just the moral aspect, either. I mean, if you screw a guy who's whoring around, there's no telling what you'll catch. Anyway, wouldn't *Tattle Tales Magazine* love to get ahold of that little bombshell? I can see the headlines now—*Pop Princess Grace Stevens: Sexless and Sad.* Oh, the irony. The entertainment world's number one sexpot doesn't even have sex." She paused and looked down for a moment before looking back up at him. "Can I ask you a question? A very personal one."

"Well, given the fact that we're lying in bed together, I don't know that anything would be too personal at this point. So, yeah — go ahead."

She hesitated. "Have you . . . well, have you ever, you know . . ." She stopped, winced, and took a deep breath. Finally, she blurted it out, "Have you ever broken your vow of celibacy?"

"No."

"Now, does jerking off count? Would that count as breaking your vow? I've always wondered about that." She picked up a piece of her bubble gum off the nightstand, unwrapped it, and started to chew.

"Excuse me?"

"You heard me — does jerking off count as breaking the vow of celibacy? Simple question. I assume you *do* jerk off. You are, after all, a guy. That's what you're programmed to do. I just can't figure out what you jerk off to. What's your material? What's your inspiration? Because you don't have any porn in the house. I've checked. Yep. I turned this house upside down yesterday while you were at work, looking for your secret porn stash. You don't have one. Looked on your computers, too. Both desktops and your laptop. Even they were clean. I was relieved. I don't like porn guys. Don't care for them at all.

"But do you — say — watch *I Dream of Jeannie* and imagine that you're Major Nelson and that you're making love to Jeannie? Oh, I love that show. I love watching all the old-time shows on the *TV Classics Network*. *The Brady Bunch*, *The Waltons*, *The Love Boat*. God, I love *The Love Boat*. It's my favorite. I like nice, clean, family-oriented shows, you know? But, anyway, getting back to Jeannie — she really had the hots for Major Nelson. And I don't know if he was gay or what, but she'd throw herself at him every episode, and he'd just flat out reject her. I mean—she was doing her damnedest to screw the man. I think she really loved him, too. But he was always, all like, *Get the hell away from me, Jeannie. You've got girl germs.* I always felt so sorry for her. That poor woman was obviously severely sexually frustrated because her astronaut wasn't blasting off for her. She must have had a teeny, tiny little vibrator in that bottle of hers. I imagine she'd sit in there at night and just go to town on it, too. I do."

"You obviously only saw the earlier episodes of the series. They had to be careful about how they presented it. They couldn't just have them in the same bed together and what-not. It was the nineteen-sixties, and the network censors weren't keen on an unmarried couple cohabitating, to begin with. I mean—take you and me, for example. A Catholic priest and a starlet in bed together? Wouldn't have flown. We could never have been a sixties sitcom. But, anyhow, on *I Dream of Jeannie*, eventually, a romance bloomed. Jeannie and Major Nelson got married in the series finale. So there. You're wrong." He stuck his tongue out at her and laughed.

He thought for a moment and added, "But, seriously, I think we should move this conversation in a more wholesome direction."

She ignored his request and continued her interrogation. "Maybe you jerk off to those female pro wrestlers. Some of them are really hot. Or maybe it's the female models on *The Price is Right*. They're pretty, and sometimes they wear swim-suits during the Showcase Showdown. Or, maybe, just maybe, you like to watch reruns of *The Jersey Shore* and get off on JWOWW or Sammi Sweetheart. Tell you what—that JWOWW has some big-ass knockers. Almost as big as mine. Almost." She stretched out her arms over her head, cracked her knuckles, and loudly popped her gum. "Any-who. Am I close on any of my guesses?"

"I'm not going to dignify that question with a response."

She nodded. "Yeah. Fine. You have every right not to in-criminate yourself. This is America, after all. Self-incrimina-tion is against one of those Commandments."

He corrected her. "Not Commandments. *Amendments.* It's against the Fifth Amendment to the Constitution. The Fifth is the one that protects people from self-incrimination."

She snapped her fingers and pointed at him. "There you go. You know all about it. That means you've almost certainly invoked it before."

"Grace. Stop it. Just stop it."

"Sure. I'll stop. I think I got most of the information that I was looking for anyway." She paused, grinned a shit-eating grin, and announced, "Yeah, buddy, you definitely whack off."

"Grace. *Enough.* Let's get off this whole topic. Please and thank you. I don't know why you're so fascinated with it, to begin with. But we do not need to be lying here in bed to-gether discussing masturbation. For the first few minutes, your little shtick is kind of cute, but it gets old real fast."

"Cute? Really? *Aw.* Thank you. Okay, well, I know I'm kind of silly. That's part of my charm, after all. Some men might even say it's more than just cute. Some might call it downright sex-ay." She batted her lashes, winked at him, puckered her lips, and kissed the air before continuing. "But, seriously, have you ever been tempted to break your vows? I'm not being a smartass anymore. It's a sincere question."

He looked at her for a long time. Her long blonde hair. Her soulful, honey-brown, doe eyes. Her lips, full but natural. Her boobs, barely contained by the teddy. Her cute little legs.

He swallowed hard and took a deep breath. *Change the topic. Get off the subject. You can't win when you're on this topic with her.* "How would you like to get out of the house for a little while tonight?"

"What did you have in mind?"

"A beach party."

"Beach party?"

"Sure. Like I told you, we're sitting on the North East River. The property backs right up to it. In the backyard, there's a small beach. I have a little fire ring set up. Sometimes, I go there at sunset if I need some extra inspiration for one of my sermons. Sometimes, I go there just to talk to God. It's the most peaceful place I know. But I've never taken anyone else down there. It's always just me and Tippy."

"Could we roast hotdogs and make our own s'mores?"

"I don't see why not."

She closed her eyes and smiled. "*Mmm.* That sounds wonderful. I've been dying to get out of the house."

"Are you sure you feel up to it?"

"Uh-huh. I'm hardly sneezing or coughing anymore. I think some fresh air would do me a world of good."

"Okay then. Good enough."

"There's no chance anyone would see us, is there?"

"Nope. Nobody will bother us down there. It's a very private area," he assured her.

"It'll give me something to look forward to while you're away."

He got up, telling her, "Well, I'm going to take a shower and get going."

She nodded. "Kay."

He started to walk out of the bedroom, stopped, and turned back around. "Grace, I just wanted to thank you for last night. You're a good friend. You made it better for me. A lot better."

She warmly smiled. "I'm glad I was there for you. Maybe God Himself wanted me in this bed with you so that you didn't have to go through that alone. After all, they say, *the Lord works in mysterious ways.*" She giggled and told him,

"Now, go. Go chase that little white ball around. Oh, and on the way home, could you pick up some hair clips and scrunchies for me? And don't forget to stop at the market and get some hotdogs and the stuff we need for s'mores."

He casually saluted her. "Yes, ma'am."

He turned to walk away, but she called out to him, "Hey, Danny—"

He turned back around. "What's up?"

"I think we could be a great modern-day sitcom. Think about it—a handsome Catholic priest and a pop diva secretly living together. Very original concept. It's never been done. Plus, you would have the whole *will they or won't they* thing to hook viewers."

He smiled and nodded. "Right. Great concept. I'll start writing the pilot tonight. I even have a wacky neighbor. And we all know every good sitcom needs a wacky neighbor. Jody Biffle. Lives in the gray Cape Cod directly across the street. A few years ago, he thought he had an oil reserve on his property, so he started drilling and hit the damn sewer line. Crap flooded the entire neighborhood for two hours."

"Wow. That's wacky, all right. We could definitely use him. But what would we call it?"

He placed his hand on his chin, thought for a moment, snapped his fingers, and pointed at her. "Okay, here you go. Try this on for size—there'd be a nosy bishop, see? Yeah, a real nosy, curmudgeonly bishop. And he'd always be poking around because he's suspicious. He knows I'm hiding *something*. So, the name of the show would be—*Please Don't Tell The Bishop*. Which is what I'm going to have to beg if anyone spots you. So, remember, keep a low profile while I'm gone today. Away from windows and such. Okay, lass?"

"*I know.* I'm not stupid. I mean—I'm from New York, not Jersey."

He took a shower and put on a powder blue sweater over

a white polo shirt. He wore navy blue golf pants and a pair of white and black golf shoes. Liberally, he sprayed on *Green Irish Tweed.*

Tippy hadn't been out yet, so he took her for her morning walk before filling her bowl with food and giving her some fresh water. He kissed the dog on the forehead and told her, "Daddy loves you. Take good care of our friend, Grace, while I'm gone." The Sheltie wagged her tail and dug into her food.

CHAPTER TEN: A MATTER OF HONOR

Danny arrived at the golf course at ten of eight. His tee time was eight sharp. Father Larkin was already waiting in the parking lot, smoking a cigarette.

Danny walked over, and they shook hands.

"Danny, good to see you," Father Larkin said.

He nodded. "Likewise, Gene."

Father Eugene Larkin. A distinguished-looking African-American priest who was some twenty years older than Danny.

Father Larkin looked up at the sky. It was perfectly blue. The sun shone brightly. "The Lord's blessed us with a beautiful day for a round of golf."

Danny nodded and reached into his chest pocket. He pulled out a pair of sunglasses and put them on. "Indeed, He has."

For the first nine holes, they talked only golf.

Danny's tee shot on the par-five, five-hundred-yard sixth hole only traveled a hundred yards. He dropped his driver, looked up at the sky, and proclaimed, "Jesus, Mary, and Joseph. I suck."

Father Larkin laughed and told him, "You're over-swinging. Remember, it's the club speed that determines how far the ball travels, not how hard you swing."

On the tenth green, Danny missed an easy two-foot putt for double bogey.

Father Larkin flashed him a look of disbelief. "You okay today? You're normally a good putter. That's the strongest part of your game. I don't think I've ever seen you get the yips like that on a two-footer."

He took a deep breath and loudly exhaled. "To be honest with you, Gene, I'm playing a bit distracted today."

"Oh, yeah? You want to talk about it?"

Danny nodded. "I think I need to talk to somebody."

They got into the golf cart and drove to the next hole.

Father Larkin pulled out a pack of *Newports* and held the open box up to Danny. "Want one? After all, all the cool kids are doing it." Father Larkin chuckled.

Danny nodded, briefly took his gaze off the cart path, and pulled a cigarette out. "Yeah, I do, actually. A smoke's exactly what I need to tell this story."

Both men lit up.

"What's on your mind, son?" the older priest asked.

Danny stopped the golf cart and gave him a hard look. Tentatively, he told him, "I . . . I met a woman."

Father Larkin laughed, shook his head, and looked down. "Aw, shit. Here we go."

"What's that supposed to mean?"

Father Larkin composed himself. "Nothing. I'm sorry. Continue. Please. So, you met a woman?"

"Uh-huh."

"And what's she like?"

"Beautiful. Inside and out. She's sweet and kind. Spiritual. And quirky." He laughed. "Has this . . . this most peculiar obsession with the hippies. I don't know what they ever did to her, but the little thing really seems to have a score to settle with them. To me, at least, even that comes off as kind of endearing. I guess maybe it's because she sounds like my grandfather when she goes on one of her hippie rants. Oh, and spunky. A spunky lass, she is. Like the little Chihuahua who thinks she's a Doberman. Funny, too. She's funny as hell. Says the darndest things. Sometimes, she can be a little on the

119

risqué side. But in a cute, innocent kind of way, if that even makes any sense. You have to know her, I guess. I'll pretend like I'm all angry with her for bringing up certain topics. I kind of have to. But on the inside, I'm laughing. Hysterically. Oh, she's a pistol, all right. A real firecracker. Curses worse than my drill sergeant from Fort Benning. Yet, she's incredibly old-fashioned when it comes to romance, believes that you should love someone before you get intimate with them, and so forth. She's from Long Island — hardly the sticks — but she has these small-town values. And that's a turn-on to me. It is. She's good for my PTSD, too. It doesn't freak her out. She's a huge comfort in that whole area." He started getting lost in the daydream, got carried away. "And it sure doesn't hurt that she's gorgeous. Looks like a young Audrey Hepburn in the face. Has a killer body. I mean, she's a tiny, petite little thing, but — day-um. A nice, round bubble butt. And her boobs are amazing. They're *huge.* And I'm a boob man, too. And I can tell those puppies are real. Not an ounce of silicone in those babies. And I can't help but want to su — "

Father Larkin interrupted and chastised him. "Danny! TMI, son. Way TMI."

It jolted him back to reality. He took a drag on his cigarette and blew the smoke out his nose. "Right. Sorry. I got carried away. But the fact is — I like her. I mean, I *really* like her."

"Yeah?"

He smiled and sighed. "*Yeah.*"

"What are you going to do about it?"

He shrugged. "I don't know. I haven't done anything yet. What do you think I should do?"

Father Larkin shook his head. "Oh — no — no — no. *No.* I can't answer that question for you."

"Why not? You've never steered me wrong before. I have the utmost confidence in your judgment."

"No. I'm not a party to this. This isn't my dilemma." He

wagged his index finger at Danny. "Listen, son—this is between you, her, and God Himself."

"But what if, hypothetically speaking, I was to eventually fall for this woman? Fall in love."

"Then you'd have a choice to make, wouldn't you?"

"Why should I have to choose?"

"Because that's the way it is."

"But is that right?"

"It doesn't matter."

"But can't you serve God as a priest in His Church and be in love, too?"

"According to Roman Catholicism—no. You knew what you were signing up for."

He nodded. "I know—I know. I just never thought I'd have these feelings."

"I'm not telling you that whatever feelings you're having are wrong. The wrong is in not making a choice. You and I both know that there are a hell of a lot of priests out there who have it both ways. They wear the Roman collar but still experience—shall we say—the carnal pleasures of life. Don't be *that guy.* There's no honor in that. And it really is a matter of honor. And what's honorable is making a choice. And it's an epic choice. The Church on the one side. A woman's love on the other."

"Yes, but don't you think God understands these things?"

"You're preaching to the choir, son. But it doesn't matter what I think. It doesn't matter what you think. Hell, it doesn't even matter what God thinks. The Roman Catholic Church is not going to change its position on celibacy anytime soon. We both know that."

Danny nodded in resignation. "*Right.*"

"Look—romantic love is a wonderful thing. Don't you think that I get lonely? I'm human, after all. I go home to an empty house every night—no one to share the day's joys and sorrows with. But I'm older than you—way older. It's too late for me. So, I stay married to the Church. And I play a lot of golf. That's why I'm so good. I'm the best golfer in the whole diocese. Easily. No one can touch me. The game keeps my mind from asking some of the questions that you're asking." Father Larkin emphatically shook his head. "But I'm telling you—it's not too late for you. You can make whatever life you want for yourself. And you're different, Danny. Look, don't take this the wrong way—but you're needier than the average person. You literally *need someone* to be there for you when the PTSD rears its ugly head."

Danny nodded but said nothing. It was quiet for a few seconds.

Finally, Father Larkin broke the silence by wagging his finger and telling him, "But before you throw it all away, just make sure she's worth it. I mean, *really* worth it. Understand? Because if she's not, then that would be a sin. But if she *is* worth it . . . well, if she is worth it, it would be a sin *not* to seize the moment. Understand?"

"Yeah. I think so."

Father Larkin winked at him and nodded. "Okay then."

"And you won't mention this to anyone?"

"Of course not. You have my word of honor that what we've discussed out here today will be held in the strictest confidence. No one will ever know about this conversation. It'll be as if it didn't happen."

They finished their round. As Danny walked to his car with his golf bag slung over his shoulder, he shook his head in disgust. *Thirty over par. And Gene finished at one under. Thirty-one strokes behind. Embarrassing. I'm getting worse at this game, not better. Oh, well. At least I can look forward to the beach party tonight. Yeah. That actually makes up for a bad day on the links—big time.* He thought about Grace. And he smiled.

CHAPTER ELEVEN: DANNY'S SECRET

He walked in the front door with his golf bag slung over his shoulder and carrying four plastic shopping bags. He'd gotten some hotdogs and all the ingredients for the s'more — the graham crackers, the marshmallows, and several chocolate bars. Grace's hair clips and scrunchies were in one of the bags.

Tippy ran down the steps to greet him. He patted her on the head. "Hi, sweetie. How's my little girl? Did you have a good day today? Hmm? Did you? Did you?"

He walked up the stairs. The dog followed. The TV was on in his bedroom. He peeked his head inside and saw Grace lying on the bed watching *Maury* and eating ice cream right out of the box. She was wearing blue jeans, a white t-shirt that depicted a kitten riding a unicorn, pink and white ankle socks, and white canvas sneakers.

"What's up?" he asked.

She looked over at him and smiled. With her mouth full of ice cream, she replied, "Hey." She swallowed the ice cream and held up the empty box for him to see. "We need more pistachio almond."

"I'll put it on the shopping list."

"How did your golf game go?"

"I ended up at plus thirty for the day."

"Sweet."

He shook his head. "No, Grace. In golf, you aim for the lowest score. Thirty over par is really bad. It pretty much means that I stink."

She shrugged and frowned. "Oh. Sorry."

Looking him up and down, she nodded approvingly and whistled a catcall. "*Oh, baby.* You got some sun. All tanned and whatnot. Mm. Sex-ay, boy." Then she looked down at her own arms and added, "And look at me. I'm pale as a ghost."

"And your skin is much healthier for it, too."

"I suppose, but I've always thought a little color looks good, you know?"

He ignored the comment and instead gestured towards the TV. "Watching *Maury*, huh?"

"Yep." She pointed to the screen and explained the episode. "This dude right here, the one with the acid wash jeans, took a paternity test and is about to find out whether he's the father of the kid who belongs to this chick here, the one who's missing her front teeth."

"That's swell."

She looked over at him. "Oh, hey, did you remember to get my stuff? My scrunchies and hair clips?"

He pulled the items out of one of the shopping bags and gently tossed them over to her. "Here you go."

"*Danke.* That means *thank you* in German. I learned that when I first toured Germany, eight years ago."

"Yeah, I already knew that. Remember, I like the song *Danke Schoen.*"

"Oh, and don't forget to keep a running count of all the money you're spending on me. Just put it on my tab. I promise—I'll pay you back."

He shook his head. "How many times do I have to tell you? I do not want your money."

"You're way too nice. You're generous to the point of fault. That's why I have to keep my eye on you to make sure you don't get used and abused."

"Well, I made it this far in life, didn't I?"

"Only by some miracle."

He dismissively waved his hand at her. "Yeah, well,

whatever."

"You know, I'm really looking forward to our beach party tonight. I've been looking forward to it all day," she said.

He smiled. "Me, too."

"It's nice to have something to look forward to. I've become so accustomed to dreading things, dreading the tours, the paparazzi, the intrusive fans, the tabloids, dealing with Kip, and each new day."

Sad. What she's describing is an existence rather than a life. She deserves better than that. Much better.

It was chilly. He waited while she put on a peach-colored hoodie over top of her shirt.

At dusk, he led her out the back door, into the yard. Tippy followed. They walked down a slight slope, and the river came into view. He took her hand and helped her over some rocks that stood between them and the beach. "Careful now," he told her. "You can easily twist an ankle on these rocks."

On the beach was a fire ring that contained some pieces of burnt wood. There was also a large rock and a log near the fire ring. Danny went back inside to get the food and drinks. He returned carrying a plastic grocery bag, a six-pack of soda, and a sand iron golf club. In his pockets, he had several golf balls.

Grace sat on the rock. "What's with the golf club?"

"Since we're on the beach, I thought I'd work on my sand shots. Lord knows I need the practice."

She took a deep breath and looked around. The crimson sun was just starting to set. It appeared to them as a huge, brilliant ball on the horizon. And it bathed them in its gentle light. "God, this is so beautiful," she declared.

"Well, I'm sure it's no Malibu, but I like it."

"It's better than Malibu." She took another deep breath. "The air here is so clean, so pure. Not like that God-awful smog we have in LA. I hate LA. I hate everything about it. I'm at the point where I'd much rather breathe clean air than million air."

He pulled out a golf ball from his pocket, set it on the beach, and stood over it with his club.

He took a practice swing and casually remarked, "Yeah, well, we definitely don't have a smog problem here." The club slowly moved backward in an arch. He kept his attention on the ball and started his downswing. At impact, the clubhead hit the sand, but the ball traveled only a few feet.

He dropped the club, looked up at the sky, and proclaimed, "Jesus, Mary, and Joseph."

Grace laughed. "Even *I* could do better than that."

He picked up the club and extended it to her. "Here, missy. Be my guest."

She stood up, took a hair clip out of her pocket, and put her hair up. Then she took the club from him. He put another ball down for her. She stood over the ball and got ready to hit it.

He stopped her. "No—no—no. You're doing it all wrong. You're not even holding the club right. You don't hold a golf club like you would a baseball bat."

"Well, how am I supposed to know? The only golf I've ever played is putt-putt. Why don't you show me?"

"Fine. I will."

He stood behind her and put his arms around her. Against his legs, he felt her backside pressing up against him. It felt good. Really good. Her hair smelled of strawberry shampoo. He took a deep breath to catch a full whiff of it.

Taking her dainty hands, he placed them correctly on the club grip. "You want to interlock your fingers," he told her. "And don't hold it too tight, okay? It's not supposed to be a death grip."

She adjusted her grip.

He nodded his approval. "Good. You'll want to bend your knees a little . . . not too much, now." He stood back and continued to instruct. "Take the club back for the back-swing . . . good. Now, swing down on the ball and try to hit the sand directly behind it. The sand itself is what propels the ball forward. If you do it right, on a real golf course, the ball will pop right out of the bunker."

She wiggled her butt, swung down, missed the ball entirely, and lost her grasp on the club. They watched as it sailed into the river.

"*Oops,*" she said as she covered her mouth.

"That was a two-hundred-dollar sand wedge," he told her.

She made a face at him. "I couldn't even see the damn ball because of my boobs. Plus, you told me not to grip the club too tight."

"Yeah, but I didn't tell you to throw it into the river."

"Look, I'm sorry. Just put it on my tab, okay?"

He laughed and shook his head. "That's not how it works."

"Oh, yeah? Then how does it work?"

He hesitated for a moment but then rushed over to her and scooped her up in his arms. "The way it works is . . . you have to go in after it, girl."

She squealed and flailed her feet in the air. "No! Don't you dare throw me into that river."

"It's full of jellyfish, you know."

"Oh, Gawd. I hate jellyfish."

He rocked her back and forth. "Here we go. A one . . . and a two . . . and a three . . ." He feigned throwing her in and lost his balance. They both fell to the ground and ended up in the sand, near the water's edge—he landed on top of her. And he felt her full breasts pressing against his own chest. He smelled his own cologne on her. She was looking at him with expectations written all over her face. But they just stared at one another, looked into one another's eyes. For the longest time, nothing was said. *Is this supposed to be our From Here To Eternity moment?*

Tippy started to walk down to the water's edge. Danny got

up off of Grace and sternly called out to the dog, "Tippy! No water! No! Water!" He turned and looked down at Grace, telling her, "Last time she went swimming in the river, she came out stinking to high heaven."

The dog turned around and walked back towards them. He held his hand out, Grace took hold of it, and he helped her to her feet.

"You really thought I'd throw you in?"

"No. I knew you wouldn't. I was just playing along. I thought that maybe . . . you know . . . maybe it was part of your plan."

"My plan?"

With a sigh, she said, "Look, forget it. Let's just eat."

He collected some kindling and started a fire. He cooked the hotdogs but asked her to make the s'mores. "I'm not crazy about s'mores," he explained. "I don't like chocolate bars. Long story. Real long story."

"What? Did they give you acne when you were a teenager or something?"

He shot her a dirty look. "I don't want to talk about it right now, Grace. *Okay*?"

"Okay. That's fine." She made the s'mores.

Tippy whined and whimpered for a hotdog. He gave in and fed her one.

After dinner, all three of them sat around the fire. Grace and Danny drank soda from the can.

They laughed and sang campfire songs, culminating with a heartfelt rendition of *Take Me Home, Country Roads*. He watched her closely as they sang. Her face was illuminated by the fire and took on a glow. *God. What a beautiful woman, the most beautiful woman in the world. She looks downright angelic. And she's sitting here with me, not more than two inches from me.*

After the song, she pulled out a pack of cigarettes and a lighter from her pocket. "Do you mind if I smoke?"

"Nah. Go ahead. As we used to say in the Army — *smoke 'em*

if you got 'em. But isn't smoking bad for a singer's vocal cords?"

"Very. But I am trying to quit." She put one of the cigarettes in her mouth and let it dangle.

He nodded and pointed to the pack of smokes. "Mind if I play with one of those things, too?"

She passed him the pack and her lighter, warning him, "Okay, but these are girly cigarettes. *Virginia Slims.*"

"Any port in a storm, my dear."

He took a cigarette and the lighter. It was a blue lighter. He lit up hers and then his own.

He looked at the lighter and commented on it. "Blue lighter. Good. Blue lighters are good. Excellent, actually. I don't use white lighters, though." He took a drag and handed the lighter back to her.

"What? Why not? What's wrong with white lighters?"

He blew smoke out his nose. "Because white lighters are bad juju. Over in Afghanistan, it was easy to start believing in what was known as *Afghan voodoo. Boonie voodoo.* Don't use white lighters. If you do, you'll get wasted. Don't eat the green pieces of candy out of the care packages. If you do, you'll get wasted. Never wash your coffee cup. If you do, you'll get wasted. And whatever you did, you *never, ever* ate the *Lucky Charms* that they'd issue as part of your field rations. You threw that shit away. You didn't even want it on your person. Very *unlucky.* Because one bite guaranteed that you'd be an angel by the end of the day. It's some crazy shit, but you start believing in it. Put people in an insane situation, and they start acting insane, you know? Some of it stays with you, too. A lot of it does, actually. I know it's irrational, but I can't help it. So, that's why I don't use white lighters."

"Wow."

"Yeah. Wow, is right."

"That seems just a little messed-up," she told him.

"It wasn't messed-up. It was just Afghanistan, that's all. As we say in golf—par for the course."

"I didn't realize that you still smoked."

"How did you know that I ever did?"

"From the picture on your desk. The one of you in Afghanistan. You had a cigarette in your mouth."

"Ah, very observant. You know, when I arrived over there, the first sergeant offered me a *Camel,* and I told him, *no thanks, Sarge, I don't smoke.* After my first firefight, I went back to him and *asked* for a cigarette. Been smoking ever since. Oh—don't get me wrong—I'm trying to quit, too. I don't buy them much anymore. Only when I get a coupon or something. They're too doggone expensive. Mostly, I just bum them." They laughed.

After they finished their smokes, she asked him, "Do you do magic?"

"A little. How'd you figure that out?"

"I saw a book about it on your bookshelf."

"Yeah, when I was a kid, I loved reading about Harry Houdini. You know, the famous magician. I was fascinated by him. I'd read about him and watch every movie and documentary on him that I could find. Houdini always had this wonderful air of mystery about him. As a kid, I always thought that there was about a ninety-nine percent chance that what he was doing was just an illusion. But there was always, like, this one percent chance that maybe, just maybe, he was doing real magic. I fell in love with that idea, the idea that magic could somehow be real."

"Yeah. I like that way of thinking. It's a nice thought . . . so can you do a magic trick for me?"

"Oh, I don't know. The routine that I do is mostly one that I break out for the kids at church. I don't really have an act for grownups."

"Well, show me a trick that you'd do for the kids. That'd be fine."

"You'd probably think it's lame."

"No, I wouldn't. Show me. Just do exactly what you'd do for the little kids. You don't have to change anything."

"Okay. Fine." He reached behind her ear. "Hey, now, what's this? I think I found something. Grace, I think I found something." He pulled his hand back to reveal a shiny silver dollar. "Well, looky here. Look what I found. That was hiding behind your ear, and you didn't even know it, did you?" He held the coin up for her to see and wagged his finger at her. "Now, if you promise to stay *in* school and *away* from drugs, you can keep that. Yeah. How about that? You can keep it. How cool is that, huh?" He handed her the coin and lightly patted her on the head.

She clapped her hands. "*Aw.* That was cute. Bravo. Maybe a little cheesy, but cute. I like your magic. It was good. I'm sure the children love it."

"Glad you liked it. But, ah, I need that coin back."

"But you said I could keep it."

"That was just part of the act. Seriously, though, I need it back."

"So, you make the little kids give the coins back?"

"The kids? No. You? Yes."

"Geez. Your act sure doesn't have very high production values," she told him as she handed the coin back to him.

He rapid-fire sneezed three times in a row.

"You catching cold?"

"Nah."

"Here. Let me see if you feel warm. You could have caught mine."

She tried to place her tiny hand on his forehead. He backed away.

She pointed her index finger at him and sharply admonished him. "*Do not* pull away from me when I am trying to check you for fever."

He rolled his eyes at her but stuck out his head. "Fine. Here. Check me."

She pressed her palm to his forehead. "Well, you don't feel warm. We'll just keep an eye on it for now."

"Grace, sometimes you treat me like a child. Like a small child. And I'm not sure whether you're trying to be my friend or my mother . . . or maybe something else altogether."

"I'm trying to be everything to you. To be perfectly frank, you haven't had enough feminine influence in your life. At least not lately. It's not normal, either. It's screwed-up, is what it is. And that's part of your problem. And it all goes back to the damn war. If you'd hadn't gone to war, you'd have a normal life. You'd be able to sleep at night. And you'd have a pretty wife, a normal job, and good-looking kids. But you *did* go to war. And that can't be changed. And all of your issues go back to that experience—every single one of them. You need a friend, yes, but you need something more, too. You need someone to look out for you, to take care of you. I don't think you can do that for yourself. You need someone who can help you heal. And I have no clue how you've managed to get along by yourself for so long. That's screwed-up, too— that you're dealing with all this shit by yourself. So, just know that it's for your own good if I ask you to do something. Don't fight me on every little thing. If you do, you'll wear me out. Okay?"

"So, in other words—do what you say."

"Just know that everything that I say is motivated by a rapidly growing affection that I have for you. Fair enough?" She warmly smiled.

He smiled back. "Yeah. Okay. Fair enough. And I'm flattered that you feel affection towards me."

She continued to pontificate. "You've never had a woman to care about you. And that's a damn shame. It's a crime, is what it is. A guy like you deserves someone really special.

You deserve a special woman, Danny."

His pride got the best of him. "*Pfft*. I've had plenty of women. When I was in the Army, I had more women than Charlie Sheen. A different woman every night. Hell, yeah — this player played."

"Yeah. Right. You expect me to believe that shit? Do you think that I'm that gullible? Do you think I give money to the Hare Krishna and the Moonies? Do you think I invite the Jehovah's Witnesses in for coffee and cake when they come a-knocking? You must."

"I'm . . . I'm just telling you the way it was."

"I know your secret, Danny. I know it. And I've known it for a while now. Me and Jesus, honey. Me and Jesus. You can't hide the truth from either of us. We both know what's up. So, why don't you just tell me instead of making me tell you, huh? We need to clear the air. This needs to be discussed."

"I don't know what you're talking about — unless you found my stash of *KC and the Sunshine Band* albums. And yes, I love the song *Boogie Shoes*." He laughed.

She accusingly pointed at him. "See, now, that's how I know I'm right. When you get nervous, you try to deflect with humor. Deflect. Deflect. Deflect."

He dismissively waved his hand at her. "Aw, you don't know what you're saying. You're out of your gourd, woman."

"It's nothing to be ashamed of. And it's not a crime. It's not. It's sweet. I just wish you would be comfortable enough to tell me. That's what's pissing me off — that you won't tell me. It kind of hurts that you won't tell."

He looked down. "I have no clue what you're talking about."

"You do. *You. Do.* You know very well what I'm talking about. Don't play dumb with me."

He threw his hands up. "What are you trying to say? Huh? Because I haven't the foggiest."

"You want me to say it?"

He yelled at her, "I want you to say it! If you think you know, Little Miss *Psychic Friends Network*, then, by all means, do share."

"Fine. But remember—it was your choice for it to come out this way."

"Duly noted."

"Okay. Okay. Fine. Here we go. I'll say it. You know that statue of the Virgin Mary you have on your desk? Hmm?"

"Yeah. What about her?"

"Well, honey, she's not the only virgin in that house."

"Shit, girl. I lost it when I was, like, fifteen."

"Bull. Shit. When you were fifteen, you *might* have been jerking off to the lingerie section of the *JC Penney* catalog, but you sure as hell weren't having sex. On second thought, I don't even think you were jerking off. When you were fifteen, I'll bet you anything you still thought that girls would give you cooties."

They stared at one another in silence for several seconds.

Finally, he asked her, "Why do you have to throw it up in my face? So you can make fun of me? Have a good laugh over it? Tease me?"

"You know me better than that. That's not why I brought this up."

"Then why did you?"

"I think you are incredibly sweet. And it makes me happy."

"It does?"

"Yeah. You have a gift to give, Danny. A precious gift. A good and perfect gift. The gift of yourself. And you can only give it once. Just once, honey. Just like the Thorn Bird only sings once. And maybe someday, you'll be ready to give that gift to a very special someone. I just wanted to say that. That's the only reason I brought it up. I swear. I won't bring it up again if it makes you uncomfortable. I promise."

"Okay. Thank you for saying that. It makes me feel better about the whole issue. Now that it's out in the open and all. Thank you. I feel like a burden has been lifted off of me. So, thanks."

"You're welcome, buddy."

"But . . . how? How did you know?"

"Combination of things. You've never had a serious girlfriend. That was the biggie because you don't strike me as a guy who's into casual sex. You're too sweet and sensitive for that. We're the same, Danny. For us old-fashioned types, sex and love go together. Plus, you weren't comfortable talking about relationships. Throw in a little woman's intuition, and it wasn't all that hard."

He nodded. "Gotcha."

"At the risk of pushing this too far, can I ask—does . . . does everything work okay down there?"

He loudly exhaled and rolled his eyes. "*Yes.* Everything works just fine. Better than fine, in fact. My Marshall Dillon can ride tall in the saddle anytime he wants, baby. Trust me."

She laughed. "Oh, snap. Your *Marshall Dillon*, huh?"

"Yeah. Like I said, I love *Gunsmoke.* Oh, and before you ask—yes. I'm sure that I'm not gay. Here. I'll prove it to you— you know the actress, Stephanie Dawkins?"

"Sure. Gorgeous woman. Pretty good actress, too."

"Right. So, when I was in the Army, she made this picture called *Some Have Entertained Angels.* Ever heard of it?"

"Sounds familiar. But I know I've never seen it."

"You should. Great little film. One of the best movies that nobody has ever heard of. Her best film, in my opinion. Should have won *Best Picture.* Anyway, she was one of my many crushes back in the day. So, I got the DVD of this film. The title comes from the Bible. Hebrews, chapter thirteen, verse two. *Be not forgetful to entertain strangers: for thereby some have entertained angels unawares.* Anyway, Stephanie Dawkins played this young, very beautiful but very jaded district at-torney. Not married, no boyfriend, because she won't let an-yone in. She's been burned by every guy she's ever allowed into her life. So, she's built up all these walls around her, see? And she pretends to be all tough. But she's really just afraid of getting hurt. So, one night, she's walking out to her car in a dimly lit parking lot when a bad guy pops out from behind a dumpster. He has a gun and is going to rob her. She gives up her purse and all. But the guy recognizes her as the DA be-cause she prosecuted him once before. And she recognizes him, too. So, he figures that he has to kill her to keep from going back to jail. He aims the gun at her head and is getting ready to pull the trigger. And right out of nowhere this guy shows up, a knight in shining armor. And he's handsome and all. And he has the most penetrating set of baby blue eyes you'd ever want to see. He knocks the gun out of the robber's hand — saves her life. The bad guy runs away. And it's just the two of them left in that parking lot. And they look at one an-other. Just stare into one another's eyes for the longest time. And then the guy just casually walks away. Like it was noth-ing. A couple of weeks later, she sees him in a coffeehouse. And she approaches him. They talk. She offers to buy him dinner to thank him. She doesn't really want to but figures it's the only decent thing to do. He accepts. And, for the first half of the film, you don't know whether this guy's even human. They mess with you a little, see? Is he, maybe, an angel, sent by God to be there for her, at her moment of crisis? I mean — the film's called *Some Have Entertained Angels*. So maybe it's going to be another *City of Angels* type of movie. But you even-tually find out that he is human. And he has his own sad story to tell. A year prior, his twenty-five-year-old girlfriend died of cancer. And he doesn't think that he'll ever be able to love again because he's scared, scared of getting hurt. So, he's as broken as she is. And as they get to know one another, he starts to move her. And, little by little, he breaks down all her walls until there's nothing left standing between them. It makes her feel uncomfortable at first. She doesn't want to let down her guard. But she can't help it. He gets to her. He just does. Because he's not only handsome but very sweet and kind, too. And she gets to him. He can see into her soul and realizes that she's not all tough. Not at all. She just wants to be loved. And so does he. And they fall in love, see? And bottom line — it's a movie about the power of love to heal broken lives. And by the end of the picture, the title makes sense. By the end, you realize that it really *is* a story about angels — that they were both angels. Human angels, but angels, nonetheless. Angels to one another. And that they were both sent by God to heal one another. But anyway, there's this scene, where they go swimming in a lake. And Stephanie Dawkins is wearing this little bikini and — *wow*. Just wow. I wore out that DVD watching her in that little swimsuit. So, that's a longwinded explanation that will hopefully convince you that I am straight. But *damn*. What a beautiful little film — brings tears to my eyes just thinking about it."

"Sounds like a great movie. Maybe we can watch it sometime."

"Yeah. Maybe on *Netflix* or something. Anyway, does that convince you that I'm straight?"

"Yeah. I never really thought that you were gay."

"So, you knew I wasn't gay, but you let me go through that whole long speech about the picture."

"You talked about it very eloquently. The way you explained the film's message kind of got to me, to be honest. So, I figured I'd just let you finish."

"Gotcha."

She cleared her voice. "Your Marshall Dillon can ride tall in the saddle. And Stephanie Dawkins turns you on. So, why then?"

"I never fell in love, I guess. That and . . ."

"And what?"

"The same first sergeant who offered me a *Camel* when I first arrived overseas also gave me some advice. First Sergeant Washington — a soldier's soldier — told me — *don't get too close to anybody, kid. Think of this as a job, just a job. And all these guys here — well, they're nothing more than coworkers. Don't think of them as anything more because some of them are going to become angels. You might become an angel yourself. Hell, I might become an angel. And life is just easier if you don't know any angels.* Oh, and just so you know — in military parlance, an *angel* is a friendly KIA. Anyhow — did I listen? Hell, no. I got close. And some of those guys did become angels. They did, Grace. So, I guess part of me is like the hero and heroine in *Some Have Entertained Angels*. You build up walls. So you don't get hurt. Hell, maybe that's the real reason that I became a priest in the first place."

They watched the sun go down and the moon come out. It was a brilliant, starlit night. They lay down on the beach next to one another. After a while, they propped their heads up on the old log and looked up at the night sky. He pulled out his phone and asked her, "Would you like to hear some music?"

"That'd be nice."

He used the light of the fire to scroll through his playlist. He selected Grace's latest single, *Sent From Above*.

She protested, telling him, "Turn it off. Turn. It. Off. Now please."

"Why?"

"Because it would be pompous for me to sit here and listen to one of my own songs. Besides, I hear enough of my music. I mean, truth be told, I don't think my voice is all that great."

"*What*? You can't be serious. You have a beautiful voice. People say you have the prettiest voice since Whitney Houston."

"I know what they say, but — I don't know — I'm self-conscious, I guess. I just don't enjoy hearing my own voice, especially on a recording. So, let's listen to something else."

He sighed. "Okay. As you wish." He again scrolled through his playlist and picked another song. "Here's something by one of my all-time favorites."

He played Elvis's *Love Me Tender*. They lay there and listened. And the only sounds they heard were the gentle waves coming ashore and the voice of a young Elvis Presley.

When it was over, he looked over at her, whistled, and commented, "*Mm*—that boy could sing."

She whispered back to him, "I don't want to end up like him. That's why I did what I did. I'm tired of being a prisoner to fame."

"I can understand that. But as you yourself said, fame isn't a toggle switch. You can't turn it on and off. Once you're famous, you're famous."

"Don't confound me with facts right now. Please. Don't ruin the evening with facts."

He nodded. "Okay. Fair enough."

They sat there and listened to the waves break, looked at the stars, and watched the fire gradually die out. When it was finally extinguished, he went inside and retrieved a bucket of water. He doused the firepit with it, just to make sure.

"Well, that's that," he said as he dusted his hands off. "Ready to head in?"

She shook her head. "No. Not really. I don't want this night to end."

He thought for a moment. "Say, I have an idea. Would you like to go for a ride?"

"A ride?"

"Yeah. A nighttime tour of beautiful downtown North East, Maryland." He bowed to her. "And I, madam, will be your chauffeur and tour guide."

"You mean you'll drive me around town?"

"Yeah. Just show you around the town. It's perfectly safe. The streets are pretty much vacant this time of night. Not a chance that anyone will see you, especially in the car. And I think you'd enjoy it."

"Sure. I'm game."

As they were getting ready to go inside, they saw the moonlight reflecting off a plastic six-pack soda ring that had washed ashore. She walked over and picked it up, telling him, "People are so damn inconsiderate. I read somewhere that ducks get these things caught around their little beaks. Then they can't eat, and they end up starving to death. I swear—I hate people. I love little duckies, but I hate most people."

"You're a good person, Grace, because the way I see it is— only an exceptional person would care about little duckies getting six-pack soda rings wrapped around their beaks."

She dotted his nose with her index finger and imitated a duck. "*Quack. Quack.*"

CHAPTER TWELVE: THE REAL-LIFE MAY-BERRY

They walked from the beach to the backyard. He took her hand and again helped her over the rocks.

The three of them walked into the house through the back door. He grabbed his car keys from the kitchen key rack. They walked into the garage from the laundry room, and he opened the passenger's side door of his blue *Chevrolet Malibu* for her. "Such a gentleman," she said with a smile as she got in. He opened the passenger's side back door, and Tippy jumped in.

He drove to the north end of town and started down Main Street, traveling very slowly and pointing out attractions and landmarks along the way.

"Look to your right. See that?"

She nodded. "Yeah. What is it?"

"That's *Herring Snatcher's Park. The Little North East Creek* runs right through it. People use it for fishing, picnicking, and generally, just people watching."

"It looks nice. At least from what I can see of it in the dark."

As they drove further south on Main, he pointed to his left. "Now, that's *Woody's Crab House.* Best crab cakes and steamed crabs in Maryland. Right here in little old North East."

He showed her the town hall, library, and police station. "The Police Department only has three officers. We don't need any more than that. There's no real crime here."

He called her attention to the *Little League* diamonds. "I

coach one of the teams. The Tee-Ball Cubs. Our season starts in a few weeks."

"Aw. You coach the little teeny, tiny guys. That's so cute."

"Yeah, well, the kids teach me as much as I teach them."

"Next thing I know, you're going to tell me that you volunteer at the local soup kitchen, too."

He laughed. "Well, as a matter of fact, I do put in some time over at *Our Daily Bread*, in Elkton."

"Oh, *Gawd*. Are you serious?"

He nodded. "But it's only one Saturday a month. It's no big deal, really."

Sarcastically, she asked, "Do you tow beached whales back out to sea, too?"

He laughed. "No. Don't be silly. I don't do that. But if we were closer to the ocean . . . maybe, just maybe . . ."

She reached over and playfully smacked him on the arm. "Smartass." She thought for a moment and turned serious. "Why do you have to be such a nice guy?"

"Beg your pardon? I thought it's better to be a nice guy than a mean guy."

"It is. But part of me wishes that you were a creep."

"Why would you want me to be a creep?"

"Because then I wouldn't like you so much. You see, our little arrangement would be so much easier if you were an uncaring louse."

He shrugged. "I am what I am."

"I know. Forget that I said that. I like you the way you are. Don't ever change, okay?"

He looked over at her and smiled. "Sure."

She reached across and grabbed his arm. "No. I'm serious. Don't ever change. Promise me you won't."

"Okay. I promise."

As they approached *Cramer's Five and Dime*, he stopped the car in the road for a moment. He emphatically pointed to the century-old building and told her, "All the kids go here for penny candy. They actually sell it by the piece, believe it or not. And they have an old-time fountain soda machine, too."

"Really? Penny candy and fountain sodas?"

He nodded. "Yeah. Sure."

She shook her head. "I've never seen anything like this in LA."

They continued along the main drag, and he announced, "Oh, and here's *Dolly's Ice Cream Parlor*. Homemade, hand-dipped ice cream. Any flavor you can imagine . . . and coming up next, on the left, is *Babe's Market*, our little ma and pa grocery store, the only grocery store in town. Old Snuffy Smith and Clayton Wanzer sit out front at the picnic table. Both Vietnam vets. They play checkers all day. That, and just watch the world go by. They talk to everyone who passes by, too. They know everyone in town by their first name. Yes, they do. Oh, and they drink soda pop. Yeah. Lots of soda pop. And they eat peanuts and *Moon Pies*. The peanuts are the kind that are shelled. And they make a mess with those peanut shells. And my understanding is that Babe is so pissed about it that he's threatening to make them start paying for the peanuts, soda pop, and *Moon Pies*. Yeah. He's *that* pissed. I mean — he's going to give them some warnings first. Just to be fair. But if, after the first twenty warnings or so, they don't start cleaning up their mess, he's going to consider invoking the nuclear option — no more free peanuts, soda pop, or *Moon Pies* for Clayton and Snuffy."

She glanced out the window, chuckled, and sarcastically told him, "Yeah, that Babe sure is one heartless bastard." *God. This is the town that time forgot. Don't these people know that places like this aren't supposed to exist anymore? Come to think of it, I don't think they were ever supposed to exist. Except in our dreams. Is this Brigadoon? Am I in Brigadoon? Dad always said it wasn't just a Scottish myth. That somewhere beyond the rainbow, it really existed. Did I by chance stumble onto it? Did the storm cause me to travel through a wormhole? Did I end up in some weird parallel universe where people actually treat one another with kindness and decency? And the legend says that if you happen upon Brigadoon and fall in love there, the Brigadoonians have to allow you to stay. Forever.*

Without even thinking about it, she muttered, "Brigadoon. It's Brigadoon. The Miracle of Brigadoon."

He turned, looked at her, and laughed. "Brigadoon? You talking about *The Brigadoon Diner*? How'd you know about *The Brigadoon*? We haven't been that far along Main Street yet. We'll be coming up on it pretty soon. It's owned by a Scottish couple, Glenn and Fiona McGavin. And the Diner's success is hardly a miracle. They make great haggis. Good milkshakes, too. I always get vanilla. I guess I'm just boring that way. They even have take-out. And on the last Thursday of the month, all vets eat for free. Maybe I can bring something home for us some time, huh? Oh, and they have this cool thing that they do. It's kind of a takeoff on the Legend of Brigadoon. You know about that legend? You should. You're Scottish."

She shrugged. "I think I might have heard a little about it somewhere once. Maybe."

"Yeah, well, here's what Glenn and Fiona do — if a proposal is made — and accepted — on the premises, both parties eat there free. Forever. They even have pictures hanging in the diner of all the couples who have become honorary *Brigadoonians*. How cool is that, huh? Cute, right?"

She didn't answer. *There's something about this place. It's not normal. Mysterious. Surreal. Sweet. Innocent. Lovely.*

Grace looked at the residential houses as they drove. They were all nice, but none were fancy. There were a lot of lawn chairs set up on front porches. And nearly every house flew the American flag.

"Dang. Look at all those flags," she noted with awe.

He nodded. "Here in North East, we still believe in flying the flag. And we make no apologies for it, either." He thought for a moment and added, "But they really should bring them in at night. Unless you can properly illuminate them, they're not supposed to fly in the evening. That's the proper flag etiquette, anyway. Mayor McKnight needs to put something in the town newsletter about that. I'll have to send him an email."

"Geez. This place looks like something right out of a *Norman Rockwell* painting," she observed.

"Doesn't it, though? People call it *the real-life Mayberry*."

Okay, Mayberry. Mayberry. Brigadoon. Mayberry. Brigadoon. Same difference, really. Mayberry's just the American version of Brigadoon. She tilted her head back against the seat's headrest, smiled, and closed her eyes. *"The real-life Mayberry.* That sounds so good. I think I want Mayberry." Her voice was filled with emotion. A tear raced down her cheek. "I don't want Beverly Hills or Malibu or Manhattan or South Beach anymore. Been there, done that. I want Mayberry." The more she talked, the more emotional she got. "I want penny candy from a five and dime and homemade ice cream. I want white picket fences and *Little League* baseball games. I want old-fashioned carnivals in the summer and church Christmas bazaars in the winter. And I want Fourth of July picnics and *Joe Corbi* pizza kits, the kind that your kids sell for the *Cub Scouts* or whatever. You know the ones I'm talking about?"

He nodded and quietly said, "Yeah. I know the ones."

She dabbed her eyes with the back of her hand and sniffled. "Tell me the truth. Am I silly for wanting those things? Am I just being sappy? Too sentimental? Does wanting to be normal make me abnormal?"

He reached over and gently patted her hand. "No, of course not. You're not silly for wanting those things. They're all good, sweet things."

She grabbed hold of his hand and squeezed it tight. "Thank you for a lovely evening. The best I've had in a long, long time."

He nodded. "My pleasure."

She leaned over from her passenger's seat and kissed him on the cheek.

They came upon *The Brigadoon Diner,* and he pointed it out. "And there you go, lass. There's your Brigadoon. How about that? There's a *Brigadoon* within the town limits of the *real-life Mayberry.* Now, if we had a *Camelot* Inn, we'd have the trifecta of magical and idyllic places, wouldn't we?" He smiled at her and winked.

CHAPTER THIRTEEN: PLEASE ASK GOD TO LOVE THEM

When they got home, Grace went upstairs to get ready for bed. She changed into a pink t-shirt and a pair of pink shorts. The shirt was her personalized one—it had her name inscribed in white script lettering. She was in her bare feet. When she walked into the living room, she found Danny sitting on the sofa with Tippy. He had changed into a plain, gray t-shirt and a pair of white shorts. He had a photo album out. The antique grandfather clock in the corner of the room chimed eleven.

"What are you doing?" she asked.

"Just looking at some old pictures. Even though it's late and tomorrow's a workday, I'm not really sleepy." He paused and asked her, "Can I tell you something?"

She sat down next to him. "You can tell me anything."

He hesitated a bit. "Sometimes . . . sometimes, I'm scared to go to sleep."

"Because you know you're going to have bad dreams?"

He nodded. "Yeah."

She pointed to the album. "What are you looking at?"

He held up the cover for her to see. It was simply labeled *Afghanistan*. "You want to look at it with me?" he asked.

"Yes. I'd like to."

"I've never shown these pictures to anyone. Except for Tippy, that is." She stared at him in silence. He opened the book and started flipping through the pages. She placed her

147

head on his shoulder, folded her right leg underneath her left, and looked on.

He stopped when he came to a picture that showed him posing with a group of six other soldiers. None of them had shirts on. Some were holding weapons. One of them was sticking his tongue out. Another was giving the camera the finger and holding a homemade sign which read, *Give War A Chance*. They all looked very young.

Danny pointed to one of the men, a blond kid toting a machine gun. "See that guy?" She nodded. "His name was Danny, too. Danny Michaels. He got killed two days before he was supposed to rotate back to the states. The chopper he was on crashed into a mountainside after it was hit with a surface-to-air missile. And it happened three weeks before Christmas. He was supposed to be home in time for Christmas. And he was all keyed up about it, too. He'd walk around Firebase Ponderosa singing that old Bing Crosby song, *I'll Be Home For Christmas*. I can still hear him singing it, like an echo in time. He came from a big family. I think there were about seven kids, and they were all supposed to be home for Christmas that year. And he told us what a big deal Christmas was in his family. They'd all go to church on Christmas Eve to see the live Nativity. He loved that because he loved animals. And, on Christmas Day, they'd get up early and exchange gifts. Then they'd have this huge dinner with extended family. He said they had about twenty people every year. His mom made everything—turkey, stuffing, mashed potatoes, candied yams. You name it. The neighbor would come over dressed as Santa for all his little nieces and nephews. And then, at the end of the day, they'd all gather around the piano. And his sister would play *Silent Night*. And they'd all sing along. Then they'd watch *It's A Wonderful Life*. They did all of that every year. And that year was going to be no different. The only difference was—that year, Misses Michaels was going to have her son home for Christmas again. And then, one day, Misses Michaels got a knock on her front door. And an Army officer in dress uniform stood there. And she knew. The woman knew. I wasn't there, but I know she knew. They *always* know. And he told her, *no, Misses Michaels, your son won't be home for Christmas. Not this year. Not any year."* He paused for a moment. "And goddamn, Grace. Just . . . goddamn." He cried. She put her arm around him.

After he'd composed himself, he pointed to another soldier, a tall, skinny one with dark hair and a winning smile. "That's Steve Piatelli. He was an Italian guy from Brooklyn." Danny laughed and shook his head. "That kid did the best John Wayne impression of all-time. I mean—he was spot-on with it. Spot. On. Oh, he was also a coach for the *Special Olympics,* by the way. Yeah, the *Special Olympics.* No shit." He looked over at Grace. "He got killed during Operation Rock Avalanche. A Taliban sniper shot him in the stomach, and he bled out before the medevac got there. We got payback, though. Even though we never actually did see the sniper, we fried his ass. Oh, yeah, we did. We knew he was in a cluster of trees, see? So, LT called me over, told me to get on the horn and get some ordinance on him. Well, guess what we did? You'll never guess what we did to that son of a bitch."

She shook her head. "What did you do?"

"We called in the Fast Movers to drop napalm. Bet you didn't even know that we still use that stuff, huh? Oh, we don't call it napalm anymore. Napalm's a dirty word, has been since Vietnam. Now, we call it the *Mark 77 incendiary device.* That sounds a lot cleaner, doesn't it? But don't let them BS you because it's basically napalm. Oh, the chemical composition is slightly different, but it's napalm all right. Better than napalm, in fact. The new and improved napalm. The heat could ruin the plastic components on an *M16,* even though we were over five-hundred meters away. When I called in the airstrike, they argued it with me. They didn't want to spend that ordinance on one damn sniper, you know? Because every time they drop one of those things, it costs the American taxpayers something like a hundred grand. But when I told them the sniper wasted one of our guys, they changed their tune. I mean—Steve's life was worth a hundred grand, don't you think, Grace? You didn't mind your hard-earned tax dollars going for that, did you? Steve was worth it, wasn't he?"

He looked at her, waiting for an answer. She said nothing, but a single tear raced down her cheek.

"Answer me, Grace. Answer me. His life was worth that much, *wasn't it*?"

She nodded. "Yes."

"Anyhow, we fried that sniper. We fried his ass. And when they dumped the *Mark 77s*, we cheered. We were all like— *yeah, die you Taliban motherfuckeeeer!* And, later, after the fire was extinguished, we walked through that cluster of trees. Or what *had been* a cluster of trees. Because we had to find the sniper, his body, that is. We had to see him, to confirm that he was dead. And, low and behold, we located him. He looked like a marshmallow that had fallen into a fire. All black. Skin charred and bubbling and whatnot. You could kind of, sort of, tell that it had been a human being. And we were happy about it. Hell, some guys even took pictures of his roasted ass. I didn't, but some did. But I was glad that he burned. I was happy that the motherfucker burned alive." He clinched his fist and thought for a moment before telling her, "I'm sorry if I come off as crass. I don't mean to. I don't talk like this anymore. But right now, I'm in another time and place. I'm eighteen again. And half a world away. So, forgive me if I come off as crude. This is how I talked back then. *Boonie Rap. Fuck that motherfucking goddamn motherfucker.* That kind of thing. It's how we all talked. I'm not proud of it. And I'm certainly not proud of talking gleefully about another human being getting burned alive by that nasty stuff. But it was what it was, you know? Back then, we wanted payback. It got real personal sometimes. The whole war — the whole damn war — came down to sending one of those little T-Men SOBs to Hell because he killed your buddy. And that's all you cared about. That constituted *winning the war*. At least to you, it did."

"It's okay, babe," she assured him. "You tell the story however you need to. It's your story. I'm just here to listen and learn."

He turned the page and pointed to a picture of a pale redhead leaning up against a *Humvee*. "Ricky Jarvis. He's in a wheelchair now. An *AK-47* round severed his spinal cord."

On the next page was a photo of a diminutive soldier. He was pointing his *M16* at the camera. On his helmet, the words *Born To Kill* were written in black magic marker. "Randy McClinton, from Denver," he explained. "He was the old man of Third Platoon. Twenty-six. Of course, he didn't join the Army until he was twenty-three. Hell, he was older than Lieutenant McKay, by a few years, in fact. A lot of the guys kind of looked up to him, too, because he actually had college. Well, a year of community college. See what he wrote on his helmet — *Born To Kill?*"

She nodded. "Yeah. What's that? What does that mean? Why did he write that?"

"That was his homage to *Full Metal Jacket*. He loved that movie. He *lived* that movie. Yeah he did. Writing *Born To Kill* on his helmet like that was not in accordance with the regs. In fact, that type of graffiti was considered *defacing government property*. But what were they going to do? Huh? Send him to the Korengal Valley?" He chuckled for a split second. "The . . . the guy was so short. I swear, he wasn't much taller than you, Grace. And he had a huge crush on Kim Kardashian. I never really got that myself. I mean — Kim Kardashian? *Way* too artificial-looking for me. I, personally, never thought she was all that attractive. But that's neither here nor there. Anyhow, we called him The Little Dipper because he was so short, and he dipped smokeless tobacco, you know that nasty stuff that makes your teeth rot and fall out? He was on his third tour. The guys would always ask him why he kept coming back. He'd just shrug and say that he didn't have anything better to go home to. That, and he couldn't hack it back in the real world anymore. He always said that he didn't know how to deal with stuff when he went home on leave. There was a story that he liked to tell about how when he went home once, at Easter time, he went to church. Well, Randy was Methodist, right? So, he went to church with his family on Easter Sunday. And he was in his dress uniform and so forth. All decked out and squared away. *Standing tall and looking good, ought to be in Hollywood.* That kind of shit. Well, it was a real nice service. And as he and his family were walking out, shaking hands and saying *hello* to the minister, Randy stopped and told the guy — *that was a great fuckin' sermon, Reverend. And that music? That was fuckin'-A. Best goddamn church service I've ever been to.* He didn't know how to talk or act in the real world anymore. He said that he could hack a war in Afghanistan a lot easier than he could hack peace in the real world. He told us that he'd just keep doing tours until he got killed. That's exactly what happened, too. One day, an IED took him out. And that was that. And I sure hope he finally found his peace, a peace that eluded him in this world.

  "Sometimes, Grace, it seemed like we were all just a bunch of guys who America didn't really care about because it was business as usual here on the home front. At least during Vietnam, people actually cared about the war. They treated the vets like shit, but at least they knew that there was a war on. In the fall of two-thousand-seven, while we were dying in the Korengal, America was more concerned about whether the New England Patriots could finish the season undefeated than it was about Afghanistan. I never really understood that, either. I mean, it was like — football. War. Football. War. Football. War. Well, football won. Don't get me wrong, I love football as much as any other red-blooded American male, but it seemed messed-up to us. Sure, Tom Brady was throwing touchdowns. But we were throwing — and dodging — hand grenades. But it was like most of the country didn't even know that there was a war on. When I got home, I told the cab driver at the airport that I had just gotten back from Afghanistan, and he was like, *oh, you mean we're still over there?* I guess you can't care about something if you don't even know that it exists, right?

"Let's see. Who else do we have here?" He flipped through the pages and stopped at a photo of a very young African-American man wearing an olive drab boonie hat and holding a mortar tube. "Oh my God. Benny. *Benny — Benny — Benny.* Benny Williams. Barely eighteen years old. We called him *Smokey* because he looked like a young Smokey Robinson. Good looking kid, right? Sweet kid. His only dream in life was to get his own puppy. He was always talking about how when he got home, he was going to get himself a puppy, you know? A Lab puppy."

She was afraid to ask but did. "Whatever happened to him? Did he get his puppy?" There were tears in her eyes. Her lower lip quivered. She already knew the answer.

He shook his head. "He smothered a live grenade with his body to save the other three guys in his fireteam. There's no greater love than that, Grace. *No greater love.* He was awarded The Congressional Medal of Honor. Posthumously, of course. His body was cut in half by the force of the blast. We had to make two trips to get his remains on the chopper."

She was at a loss for words. *God. What are you supposed to say to that?* She just looked up at him with tears running down her cheeks. For a few seconds, the room fell silent.

Finally, he spoke. "He was just like you and me — he was

an only child, his mother's only child. When he died, I wrote a letter to his mom, you know? Because I wanted her to hear from someone who was actually there when her son died. I wanted her to know that, even though he was so very far from home, that he didn't die alone, that he died with the only brothers he ever had. He never had a chance to fall in love or have kids or any of that good stuff. And, now, his face is frozen in time. Forever young. Young until Kingdom Come.

"Whenever something bad happened over there, we'd always tell each other — *it don't mean nothing. Not a thing.* Well, we said that because it meant so much. It meant everything, Grace. *Everything.*"

She broke down and started sobbing.

As she cried, he added, "And do you know what pisses me off the most about Benny's death?"

She shook her head, sniffled, and used her index finger to dab her tears. "Uh-uh. What?"

"That the world will never know who he was. He's just another name on some memorial wall. Well, he's more than a name on a wall. He's a hero, a *real* hero. Not one of these fake heroes that our society loves to manufacture and prop up. But a real one. And he died at eighteen, seven-thousand miles from home, on some godforsaken hillside in Afghanistan. And only his family and those of us who served with him will ever know what a fine man he was. And that pisses me off to no end."

Softly, she told him, "Now, *I* know. At least *I* know who he was. Thank you for sharing Benny's story with me."

He closed the book and held it up to her. "This is part of who I am. Do you understand that?"

She nodded and sniffled again. "Uh-huh."

"We came from all different backgrounds, Grace. Black and white. Rich and poor. City slicker and country bumpkin. College degrees and GEDs. But none of that mattered. Because war is very egalitarian. It doesn't play favorites. It offers all of its participants the same chance. The same random chance . . . the chance to die.

"It was the worst experience of my life. It's a surreal feeling to hear a bullet whiz by and know that that bullet was intended for *you*, that someone was just trying to kill *you*. But here's the kicker—I wouldn't trade that experience for anything in the world. I was there. I was with these guys, these magnificent guys, on Saint Crispin's Day. Maybe they weren't the Greatest Generation. But they were the greatest of *their* generation. And they didn't need some slick Hollywood PR machine to concoct an *image* or *narrative* for them, either. Sometimes, Grace, the so-called heroes don't live up to it. Because they were never really heroes, to begin with. But these guys? These guys? God Almighty! These boys—these *men*— they lived up to it. Believe that. When it came time to perform for America and each other, they *did*. In spades. And some made it home. And some didn't. But all were changed. I'm proud that I served with them. I'm proud that I fought for this country. It was an *honor* to fight for this country, not a burden but an *honor*. But my demons don't give me much of a break. They come at night, in the darkest part of the night—in my dreams. And they take me back in time. And suddenly it's two-thousand-seven again. And I see guys like Benny Williams die all over."

He paused and looked her square in the eye. "My reason for telling you this, my whole reason for telling you all of this is—I love these guys, these wonderful, heroic guys. Like brothers, I love them. And I'd like for you to love them, too, Grace. And, tonight, if you bow your head . . ." There was a long pause. "Please ask *God* to love them."

She started to wail. She put her arms around him and nuzzled her head against his chest. Her tears got his t-shirt wet. "You always get me crying. I swear, I've cried more since I've been living here than I have in the last twenty years," she told him.

"I'm sorry."

"Don't be. I cry because you get to me. You get into my heart. And my soul. Yes, you get into my soul, too. And that's a special thing to a woman." She smiled through her tears.

She took the album out of his hands and set it on the coffee table. "Let's go to bed, Danny." She got up and took him by the hand.

He hesitated. "You know, I've been thinking about the sleeping arrangements around here. And I've come to the conclusion that we should sleep in separate beds from now on. Last night wasn't a good idea."

She protested. "But we didn't do anything wrong."

"The optics, Grace. The optics aren't good."

She laughed. "What optics? Who's going to see? What? Is Tippy going to squeal on us?"

"God sees everything."

"Oh, Danny. Do you really think God is angry because we shared a bed last night? Are you telling me that with all the awful, shitty stuff He has to deal with that He's ticked off because Grace and Danny slept in the same bed?"

He looked down and didn't answer.

She pressed her case. "Look—I've never studied theology or the Bible or anything like that, but I can't imagine a loving, compassionate God having an issue with that."

He shook his head. "It's not that simple."

"It *is* that simple. You're letting that good old-fashioned Catholic guilt get to you." She held up her index finger. "Give me one good reason why it's wrong for us to sleep in the same bed."

He said nothing.

Quietly, she said, "Let me ask you something—did you get comfort from having me in bed with you last night? Be honest now."

He nodded. "Yes. I did. Great comfort."

"I got comfort from it, too. So, what's wrong with two lonely people finding comfort in one another's company?"

He loudly exhaled and shook his head. "I guess nothing."

She smiled, reached down, and again pulled him by the hand. "Well, come on, then. Let's go." She led him up the staircase. Tippy followed.

When they got to his room, he turned down the bed and explained to her, "Now, listen, we need some ground rules. You get half of the bed, and I get half. And we have to stay on our respective sides." He took his index finger and drew an imaginary line down the center of the bed. "See this?" he asked.

She nodded. "Uh-huh."

"Well, this is *no man's land*. This is the dividing line. Neither of us are allowed to cross over into *no man's land*. Understand?"

"No problem. But I call dibs on the left side of the bed. I'm a left-side sleeper."

"Fine. You can have the left side."

Grace climbed into bed. Danny kneeled at the foot of the bed and said the Our Father before he clapped off the overhead light and got in with her.

She reached across the bed to turn out the light on the nightstand. As she did, her left breast brushed his cheek. She giggled. "Sorry. I didn't mean to hit you in the face with my boob."

"No problem. Too bad *The Clapper* doesn't work on the nightstand light. Then you could have just clapped it out."

"Nah. I like doing the good old reach-across. I'd think you'd like it, too. I mean, you get a free feel each time. And my boobs could, conceivably, pop right out when I reach across like that. Then, you'd literally have them right in your face. What would you do if they were right there in your face? Would you motorboat 'em?"

"Grace — please. Let's not speak of such things. Okay?"

She laughed. "*Let's not speak of such things.* For some reason, that sounded incredibly adorable."

"I was completely serious."

"All right. Fine. I'll stop. After all, I don't want you to have a wet dream and ruin your shorts — don't want to be responsible for that. No siree Bob."

"*Grace.* It's time to say goodnight."

She reached over and gently caressed his cheek. "Okay. Fair enough. My shy guy is embarrassed. Goodnight, Danny."

"Goodnight, Grace."

Tippy jumped up on the bed and lay down at its foot. Grace called out, "Goodnight, Tippy."

Danny chimed in, "Oh, yeah, goodnight, Tippy."

Grace snickered. "Goodnight, Jim Bob. Goodnight, Mary Ellen. Goodnight, Elizabeth. Goodnight, Erin. Goodnight, Jason. Goodnight, John Boy."

Danny laughed. "You forgot Ben."

"No, I didn't forget him. I just didn't want to disturb him. See, he likes to lie in bed at night and . . . you know."

They both laughed. "You're naughty, girl."

There was silence for about half a minute. Finally, he called out, "Grace?"

"Yeah?"

"Can you sing me a song while we're lying here? Your voice relaxes me. You have the voice of an angel."

"Aw, bless your heart. Of course, I'll sing for you. What do you want to hear?"

"Surprise me."

She thought for a moment. "Okay. Let's see how you like this one." She cleared her voice and sang *Somewhere Over The*

Rainbow.

When she was finished, he clapped. The light came back on. They laughed.

"Thank you. That was gorgeous. I'm glad you're here in bed with me. It feels really good to have you with me like this."

"It makes me feel good, too. And I hope that, tonight, you have only sweet dreams."

"Me, too." He again clapped the light off.

After a few minutes of silence, he again called out to her and gently tugged on her shirt, "Grace?"

"Yeah?"

"Can . . . can I . . . can I kiss you?"

She sat up in bed. "You want to kiss me?" *Yes!*

"Yeah. Just a little peck on the cheek."

She was mildly disappointed. "Well, that's not a real kiss, Danny. That's a *daddy kiss*. That's how a girl's father kisses her."

"Oh."

"Do you want to try a real kiss? We don't have to French or anything. At least not yet. But we could at least kiss on the lips. You want to try that? Hmm? I'm a good kisser. Never any complaints. Only compliments. I think you'd like it. I really do. Very romantic. Very sensual. Very comforting. All those things. And I promise not to give you any *girl germs*."

"No. Not on the lips. Just on the cheek. I think I need to crawl before I can walk."

This is good. This is progress. Now, give him some positive rein-forcement. "Oh . . . oh . . . okay. Okay. It's very brave of you to take that first step towards exploring your feelings, by the way."

"*Brave*? Really? You think so?"

"Oh, absolutely."

"Thanks. That makes me feel better about the whole thing."

She lay back down, flat on her back, and presented her left cheek to him. "Well, here. Kiss away."

He leaned over and tenderly pressed his lips to her left cheek.

"That was nice. Your skin is so soft. You smell good, too. I liked that. I did. You make me feel good. You make me feel safe. A little five-foot woman who barely weighs a hundred pounds makes me feel safe." He laughed.

"I'm five-two," she corrected him. "Don't cheat me out of those last two inches, bub."

He chuckled. "Sorry. Yeah, you're five-two. But you do make me feel safe. You're a good person, Grace. You're special. Very special. And not because you're Grace Stevens. But because you're . . . Just Grace."

"You remember when I said that Forrest Gump was the sweetest man who ever walked the face of the earth?"

"Yeah."

"Well, I was wrong about that. I . . . I was wrong. Just—I was wrong. Okay?" She sniffled.

Chapter Fourteen: Jesus of North East

Later that night, Grace was jarred awake by a noise that sounded like it was coming from the outside. She looked at the clock—one-thirty in the morning. As she sat up, she nudged Danny's arm. "Danny . . . Danny," she called out in a whisper. She poked his arm. "Hey, come on, wake up."

He was startled and popped up. "What? What? What's going on?" He yawned and rubbed his eyes.

"I think someone's outside. I heard a noise."

He listened for a moment. Nothing. He shook his head. "I don't hear anything." He started to lie back down.

A few seconds later, they heard the sound of metal hitting the sidewalk. Danny sat back up. "Okay. I *did* hear that." Tippy woke up and started barking incessantly.

"Told you. There's someone out there."

"It sounded like someone knocked over the trashcans. Probably raccoons. But I'll go down and have a look, if it'll make you feel better." He got out of bed and started to walk out of the room. Grace got up, too, put on his bathrobe, and cinched the belt tight to cover herself.

"Be careful," she told him.

"I will. I'm sure it's nothing, though."

She walked over to his golf bag, sitting in the corner of the room, and pulled out the driver. She tried to hand it to him. "Here. Take this. It could be a prowler, a burglar."

He shot her a leery look and waved off the club. "We don't

have prowlers or thieves in North East. Remember, this is Mayberry."

As he started to walk out the door, he turned, pointed to her, and said, "You stay up here with Tippy."

She nodded. "Kay."

He walked out the door. Grace walked to the top of the stairs, sat on the hardwood floor so she could see into the living room, and waited. Tippy lay down with her and whimpered.

For several minutes, she heard and saw nothing. She was getting worried.

Finally, she heard the front door open. Then she heard voices—Danny's and someone else's. She saw the living room lights come on. Tippy took off down the stairs, barking incessantly.

A man came into her view. He looked to be in his early thirties and was handsome. His features were soft, even delicate. He had long brown hair and a beard but was dressed in shabby clothing. With one hand, he clutched a teddy bear that was falling apart. With the other, he pulled a red child's wagon. In the wagon sat an old Rottweiler. She noticed that the dog didn't appear to have any hind legs. *Poor thing. Probably born that way.*

Tippy ran over to the dog, and they began to sniff one another's behinds.

She heard Danny say, "Yes, Tippy, your old friend Jake's come to see you." Then she saw Danny walk over to the wagon and pat the Rottweiler on the head.

The man pulled the wagon over to a *Lazy Boy* recliner and sat down in the chair. He walked with a limp.

Danny walked away and returned a minute later with several cans of dog food. "Here you go," he said as he handed the food to the man. "Ten cans. This should hold old Jake for a little while. And when you run out, just come back, and I'll set you up with more." *Aw, he's giving the homeless guy food for his dog. God Almighty. This guy's getting to me. He's getting to me in ways that no man ever has.*

The man nodded. "Thank you, Danny."

Danny stood in front of the man with his hands in the pockets of his shorts. "Is there anything else you need, Mike?"

He looked up at Danny. "I'm not *Mike*. You always call me *Mike,* and I don't know why."

"Well, that's your name. Mike. Mike Jameson." Danny paused and continued. "You graduated from North East High School. Then you joined the Marines. Remember? You fought in Iraq, at a place called Fallujah. Back in two-thousand-four. That's why you walk with a limp. You got hit with shrapnel, just like me. I was in Afghanistan. You were in Iraq. I got hit in the shoulder. You got hit in the leg. Remember?"

He shook his head. "I'm sorry, but I don't know who this *Mike Jameson* is. And I've never fought anywhere. I would never fight anyone. I have no enemies. I love everyone." He paused for a moment, looked directly at Danny, and finally continued. "Every time I stop by, we end up having this same conversation. I tell you who I am, but you never believe me. So, I'll tell you again—I'm Christ, Danny. *Jesus. Christ.* Don't you know me, son?"

Danny shook his head. "No, Mike. Jesus died on the cross two-thousand years ago and rose to Heaven."

Mike spoke quietly and gently. "But I said I would come back. I always said I'd come back. As a man of faith, why are you unwilling to believe that I've fulfilled my promise?"

Danny shrugged. "I don't know—it just seems that if Jesus came back, he wouldn't come to little old North East, Maryland."

"Nazareth was a small town, too."

Danny ran his fingers through his hair. "Why don't you let me take you to Perry Point? They have some really good programs for vets, in-patient programs. I could take care of Jake for you while you're there. That would be no problem at all."

He shook his head. "No—no. I have work to do. I have to get my message out before it's too late."

"What's your message?"

"That God is love."

"That's it?"

"Isn't that everything?"

Grace sat there at the top of the stairs and watched the bizarre scene unfold with her mouth open. *This is weird. Really weird. Twilight Zone weird.*

"Do you have a place to stay tonight, Mike? Is Reverend Mullins over at the Methodist Church still letting you stay at his place?"

He nodded. "Yes, I stay with Richard in his guest room. I just needed some dog food for Jake. He's my best friend, you know."

Danny nodded. "I know what you mean. I wouldn't know what to do without Tippy."

"Yes, animals live closer to God than most humans. And they're a source of great comfort and companionship. But you're still a lonely man."

"Excuse me?"

"Lonely. You're extremely lonely. And haunted, too, haunted by the war. You can't hide your feelings from me. I know what's in everyone's heart."

"Why are you telling me this?"

"Because I want you to find peace. And love. Yes, love, too. That's my will for you. That's my will for all of my children. You're all the same to me. I want you to be loved. But I can't force you to. I can die for you, but I can't live for you. Please, son, open your heart to accepting love and peace."

"Yeah, well, love and peace aren't easy things to come by in this world."

Mike held up his teddy bear. "Can I borrow some heavy-duty tape? Max's stuffing is starting to come out again. I need to tape him up."

Danny nodded. "Sure. I think I have some in one of the cabinets in the kitchen. Let me take a look real quick."

Mike added, "I'm sorry I came over so late. I stopped by earlier, but no one answered the door. And I'm sorry I knocked over your trashcans and caused a commotion. I probably woke up the entire neighborhood."

Danny started to walk away toward the kitchen but called out to him, "Hey, no problem, man. It's all good."

Mike got up from the chair and limped out of Grace's view. She could tell, though, that he was still in the living room.

To get a better view, she lay flat on her belly and slid herself down the first three steps. But she underestimated how difficult it would be to get her bare feet anchored to the hardwood floor. She lost control and slid all the way down on her stomach. "Whoa!" she cried out as she traveled to the bottom of the stairs.

Danny heard the commotion and came running out of the kitchen. He ran over to her. "Are you okay?"

She nodded as she got up and brushed herself off. "My boobs broke my fall. Those suckers are like airbags," she nonchalantly noted as she looked down at them.

He flashed her a scowl. "Why do you always have to work your breasts into every conversation. *My boobs this, my boobs that.* You talk about them like they're your darn superpower. And I thought I told you to stay upstairs."

"You did, but I kind of fell down the stairs . . . when I was eavesdropping." She shrugged. "What can I say? I'm an eavesdropper. And let's not fight when company's over. Kay?"

She tilted her head to one side and flashed Mike an outrageous, exaggerated smile, showing both her top and bottom set of teeth.

Mike limped over to Grace. *Oh, shit. My cover's about to be blown — the jig's up.*

He smiled at her and looked directly into her eyes. "Hello, child."

Grace meekly raised her hand and waved. "Hey." *His eyes. His eyes are penetrating. I'm scared of him.*

Danny jumped in. "Ah, Mike, this is a friend of mine. She's staying with me for a while. But, you know, she's a very private person."

Grace interjected. "Yes. *Very* private."

Danny nodded. "Right. So, she doesn't want anyone to know she's in town, you understand? She's tired, just wants to rest. Can I count on you to make this our little secret?"

Mike nodded. "Of course. Confidentiality is one of my specialties."

"Thank you," Danny said.

Grace added, "Yeah. Thanks."

Mike looked at Grace again, stared at her for several seconds. It made her feel awkward. Finally, he tenderly said to her, "*Blessed are the pure in heart, for they shall see God.*"

She smiled and laughed a nervous laugh. "I know, right?"

Danny taped Mike's teddy bear for him, and he got ready to leave. He placed the dog food inside the cart. He gently set the teddy bear down in the cart as well. Danny and Grace stood next to one another.

Mike looked at them and warmly smiled. He walked over to Danny and placed his hands on Danny's head. "Bless you, Danny, for your kindness. I'll remember you when I come into my kingdom."

Then he placed his hands on Grace's head. Again, she felt uncomfortable. She nervously looked upwards as his soft, warm hands settled on her head. He spoke in a near whisper. "And bless you, Grace, God's Grace. Bless both of you. May you both find peace, happiness, and love."

Before he left, he reached into his wagon and pulled out two copies of a children's Christian magazine called *The Little Shepherd*. He handed them each a copy. They thanked him.

They watched as he limped out the front door, pulling his dog along in the wagon. Danny closed the door, leaned against it, and took a deep breath.

Grace pointed to the door that Mike had just walked out of. "Okay, what the hell was *that*?"

"Come on. Let's have a cup of coffee, and I'll tell you the whole story."

He made some coffee. She took off her housecoat. "It's really warm in here," she noted as she fanned herself with her hand. They sat at the kitchen table and drank the coffee.

He looked in his cup and casually commented, "I sure hope this doesn't keep me up the rest of the night. I have to go to work tomorrow, or should I say, later this morning."

"Yeah — yeah — yeah. Now tell me about that character who was just here."

He shrugged. "His name's Michael Jameson. He served with the Marines in Iraq. Saw lots of combat, was wounded pretty bad. He's a legitimate war hero, won a ton of medals. Anyway, now he thinks he's Jesus Christ. He's known all around town. Everyone calls him *Jesus of North East*. The whole town kind of looks after him. Everyone does their part, you know?"

"That poor man. He's delusional."

He took a sip of coffee and nodded. "Yep. Delusions of grandeur. And he's never gotten the help he needs, either."

"How sad."

"Isn't it, though? I think what happened to him was that he decided that he had had enough of war when he got back from Iraq, enough of the killing. So, he tricked his mind into believing that he's Christ. The man who has no enemies, loves everyone unconditionally, renounces all violence, etcetera, etcetera."

"You don't think he recognized me, do you?"

He shook his head. "Nah. Not a chance. He's in his own

167

little world. Almost literally. My understanding is that he lives a very monastic lifestyle—no TV, no cellphone, no radio, no computer, no internet. No nothing. They say he hasn't had any of that stuff in years, gave it all up to devote himself full-time to his *ministry*. As a matter of fact, someone told me that he doesn't even know who's president of the United States. That's how out of touch he is. He's probably one of the few people who wouldn't have a clue as to who you are. And even if he did, he wouldn't say anything after promising not to. After all, Jesus would never go back on his word. That wouldn't be very Christ-like, now would it?"

She felt relieved. "Well, that's good. I feel better knowing that."

She thought for a moment, scratched her head, and asked, "But you know what freaked me out about him?"

"What's that?"

"That he knew my name. You never introduced me by name. You introduced me as your *friend*. How did he know my name, Danny? That gave me the chills."

He pointed to her shirt and laughed. "Your shirt. Your name is right on that shirt I bought you."

She looked down and laughed. "Oh, yeah. You're right. It is. *Duh*. I forgot all about that. Okay. *Whew*. That explains it. Totally *not* Jesus Christ, right? Just a sad, delusional man who can read."

Danny nodded. "Right."

They went upstairs and got back into bed. Grace clapped out the lights. They said goodnight to one another. A couple of minutes went by, and Grace sat up in the bed. "Danny," she called out. "Are you still awake?"

"Yeah. What is it?"

"When I was talking to your friend, Mike, I had your bathrobe on over my shirt. And it was pulled tightly shut."

He turned and looked at her. "Seriously? Are you sure?"

She nodded. "I'm positive. I didn't take it off until we went into the kitchen for coffee."

"Well, maybe he did recognize you, after all."

"Maybe. But if he's as isolated and out of touch as you were saying, I think it's doubtful he would have known me. I mean, seriously, if the man doesn't even know who's president of the United States, I doubt he knows much about entertainers."

"Listen, it doesn't really matter. Whether he recognized you or not, the bottom line is he's not going to say anything. Our secret is safe. That's really all that counts."

"Yeah. I guess." She thought for a moment and added, "Oh, I know — there's something else I wanted to ask you. What did he mean when he told me — *blessed are the pure in heart, for they shall see God?* What did he mean by that stuff? That creeped me out, too."

"He was quoting one of the Beatitudes. He was paying you a tremendous compliment. In his eyes, you're pure in heart. So, God blessed you. He allowed you to see Him, to see the Face of God. Because only pure eyes can look at God and live. He was saying that the Beatitude was fulfilled when you looked at him." With a touch of sarcasm, he added, "So, congrats, Grace. The Man Himself thinks you're pretty awesome."

"Don't be sarcastic about this."

"Oh, I'm not. Look — I love Mike, known him for years. He's a wonderful guy. Literally wonderful. And he's totally harmless, except to himself. Heck, he's a better Christian than anyone else on the planet because he's convinced that he's the one who started it all. It's like the weekend duffer who's convinced that he's Jack Nicklaus. The guy's probably going to play better because he's brimming with confidence and such."

"Just the same — it was weird. The wee hours of the morning and all." She paused, thought for a moment, and asked,

"Hey, doesn't the Bible say that He'll come back in the wee hours of the morning or something like that?"

He didn't immediately answer, just stared at her. Finally, after several seconds of silence, he said, with great deliberation, "*Like a thief in the night.*"

She shuddered and shook her hands. "Oh, God. It's giving me *freaking chills.*"

"All right, I'll admit—it might have come off as a little weird, especially to someone who's not familiar with Mike. I'll admit that much. But, really, he's a man. Just a man. A sweet, lovable, mentally ill man. One who carries a broken teddy bear everywhere he goes. And pulls his disabled Rottweiler around in a kid's wagon."

She scooted over close to him and put her head on his chest.

He looked at her sternly. "You crossed into *no man's land.*"

She pointed to her breasts. "As I know you've noticed— I'm not a man, *man*. So, it doesn't apply to me." She stuck her tongue out at him, adding, "Besides, you should give me a pass on that tonight anyway . . . because shit's getting just a wee bit spooky around here."

Chapter Fifteen: The Last Five Minutes of *Breakfast At Tiffany's*

Danny arrived home from work on Tuesday evening carrying two bags, a white shopping bag and a small, brown paper bag. After emptying the mailbox, he walked in the house with his head down, flipping through the various pieces of correspondence — a credit card statement, some coupons for *McDonald's. The Veterans of Foreign Wars* wanted a donation, and so did *St. Francis of Assisi Animal Sanctuary. I'll send them both a little something next payday.*

As he entered the living room, he was greeted with the unmistakable aroma of meatloaf in the oven. He walked into the kitchen to find Grace placing some brown and serve rolls on a baking sheet. Her hair was up. She was in her bare feet, wearing a pair of black shorts and a tight-fitting white tank top. It was obvious she wasn't wearing a bra. Tippy was lying at her feet. "Hey," she called out.

"Hey there," he replied. He looked at the oven and pointed to it. "That smells like meatloaf. Are you cooking a meatloaf?"

She smiled and nodded. "Uh-huh. I found some ground beef in the freezer, so I thawed it out and made a meatloaf. Oh, and I found some instant mashed potatoes, so I made them up. Plus, some peas. And as soon as the meatloaf is done, I'm going to put these dinner rolls in. You don't mind that I took it upon myself to make dinner, do you?"

"No. Not at all. I didn't know you cooked. I guess I just figured a big star like yourself would have a personal chef on staff."

She shook her head. "Nope. This Long Island girl likes to cook her own meals."

"That's very Roosevelt of you."

She chuckled at his wisecrack, then turned serious. "I just thought you might like a home-cooked meal for a change. I'll bet you don't get many of those, huh?"

He shook his head. "No. I don't. Almost never."

She walked over to him and patted his stomach. "You need to eat better. You're too thin."

"I weigh a hundred and seventy," he retorted.

"Yeah, but you're what? Six-foot-three, six-foot-four?"

"Six-three."

"Yeah, so you can stand to put on a little weight."

"Yes, Mom."

She took a dish towel that she was holding, rolled it up, and snapped it at him. It hit him in the rear end. The impact made a loud popping sound.

"Ouch. That stung, girl." He feigned pain and rubbed his backside.

She pointed to the bags he was carrying. "What do you have there?"

He looked down. "Oh, yeah. I stopped at a couple of places after work. Picked up some things."

He pulled out a tub of ice cream and held it up for her to see. "I stopped at *Dolly's* and got some homemade ice cream."

Grace looked at the carton and read the name of the flavor out loud. "*Georgia Peach*, huh? Is that supposed to be better than regular peach ice cream?"

"Yeah. I think it is, actually."

"Well, I love peaches. We can have it for dessert." She took it from him and put it in the freezer.

"Oh, and this is for you." He held out the small, brown bag to her.

She took it from him, peeked inside, and smiled. *"Aw,* you got me some candy."

He pointed to the bag. "Now, that's not just any candy. That's old-time penny candy from *Cramer's Five and Dime.* You said that you wanted some."

She looked into the bag. "That was very kind of you. Let's see what you got me."

She dumped the contents on the kitchen table and started to sort through it. "Oh my God. Look at this. You got some of those caramel chews that have the cream in the center. What are they called?"

"Bullseyes."

"That's right. *Bullseyes.* Those things are, like, *so* freaking good."

"I know, right? I love them. You can never eat just one."

She continued to go through the candy. "And let's see . . . what else do we have here? We have some strawberry string licorice . . . and some *Mary Janes* . . . and *Swedish Fish.* Oh, God, I love *Swedish Fish* . . . root beer barrels, and a whole bunch of other stuff. I'm really going to enjoy this." She unwrapped one of the *Bullseyes,* popped it in her mouth, and chewed.

He smiled. "See, now you can say you've had the world-famous *Cramer's* penny candy."

She nodded and talked with the candy in her mouth. "Right. *Cramer's* penny candy from the real-life Mayberry."

"Exactly."

He helped her put the finishing touches on the meal and made some fresh, southern iced tea. They sat at the kitchen table and got ready to eat. Tippy sat on the floor and begged for table scraps.

Grace took a knife and prepared to cut a piece of meatloaf for him.

He pointed to the loaf. "Give me one of those burnt ends. I

love the burnt ends."

She cut off the burnt end and set it on his plate. He picked up a bottle of ketchup and drowned his hunk of meatloaf in it.

"Danny, it already has ketchup in it, sweetie." She pointed to it with her knife. "That's what that red stuff is on top."

He smiled. "I know. But I like extra ketchup on mine. *Lots of extra ketchup.*" He used his fork to sever off a big slice and put it in his mouth.

As he sampled it, she looked at him with anticipation. "Well?"

He swallowed, took a drink of his tea, and pronounced her meatloaf, "Delicious . . . *delicious.*"

She smiled. "You really like it? You're not just saying that to be polite?"

"No. Of course not. Your cooking would put Aunt Bea to shame, girl."

She laughed. "Good. That makes me happy. I enjoy cooking for the special people in my life."

After dinner, they cleared the table and did the dishes together.

"Can we take Tippy for a walk down by the beach tonight?" she asked.

"I don't see why not. But give me an hour or so to work on my homily for next Sunday, okay?"

"Sure. No problem. I can wait. In fact, I'd rather wait until after sunset. *The Weather Channel* said it's supposed to be a full moon tonight. And I *adore* full moons. They're lovers' moons."

He retired to his den and sat in front of a desktop computer, twiddling his thumbs. The topic of the sermon was *Romantic Love – A Catholic Perspective.* He sat there and stared at the blank page. *What do I know about love, romantic love? Nothing. That's what. How am I supposed to preach to people, instruct people on a topic that I know nothing about?* He sat there and thought about Grace. Grace in her cute little shorts. Grace in her tight tank top, nipples practically bursting through the material. Grace with her beautiful smile. Grace with her sweet soul. He tried to focus on the task at hand, but his mind constantly wandered into a daydream. And it was always the same daydream. He was holding her in his arms, kissing her, caressing her . . . making love to her. *Stop it. Just stop it. You're not supposed to have these thoughts. Having the thoughts themselves are wrong.*

After an hour of futility, he minimized *Word. To hell with this.* He went to *YouTube* and looked at a clip that showed the end scene of one of his favorite films, *Breakfast At Tiffany's.* He watched George Peppard kiss Audrey Hepburn in the pouring rain of old New York. He nodded. *Wow. Grace really does look like a young Audrey Hepburn, only with a much better body.* He imagined kissing Grace in the rain, in torrential rain.

Just then, she walked in and stood behind him. "Hey, I thought you were supposed to be working on your sermon."

"I took a break," he said quietly, keeping his focus on the screen.

"That's the ending of *Breakfast At Tiffany's*, isn't it?"

"Yep. Sure is."

"It's a beautiful scene — one of the most romantic scenes in the history of Hollywood. God, I wish they still made old-fashioned love stories like that today," she said.

"Tell me about it."

"You know, I've always dreamed of having my own *Breakfast At Tiffany's* moment."

"*Breakfast At Tiffany's* moment?" He took his attention off the computer screen and turned around to look at her.

"Uh-huh. I fantasize that some guy, some sweet and handsome guy, would chase after me in the rain to tell me that he loves me. And that he wants to be with me and only me. Forever. And we'd kiss, a passionate but supremely tender kiss.

And then the credits roll, and *Moon River* plays. I know it's cliché, but sometimes clichés can be so lovely." She clutched her chest and looked upwards. "And then we'd go inside and make love all night long. *All. Night. Long.*" She giggled for a second or two but then turned serious. "I mean it. I'd give anything, all my fancy houses, cars, private jet, entourage, and money. Yes, my money, too. Anything. I just want the last five minutes of *Breakfast At Tiffany's.*" She smiled at him. "I'm silly, aren't I?"

He shook his head. "Totally not silly. In fact, it's as far from silly as you can possibly get. It's never silly to want to love and be loved."

They stared at one another, looked each other in the eyes. She licked her lips. His gaze slid downwards, to her chest. He ogled her breasts.

"Do you want me to just take the shirt off, so you can finally see them in the flesh? After all, you gawked at them all through dinner."

"You're not even wearing a bra, for God's sake."

"Does that *oh-fend* you? Do you need a *safe space* from boobies?"

He just rolled his eyes and shook his head.

"Look—I am sorry for not wearing a bra, but I thought that maybe—just maybe—you'd enjoy it. Yes, there you go. I wanted to give you something to look at. I'll admit it. Okay?"

Sheepishly, he confessed, "I did enjoy it. It turned me on. Big time."

"Really?"

"Of course, it did. Come on, Grace, don't play Little Miss Innocent. You know your power. You know darn well that any straight man would have been turned on by that."

She threw up her hands. "Okay, then, so what do either of us have to be sorry about? What's the BFD? I wanted you to be mesmerized by my tits and you were. So, it was a win-win, wasn't it?"

"You don't have to rub it in."

She smiled a naughty smile. "Do *you* want to rub it in?" She thrust her chest forward and shimmied her shoulders, so her breasts jiggled. "Do you want to rub some baby oil in on these puppies and then slide your Marshall Dillon in between?"

"*Graace.*"

She looked down and fiddled with her nails. "Sorry. I know I'm bad sometimes. But I'm a woman. A woman who's in her sexual prime. I get horny. I do. It happens. It's perfectly natural, too. And just so you know — I wouldn't be doing this with any other man because I *am not* a slut."

There was silence for a few seconds.

Quietly, he told her, "I don't have any baby oil in the house right now. I'll have to put it on the shopping list."

They snickered.

She gently caressed his shoulder and asked, "Are we going to take Tippy for her walk or what?"

He nodded and got up. "Yep. Let's take Tippy for her walk. Maybe the fresh, evening air will help stimulate my thinking as far as this sermon goes."

CHAPTER SIXTEEN: WILLY WONKA AND THE CHOCOLATE BAR

She put on her sneakers, a pair of blue jeans, and one of Danny's hoodies, a white one with a picture of an American flag on it. The inscription read *If You Love Your Freedom, Thank A Vet*. Like everything else of his that she wore, it was way too big. Her hair was still up, held in place by one of the brown clips he'd bought for her.

They walked out the back door and Tippy ran ahead of them toward the beach. The night air was cool and crisp. Danny wore a black sweater over his clerical shirt and Roman collar.

When they got to the beach, they saw the full moon reflecting off the water.

"Pretty, huh?" he asked.

She raised her eyebrows and nodded. "Very."

Tippy walked to the edge of the water. Danny loudly clapped his hands. "Tippy! No! No water! Get over here. Come on." He turned to Grace, shook his head in disgust, and observed, "For some reason, she loves that filthy water, that filthy river water."

The dog walked back over to Danny and Grace, who were by now on the beach.

Grace took off her shoes.

"When I was a little girl, on Long Island, we'd go to the beach on the Fourth of July and watch the fireworks. Every year. It was a family tradition. Do you like fireworks?"

"When I was a kid? Yeah. Now? Not so much. A lot of combat vets don't care for them."

"Oh, God, I didn't even think about that. I'm sorry."

"It's okay. Maybe one day I'll be able to enjoy them again." He thought for a moment and added, "Aw, who am I kidding? They'll always freak me out. It's not just the fireworks themselves. I mean—they're bad enough. But combine them with the fact that they always put them off at night, and it gets real spooky for me. See, over there, we held the day. But they owned the night. They absolutely *owned* the night." He paused and stared at her for a moment. "Do you want to know what combat is like?"

"Tell me. I feel like I have to know. To be closer to you, I have to know."

"It wasn't like the movies. The movies never really get it right. Some come close, but no movie has ever captured what it's truly about—the sound. The sound of combat is always what stood out the most to me. You have no idea how loud war is until you're in the middle of it. You couldn't hear anything. It was a deafening symphony of chaos. You had small arms fire, machine guns, RPGs, mortars, artillery. You had the LT yelling out orders, trying to be heard. You had Air Force Fast Movers streaking super-low across the sky, dumping bombs. Sometimes, when it got really bad, they'd bring in the Buffs—the *B-52s*—to carpet bomb." He paused and chuckled. "Carpet bombing—the greatest political reeducation tool ever invented. There was nothing like a carpet-bombing run by a *B-52* to convert those little Taliban bastards to *our* way of thinking. Anyway, the freaking earth would shake when the *B-52s* bombed. Like it was the damn Apocalypse. Knocked you flat on your ass. It did. I saw guys bleed from the nose and ears. Hell, it was so bad you almost felt sorry for those sons of bitches who were on the receiving end. Almost. Then, you had Cobra gunships firing off their ordinance—they spewed death from above. You had guys who had been hit crying out in pain. They called for Doc Meadows. Some called on Jesus Christ to help them. Some just cried for their moms. Yep. That's true, all right. It's not just a movie myth. Guys really do cry for their moms. Oh — we had this one guy, Mason. Corporal Mason. He had this big boombox, and he'd play AC/DC's *Hells Bells*. He'd turn it all the way up. The Taliban supposedly hated that decadent American Heavy Metal shit. Of course, I don't know that they could hear it over the rest of the noise. Oh, yeah — there was lots of cursing, too. A lot of *goddamns* and *motherfuckers* and *bastards, sons of bitches* and so forth. But more *goddamns* than anything, really. Yeah. A lot of guys ordering God to *damn* various things. You had the enemy taunting you over their megaphones, telling you, in broken English, that they were going to cut off your *fucking* head and mail it home to your girlfriend. They'd also tell us — *the Twin Towers are no more, and your precious Lady Liberty is a filthy whore.* And all the plans went right out the window. And you just held on for dear life. We held onto each other. Like brother-to-brother. Because that's the only thing we had. And we weren't fighting for American foreign policy, or apple pie, or cheaper gasoline. We were fighting for each other. I fought for the guys of Third Platoon. They were my cause, my only cause. And while the rest of America worried about getting its hands on the newest cellphone or digital camera, we worried about whether our parents would be able to give us an open casket funeral if we got wasted by an IED. Because, in the Korengal Valley, when your time was up, *your time was up.* Simple as that. Amen. And that's the *Cliff Notes* version of what combat in Afghanistan was like, Grace." He paused. Tears filled his eyes as he looked up at the night sky. "But it don't mean nothing, you know? *It. Don't. Mean. Nothing.* Not a thing."

He wiped the tears away and continued. "When I showed you my scrapbook the other night and told you about all the guys who didn't make it, there was one death that I left out. But I have to talk about it. I've never talked to anyone about this one. And it's eating me up. It's eaten me up for the last thirteen years. Can I tell you about it? Would it be too much of a burden? It's an ugly, sickening story, Grace. It's filthy. Worse than the worst parts of *Saving Private Ryan*. It might literally make you sick. And I don't want you to be haunted by it the way I am."

Without any hesitation, she said, "Tell me."

"You sure?"

"Yes. Danny, when you lo—" She paused and restarted. "When you care about someone very deeply, it's not a burden. So, tell me. Please. I want to hear it. I *need* to hear it. Share it with me. We can share the experience."

He took a deep breath and loudly exhaled. "Okay. Here we go. So, there was this kid—James. Specialist James Balado. Twenty-two. From Akron, Ohio. Another Italian kid. I swear—all the Pisans bought it over there, every one of them. He was married, married his high school sweetheart. His wife's name was Lauren. Pretty girl. Something like seven months pregnant when this happened. Anyhow, we called James *Willy Wonka* because he was a chocolate addict, always eating chocolate. Hell, for Thanksgiving, when we had turkey, he melted some chocolate bars to make a sauce and poured it right over his turkey, potatoes, and stuffing. Gross, right? We all thought so. But he lapped it up. Well, he was a good guy. He had a soft spot in his heart for the little Afghan children. He'd always say he felt sorry for them, being born into war and whatnot. And he'd sing to them. He'd sing *Puff the Magic Dragon*. He had a terrible voice, but that didn't really matter, you know? Most of them couldn't understand him anyway. Didn't matter to him. He'd tell them—*never outgrow your magic dragon. He'll cry if you do, just like Puff cried when Jackie forgot about him.*" Danny teared up again. "Jesus Christ. I can't take this, Grace. I can't take it." He paused, took another deep breath, and went on.

"So, one day, we were making a sweep through this vil. And you never knew. You just never knew. Friend or foe? The people in these villages would smile and wave at you by day and try to sneak up on you and slit your throat by night. So, we were in this vil. And I had a bad feeling about it. A real bad feeling. Like we were poking at a hornet's nest. And the LT was meeting with the village elders, trying to smooth everything over with them. Because we knew they were at least letting the Taliban operate from inside their walls. Well, we're taking a break because we'd been humping all day. Once LT was finished with his little power convo, we were going to complete the sweep and call it a day. Me and Willy Wonka were sitting down, just the two of us, leaning up against this old, dilapidated shed. I was smoking a *Camel*. And Willy Wonka saw this little Afghan kid, a little boy, no more than ten years old. Ten—tops. And he pulled out a chocolate bar and held it up for the kid to see. And he yelled to the kid— *here you go, little buddy. You can have some chocolate. American chocolate. It's good.* He set down his rifle and walked over to the kid. The boy was, like, maybe ten or fifteen meters away. I told him not to. We weren't supposed to. But he was all like— *Christ, O'Connor. I'm just going to give the kid a chocolate bar. Goddamn. Chill the fuck out, dude.* When he got to within about five meters of the kid, he started kind of waving the chocolate bar, so the child would know that he just wanted to give him the candy. Oh, and the kid had a *Power Rangers* shirt on. I'll never forget that. Yeah. The *Power Rangers*. Well, Grace—that kid reached into a bag he had slung over his shoulder and pulled out an old *Makarov,* Soviet-era pistol and pointed it at Willy Wonka. And everything got real slow at that point. Slow-motion. It seemed like an eternity, but, in reality, it all unfolded in just a few seconds. The boy was having some trouble with the magazine. Now, mind you, Willy Wonka didn't have his rifle with him at that point. He laid it down before he approached the kid. So, he was unarmed. And I pointed my *M16* at the kid. And I told him to put the gun down. But he didn't. Hell, I'm sure he didn't even understand what I was saying. Not that it would have made a difference. Willy Wonka shouted, *come on, Danny! Shoot him! Shoot him, for God's sake!* He begged me to shoot the boy. But I froze. I hesitated. I couldn't pull the trigger on a little ten-year-old kid—couldn't do it. *Could. Not. Do it.* If I had had five minutes to think about it, I would have shot the kid. But I didn't have five minutes. I didn't even have five *seconds*. And the kid got the magazine in right. And don't you know that that little boy pulled the trigger and shot Willy Wonka in the chest? Shot him six times. *Pop! Pop! Pop! Pop! Pop! Pop!* Six fucking rounds. Then he pointed the pistol towards me. And I still couldn't pull the trigger. And that's when Morgan showed up. He'd heard the shots. And he had a fucking *M249*, a SAW. Squad Automatic Weapon. A light machine gun. You don't have to be in the prone position to fire it like most machine guns. You can literally shoot from the hip. Nasty weapon—the SAW. A real mayhem maker. Well, Morgan opened up on that little boy. He really lit him up, went fully automatic on his tiny, little ass. He shot him full of holes and filled him full of lead. Yes, he did. And that little boy did a dance, too. My *God*—he did a dance! Looked like some crazy modern dance interpretation or something. I don't know. I think he actually left his feet for a split second. Like he was levitating. It was like he'd been electrocuted. All kinds of crazy, spastic jerking movements, and so forth. When the smoke cleared—and, yes, there was literally smoke from the SAW—Willy Wonka was dead. Just as dead as he could be. And so was the kid. The kid . . . he was . . . he was . . . he was just a mess. A fucking mess. All chewed up. Brains all hanging out. I'll tell you what it looked like—it looked like one of those cans of cheap lasagna that you get at the supermarket.

You know — the ones that only cost ninety-nine cents. The crazy thing was that one of his eyeballs was sitting on his forehead. Just perfectly balanced there on his forehead. Looking up at us and whatnot. I mean — what were the chances, you know? And Morgan screamed at me, *why didn't you waste him, goddammit*? So, I screamed back at him, *because he was a kid. He was a little fucking boy*! And Morgan screamed back, *he was a fucking warrior! A Taliban warrior! They start em' young over here, for Christ's sake! I don't care how fucking old they are. When they pick up a gun, their ass is done!* Me and Morgan just stared at the kid for a while. Then we looked over at Willy Wonka. He had this look of utter shock frozen on his face. His eyes were open. So was his mouth. And it was like he couldn't believe it. And I don't know whether he was shocked that the kid actually shot him. Or whether he was shocked that I didn't shoot the kid to save his life. To this day, I honestly don't know. We looked back at the kid again. And Morgan casually lit up a *Lucky Strike* and changed the drum on his SAW. He looked at me and patted me on the back. And his eyes got big. I mean *real* big. Like he was coked-up or something, which he wasn't. And he laughed. *Woo! That's whassup, baby! That's whassup!* he said. And he added, *ain't war hell*? Then he laughed again. Bobby Morgan. He tried to John Wayne it, Grace. He tried to act all nonchalantly about it. But he wasn't really a callous guy. He wasn't. He was a good guy put in a bad situation. An insane situation. And he never got over it. Never got over having to grease that kid, even though they ruled it a *legal kill*. That little Afghan boy, that tiny T-Man, became his own personal ghost, followed him everywhere. Every time he saw a ten-year-old kid, he saw that little boy he wasted. He killed himself a few years ago. Bobby Morgan put a nine mil in his mouth and pulled the trigger. I guess that was his penitence. Wars have consequences. Bobby was one. I guess we all were. That place took our magic dragons away from us. I want my magic dragon back, Grace."

He cried. "But Morgan was right. The kid *was* a warrior. And I should have killed him. And because I didn't, Willy Wonka—*James*—died. And that's a hell of a thing to live with, Grace. To know that you could have saved your buddy's life—but didn't. And that haunts me every day. And every night. Every night, I see that kid pour half of his mag into Willy Wonka. And then I see Morgan turn the kid into swiss cheese. And the craziest thing about it was that after it was over, another kid came along, about the same age as the one Morgan killed. And he picked up the chocolate bar that was still sitting there on the ground. And he unwrapped it and ate it just like nothing had happened. I guess the little guy was used to that kind of crazy shit. Anyway—James *Willy Wonka* Balado, that's the one death that I can't live with. Because that's the one that I could have prevented. And that day, I made both a widow and an orphan—a wife who never saw her husband again. A little girl—I heard that's what she ended up having—who never even met her father. All because of me. Hell, Morgan killed himself because of me, too." He paused for a second and added, "Ain't war hell, indeed. But, you know, it don't mean nothing. Not a thing. *Not. A. Thing.*"

She cried and put her arms around him, pulling him into her. He put his arms around her, too. And they stood there in an embrace and cried together.

CHAPTER SEVENTEEN: LET THIS HAPPEN

They sat on the beach. Grace rolled up her pant legs, buried her toes in the brown sand, and asked, "So, do you think we'll have any late-night visitors tonight?" She sniffled.

He wiped a remaining tear from his eye and chuckled. "You never know."

"Are there any other eccentrics in this little town besides Jesus that I should know about?"

He thought for a moment. "Well, let's see. There's old Pud Benjamin."

"Who's he?"

"The town drunk. He shuffles down Main Street with a bottle of *Thunderbird* in hand."

She shot him a confused look. "What's *Thunderbird*?"

He laughed. "You mean you've never heard of *Thunderbird*?"

She shook her head. "Nope."

"They call it bum wine. It's a cheap, potent form of alcohol. It'll get you very drunk, very fast, and at a very attractive price point. Hence, the nickname. Sometimes, he mixes it with grape *Kool-Aid* and a splash of rubbing alcohol."

She made a face. "Oh, Gawd."

He thought for another few seconds and started laughing again. "You know, once when Pud was hard up for cash, he walked right into the church — we always keep it unlocked for prayer and meditation — and stole the Communion wine."

"Nah ah."

"Oh, yes, he did. We didn't press charges, though."

"Why does he drink like that?"

"Disappointed in love. At least that's how the story goes. Supposedly, when he was a young man, his girlfriend jilted him. That started him drinking, and he's never stopped."

"Yeah, well, being disappointed by love can be a pretty traumatic thing. When I found out Orion was cheating on me, I was devastated. And you know who he was screwing?"

"Who?"

"Bridgett McMahon. You know, the actress. She was in *Double Rainbows*. That's the movie set in the sixties, and it's about the hippie chick who falls in love with the Marine, who's about to go to Vietnam. Sad story. He dies over there. You know the picture I'm talking about?"

He nodded. "Oh, yeah. I saw that one. She was good in that movie."

Angrily, she told him, "She's a *slut*. She knew that Orion had a girlfriend when she hooked up with him."

"Still, it takes two to tango."

"Oh, yeah. I know. Don't get me wrong—I'm not making excuses for him. He's a male whore. I'm just glad I found out before we got married. Because that's one thing I'll never put up with—someone who cheats. I believe in fidelity. I give it in a relationship and expect it in return. That's not too much to ask. You know?"

"Yeah. Sure. Absolutely. You should never have to put up with a cheater. But what I can't understand is why anyone would ever cheat on you, to begin with."

"*Aw.* You really mean that?"

"Sure I do. You're smart and pretty. And you have a good heart . . . and you make a killer meatloaf." He winked at her.

"Very sweet. You're a total sweetheart. I like you. *A lot.* I like you a lot."

"I like *you* a lot."

They smiled at one another.

She got up and pulled him by the hand. "Come on. Let's dance."

He resisted and remained seated on the beach. "Oh, I don't know about that. I'm not a good dancer."

"Who cares? I sure don't."

"No. You don't understand. I never really learned to dance. I'm a dancing virgin, too."

"I can teach you." She again pulled him by the hand. "Come on. Up. On your feet, mister. Professor Grace's Dance 101 is now in session."

He reluctantly got up but protested by telling her, "This is stupid. I'll feel stupid."

"Nonsense. You'll do fine."

They stood face-to-face, about two feet from one another.

"You like my hair up or down?" she asked.

"Um . . . doesn't matter. It looks dynamite either way."

"*Aw.* So sweet. Okay, well, I'm going to let it down." She removed the hair clip, shook her head, and her hair cascaded down to her shoulders. It shone in the moonlight.

She began to instruct him. "You need to come closer to me. We're way too far apart."

He moved closer, leaving a gap of about a foot between them.

She shook her head. "Nope. Still too far apart. We have to be in the same zip code, buddy."

He inched still closer.

"Keep it coming." She used her hand to wave him forward, like a cop directing rush hour traffic. "Keep it coming. Come on. Don't stop until you feel my boobs pressing against your own chest."

He laughed a nervous laugh, to which she replied, "I'm quite serious."

He took a deep breath and slowly lurched forward. Finally, he felt her breasts pressing against him.

She smiled at him and spoke softly, almost in a whisper. "Good. Now, I want you to put your arms around me."

Awkwardly, he threw his arms around her neck.

"No. That's too high up. You want to go lower."

He adjusted his arms so that they rested on the center of her back.

"Is that better?"

"No. You're still too high. Put your hands on the small of my back."

"Small of your back, you say?"

"Yes."

He let his hands slide down farther. They settled at the base of her spine. He swallowed hard. "How's that? Is that good?" His heart raced.

"That's good." She put her arms around his neck and looked up at him before continuing to teach. "Okay, we're going to sway, just gently sway, back and forth. Nothing fancy."

"Don't we need some music?" he asked.

"I'm going to take care of that." She gently brushed his hair with her hand. "I have a song I want to sing for you. Just for you. Only for you. Okay?"

He nervously laughed. "Yeah. Okay."

She looked up at him. He looked down at her, gazed into her big, honey-brown doe eyes.

She started to sway, and he followed her lead. She began to sing. He recognized the song right away. It was Alabama's *Angels Among Us*. Her voice was choked with emotion, passion.

He felt the heat of his skin blushing and looked down at the sand. She kept singing while she took her left hand and placed it under his chin. Gently, she pushed his head back up so that he was again looking at her.

He stared at the beautiful woman who was standing mere inches from him. And he wanted her. Badly. *Such a lovely voice. And she's singing just to me. She's performed for millions. But tonight, it's all for me. God. That's heady. And she doesn't care that I'll never be normal.* He felt goosebumps on his arms and a tear roll down his cheek. He closed his eyes and absorbed every word she sang.

When she was finished, there was silence, except the sound of gentle waves breaking and frogs croaking. They each leaned forward so that their foreheads touched. She moved her hands down to his waist and squeezed him tight, burying her head in his chest. And they stayed just like that for a good minute or so.

Finally, she looked up at him. She softly caressed his cheek. He pulled back a little.

"Hey, come on, now. Don't be afraid," she whispered.

He backed up even more.

She closed the gap. "Why are you afraid of me? Hmm? Why is a big guy like you scared of a little tiny girl who's only five-two and weighs a buck eight."

"I'm . . . I'm not scared of you."

"Then don't pull away."

She nuzzled his neck and whispered, "Let this happen, Danny. Okay? Just let it happen. It was bound to happen. It's supposed to happen. It *needs* to happen. Don't fight it. Don't fight *me*. You've done enough fighting for an entire lifetime. So, stop the fighting. *Please.* Let's be angels to one another, just like in the movie. Let's be two angels. Angels who've been rescued from The Fall. Who've rescued one another."

He took a deep breath and looked up at heaven, at the stars and the full moon. Then he looked back down at her. He could read her eyes. They were full of anticipation. Tentatively, he whispered back to her, "Okay, I'm going to let it happen. We can both be angels tonight. Angels to one another. I want you. I want you so bad." He cupped her face in his hands and slowly leaned forward towards her lips. She closed her eyes and opened her mouth wide.

Then... his phone rang. His ringtone was Britney Spears's ... *Baby One More Time*. It snapped him out of the trance he'd fallen into. He reached into his back pocket, pulled out his phone, and answered the call.

It was Mrs. Sutton, one of his parishioners. Her husband, Harry, had suffered a bad heart attack. He had been taken to *Union Hospital* and was in pretty rough shape. She needed Danny to come to the hospital right away. "I'll be there in twenty minutes," he promised.

He hung up and looked at Grace.

"I have to go. A member of the congregation was just rushed to the hospital and is in serious condition. Heart attack."

"When will you be back?"

"I don't know. Probably late, maybe very late. Don't wait up."

"But aren't you off-duty now?"

"It's not a nine to five job. There's really no such thing as being *off-duty*. I get these kinds of calls a lot, sometimes in the middle of the night. I have to go when a member of the parish needs me."

"What about me?"

He ignored the question. "Look, I really do have to go." He turned to walk away. She pulled him by the hand and spun him around.

"To be continued?" she asked.

"We'll talk about it tomorrow," he said. He called out to the dog, "Come on, Tippy. Time to go inside." She ran over to him, and the two of them walked away from the beach.

He got home from the hospital at one-thirty in the morning. He yawned and scratched his head. *Dang. I have to get up in just a few hours. I'm tired as hell, too.* Tippy came running to the front door as he walked through it. He patted her on the head and walked into the living room. There, he found Grace. She'd changed into a royal blue lace teddy and was asleep on the couch. On her chest was his laptop computer. He picked it up, closed it, and set it on the coffee table. *Aw. So cute. Bet she tried to wait up, but the poor little thing got all tuckered out.*

He nudged her arm. "Grace," he called out. No response. He gently shook her arm. "Grace. Hey, Grace. Come on. Come on, Grace. It's time to go to bed." She stretched her body out but still didn't open her eyes.

He reached down, scooped her up, and carried her up the stairs. About halfway up, she started to wake up. She opened her eyes and yawned. Still groggy, she smiled and said, "Hi-ya."

"Hi yourself."

"I fell asleep on the couch, didn't I?"

"Yeah. You sure did. And that couch will kill your back."

"I was watching *Breakfast At Tiffany's* online. The last five minutes of *Breakfast At Tiffany's*. Over and over again, I watched it."

"Yeah?"

She smiled a big smile. "Yeah," she whispered.

As he carried her towards the bedroom, he noted. "Boy, you really are just a tiny little thing, aren't you?"

She nodded her head and flashed him puppy dog eyes. She spoke in her baby-talk voice. "Uh-huh. I'm just a *tiny* little thing."

When they got to the bedroom, he gently set her down on the bed.

"What time is it?" she asked

"About one-thirty."

"How's the guy who had the heart attack?"

"It looks like he's going to pull through."

"Really?"

"Yeah."

"That's good."

He lay down next to her, still in his clothes. "Before I left, he was awake and talking. He saw me and swore that he's going to start attending Mass more regularly instead of going to the racetrack on Sunday mornings. I guess seeing a priest standing over him, ready to administer Last Rites, put the fear of God into him."

He closed his eyes.

For a couple of minutes, there was silence in the room. Tippy jumped up on the bed and settled herself down at its foot.

Finally, Grace called out, "Danny?"

"Yeah?"

She snickered. "Your ringtone. . . . *Baby One More Time*. Seriously?"

He laughed and sheepishly admitted, "Okay, so now you know another one of my guilty pleasures. Back in the day, when I was a kid, I had a huge crush on Britney Spears. There. I said it. Nowadays, it's just about nostalgia. Anyhow, I alternate my ringtones. I go back and forth between . . . *Baby One More Time* and *Oops! . . . I Did It Again*."

"That's so two-thousand."

"Hey, two-thousand was a good year."

"Yeah, it was."

"You know, when I was a little girl, I had a big crush on Lance Bass from *NSYNC*."

"Really?"

"Yep. Turns out, he's gay."

"Yeah. I remember when he came out."

She sighed. "Yeah, you know what they say, don't you? *All the good ones are married or gay.*"

"That is what they say."

She turned on her side, so she was facing him, and added, "Or they're Catholic priests." She frowned.

He didn't say anything.

"We need to talk about last night."

"When I get home from work today, we'll talk."

"Promise?"

"Promise."

"Okay. That's good enough for me."

The room fell silent for a few seconds. Eventually, she poked his right arm and said, "Oh, hey, do you think you could stop off on your way home tonight and grab me something to read? I love to read."

"Sure. *Cramer's* has books. What do you like to read?"

"Novels, romance novels. I love a good romance. Since I don't have a love life, I live vicariously through the characters. Whenever I'm on tour, on a bus or plane, I always read."

"What kind of romance books do you like?"

"Good ones."

He laughed. "You'll have to be a little more specific. I don't read romance novels. How am I supposed to know which ones are good?"

"I don't know — look at the cover, read the back. But do me a favor — don't get me one of those ones where everyone is having sex with everyone else — threesomes and orgies and whatnot. I hate those. I like sweet romances. Some sex is okay, but it has to be in the context of a committed, monogamous relationship. Okay?"

He nodded. "Okay. No threesomes or orgies — got it. I wouldn't be comfortable buying a book like that anyhow. Besides, I don't think *Cramer's* even sells that kind of material."

She propped her head up with her hand. "You know, when I first became a big star, I was dating one of my backup dancers — a guy by the name of Dan Johnson. Well, he approached me about having a threesome. Me, him, and one of my female backup dancers — a pretty little thing by the name of Kim something-or-other."

"Let me guess—you slapped him in the face and stormed out, right?"

"Kicked him in the nuts and stormed out. That's what I do when men get obscene with me. I kick them in the balls. Broke up with him on the spot and fired his ass to boot. Grace Stevens don't play that shit."

He chuckled. "I didn't think she did."

"And she never will," she added.

"Good for you."

"I mean—don't get me wrong—I love sex as much as anybody else. I'm no prude. Matter of fact, I'm a very sexual person. But, when it comes to sex, two's company, three's a crowd, and any more than three is just a freaking mob. I'm only into one-on-one sex. I'm totally straight, too. I'm *strictly dickly*. Not even bi-curious. And I *have* to be in love to screw someone. I guess a lot of people don't believe in that anymore, do they? I mean—a lot of people don't believe in linking sex to love."

He shook his head. "Nope. A lot of people don't believe in it. But I admire your values. I feel that same way. Exactly."

"I guess—you and me—we're just a couple of romantic fools, huh?"

He nodded. "Yep. Romantic fools."

"I know I have a filthy mouth and all. I sometimes talk worse than a drunken sailor. I know that. I do. But I have a real soft spot in my heart for all things that are sweet and innocent. Maybe that's one of the reasons that I like you so much. I have no idea how you do it. With all that you've seen and been through, you still manage to have this air of innocence about you. It would have been so easy to become jaded about life. But you didn't. That makes you very special. Rare. Like a unicorn. Like one of those dimes that dude was trying to sell on TV for three-hundred bucks."

He smiled at her but said nothing.

She continued. "But there's not much sweetness and innocence left in the world, is there?"

He shook his head. "Nope. Not much."

"I miss it, Danny. But I guess the world grew up, huh?"

He nodded. "The world grew up."

She shook her head in disgust. "What a shame. What a goddamn shame. And pardon my language. I know I just took the Lord's name in vain." She looked up and added, "*Mea Culpa.*"

He chuckled. "You're absolved."

A quizzical look came over her face. "When did it change? When did we lose that innocence?"

"I suppose for every generation, it's different. Every generation loses its innocence, Grace. For our grandparents, it was the Kennedy assassination and Vietnam. For our parents, it was Watergate. For our generation, it was September eleventh. That's when the world officially went to hell. Then came all the wars."

She reached over, tenderly rubbed his chest, and started singing *The Shoop Shoop Song*. After a few bars, she stopped and asked, "Do I sing that better than Cher? Because it was one of her big hits."

"Hey, come on, now. Don't be silly. Of course, you sing it better than her. It's not even close." He brushed her hair with his hand. "Compared to you, *Cher* is only *fair*."

"*Aw.* You support me and only me. I love that."

"Damn right. And if it were up to me, you'd win every *Grammy*, every year. They'd be all like – *and, now, for this year's Best Rap Album, the Grammy goes to . . . Grace Stevens.*"

"But I don't sing rap. I sing pop."

"Right. But if you *did* sing rap, you'd be the best, so I'd go ahead and give you the award anyway, girl." He made a sideways *V* sign with index and middle fingers and said, "Yo. Word to ya mother."

She giggled. "What do you know about rap music? I'll bet

you can't even name three rappers."

He shot her an incredulous look. "Say *whaaat?* Of course, I can. Let's see here—there's . . . Eminem . . . Slim Shady . . . and Marshall Mathers." He cackled.

She playfully smacked him. "Oh, Gawd. You're full of shit, boy. You know that?"

He turned serious. "And you're full of beauty. You know that? You're beautiful, Grace. Inside and out."

"Aw. You're going to make me cry again." She reached over and gently brushed his cheek with the back of her hand. "Getting lost on the interstate that day might have been the best thing that ever happened to me. By getting lost, I got found."

He smiled. *Best thing that ever happened to both of us. I want you, Grace Stevens. Not just for a little one-nighter, either. I want you and only you. Forever. These feelings are getting harder to fight. Not sure how much longer I can do it. I'm only human, after all.*

He watched as she drifted off to sleep. He lay there, awake, staring at the ceiling. He had to get up in a couple of hours and was exhausted. But he still couldn't sleep. All he could think about was dancing with her on the beach. He knew what would have happened if he hadn't gotten that emergency call from Mrs. Sutton.

He shook his head. *Only Harry Sutton's severely clogged arteries prevented me from breaking my vow of celibacy last night. And all I can say is that I wish the man had lived healthier. Laid off the red meat and quit smoking those cigars and whatnot.*

CHAPTER EIGHTEEN: GRACE'S PRAYER

Grace curled up in bed with Tippy and watched the news. She wore a pair of Daisy Duke jean shorts, a baby blue t-shirt, and canvas sneakers. Her hair was up. Periodically, she ate pieces of penny candy. There was a large pile of wrappers sitting next to her.

She'd been avoiding the news reports of her disappearance — she hadn't wanted to deal with it and still didn't. But curiosity finally got the best of her. The first thing that struck her was that they had made up a special graphic that flashed on the screen whenever they talked about her. It was a picture of her with a caption that proclaimed — *Grace Stevens: Without A Trace. Do they have to be so damned melodramatic?*

There were still no leads in her disappearance. The FBI was now involved. *Leave me the hell alone. I'm actually happy.* They showed footage of her fans holding a candlelight vigil outside of her Malibu home the previous night. *Oh, come on, people — get a life.* Her case was being compared to that of Jimmy Hoffa. *Who's Jimmy Hoffa? Note to self — Google him.*

She turned off the TV, happy and relieved that the world still had no clue as to her whereabouts.

A few minutes later, she found herself in the parlor, sitting at the old *Baldwin*. In her mind's eye, she tried to take herself back to a time when performing was still fun. It had been so long that it was hard to remember. For a while, she just sat there. Finally, she played a litany of songs, some that were her own, others, ones that she'd covered. She finished the session by playing a particularly soulful rendition of *Can't Help*

Falling In Love. I want that played at my wedding.

She walked into the living room. There was a large pewter crucifix hanging on the wall. Right next to it hung an oil painting of the Virgin Mary. Grace looked up at the crucifix, cleared her voice, and quietly talked to it. "Ah . . . hi. It's me. Grace. I'm not sure whether You remember me or not. It's been a long, long time since we last talked. And I haven't been to Mass since — well . . . since forever. But I wanted to talk to you about my friend, Danny. I know You know him. After all, he works for You. Danny hasn't had an easy life. He's been to war, You know. And he's seen things that no one should have to see. And those things haunt him. Every day, they haunt him. He's a very lonely person. Well, I guess I am, too. But he's a good guy. One of the best You've ever made, in fact. He's sweet and kind and gentle. And he doesn't care that I'm a big star. To him, I'm just Grace. And to me, he's just Danny. Together, we're just Grace and Danny, You know?" She looked down and thought for a moment before lifting her head and continuing. "But here's the thing — You say that You love Your children. And I know You have to love Danny. I mean — who wouldn't love Danny, right? But if You love him — if You really love him — love him enough to let him go. And let him love someone else. Okay?" She looked at the picture of Mary and pleaded with it, too. "You're a woman. You *know* a woman's heart. I'm sure you must understand. So, I'll ask you — woman-to-woman — can you put in a good word for me? Please. Because sometimes, a son will listen to his mother when he won't listen to anyone else." She started to cry and took a deep breath. She looked at both the crucifix and the painting. For a few seconds, she just stared at them. Finally, she said, "Well, okay. That's it. Thanks for listening. Amen or whatever." She crossed herself and walked away.

When Danny arrived home from work, she met him at the door. He carried a plastic shopping bag.

"Hi-ya, kiddo," he called out to her.

"Hey. How was your day?"

"Mixed bag. Mister Reynolds died today. They found him dead in bed. He'd been a member of Saint Mary's for over sixty years. On the other hand, Hannah Cartwright delivered a healthy baby girl."

"Sorry about Mister Reynolds."

"It happens. It's part of the job. He was old and lived a full life. People are born—people die. *To everything, there is a season,* you know?"

She nodded and looked down at the bag. "Is that my book?"

"Oh, yeah. Yeah, it is. I picked one out for you. Hope you like it."

She took the bag and pulled out a paperback book. The cover showed a handsome blond man in an Army uniform embracing a pretty brunette holding a toddler. The title was *His Instant Family.*

Danny gave a quick synopsis. "It's about a soldier who returns from deployment and falls in love with a widow who's raising a small child. I checked it out pretty thoroughly—no threesomes or orgies. Looks like a wholesome book. It's really long, too. Over four-hundred pages. That ought to keep you busy for a while."

She examined the cover and said, "Yeah. You can almost always tell from the cover. This definitely looks like a sweet romance—just the kind I like. You did good. Thank you." She kissed him on the cheek.

They had cold meatloaf sandwiches for dinner, after which Danny retired to his den to work on his sermon again.

She lay on the living room sofa and read her book. After an hour, she put it down and knocked on the den door. She could hear music playing inside.

"Come on in," she heard him say through the door.

When she walked in, he was sitting in a black leather office chair. He was turned away from his computer. His hands were clasped together behind his head, his eyes closed. The music was coming from a portable CD player that sat on his desk. The song that played was *Mother's Pride*.

Grace said nothing, just listened. It was the most painfully beautiful thing she'd ever heard. When it was over, he opened his eyes and told her, "I hate that song. It hurts — almost physically — to listen to it. It dredges up so many memories, all about young men dying. But God help me, I can't stop listening to it. Sometimes, I'll just listen to it over and over and over and over."

"Oh, Danny. If I could take away all your hurt and put it on myself, I would in a heartbeat."

"You would? Seriously?"

"Yes. Seriously."

He shook his head. "I would never want you to do that. But it means everything to hear you say it. I mean — that's something that you'd only say to someone if you really l — "

"If you really what?"

He said nothing but just looked at her.

She sat on his lap and put her arms around his neck. "You've got a lap full of girl, mister. What are you gunna do about it? Huh?" she ask as she dotted his nose with her index finger.

He didn't answer but smiled.

She brushed his hair with her hand as she quietly talked to him. "You know, I've been thinking."

"About what?"

"About Benny Williams. And all those like him."

"And?"

"I want to do something for them."

"Like what?"

"Start a foundation, a charitable foundation, to benefit

201

Gold Star families."

He nodded. "That sounds wonderful."

"I even have a name for it. Tell me what you think — *The Benny Williams No Greater Love Foundation.*"

"I like it. I love it, in fact. But it takes a ton of money to start something like that."

"I *have* a ton of money. And I want to use it to do some real good. Doesn't the Bible say something like, *where your money is is where your heart is?*"

"*For where your treasure is, there will be your heart also.* It's Matthew, chapter six, verse twenty-one."

"Right. Anyway, I'd need somebody to run it. Preferably, someone who's an actual combat veteran. Have any suggestions?"

"Is that your way of offering me a job?"

"Uh-huh. What do you say?"

He shook his head. "I'm a priest."

Tersely, she replied, "You're a man."

"I'm a man of God."

"But you're not God."

He took a deep breath. "I guess now is as good a time as any to have that talk about last night."

She got up off his lap. "What happened last night?" she asked.

"You tell me."

"We almost kissed. If your damn phone wouldn't have rung, we would have. You know it. I know it. And after that? Well, after that, we would have made love. Isn't that so?"

"Aw, Grace."

"*Aw, Grace,* nothing. Don't you want me?"

He loudly exhaled. "That's not the question."

"It *is* the question. Either you want me, or you don't."

"Listen, when I became a priest, I took a vow, and —"

She cut him off. "I don't want to hear about your damn

vows."

"Well, you're going to hear about them because I take them seriously."

"Why do you have to be so damn honorable? I swear—it's stuff like this that keeps me from fully embracing the Catholic Church."

He didn't respond.

She continued to make her case. "Can't we try it? Just once? Please." She paused for a moment. "Look, I know you like the Old West, so let me put it in terms that you can relate to—my Miss Kitty wants your Marshall Dillon to visit her, in her house, inside her house. She wants him to come over. And, in fact, I think she'd probably like him to come by and visit quite often. Sometimes, maybe even twice a day. And he wouldn't even have to wear a cowboy hat because Miss Kitty trusts him. You get my drift, big boy?" She smiled and winked at him.

"It wouldn't be a good idea."

"You don't play fair."

"What are you talking about?"

"You lead me on and lead me on and lead me on. And then when it comes time to do something about it, you run away."

"And how, pray tell, have I led you on?"

She held up her hand and started counting off reasons with her fingers. "Okay, well, first of all, you let me sleep in your bed—that's a biggie right there. Second, you let me hug you. Third, you gave me a leg massage. Fourth, you danced a slow dance with me. Fifth, you told me my meatloaf was good."

"*Meatloaf?* Are you serious? You see the fact that I liked your meatloaf as a sign of flirting?"

"Yes. Everyone knows that—for guys—there's a connection between food and sex. You cook them a nice, big meal, and they'll screw you all night long. Throw in dessert, and they'll even go down on you. And, by the way, putting extra catsup on meatloaf is just plain wrong. It ruins the flavor. And only an uncouth Neanderthal would do such a thing. So there." She stuck her tongue out and blew raspberries at him.

He ran his fingers through his hair. "Oh, brother."

"Do you know how many guys would love to be in your shoes? I'm throwing myself at you."

"Yeah, well, that's not good."

"It's not something I've ever done before, but I'm trying to make it easy for you. I know you're shy. And that sex is all new to you. Furthermore, I happen to think you're worth it. Plus . . . you make me horny, boy."

"Don't say that."

"I'm sorry, but you do. If it's wrong for me to feel that way, then I guess God can strike me down with lightning."

He was still sitting in his leather chair. She sat back on his lap. This time, she was facing him. With her legs, she straddled him and placed her arms around his neck.

"You've already touched my soul. Now, I want you to touch my body," she whispered.

He whispered back. "Why? Why would you be interested in a guy like me? Me and all my baggage. Don't you want a guy who you can sleep next to without being woken up two and three times a night by his nightmares? Don't you want a guy who can watch the Fourth of July fireworks with you? Don't you want a guy who's nice and normal?"

"Well, in case you haven't noticed — I'm not quite perfect, either. And that's an understatement. I'm far from perfect. I'm perfectly imperfect. I know that. But no human being is perfect. And I want to be there for you. I really want that."

He loudly exhaled. "God. I don't know what I want."

"I do. I know what you want. You want *me*. Bad. I see the way you look at me. I'm not blind, you know. A woman notices those things. I see you staring at my boobs and ass and legs. Don't even *think* I don't notice your staring."

"It's hard not to, missy. You prance around here in bra and panties half the time."

"Yeah. Bras and panties that *you* bought for me."

"Oh, so because I bought them, I'm responsible for how *you* choose to wear them? Oh, that's rich, honey. It makes no rational sense whatsoever."

"Bingo, smart guy! This isn't about reason or logic. It's about emotions. And you're toying with mine. And I don't appreciate it."

"Look, I'm confused. I'm feeling things that I haven't felt before. And, yes, it's because of you. It's exciting, but it's scary, too. As we used to say in the Army—cut me some slack, will you? Please."

She got off him and walked over to a coatrack, which sat in the corner. His black fedora hung there. She put it on and pulled the brim down over her eyes. Then she walked over to his desktop computer and got on *YouTube*. She dialed up Elvis's *A Little Less Conversation* and turned up the speakers. Her hips swayed back and forth to the music. She improvised a sexy dance for him, just like the ones she performed at her concerts.

He watched her with big eyes.

She giggled and talked over the music. "Too bad you don't have a stripper's pole in here. Then, you'd see some real magic, fella." She winked at him.

Again, she straddled him and threw her legs around his. Looking him in the eye, she purred to him, "God, I need this. You do, too. This is going to be good for both of us, Danny. *So* good. Trust me, okay? I'd never do anything to hurt you. Just give me your trust, sweetie."

She threw her head back, and the fedora fell to the floor. Next, she let her hair down and ran her fingers through it. And then she started moving her hips back and forth, side to side. All while still straddling him. She started grinding on him — a dry hump.

After about thirty seconds, she felt his erection beneath her. "Oh, you like that, do you?" she asked with a naughty smile. Then she added, "You're a big boy. I knew you were. Yeah. I knew you were. You have big hands. You're big, and I'm like Ebenezer Scrooge. I'm tight, boy. That's one advantage to being petite. Petite women are quite often very tight. Did you know that, Danny? It's not a myth. Really, it's not. It's generally true."

"Ah, no. I didn't. I didn't know that. That's a fun fact."

She giggled and shook her head. "A *fun fact*. God, you're too much. You're adorable, is what you are."

She started to grind harder, and she growled as she did. The growling turned into primal, guttural vocalizations.

She looked at him. He'd thrown his head back, his eyes were closed, and he was breathing heavy.

She stripped off her top, leaving a red bra on, and continued to hump. "Come on, baby. Let me make love to you. I know you want it. Don't lie. Lying's a sin, isn't it?"

He nodded. "Uh-huh. It's against the Eighth Commandment." He brought his head forward and opened his eyes.

"Well, there you go then."

She started to remove her bra. "I'm going to get my tits out for you. Yeah, I'm getting these puppies out. I know you're a boob man. I know you are. My girls want to meet you, too. I call them the Hooter Twins, and they absolutely adore *you*. Yup. They've been all like — *Grace, when do we get to meet Danny*? And I've been all like — *girls, you have to be patient with Danny. He's shy.*" She tee-heed.

"Grace, please —"

She angrily interjected. "*No!*" She unhooked her bra and slowly let it fall. Big, brown areolas and nipples capped her 34DDs. She shimmied her shoulders, and they jiggled.

He stared at them with his mouth open. "Oh, God."

She smiled. "You like?"

He said nothing.

She answered for him. "Yeah, *you like*. You like the Hooter Twins. Why don't you go ahead and touch them? I want you to. A guy sure could have a lot of fun with them. They're extremely sensitive." She cupped her breasts and squeezed them together. Her nipples were hard and erect.

"Grace, I want this, too. *I do*. God, I do. But I'm not *supposed* to want it. And that's what bothers me. Maybe . . . maybe you should put your clothes back on. You know — maybe . . . or . . . or maybe not. That could work, too." He thought for a second. "On the other hand — maybe you should."

"No. I won't put my clothes back on . . . oh, God. I feel you. I feel you underneath me. You're totally hard for me. Hard as a rock. I love it. I freaking *love it*. It's the ultimate physical compliment a guy can give a girl." She was still grinding hard. "Come on, baby, give Momma some sugar now. Sugar. *Shug. Ger*. Just a little bit. You act like she's a damn diabetic, and she's not. Let me make love to you. Come on, baby — show me how you want it to be." She raised her arms over her head for a few seconds as she humped him for all she was worth. Then, she brought her hands back down and squeezed her own breasts and gently pinched her nipples, still grinding on him all the while.

He yelled at her, "Damn it, Grace! You're trying to get me to break my vows — my promise to God. I can't resist this temptation much longer. And you *know* that. You absolutely know it. You know I want you. You know you have power over me. And you're using that against me. Instead of laying off, you're pushing harder. I mean — are you trying to ruin me as a priest?"

"I'm trying to *help* you as a *man*. Now shush. Just shush. You don't have anything constructive to say."

"You're going to make me squirt in my pants here in about

another ten seconds."

"Oh, so you don't want to squirt in your pants?" She was breathing hard.

"No. They're brand new boxer shorts. *Ralph Lauren Polo.* Almost twenty bucks a pop."

"Well, then let's take them off. And I'll take my shorts and panties off."

"But then we'll be naked."

"Customarily, that's how sex is had, dear."

"My shoulder hurts tonight."

She stopped humping and kissed his shoulder. Her bare breast brushed against his chest. "Then let me make it better."

"You can't. You can't make it better. I wish you could."

"How do you know? You haven't allowed me to try." She paused for a second, threw her hands up, and continued. "Danny, I know I've been a little silly, talking about the Hooter Twins and Miss Kitty and Marshall Dillon and what-not. I guess I'm just trying some humor. I don't know what else to try at this point. But all kidding aside—this can help you heal if you let it. But only if you let it. So . . . let it. Okay? Just *let it.* Honey, you're broken. I'm broken, too. We are both broken. This fucked-up world, this incredibly fucked-up world, has broken both of us. The world does that to people. But we can rise above it. The world doesn't have to win. We can. This isn't about some cheap, one-night stand. I don't want to *fuck you.* I want to *make love to you.* And there's a difference, a world of difference. Sex is a biological function. Making love, on the other hand, is spiritual. We can have a real life together. But it has to start somewhere. It has to start here. We have to start by being as close to each other as possible—by giving ourselves to each other. And there's only one way to do that. It has to be this way. This is how God made us. And I would be super-duper gentle with you. I promise. I want to *show* you how much I care because words aren't enough. There. I said my piece. What do you say?"

"I can't, Grace . . . or maybe I can. Yeah. Sure, I can. Why . . . why not?" He paused, loudly exhaled, and rubbed his eyes. "No, I just can't. Oh, hell. I don't know. I'm sorry. I'm very sorry. I want to. God literally knows—I want to. But I don't think it's a great idea. And I feel horrible. I feel like I'm being unfair to both God and you. Like I'm being disloyal to both of you. And it makes me hate myself. I mean—I want you. I really, really do. I want for this to happen. I want to make love to you, Grace. There. I said it. But I've made a commitment. I'm just . . . confused. I am. I know I'm not making much sense right now and I'm sorry for that, too. But I think we should probably stop this. Now. Before it goes any further. Because we are rapidly moving towards *the point of no return. Crossing the Rubicon,* as they say. I'm teetering on the brink. And I can't hold out much longer. I think you should get off me. At least for now."

She climbed off of him and cried. "I'm a sensitive soul, you know. And the heart wants what it wants. And now, you're rejecting me, and I feel like a fool."

She started with an ugly cry. "You don't want me. I tried to give myself to you, and you don't even want me. I'm a failure as a woman. You make me feel like a failure as a woman. I just want to make love to you. I just want to do what any woman would want to do for her man."

He got up and put his arms around her. She could see and feel that he was still semi-erect. His arms brushed the sides of her bare breasts. She could also feel a touch of moisture around his crotch.

He gently stroked her hair and kissed her forehead. "Aw, come on. Don't cry. Please, don't cry. I hate to see you cry. I'm sorry for giving you mixed signals. I'm very sorry. And you're not a failure as a woman. Don't you dare think or say that. You're the exact opposite of a failure. Why, if there were a

Nobel Prize for Womanhood, you'd win it every year. Hands down."

She sniffled a couple of times, and the pace of her tears slowed. "I . . . I . . . I would?"

"You sure would, girl," he said with a warm smile.

She started to compose herself a bit. "The Nobel Prize for Womanhood? That's a little cheesy, Danny. Very cheesy, actually. But I'll take it."

"Yeah, I guess it was kind of cheesy. But the sentiment was sincere."

She caressed his cheek. "I know it was."

He gently stroked her hair with his hand. "Listen, you just have to try to see this whole thing from my point of view. This is all new to me. I feel lost. I feel conflicted. It's like there's a tug of war. God's pulling me in one direction, and you're pulling me in another. You need to give me time to figure this out. Give me some space. Okay?"

She looked up at him, sniffled, and said, "So, is that a *maybe*?"

He nodded. "It's a *maybe*. I have a lot to think about. I will say this, though—right now, I want to carry you upstairs . . . and make love to you all night long. I do. God, I do!"

"Well, that's encouraging."

He smiled, nodded, and reached out towards her left breast. When his hand got to within an inch of her areola, he stopped, withdrew it, and clinched it into a tight fist. "I'm just not quite ready, yet. I'm getting there, but I'm just not quite ready. I'll have to pray on it, I suppose."

She nodded. "You know, I prayed today myself. For the first time in a long, long time," she confessed.

"Is that right?"

"Uh-huh."

"That's good. Praying's good."

"Do you think that God answers all prayers?"

He got a faraway look in his eyes. "When I was in Afghanistan, I prayed that me and my buddies would all make it home safe. I prayed that prayer every day. Well, you know how that worked out."

"So, you think that God doesn't answer all prayers?"

"He answers them all, Grace. Sometimes He just says — *no.*"

Chapter Nineteen: When You Care Enough To Get Pissed Off

On Saturday afternoon, Danny and Grace were sprawled out on the living room floor playing *Risk*. Grace wore a pair of blue jeans and a red tank top. She was in her bare feet. Danny wore jeans and a plain gray hoodie. They ate takeout pizza and drank orange soda from the can.

He gleefully rubbed his hands together. "Ha. I've driven you out of Africa, steamrolled through Asia, and have your armies in Europe on the brink of complete and total collapse."

"You're not a very gracious winner."

"You don't have to be gracious when you're on the verge of world domination." He did his best mad scientist laugh. "*Bwahaha.*"

"Whatever, dude. You win. Let's put in a movie."

"What do you want to watch?"

"*Silver Linings Playbook*. I think I saw that one in your DVD collection."

"Yeah, I have that one. It's my favorite Jennifer Lawrence film. De Niro was great in that picture, too."

"It's very romantic."

"Yep. It's about two lost souls who find one another and fall in love."

"Yeah. Two lost souls. Imagine that."

"Why don't you run upstairs and get it, and I'll put the game away."

"Kay. Be back in a flash." She ran up the stairs.

When she came back downstairs with the DVD, he was on the phone.

She sat on the floor, cross-legged, and listened to him talk.

"No — no — no, Marie. It's fine. Really, it is. Don't feel bad. It's no imposition at all. Give me a half-hour or so and I'll be over, okay?" There was a pause. After about five seconds, he started talking again. "Yeah, I know where you live — that big house on Beaver Trail Road. I'll be leaving shortly, so I'll see you in just a little while. Keep your chin up, okay? Bye now." He put down his phone.

Grace was angry and pouting. "Who were you talking to, huh? Who was that? Who?" She stood up.

He smiled. "It was . . . Jake from *State Farm*."

She shook her finger at him. "Do not be a smartass to me. I heard you say *Marie*. Was that that Marie Gianelli? Was it?"

"Okay. So it was Marie Gianelli. So what?"

"What did she want?"

"Look, I have to go over to her house for a little while this afternoon, that's all."

"Why?"

"She's very upset, very despondent, over the split with her husband. She said she needs someone to talk to, someone she can trust."

"You're going over there right now? To freaking commiserate with her and such?"

"Yeah. I told her I'd be right over."

"But what about our movie?"

"We can watch it when I get back."

"When will that be?"

"I don't know. Whenever I'm done."

"But it's Saturday. This is your day off."

"I've already told you — in this line of work, there's no such thing."

She crossed her arms, tapped her toe on the floor, and

declared, "I don't like that dame. I don't like her at all. Not one bit."

He nodded. "I'm well aware."

"I thought you told me that you weren't going to see her anymore."

"No. I said she wouldn't be coming over *here* anymore. And she's not. I'm going to her place."

"It's a trap," she confidently announced.

"Beg your pardon?"

"It's. A. Trap. She's trying to lure you onto her turf so she can have her way with you. A lioness always prefers to hunt on her own territory. It's her fantasy, for God's sake. *Dear Diary, well, today's the big day, the day I finally* boink *my priest.*"

"You don't know what you're talking about."

"I *do* know, and soon, you will, too, buster."

He shook his head. "She's a very depressed woman who's in need of pastoral care."

She yelled at him, "She's a cougar, and she's trying to *fuck* you!"

"Hey — hey — hey! Now, that's enough of that kind of talk, missy."

"I have her all figured out."

"You do, do you?"

"Yep. I've thought about this a lot and have come to the conclusion that she's a mafia princess."

He laughed. "A mafia princess?"

"That's right."

He folded his arms. "Okay, Lucy, let's hear the explanation behind this one. It has to be a doozy. Geez, I so feel like Ricky Ricardo."

"Fine. I can give you a perfectly logical argument. First of all, she drives a *Cadillac*."

He threw up his hands. "So?"

"Danny, mafia princesses *love Cadillacs*. You could offer

them a brand new *Rolls Royce* or an old beat-up *Cadillac,* and they'd pick the Caddy every time. I swear, it's in their DNA."

"Okay, besides the *Cadillac,* what else?"

"How about Sinatra? Does she listen to Sinatra? Mobsters worship that man, you know."

"Well, come to think of it, when she was over here, her phone rang, and the ringtone was *Fly Me To The Moon.*"

"Fur coats. I'll bet she wears them."

"Only in the fall and winter."

"And how about jewelry? She probably likes really gaudy jewelry."

"Well, she does wear those huge hoop earrings. And a big diamond, too."

"*Yes.* They *adore* hoop earrings and big diamonds."

"You're letting your imagination run wild. Besides, what would the mob be doing in a little town like North East?"

"It's the perfect place to set up shop. Virtually no cops around."

"Aw, you're coo-coo, girl. Are you convinced that you overheard Jack, Janet, and Chrissy plotting to kill Mister Furley, too? Because they were actually talking about getting rid of the roaches in the apartment."

She ignored his sarcasm. "Does she use the word *yous* instead of *you?* For example, does she say, *hey, how yous doin'?* Does she say that?"

"Yeah, but I think she told me that she's originally from South Philly. People in South Philly talk that way. It's part of their charm."

"Jesus. South Philly?"

"What's wrong with South Philly?"

"Danny, that's, like, their capital. South Philly is to the mob what Washington DC is to the United States."

"No—no—no. You've got her all wrong."

"Okay, next question—what does she do for a living?"

"Come to think of it — I don't think she works."

"Nope. Mafia princesses don't. That's because their husbands want them barefoot, pregnant, and in the kitchen. And speaking of husbands — what does hers do? Does he run a nightclub or casino?"

"No. Certainly not."

"What does he do then?"

"I think he's a union rep."

"Oh, *shit*. They like that kind of stuff, too. They're always getting involved with the unions, trying to infiltrate them and such. When I performed in Vegas, I'd hear stories of how they'd plant their people inside of the casino workers union."

"You're jumping to all kinds of conclusions, lassie."

"Her husband — does he wear a pinky ring?"

"Well, as a matter of fact, he does. Paulie does wear a big, gold pinky ring."

She threw up her hands. "His name's *Paulie and* he wears a pinky ring? *Ding! Ding! Ding!* Jack-freaking-pot. We have a winner. That's the clincher. Let's face it — the whole family's *Cosa Nostra*."

"You've seen *Goodfellas* too many times."

"Yeah? Well, that was based on a true story."

"Look, I can vouch for the family. They're always in church. Their kid, little Paulie, gets confirmed next month."

"Of course, they go to church. Mafiosos are deeply religious. They have to be in order to cover their asses for all that crime they commit. They figure that if they just slip a couple of hundreds into the collection plate, God will look the other way. Everyone knows that. *Duh*. And they're always Catholic. *Always*. After all, you don't see too many Mennonite gangsters."

He rolled his eyes. "Oh, brother."

"Don't you *oh, brother* me, boy. I know what I'm saying. Have they ever given you a gift?"

"Yeah. Why?"

"What'd they give you?"

He nervously laughed. "What difference does it make? I mean, a gift's a gift, right?"

"What did they give you?"

"Well, last Christmas, they gave me a . . . ah, you know, a nice, crisp . . . hundred dollar bill. But it was in a lovely card that had a picture of the Virgin Mary on it. Nice . . . nice card, you know? Very nice card."

She pointed at him, gasped in horror, and covered her mouth. "Awwwww, Dan-ney. You took money from the moooob. That's tainted money, too, mister. It probably came from money laundering or a numbers racket. Or . . . oh my God . . . prostitution. Maybe it came from prostitution. Some poor young girl sold her body so you could get a brand new putter at the *Dick's Sporting Goods* Day After Christmas Sale. I hope you can live with yourself knowing that."

"For your information, I donated that money to charity. To the *Saint Jude's Children's Hospital*. And what am I supposed to do? What do you want me to do, huh? Tell her I can't be her priest because the runaway celebrity who's hiding in the rectory doesn't like her and thinks she's mafia? You want me to tell her that, do you?"

"I'm just looking out for you. I'm telling you—you go over there, and she's going to try to make you an offer you can't refuse."

"She's looking for a friend."

She screamed, *"She's looking for a nooner!"*

He dismissively waved his hand at her. "Aw, fuggedaboutit."

She stuck her tongue out at him.

"Look, I promise, as soon as I'm finished, I'll come straight home, and we'll watch our movie."

"Promise?"

"Sure do. Assuming that I don't get eaten alive by the big,

bad barracuda." He cackled.

Grace was lying on the sofa in the living room, working on a crossword puzzle, when she heard him come in. Tippy ran to the door to meet him.

He walked into the living room and took off his blue windbreaker, tossing it in the recliner. Next, he took his keys and dropped them on the coffee table.

Grace looked up. "Hey, I need a fourteen-letter word that means *representing the most perfect or typical example of a quality or class*. Come on, college boy. Help me out."

"Hmm. Let's see. How about *quintessential*. Does that fit?"

"Spell it for me."

"Q-u-i-n-t-e-s-s-e-n-t-i-a-l. Here. I'll even use it in a sentence for you. I was the *quintessential* fool for going over to Marie Gianelli's house this afternoon. God, I'm stupid. Such a sucker."

She put the puzzle down, sat up, and looked up at him. "What's wrong? You weren't gone very long. Did something happen over there?"

He threw up his hands. "You were right. There. I said it. Go ahead and gloat. Tell me *I told you so*."

"What are you talking about?"

"I'm talking about Marie Gianelli. You. Were. Right. Ya happy pappy?"

"You mean I was right about her being a mafia princess or right about her being a cougar?"

"Well, she's probably in the mafia, too, but, ah, yeah, she's a cougar. Most definitely a cougar."

She patted the sofa seat. "*Oh. My. God.* Here. Sit down and tell me the whole story."

He sat next to her and started talking. "Well, I got to her place, and she has this intercom system. So, when I rang the doorbell, her voice came over the PA, and she told me that the door was unlocked and that she was upstairs. She told me to meet her up there. All the lights were off in the house. There was nobody else around. It was quiet, eerie even." He paused.

"And?"

"So, I walk up the stairs, and when I get to the top, I hear her voice coming from the master bedroom." He imitated a woman's voice. "*I'm in heeeere. Come on iiiiin.* And I can already hear this mood music playing in the background. It was Marvin Gaye."

"Which song?"

"*Let's Get It On.*"

"*Daang.* The slut was literally broadcasting her intentions. So, what happened next?"

"Well, I walk into the bedroom, and she has this weird wood paneling thing going on and leopard print bed sheets and—"

She interrupted. "Leopard print bed sheets? *Very* mafia. Also, very swinger. Sorry to interrupt, but I had to make that point. Continue. Please."

"Yeah, anyhow, when I got to the bedroom, she was lying on the bed in this little blue negligee, wearing four-inch spike heels and—"

She again interrupted. "They're called *fuck me heels.*"

"Right. So, she stood up and took off the negligee. Then, she lay back on the bed, and she spread her legs wide open. And I mean *wide* open."

"Was she waxed? Just curious. Because women should always wax. I do. Everyone should, really."

He nodded. "A Sphynx. Her kitty was a Sphynx. And I actually do wax, too."

"Great. I figured you probably did. So, getting back on track here—could you see pink?"

"Oh, *yeah.* Most definitely. I saw more pink than you'd see inside a cotton candy factory."

"Oh my God! You saw her whole *who-ha.*"

He nodded. "I saw her whole *who-ha.* Well, next thing I know, she's telling me that she needs me to *exorcise* her *demons.*"

"That's what she called it?"

"Yeah."

"Very original. I will give her credit for that. I don't think I've ever heard it called that before. What happened next?"

"She told me that she wanted me to *squirt* my *ranch dressing* into her *Hidden Valley.*"

Grace gasped and covered her mouth. "Oh, *shit.* You know what that means, don't you? She wanted you to come inside of her."

"I'd never heard that expression before, but, yeah, I kind of inferred that that's what she was talking about."

"What happened next?"

"Next came the coup de grace. She walked up to me and groped my manhood."

"Nah ah. No way."

"Ya-ha. Yes way."

"Good Lord. She grabbed your Marshall Dillon?"

"She did."

"That *bitch!*"

"I got all tongue-tied at that point. I totally spazzed out. I mumbled some gibberish about how nice the house was. And then I babbled some crazy shit about how I thought I saw the girl who played Sydney on *Melrose Place* at the *7-Eleven* buying scratch-offs on my way over. And then I just ran out. And that's how it ended."

"Oh, you poor thing. Danny, that was a sexual assault. Did you call the police?"

"No. Look, I'm just going to let it go. I don't want to make a big stink over this."

"I'm so pissed. I knew that skank was up to no good. I just knew it. Well, she's not going to get away with this. I'm going to hunt her down and bitch-slap her." She curled her tiny hand into a fist, shook it, and continued her tirade. "I'll go all *Ike Turner* on her ass! She needs to learn to stay the fuck away from other women's men."

He didn't say anything, just stared at her.

She grabbed for his cellphone, which was in his pocket. "Here. Give me your phone. And give me this whore's number."

He put his hand over his pocket to block her. "No. It's not your problem. I don't need a woman to fight my battles for me. It's very emasculating."

She held her hand out. "Danny, give me the phone. Now please."

He shook his head. "No. It's not a good idea."

"Give me the *fucking* phone and give me her *fucking* number. Because I *am* going to call the *bitch*. I want to tell her that she's going to spend an eternity in Hell for this. Because that's what happens to women who put their filthy paws on other women's men—*they burn in Hell*. Says so right in the Bible. There's an entire chapter on skanks. That tells you right there that God has an ax to grind against them. Now, give me the *damn* phone. Please and thank you. Because I am going to call her or at least text her."

"I don't think there's a chapter of the Good Book devoted to skanks. In fact, I don't think the word is ever mentioned."

"Then you'd better study your Bible, padre, because it's in there. It's right before the chapter that tells about what happens to men who send dick pics to women. Oh, God. That's so gross. What possesses men to do that?" She pretended to vomit.

"Be that as it may, my point is—you most certainly are not going to call or text her. That'll just make things worse, stir up more trouble. I forbid it."

"Fine. I'm creative. I'll find another way to make my point." She thought for a moment. A big smile crossed her face. "Oh, I know. I'll create a fake *Facebook* profile, go to her timeline, and post that she has both crabs and Hep C."

"You'll do no such thing. Drop it, okay? Just drop it. Jesus always turned the other cheek."

"Oh, so you're trying to be just like Jesus, are you?"

He emphatically nodded. "Yes. Certainly."

"Well, here's a news flash for you, bub—Jesus never had a cellphone, didn't play golf, and walked everywhere he went. Hell, he probably didn't even have premium cable. So there." She made a face at him.

"Enough of your sass. Enough."

"No. It's not enough. It's not even close to enough."

"I'm not even sure why you care. So, I saw her who-ha. So what? You think that's the first who-ha I've ever seen in my life? You think that just because I'm a virgin, that I haven't even seen a who-ha? Why, just last week, I was paging through an issue of *National Geographic,* and they had a feature on this tribe in West Africa that doesn't wear any clothes— nothing at all. Never. It's against their religion. *And I saw some who-has, baby.*"

"But it's not fair."

"What's not fair?"

"That you saw her who-ha, but you haven't seen mine. That's not fair."

"Aw, let's not go there right now."

"We *will* go there, buddy. She robbed me of something, stole something from me. And I *hate* her for it." She folded her arms and pouted.

"Right now, I'm not too proud of you. You're acting like a vindictive little monster. If being nasty were an Olympic sport, your face would be on a *Wheaties* box. And hate's a strong word. You should never hate. Hate will destroy you."

"Don't you preach to me. I'm not a member of your congregation. And you're not a woman. You wouldn't understand. This shit is as primal as it gets."

He looked upwards. "Jesus, Mary, and Joseph."

"Listen, you should be happy, flattered even, that someone cares enough to get all pissed off over this. I'm trying to protect you, to show you how much I care."

He started to calm down. "I know you are. And I appreciate it. I'm not really angry with you. I'm angry with myself. I just can't believe I was so stupid." He looked over at her. "But you knew. I should have listened to you. You definitely had her pegged right. I'm sorry I didn't pay attention to your warnings. I was flat-out wrong about her. And you were spot-on right."

She gently massaged his shoulder. "You don't know how to read women, that's all. I guess you just never learned. Now, granted, we're not always super easy to read. We can be cryptic and mysterious, but that's part of our lure. But in this case, the red flags were there. I saw them. And I didn't want to see her treat you like a piece of meat. You're much more than that. You deserve so much better from a woman. I was only trying to fight for you. After all, you went overseas and fought for me. There. I had to get all that off my chest."

He looked at her breasts with mock suspicion. "I don't know, girl. By the looks of you, you still have an awful lot *on* your chest."

She smiled a naughty smile. "Then why don't you play with them? They're *more fun than fidget spinners*. At least that's what Orion used to say."

He shrugged. "Frankly, I'm not sure that's really saying too much. I never understood that fad. Never thought fidget spinners were that much fun."

She cupped her breasts and gently squeezed them. "Yeah?

Well, these babies will make your *head spin*."

"Oh, is that so?"

She raised her eyebrows, smiled, and nodded. "*Mm.*"

"Well, then maybe I *will* play with them. Maybe I'll knead on them like a little kid playing with a big old thing of *Play-Doh*."

"Good. That would make me feel good because my tits are very sensitive. I can get off just by having them fondled. And I could make you feel good, too."

"I'm sure you could, Grace. And I want that. I want that so bad. I want it more than you could possibly imagine. In my mind, I've made love to you a dozen times already. I'm just not quite ready yet for the real thing . . . okay?

She reluctantly nodded. "Yeah. Kay."

"And thank you for caring, by the way. It's actually nice to have someone to look out for me. I haven't had that since my days in the Army."

"I'll always have your back."

"But do me a favor, will you? Don't mess with Marie Gianelli, all right? No calls. No texting. No social media posts. As *The Beatles* once said, *let it be.* Just let it be. Please. Can you promise me that you'll do that?"

"But she disrespected you."

"Yes. She did. But I'm willing to let it go."

"What if she tries it again?"

"We'll cross that bridge when we get to it. If anything, we should pity her. She truly is a lonely soul. And she's trying to elevate her self-esteem through casual sex. That's quite sad, don't you think?"

"Fine. I'll drop it. For now. But if she ever lays a hand on you again, I'll beat her ass. Because even though I'm tiny, I'm scrappy. I'm Scrappy-Doo. Remember him? He was Scooby's little nephew."

He laughed. "Yeah, I remember him. And, yes, you are

scrappy. That's one of the many qualities that I admire in you."

"You do?"

"Yeah. I find it sexy."

"Sexy?"

"Most definitely."

"Aw. Thank you."

"Ready to watch our movie?"

She sniffed the air. "Yeah. As soon as you take a shower."

"Why? Do I smell like a hippie? I took a shower this morning."

"I know. But I can smell her on you. Her perfume. Her house. *Her*. And it's kind of freaking me out. Would you mind too awfully much going up to the shower and washing her off you?"

"You can seriously smell her on me?"

"Yeah. I can. It's a woman thing. Trust me."

"Fine. I'll take a shower." He started to walk up the stairs. After he took a few steps, he stopped and turned around. "Hey, Grace—"

She looked up at the staircase. "Yeah, babe?"

"Thank you for caring enough to get upset."

"*Pissed off.* I cared enough to get pissed off. I get *upset* when someone says *I could care less* when what they really mean is *I couldn't care less*. I get *upset* when people insist on constantly using that damn phrase—*at the end of the day*. God, that gets on my nerves. Like nails on a chalkboard. But when some dirty, filthy jezebel tries to mess with my guy, I get *pissed off*."

"Right. Well, thank you for caring enough to get *pissed off*."

She smiled at him and winked. "Welcome, buddy."

He started walking back up the stairs.

Grace called out to him, "Oh—hey, Danny."

He stopped and looked down at her. "Yeah?"

"One more thing—do you think it was really the girl who

played Sydney on *Melrose Place* who you saw at the *7-Eleven*?"

"If it wasn't her, it was her twin. She bought three-hundred bucks worth of scratch-offs, five packs of *Capri Lights*, some *Five Hour Energy*, a hotdog, a grape *Slurpee*, and a *Three Musketeers* bar. Oh, and a copy of *Boy Toy Magazine*, too. She smelled like *Cheetos,* too — her fingers were all orange and whatnot. She tied up that line for a good fifteen minutes with those damn scratch-offs. She won, like, twenty bucks on one of them but gave it right back, bought more tickets. You know how they do — they win a little but *invest* it right back into their gambling. And then they lose that, too. I watched her leave. She got into an old purple *Dodge Neon*. The bumper was held together with duct tape. She peeled out of that parking lot like a bat out of Hell." He laughed.

"That's quite a story, fella. Very exciting for little old North East. I mean — to have a big star like the girl who played Sydney on *Melrose Place* in town for no apparent reason."

"Yeah, well, all-in-all, quite a day, huh? It was a real show. Anyway, I'm going to go up and wash Marie Gianelli off me. And then we'll watch *Silver Linings Playbook*."

"Kay, sweetie."

He continued up the stairs only to stop again. He looked down, and told her, "You know, the girl who played Sydney on *Melrose Place* might be a big star and all. But she can't hold a candle to you. Because, baby, you're the *only* star in *my* galaxy."

"*Aw*. That was the cheesiest line in the history of humanity. I mean that quite literally, too. It was bad. Real bad. *So* bad. But, somehow, it still came off as being incredibly sweet. Thank you, honey." She blew him a kiss. He pretended to catch it and then continued his ascent up the stairs to wash Marie Gianelli off of him.

CHAPTER TWENTY: EVERY GOOD AND PERFECT GIFT

Seventeen Days Later

It was nine o'clock in the evening. Danny had just gotten home from coaching his first *Little League* game of the new season. Carrying a green duffle bag full of baseball equipment, he walked up the stairs. He wore a blue baseball jersey that said *Cubs* in white script lettering, a pair of blue jeans, sneakers, and a blue ball cap with a white C on it.

He walked into his bedroom carrying the bag and set it down at the foot of the bed. Grace was sitting on the bed painting her fingernails while watching TV. She was in her bare feet, wearing a pair of baby blue terry cloth shorts and a white halter top.

"Hey," he called out.

She looked up. "Hey. How'd the game go? Did we win?"

"You don't keep score in Tee-Ball," he explained. "Our motto is *everybody's a winner.*"

"Aw. That's adorable. I love that motto. I was starting to wonder when you'd be home. It's been dark for a while now."

"Well, after the game, I took the team out for pizza."

"Does the league pay for that?"

He shook his head. "No."

"Well, who pays?"

"I do."

"*Aw.* Taking the little guys out for pizza. So sweet."

"I want them to have the full Tee-Ball experience. And postgame pizza parties are kind of a *Little League* tradition."

She wagged her index finger at him. "You would be a great father, Father."

He laughed. "Thanks. And you'd be a good mom. You're very nurturing."

She made a face. "I feel like my biological clock is tick, tick, ticking away."

"How many kids do you want?"

"Two. At least two." She elaborated. "And if I have a boy, he's not playing football. Already decided that."

"No? I think we—I mean *you*—should reconsider that. Football teaches valuable lessons—teamwork, discipline, perseverance. All admirable qualities."

"Yeah. And I've seen on TV the way those big goons chase each other around that field, how they hit one another—broken ribs, concussions. No way. Not my boy. In fact, my son's not going to play any sports at all." She pointed to her head. "He's going to make his way in life by using his brain. Sports just make you all hot and sweaty. And you end up stinking. Well, my son's going to be a thinker, not a stinker. And I'll tell you something else, too, while we're on this topic—he's not going to be a soldier. Never. My son's not coming home wrapped in an American flag. No. I am not going to be presented with that folded flag at a graveside service and be told by a member of some Army Honor Guard—*this flag is presented on behalf of a grateful nation.* The *grateful nation* can go to Hell. Not happening. My son's going to be the president of the United States. Or come up with the cure for cancer. Or at least invent *Styrofoam* packing peanuts that don't make a mess everywhere."

"I think someone already invented ones that dissolve in water or something like that."

"Fine. Then he can invent a kitty litter that cats can't track outside of the box."

"Say, now, that idea's gold. Pure gold."

"Oh, and if I have a girl, she's not dating until she's, like, fifty. Too many assholes out there."

"Yeah. I'm right there with you on that one."

"And, of course, I'd have to go to the parent-teacher conferences. And I'd want to be involved in the PTA, too. But my children are *not* going to public school. They'll go to Catholic school. Someplace where values are taught. Public schools are afraid to teach values. They're all freaking paranoid that they might *oh-fend* someone. I mean — God forbid that kids actually learn right from wrong. Nope. We certainly can't have *that*. And, besides, too much crazy shit goes down in the public school system. Ever notice how all these shootings *always* happen in public schools?"

"Yes. Very true. You are right about all that. I don't know of any that have happened in Catholic schools."

"And my kids are going to college. I never went, but my kids will. And none of my children will ever, under any circumstances, get involved in the entertainment industry. I'll forbid it."

"Well, I understand your reservations, but, ultimately, children have to choose their own paths in life."

She ignored his point and continued to fantasize. "I'd take them to the Grand Canyon and Washington DC. And while we're in DC, I'd take them to Arlington National Cemetery so they can learn about the sacrifices that our soldiers make for our freedom. Oh, and the birthday parties would be at *Chuck E. Cheese*. And I'm not spending too much time at my folks' place because their neighborhood's going to shit — too much dope. You've got people walking the streets barking like dogs because they're high on PCP. I've offered to move them out of there, but they've been there their entire married life. They don't want to leave. Oh, and, by the way, when I become a mom, I'm cleaning up my potty mouth. I'd be done with cussing. I don't want my children picking up that shit."

"That all sounds real nice. Other than the PCP addicts in your parents' neighborhood, that is."

"God, Danny, I want a child. I can't help it. I have a strong maternal instinct. I see something that's vulnerable, and I just want to mother it."

"I know you do. I've seen that side of you firsthand."

"I would be a good mom, wouldn't I?"

He nodded. "You would. The best, actually."

"Aw, I want a baby, baby."

"There's plenty of time for that. You're only, what, twenty-seven?"

She shook her head. "As of tomorrow, I'm twenty-eight. Tomorrow's my birthday."

"Oh. Wow. Tomorrow's your birthday? We need to do something special."

"What do you suggest?"

"I could cook for you, and then we could have a little party."

She shot him a leery look. "You cook? Ha. I haven't seen you cook yet. Putting stuff in the microwave doesn't count. With the exception of when I made the meatloaf, we always get delivery."

"That doesn't mean that I *can't* cook. What's your favorite meal, your fantasy meal?"

"Um, let's see. Fried chicken, extra crispy, mac and cheese with extra cheese, mashed potatoes, and cornbread."

He shrugged his shoulders. "I could make that. Easy."

"Yeah? In that case, I'll take you up on your offer. Tomorrow, you can cook for me."

"We'll need to get a cake, too. You should have a birthday cake. I can run over to *Walmart* and get one from their bakery. What kind do you like?"

"Red velvet."

"Okay. Consider it done. Now, what do you want for your birthday present? I'd like to give you something."

She looked at him with a naughty grin. "I'd like you to give me something, too."

"Oh, Grace. What am I going to do with you?"

"I have plenty of ideas."

"Stop. Just stop."

She put down her nail polish and held her fingers out for them to dry. "You really want to give me a present?"

"Of course."

"Fine. I want a kiss."

"A kiss?"

"That's right. But not a baby kiss. Not a peck on the forehead or cheek. I want a *real* kiss. I want an open mouth, tongue, saliva. Passion. The whole nine yards. I want a bubble gum kiss."

"A bubble gum kiss? What's that?"

"Okay, well, that's where I chew some bubble gum. And then after I've chewed for a while, we kiss, see? And during our kiss, I transfer the gum from my mouth to your mouth. And then you chew it until it goes stale. And you just eventually spit it out like normal."

"Sounds like a good way to pass germs back and forth."

"Sure it is. That's the whole point. If you really, really, really, really, really care about someone, you'd want their germs. I mean—my germs are your germs. Your germs are my germs. Our relationship is so intimate that we even share germs. That type of thing."

"Interesting concept. Very interesting. I've never heard of the phenomenon before."

"Can we do it?"

"Well . . . I don't know . . ."

"Oh, please. Just one. That's all I want for my birthday. If you give me that, you don't have to give me anything else. One bubble gum kiss. What would the harm be in that?"

"And what if it doesn't stop with one *bubble gum kiss?*"

"What's the matter? Don't you trust yourself, padre?"

"To be perfectly frank, no. I don't."

"Well, in that case, I promise you the best night of your life."

Grace woke up at one o'clock in the morning to the sound of Danny screaming in his sleep.

"Lion King, Lion King — this is Super Serpent Six. London Bridge is falling down! I say again — London Bridge is falling down! We need immediate close air support. I need you to burn em' out on hilltop x-ray, tango, whiskey — one, five, zero. That's x-ray, tango, whiskey — one, five, zero. Dump it right on top of us . . . because there ain't no fucking lines! They're all over us. Over."

He popped up in bed, drenched in sweat and out of breath. His bottle of *Ativan* was on the nightstand. He reached over and grabbed it along with some bottled water. She put her arms around him.

He explained his dream. "They got into our perimeter. We were getting overrun. They were everywhere. Taliban. Hundreds of them. Thick as fleas. They were going to wipe us out." He tapped out a pill, popped it in his mouth, and took a sip of water.

"It's okay. It's okay. Listen to me. There's no Taliban here, babe. We're in your bedroom. It's just me, you, and Tippy. No bad guys. I promise."

He rocked back and forth. "I'm scared, Grace. I'm scared."

She pulled him into her bosom and kissed him on the forehead.

"I won't be able to sleep anymore tonight," he told her.

She stroked his head. "Yes, you will. You'll see."

Gently, she pushed him back down on the bed and lay

down with him.

She held him in her arms and turned on the TV. They watched an infomercial for a set of knives. After that, *Generation Kill* came on. She turned off the TV.

"I'm going to sing you a song. And by the time it's over, you'll have fallen asleep. Okay?"

He turned his sad eyes up to her and nodded.

She sang *Bridge Over Troubled Water*. When she finished, she looked at him. He was sound asleep. She held him for the rest of the night.

Later that afternoon, Danny sat behind his office desk in the Church's Administrative Building, on his lunch break. He went online and ordered Grace some flowers for her birthday. A dozen yellow roses. He paid the extra twenty dollars to ensure same-day delivery.

Tired, confused, conflicted, he walked over to the church. It was cold and rainy, a typical April day in Maryland. Once he got inside, he walked up to the altar and kneeled. The life-sized crucifix hung just above him. He crossed himself and said the Our Father.

He gazed upward towards the crucifix. He turned his head around to make sure that he was alone. Once satisfied that the building was empty, he talked out loud, addressing the image of Jesus on the cross.

"I've gotten myself into quite a situation and could use Your help," he began. "Why does the world have to be so complicated? Why does life have to be so hard? Why couldn't You have made it easy? After all, easy is better than difficult. I feel like I'm caught between You and her. And that no matter what choice I make, it'll be the wrong one. I *want* her. Don't You understand that? And not for some cheap, one-night stand. I want her forever. When I made my vows, I didn't know anything about these kinds of feelings. But now I do." He shook his index finger at the crucifix. "You know, Your trouble is that You don't know. You can't relate. Though You loved, You were never *in love*. To be honest, I'm a little resentful. You expect me to live up to Your standards? I'm not You. And, frankly, I don't want to be You. And now I'm questioning everything, even my vocation. As we say in golf, I want a mulligan. I want to start over. Could we start again, please?" He thought for a moment before adding, "But we made a deal, didn't we? I made a bargain with You that night in Afghanistan. You got me out of there. You kept Your end of the deal. So, I guess now it's up to me to keep my end, huh? Is that how it is? Are You going to be a stickler and hold me to the exact terms of our little contract?"

He heard the door open, quickly got up, and turned around to see who was there. It was Mike Jameson. His hair was soaking wet, as he had no umbrella. He wore a pair of jeans rife with holes and a camouflaged military field jacket that wasn't zipped up. Underneath his jacket was a white t-shirt. The shirt had a yellow smiley face on it, and the caption read — *Smile, God Loves You*. He pulled the red wagon with his Rottweiler in it. The dog shook the water off his coat.

"Did I startle you? I hope not. I wasn't trying to," he called out to Danny as he closed the door.

"Hey, Mike. Yeah, you might have startled me a little, but that's okay. What's up? You need some more dog food?"

"No. Mrs. Cavanaugh just gave me a whole case of *Iams*. That's excellent food. Jake should be good for a while."

"You need something else?"

"No. I don't need anything today. I came to see you. There's a new issue of *The Little Shepherd* out. Hot off the presses. I thought I'd drop off a couple of copies. One for you and one for your friend." Mike pulled a clear, plastic bag from his wagon. The bag contained two copies of the magazine. He limped up to the altar and handed the periodicals to Danny.

"Thanks, Mike. I appreciate it." He removed the magazines from the protective bag, rolled them up, and placed them in his back pocket.

"How's your friend? The one who's living with you that is. Her name is Grace."

"Well . . . she's not really *living with me*. She's just kind of staying with me for a little while."

Mike shrugged. "Same difference."

Danny paused and cleared his voice before continuing. "Listen, you didn't say anything to anyone about Grace being in town, did you?"

"Of course not. I promised I wouldn't. I never go back on my promises."

"That's good. Keeping promises is a good thing."

"Would you please tell her I was asking for her?"

Danny nodded. "Sure, I will. Today's her birthday."

"Are you going to give her a gift?"

"Yeah. I'd like to. Only trouble is, I'm not sure what to get her. She kind of has everything."

Mike shook his head. "She doesn't have everything."

"Yeah, Mike, she pretty much does. I was thinking about going to a nice jewelry store and getting her a gold woman's cross. Real gold. Twenty-four carat. What do you think?"

Mike shook his head. "No. I don't think she'd want that."

"No? Do you have any suggestions? Do you know anything about the types of gifts women go for? Because I'm totally at a loss. And I don't have much time."

"Give her what's in your heart."

"What's in my heart?"

Mike nodded. "Yes. It's that simple."

Danny emphatically shook his head. "No. It's not that simple. This world is a complex place, Mike. Incredibly complex."

"I'm not concerned with the ways of the world. My kingdom isn't in this world. It never was."

Danny chuckled. "I wish I could be that carefree. It must be liberating."

"The truth *will* liberate you."

"Right."

"Well, I have to be going. I just wanted to stop by and drop off those magazines."

"Do you need a ride back home? It's raining out."

"I wouldn't want to put you out."

"You're not putting me out. I know it's not a long walk but, still, with the rain and all, it'd be a lot more pleasant to ride. Not just for you, but for Jake, too."

"Are you sure you don't mind?"

Danny smiled at him. "Sure, I'm sure. Come on. Let's go."

Danny got his car from the rectory garage and drove it to the church. He lifted Jake out of the wagon, gently set him in the backseat, and placed the wagon in the trunk. Mike got in the front passenger's seat. They drove to the Methodist Church, at the north end of town.

While they were enroute, Danny heard some commotion in the backseat. He took a quick look over his shoulder. Jake had found one of Tippy's toys. It was a pink, corduroy plush pig. The dog picked it up in his teeth and chewed on it. When he did, it squeaked.

Mike turned around and gently admonished his dog. "Jake! Put that down. It doesn't belong to you. We don't take things that don't belong to us."

Danny told him, "He can have it. Tippy has a million toys. She doesn't even play with half of them."

"He can have it?"

Danny smiled. "Sure he can."

Mike again talked to the canine. "Okay, well, in that case, you can keep playing with it. Our friend, Danny, has given it to you as a gift. You now have your very own toy." Jake continued to gnaw on the pig.

Mike turned back around and told Danny, "He's never had his own toy before. I've never been able to afford one. He's always wanted so much to be like other dogs and have a toy. Now, thanks to you, he does. That was a perfect gift. A good and perfect gift. Thank you."

Danny had to fight back tears. He found something profoundly sad in what Mike had just told him. *Every dog deserves a toy*. He found it poignant that Mike was making such a big deal over something as simple as a little, squeaky toy.

When they arrived at Reverend Mullins' house, Danny got the wagon out of the trunk. He lifted the old Rottweiler out of the backseat and placed him inside. Jake's new toy had gotten stuck under the rear seat floormat. He retrieved it and handed it to Mike, who put it in his jacket pocket.

"Well, that was a lot better than walking, wasn't it?" Danny asked.

Mike smiled. "Yes. It was."

Danny got back in his car and started it up. He rolled down the window and called out, "Are you all set now? Do you need anything else before I take off?"

"No. Thank you for the gifts — the dog toy and the ride over here. The ride — that was a gift, too."

Danny nodded. "I'm glad to do it. Do you want some help pulling the wagon up to the house?"

"No. I can take it from here." Mike started pulling the wagon towards the parsonage. After a few steps, he stopped, turned around, and walked back to the car.

Danny poked his head out the window. "What's up? Did you forget something?"

"No. I just wanted to check and see how you liked my gift to you."

"Your gift?"

Mike nodded. "Yes. I've given you a gift."

He drew a blank for a few seconds. Finally, it registered. *Oh, yeah. The magazines. He gave me the magazines.*

He reached into his back pocket and pulled out the two copies of *The Little Shepherd*. He unrolled them and told Mike, "Yeah. This is a nice little magazine. I was thinking about getting a subscription for Saint Mary's so we can use it in our CCD program."

"No. That's not the gift I was talking about. I don't think you understand yet." Without saying another word, he turned and pulled Jake's wagon up to the front door. Danny watched as the two of them disappeared into the house.

That night, when he got home from work, he was carrying a black umbrella and four plastic grocery bags. Grace and Tippy raced down the steps to meet him in the living room.

She was wearing a pair of black sweatpants, a pink hoodie, and her white sneakers. Her hair was up.

"What's up?" she called out.

"Hey. There's the birthday girl." He held up the grocery bags. "I went to the store and got all the fixings for your birthday dinner. I got the cake, too. They only had one red velvet cake left, and I snagged it. Oh, and I even got some ice cream. Mint chocolate chip."

"Cool. Still raining?"

He shook the excess water off the umbrella. "Yeah. Pretty hard, too. It's supposed to rain all night. Listen, before I start dinner, I'm going to go change."

"Want me to help you?" she said with a smirk.

He did his best Austin Powers impression. "Oh, behave, baby."

She giggled but seriously added, "You're the complete package—looks, personality, and even a great sense of humor."

He nodded. "Thanks . . . oh, by the way, Mike Jameson says *hello.*"

She squinted and wrinkled her nose. "*Who?*"

"Mike Jameson. You know—Jesus. The guy who thinks he's Jesus."

"Where'd you run into him?"

"He actually came to the church to see me. Brough over a couple of copies of that kid's magazine that he likes." He retrieved one of the copies from his back pocket. "Oh, that reminds me—he wanted you to have one." He handed it to her.

She set it on the coffee table and shook her head. "There's something about that guy that scares me."

He laughed. "You're scared of a disabled homeless man who carries a teddy bear with him everywhere he goes?"

"I don't mean *scared* in that way. I know he's perfectly harmless and wouldn't hurt a fly."

"Well, then what do you mean?"

"There was something about him. His eyes. His smile. I don't know. He smiled at me like, like . . . like Jesus to a child. Exactly like that."

"Aw, you're just freaked out because he knew your name. He probably recognized you."

"No. I don't think he recognized me at all. I think he just *knew.* He *knew,* Danny. I know that he knew."

"What? You want to be one of his followers? He doesn't have any, you know. You could get in on the ground floor, be his first groupie." He laughed.

"There was a power about him," she insisted.

"Power? He has no power. He's as powerless as they come. I don't think he even wants any power."

"The power to reject power might be the greatest power of all."

He rolled his eyes. "*Geez.* This conversation is getting way too heavy for me. Sorry, but I don't have a PhD in philosophy."

He went upstairs to change and came back down five minutes later. As he came down the stairs, she looked up at him. The expression on her face was one of disbelief.

He was wearing a pair of blue jeans, black cowboy boots, a fancy black western shirt with embroidered red roses around the top, and a straw cowboy hat. He wore a black belt with a huge silver buckle that featured a pair of mini steer horns protruding out.

He tipped his hat to her. "Howdy, ma'am."

She laughed and pointed. "What the *hell* are you wearing?"

He looked down at himself and shrugged. "It's your birthday—a special occasion. Sometimes, on special occasions, I like to get dressed up. Remember, I told you I'm a big fan of the Old West."

"You look like Toby Keith."

"You don't like it?"

"No. I don't. I honestly thought you had better taste."

"You want me to change?"

"Yes, please. I am, after all, the birthday girl. And I think that entitles me to some say over the dress code at my own party."

"Okay. Well, I guess I'll change then."

She emphatically nodded. "Yeah. Mosey yourself on upstairs pardner, and don't come back down until you lose that look."

He slinked back up the stairs. When he got half-way up, he turned around, looked down at her, and said, "You know, I actually like Toby Keith. I really like him. He came to Afghanistan on a USO tour and did a show for us."

She gave him a hard stare for a few seconds. Finally, she spoke gently to him. "Don't worry about changing. Don't. I don't want you to. Come on back down here."

"You sure?"

"Yes. I'm sure. You're sweet. The sweetest man I've ever met."

"I am?"

"Uh-huh. Absolutely."

They went to the kitchen. He took off his cowboy hat and put on an apron that said, *Kiss Me – I'm Irish*. She sat at the table, reading her book. He started preparing the meal by getting the chicken ready.

He looked over at her. She was sitting on the chair with one leg bent and folded underneath the other.

"How's the book?" he asked

She looked up at him and smiled. "It's good. Really good. You picked a winner."

"I'm surprised you haven't finished it yet. Didn't I get that for you a couple of weeks ago?"

"Yeah, but it's four-hundred-plus pages. Not only that, but I read in spurts. One day, I'll read, like, all day. Then I won't read at all for three or four days. I'm about half-way through. And it's really good."

He nodded. "Glad you're enjoying it."

"I am. But I'm still waiting for that first kiss. The two main characters haven't kissed yet. There's plenty of sexual tension but not much real action so far." She put the book down, stared at him for a few seconds, and added, "Oh, how art imitates life."

"Well, you have to figure that when they do finally kiss, it'll be all the more special because everything has been building up to that moment. Right?"

"I suppose." She threw her head back and sighed, adding, "But I'd be lying if I said it didn't have me all hot and bothered. I mean – if I get any hornier, I'm going to have to send you back to *Walmart* to get me a BOB."

"What's a BOB?"

"A Battery-Operated Boyfriend. A vibrator. And if you

think getting those tampons was embarrassing, just wait until you have to stand in the checkout lane with BOB in your cart."

"Well, hopefully, it doesn't come to that. Hopefully, something will happen soon. You know — an explosion of passion. They'll just give in to their desires. And, of course, they'll say their *I love yous*, ride off into the sunset together, and live happily ever after. All that good stuff."

She threw up her hands. "That's what I'm waiting for."

"It'll happen. You'll see."

"Are we still talking about the book?" she asked.

"Ah . . . yeah. Yeah. I mean — I was. Weren't you?"

She rolled her eyes. "Yeah. That's totally what I was talking about. Totally. I'm going to go watch TV. Call me when dinner's ready, okay?"

"Yes, ma'am."

She marked and closed her book, set it on the table, and left the room.

Just as he was putting the cornbread in the oven, the doorbell rang. It was the *FedEx* man. He delivered Grace's flowers.

Danny took the box into the kitchen and set it on the counter.

It took him an hour and a half, but he finally had everything done. The chicken. The macaroni and cheese. The potatoes. And the cornbread. He was proud of himself. It was the most elaborate dinner he'd ever made. He mixed up some iced tea and called Grace to the table.

"Prepared to be dazzled," he told her as he pulled out her chair for her.

She looked over at the long, white box sitting on the counter. Pointing to it, she inquired, "What's that?"

"It's for you. I'll show you after we eat."

They sat at the table, across from one another. He took her hands in his and told her, "I, ah, I want to say a special grace tonight. Would that be all right?"

She nodded. "Yeah. Sure. Whatever you want is fine by me."

They both closed their eyes and bowed their heads. He prayed. "Dear Lord, I'm not going to thank You for the usual stuff tonight, the food and so forth. I think You know that we appreciate that. Instead, tonight, I want to say this special grace to thank You for a special Grace. So, thank you. Thank you so much. Amen."

They opened their eyes and raised their heads.

She dabbed her eyes. "Jesus, that was sweet. So sweet. So sweet that I want to take you upstairs right this minute and screw the hell out of you for, like, the next two hours. At least the next two hours."

He laughed.

"Don't. Laugh. I'm completely serious."

"You don't need to say that kind of stuff, Grace."

"Then you don't need to say the kind of stuff that you're always saying."

"What has you all fired-up tonight?"

"What has me fired-up is that you say all this lovely, sweet, beautiful, romantic shit to me, but you won't even give me a real kiss. That's what has me all fired-up. It would have any woman fired-up. I am sexually frustrated. Understand?"

"Aw, come on."

"No, you come on. I am not a toy. I am not something to be played with. I have emotions, feelings. *Real* emotions and feelings."

"Let's not ruin your birthday dinner, okay?"

"Fine. Sorry. Sorry, I brought it up. Let's . . . let's just have a nice dinner. Let me get out of this foul mood."

He winked at her. "That's my lassie."

He took her plate and filled it with generous portions of each dish.

She looked down at her food but hesitated.

"Go on. Dig in," he enthusiastically commanded.

She tentatively scooped up some potatoes with her fork. They were watery, so watery that they slid off the utensil. Nervously, she smiled and told him, "I might need you to pour these into a glass so I can drink them." She gave it another go. When she got the potatoes on her fork, she quickly stuck them in her mouth. "Potato soup has more consistency," she noted with her mouth full.

After she swallowed, she made a face.

He eagerly looked on in anticipation of her evaluation. "Well?"

"Interesting texture. Very interesting. Did you add salt to this? Like, a lot of salt? A whole lot of salt?"

He nodded. "I added some. I did. Why do you ask?"

"Because it tastes like the freaking Dead Sea."

"Sorry."

She sampled all of the food. A thick layer of grease covered the chicken. The macaroni and cheese was all clumped together in one big ball. The cornbread was burnt on the outside but not fully cooked on the inside.

After she had tasted everything, she told him, "This is certainly a unique interpretation of the traditional chicken dinner, Danny."

"You don't like it," he said with a frown.

She laughed and held up a piece of cornbread for him to see. "It isn't even fully cooked on the inside."

"It said to cook it at three-hundred-seventy-five degrees for twenty minutes, but I figured if I cooked it at five-hundred degrees, I'd only have to have it in there for, like, twelve minutes. I guesstimated."

"And I'm guesstimating that you've never cooked cornbread before."

He put his head down. "You're right. I haven't. But I thought I could pull it off. I guess I got a little cocky. I thought

I could draw from my experience of those two weeks in the summer of oh-four when I was a cook at *KFC*."

"Why'd you only last two weeks?"

"I took the initiative to create a new dish without getting management's approval—Chicken Tartare. It didn't go over so well." He shook his head. "People just love to sue, you know? Anyhow, I ruined your birthday."

She reached across the table and took his hand. "No. You didn't. You tried, and that means more to me than anything. You tried to do something special. That's all that matters. This was a lovely gift. Or at least a sincere attempt at one."

"Really? You're not too disappointed?"

"No. Besides, we can still order pizza from *Frank's* later."

He nodded. "Yeah, we can do that. Thank you for being so understanding."

"You bet, buddy."

They threw the food out, the entire lot of it.

He excused himself and went upstairs. After less than a minute, he returned to the kitchen carrying a pink envelope.

"For you," he said as he handed it to her. She opened it and pulled out a birthday card. There was a picture of a couple walking hand-in-hand on the beach at sunset on the front cover.

She opened the card and read aloud the handwritten inscription he'd authored.

"Dear Grace, I am glad you came into the world, and I'm even more glad that you came into my world. You are the most beautiful and the kindest woman I've ever met. You are special. Not because you're famous. Not even because you can sing so beautifully. But because you have the sweetest of souls. Yours Always, Just Danny."

She dabbed her eyes with her finger and sniffled. "Those are lovely words. Thank you. Thank you so much. I'll keep this card always. I'll treasure it."

He picked up the white box from the counter and handed it to her. "Also, for you."

She opened the box and pushed aside the white tissue paper. "Roses," she said. "Yellow roses. Yellow roses mean . . . friendship." She set the flowers down. "They're gorgeous, but I'm confused," she declared.

"Confused?"

"Yes. Confused." She picked the card up with one hand and the box of flowers up with the other. She held both up for him to see.

"You give me a card that oozes romance but flowers that say *I just want to be friends.* Why?"

"Maybe because I'm confused myself."

"I think you want it both ways. You want to be the pious priest, Father Faithful, but you absolutely *love* all the attention you're getting. You love having me fawn over you. You can try to deny it, but I know the truth."

"Oh, come on. That's not fair."

"What's not fair is the way you're playing me."

"*Playing you?*"

"That's right. You're a player. And you're good at it, too. You could give lessons. You walk right up to the line, so close that your toes are touching it, but you don't cross it. You know exactly what you're doing."

He looked at her in silence.

She got in his face and yelled at him, "*I need you to cross a line!*"

He still said nothing, just stared at her.

"Say something," she commanded. "*Re. Fucking. Spond,*" she screamed.

He loudly exhaled. "Fine."

He took her by the hand. "Come on."

"Where are we going?"

"You'll see."

He picked up a pack of *Hubba Bubba* sitting on the kitchen

table and walked her out the back door. The rain was coming down in sheets — a torrential downpour. The wind was blowing hard, too.

"What the hell are you doing? We're going to get soaked. At least go back and get an umbrella." She put her hood up, pulled the drawstrings tight, and tied the strings in a bow.

"Nope. No umbrella."

He walked her down to the beach.

"Oh, God. It's cold out here. We're both going to catch pneumonia."

"No, we won't."

When they got to the beach, they looked out at the river. The water was rough and whitecapped.

"Why did you bring me out here?" she screamed.

He opened the pack of gum and handed her a piece. "Here. Chew this."

"Oh my God. Really? Are you serious?"

"Yeah. I'm serious. Now, go on. Chew it."

She unwrapped the piece of gum, put it in her mouth, and started to chew.

After a few seconds, he asked, "Ready?"

"Nope. Not yet. You have to work a new piece of gum a little before you can start chewing in earnest."

"Okay. Fine." He placed his hands in his pockets and whistled *Yankee Doodle* while she chewed.

After another few seconds, he again asked, "Okay, how about now? Now, are you ready?"

"Almost. Give me a few more seconds here." She bobbed her head from side-to-side as she worked the gum and sang the words to *The Macarena*.

Finally, she said, "All right. Now I'm ready."

He pulled the drawstrings of her hoodie loose and untied the bow.

He locked eyes with her and warmly smiled. And he

pushed the hood back so that it no longer covered her head.

"God, it's raining so hard. I'm getting soaked."

He nodded. "I know. So am I."

"It's going to be just like the ending of *Breakfast at Tiffany's*, isn't it?" she asked.

"Yep. That's the idea."

She licked her lips and flashed puppy dog eyes. "Kay."

He removed the hair clip from her hair. She shook her head. Her hair fell down and into her eyes. He pushed it to the side. Gently, he caressed her cheek and ran his fingers through her wet hair.

"I've been saving this up for a rainy day," he told her. He paused for a few seconds before adding, "Happy birthday, Grace."

She stood up on tippy-toes, put her arms around his neck, closed her eyes, and opened her mouth.

He inched closer to her, opened his mouth, and pressed his lips to hers.

"Ow!" she cried out.

"What's wrong?"

"Your damn belt buckle. I got poked in the ribs with those little, tiny steer horns." She rubbed her side.

"Sorry. Here. I'll push it over, so it's not aimed at you." He tried to turn the buckle to the side.

She intervened. "No—no. That's not going to work. You're going to have to just take it off. Take off the whole belt."

Very carefully, he tried to undo the buckle—to no avail.

"It's stuck," he told her as he continued to work on it. "I always have a problem getting this off."

She started to jerk on the buckle. "You're not pulling hard enough. You can't be all delicate with these things, Danny."

"Hey, be careful. This belt cost me three-hundred bucks."

She momentarily stopped pulling and looked up at him. "You paid three-hundred dollars for this thing?"

"Yeah, I did."

She rolled her eyes. "Oh. God. I can see that I'll have to handle all the cash. And, yes, I said *cash*. Not hash."

She went back to haphazardly yanking on the buckle, cursing it, "Come off, you son of a bitch! Come off, I said!"

Finally, with a mighty tug, she pulled the hook from the hole. All of her momenta was going backward. She reeled and was unable to keep her balance and fell to the ground, landing in a puddle.

He picked her up. "Are you all right?"

"I'm fine. Only my pride is hurt." She brushed wet sand off her backside and pulled the belt off his waist. Once it was off, she held it up for him to see and said, "I don't like this thing." Then she angrily threw it to the ground and cursed it. "Bastard!"

He went to pick it up.

"*Dan-ney!*"

"Right. I can pick it up later. Now, where were we?"

She stood back up on her toes and put her arms around him. Again, she closed her eyes and opened her mouth.

He put his hands on her cheeks and kissed her—an open mouth kiss, but a short one. He withdrew. She opened her eyes, shook her head, and told him, "That's not enough. Not even close to enough." She pulled him back, closed her eyes again, and kissed him. They both opened their mouths and went all-in. Their tongues wrestled one another. They swapped spit, gum and generally tried to inhale each other. They just kept kissing and kissing and kissing. And the rain kept pounding and pounding and pounding. They didn't care. She moaned a husky moan. Without breaking the kiss, she used her athleticism to leap up and wrap her short legs around his waist. He clutched her backside to support her. They were both running out of oxygen, so they unlocked their lips. When they did, he opened his mouth to reveal that they had successfully transferred the gum from her mouth to his. They smiled, and she giggled. She threw her head back, exposing her neck to him. He started kissing it, kissing it and even sucking on it. After a couple of minutes of this, she took short gasps of breath. He opened his eyes. Momentarily, he stopped when he noticed that her skin was turning red. It felt warmer, too.

"Don't stop," she said in a raspy voice. "I'm almost there. Come on, boy. Get me across the finish line."

"Finish line?"

"My neck, Danny. Get back to my neck," she commanded.

He started back on her neck. And he added a new kink. In addition to kissing and sucking on it, he gently licked it, too.

Once the licking started, she clenched her teeth and called out, "Oh, God, yes!" She breathed heavily. He looked at her and saw that her eyes were rolled back, her lashes fluttering. She started bucking her hips against him. Hard. She howled like a banshee.

Then, slowly, her breathing returned to normal, as did her skin tone. She shivered. *"Aye yai yai."*

She shuddered hard, took a deep breath, loudly exhaled, and looked up at him. With one arm, she held on tight to him. With her free hand, she took her French manicured nail, brushed the tip of his nose, and told him, "I don't think you'll have to buy me a BOB after all. No BOB could make me feel this way. That was freaking intense, dude. You made me come. You made me come hard."

"I . . . I did?"

She unwrapped her legs from around his waist and slid down so that she was standing on her own two feet. "Oh, yeah. God, that felt so good. Such a release. I needed that. It cleared my mind. All that pent-up energy that had nowhere to go. Now, it's finally gone. Oh, that was the best. Just thee best." She turned her gaze upward. "I mean—wow! *Oh là là!*"

"How did you have an orgasm without actually . . . you know . . . *doing it*?"

"How did Mary get pregnant without actually . . . you know . . . *doing it*?" she countered.

"Are you saying that your orgasm was a miracle?"

"No, I'm just teasing. Maybe that joke wasn't in good taste. But to my point — women can have orgasms without penetration."

"They can?"

"Yes. It's possible."

"Do you think that what we just did counts as having sex?"

"I would say no. But some people might disagree. It might be a gray area."

"Gray area? Oh, God. I didn't realize that it might count as having sex."

She softly stroked his cheek and told him, "There was no wrong in what we did." She leaned her head forward so that it brushed up against his chest. Putting her arms around him, she squeezed tight. They were both completely drenched.

He chewed the gum and blew a big bubble. She looked up and playfully poked it, causing it to burst all over his face. It left him with a bubble gum mustache. They laughed.

Then, she turned serious. "You gave me a gift tonight. It was a good gift, a perfect gift. And every good and perfect gift comes from Above. That's one of the few Bible verses that I remember from CCD." She paused for a few seconds and added, "Thank you, Danny. You yourself are a gift."

Chapter Twenty-one: Tears From Heaven

When they got inside, they both changed into jeans and a t-shirt and towel-dried their hair. He ordered pizza, and got her cake out and set it on the table. He called Tippy. "Ti-peeee, come on, girl. Time for Grace's party." The dog came running. He put seven candles on the cake.

"Why seven?"

"Good luck. Seven's the number of perfection. God's number. You know, the seven days of Creation and so forth. But the number *six* — well, that's the Devil's number. And if you ever buy a random pick three lottery ticket, and the computer spits out the number *six-six-six*, tear it up. Seriously. Only a Satanist would keep that ticket because that's the number of the Antichrist from the Book of Revelation. I hated the fact that in Afghanistan our call sign was *Super Serpent Six*. More Afghan voodoo, I suppose. But maybe that's why we had so many casualties in our unit. Maybe if we had been *Super Serpent Seven*, nobody would have died, you know? That call sign put too much bad juju on us. I know it did. I know it. And you don't need any bad juju in a combat zone." He shook his head.

He sang *Happy Birthday* to her. She blew on the candles, but every time that they appeared to be extinguished, they'd flicker back on after a second or two. They were trick candles.

He cackled. "You better quit that smoking, girl. You can't even blow out your own birthday candles."

She shook her head. "You are such a smartass." With her index finger, she scooped up a generous portion of vanilla icing off the top of the cake and dotted his nose with it. "There. How do you like that? Huh?" She stuck her tongue out at him.

He took her in his arms, and they kissed some more. Their noses touched, and she got icing on her nose, too.

After the party, they cleaned up the kitchen together. He washed the dishes, and she dried them.

"Did you enjoy your birthday?"

"Oh, it was my best ever. Best. Ever. Thank you."

"My pleasure. Literally, it was my pleasure." They laughed.

"You're a good kisser. And I loved it when you started licking my neck."

"That was total improv, by the way," he proudly announced.

"You know, we still aren't finished," she told him.

A confused look came over his face. "Come again."

"I'd like to."

It took him a moment to get her joke. He nervously folded his dish towel.

She turned serious. "Danny, a relationship is sort of an agreement between two people. Kind of like a contract almost. Are you following me so far?"

"Uh-huh."

"Okay. Well, every contract has to be signed before it can be finalized. You have to seal the deal. Do you know how you *seal the deal* in a relationship?"

He nodded. "I think so. I think I know what you're talking about."

"Which is?"

He shrugged his shoulders. "The birds and the bees, I guess. A little *hey-hey*, as we called it in the Army. You know, sex, or . . . whatever."

She giggled. "The birds and the bees, huh? You don't hear it called *the birds and the bees* much anymore. And I've never even heard the term *hey-hey*. But, yes, I'm talking about sex. How do you feel about that?"

He ran his hand through his hair. "Oh, brother. I don't know."

"Don't you want to be close to me? Sex is as close as two people can be. It's sort of like two people becoming one. That's why it's so special. And it changes the dynamic of the entire relationship. Do you want to be one with me, Danny?"

"I want to be one with you."

"And I want to be one with you," she told him with a warm smile.

"So, I guess we should go for it, huh?"

"I think so. But I want you to be good with it."

"What about the Church? What about God?"

"You and I are different when it comes to God. You're *religious*, whereas I'm *spiritual*."

"What's the difference?"

"The difference is that I don't really care what the Church would think. I only care about what God would think."

"And what would that be?"

"I think He understands. I think He loves you so much that He wants you to be happy. And that He's willing to let you go. So, you can love someone else. At least that's what I hope He's thinking. That's what I prayed for, anyway."

"That's what you prayed for?"

"Yes. Maybe that's why it's raining tonight."

"I don't follow you."

"Well, maybe the rain is God weeping down tears of joy. Maybe He's watching us the way we watch romance films on TV. Who knows, maybe we're God's own, personal *Romance Channel* movie."

"That's a real interesting take on it."

"So, what do you want to do? You tell me."

He stared at her but said nothing.

She set her dish towel down and took his hands in hers. "Please. We owe it to each other."

He cleared his voice. "You were telling me before that this can help heal. Is, is that really true?"

"Yes."

"Then I want to heal."

"I do, too. We can heal each other. Okay?"

He nodded and swallowed hard. "Yeah. Okay."

"I'll never hurt you, Danny. Never."

"I know. I trust you."

"Good. Trust is good."

He took a deep breath. "Yeah. Trust is good."

"But you're nervous, huh?" She brushed his hair with her hand.

"Yeah. I'd be lying if I said I wasn't."

"That's perfectly natural, too. But you don't need to be. It'll be fine. You'll see."

"Right. It'll be good."

She purred to him. "*So good*. It's what we both need. It really is."

"I know. I know it's what we both need."

"So, are you all-in on this? Because I need you to be all-in. I am."

"I'm all-in," he assured her.

"Okay, then. Listen, I'm going to go take a shower to get some of this sand off me. After that, we'll go to bed, okay?"

"Yeah. And I'm going to take a shower, too."

"You want to take one together?"

He shook his head. "No. I want the anticipation to build a little more. I don't want to see you naked until we're in the bedroom. See, when I was a kid, at Thanksgiving, I'd always eat the stuffing last because that was my favorite part of the meal. And I wanted to save it for as long as possible. So I could anticipate how good it was going to taste when I finally did eat it. This is kind of the same principle."

She placed her hands on her hips and, with mock indignation, told him, "Oh, so you're saying I'm like turkey stuffing?"

"Oh, no—no. I didn't mean for it to come out that way. Gosh, I'm sorry, Grace."

She smiled and shook her head. "I know what you meant, sweetie. I'm just teasing, that's all."

"Whew. For a second there, you had me going."

She put her arms around him and joked some more. She started with some bawdy talk. "Speaking of stuffing—are you going to stuff *me* tonight? Huh? You going to fill me up, are you? Make me feel fuller than Elvis at an all-you-can-eat buffet?"

He laughed and played along. "You told me that Momma wanted some sugar. Well, Papa just opened a candy factory, baby."

"Talk to me, boy. Talk to me."

"I'm going to give it to you good, girl. Real good. The Dan Man's got a plan."

She tee-heed. "Oh, *shit*. Listen to you talk. A little *cocky*, eh? Pun intended. I like it, though. I like that bedroom confidence—*I'm going to give it to you good, girl. Real good. The Dan Man's got a plan.* Yeah, babe—you tell me just how it's going to be. You Tarzan. Me Jane."

"I didn't want to come off as cocky. Honest, I didn't. I just want to please you. I'll do anything to please you, Grace. I'll even, you know, go *down south* on you." He raised his eyebrows, winked, and smiled.

She threw back her head and howled. "Oh, you will, will you?"

"Certainly, I will."

She nodded approvingly. "Okay, I'll take you up on that. I

like that as much as any other red-blooded American girl. And I can teach you how to do it right. Some guys do it — but they don't do it *right*. And if it's not done right, it can actually be quite unpleasant for the girl. You see, you have to be careful when you go *down south* because that southern region is really sensitive. If you're too rough, you can rile up the *south*. And when the south gets all riled up and pissed off and so forth, well — that can lead to a civil war."

"Well, we certainly don't need a civil war."

"That's why I'll teach you before we try it. I'll give you a little class on it. Sound good?"

"Yeah. That'll be good. I just want to make you happy, that's all. I want to satisfy you."

"Aw, you're so sweet. And while we're talking about the details of how we want this to happen, I was wondering — can I be on top? Would you mind that? I love being on top. It's my favorite position — always has been. Some girls like it doggie style. Some girls like the good old standby — missionary position. Me? I like it cowgirl — *yee-haw*. I'll ride you — and ride you hard. And I'll ride you all freaking night. And by the time I'm done with you, little buckaroo, you'll know that you've been ridden. Because this cowgirl will tame you, you wild mustang."

"Hmm. That sounds like a challenge. I'm up for it, too."

"You'd better be *up* for it. And you'd better be prepared to stay *up* all night."

"Oh, yeah, girl? Well, Marshall Dillon's in town. And he's not shooting blanks."

She laughed. "We're getting silly, aren't we?"

He laughed, too. "Yeah, we are. But it's kind of fun."

"I know, right? Sometimes, when you're with the right person — and you have to be with the right person — it's fun to just let go and talk a little dirty, right?"

"Yeah. It's fun."

She brushed his nose with the tip of her finger. "I adore you. I freaking adore you. You know that, don't you?"

"I adore *you.*"

"Here. Let's just hold one another for a minute or two, okay? Just hold me, all right?"

"Yeah. I'd like that."

They wrapped their arms around one another and she squeezed tight. His arms around her felt like a protective barrier—like a forcefield—that would insulate her from any harm. A wave of sensations and emotions washed over her. She got chills on her arms and butterflies in her stomach. A tear welled up in her eyes. *I feel loved. This moment, this very moment, is what life is all about. This is the feeling that everyone chases. Because for the first time in my life, I feel that a man really loves me.* "Oh, Danny boy. My Danny boy." She looked up at him with her honey-brown doe eyes. She sang the opening bars of *Danny Boy* to him.

He looked down at her and quietly asked, "This is what real romance is like, isn't it?"

"It is."

"I thought it was. But I've never had that, so I wasn't sure."

They again passionately kissed.

She sat in the living room and petted Tippy while he took his shower. He came down the stairs wearing a pair of black shorts and a gray t-shirt that said, *US Army* in black lettering.

She took her shower, washed her hair, and slipped on a black teddy. As she dried her hair in the bedroom, she felt the excitement building inside her. And she felt herself getting aroused by the anticipation. *It's really going to happen. All my hard work paid off. Tonight, I get my reward. He's mine. All mine. No more sharing him with the Roman Catholic Church. Grace 1, Pope 0.*

She put her hair up and wondered whether she should put on makeup. After pondering it for a moment, she decided to go with a minimalist look, just a little bit of eyeliner and mascara. *He likes a more natural look.*

When she got downstairs, he was sitting on the sofa in the living room with his laptop out.

He looked up at her and whistled a catcall. *"Woo,* Lord have mercy, girl. Is it hot in here, or is that just you? And I love that black teddy. The person who bought that had really good taste, huh?" He laughed and winked at her.

"Oh, Gawd. Do you want some wine to go with that cheese?"

"Your beauty is intoxicating enough." He grinned.

She rolled her eyes and shook her head. "So, are you ready to do this, dude? Or should I say — are you ready to do *me*?"

He nervously laughed. "Yeah. I just want to finish going through the rest of my emails."

"Kay." She sat down next to him and put her head on his shoulder.

He explained each piece of correspondence to her. "I see where *Home Depot* is having a big sale this week. They're calling it a *blowout sale.* I guess that's better than a regular sale. Let's see. They've got *big savings* on bags of mulch. And they're *slashing prices* on *John Deere* tractors, too. Ever ride a *John Deere?*"

"Nope. But I'm about to ride a Danny O'Connor." She giggled. He laughed but also turned red.

She just shook her head and told him, "You're too cute, you know that?"

He kept scanning his messages. "Oh, look at this one. I get these all the time. I'm almost tempted to order just to see if it's legit. *Upinsmoke.com.* They sell cartons of name-brand cigarettes via mail order. Real cheap prices, too. You can get an entire carton for, like, fifty bucks."

She shook her head. "No, delete that one. Delete — delete — delete. You don't want to get mixed up in that. You know where those cigarettes come from?"

"Where?"

"Russia. That shit comes from *Russia*. And it's illegal as hell. I once had a girlfriend who ordered from one of those sites. The cigarettes are counterfeit, and they taste terrible. It's like smoking rope. Plus, the ATF showed up at her door one day."

"Dang. I don't want the ATF at my door. I'd hate for them to find my moonshine still. I'll, ah, I'll just mark that one for deletion."

She laughed. "*Moonshine still*, huh?"

"That was a joke. I don't really have one."

"I know. Now, getting back on topic — this is why I worry about you. I mean, I know you're a smart guy and all. But you're book smart. You're not street smart. And you can be naïve. Too much of a Pollyanna. If I hadn't been here, you might have ordered that crap."

"Yeah — yeah — yeah. I know. I'm a rube. A rube from Mayberry."

"Maybe a little bit of a rube. But you're *my* rube." She leaned over and kissed him on the cheek.

He continued to scroll. There was a message from *Camp Bow Wow*, a doggie day camp business. "Hmm. *Camp Bow Wow*. I've been thinking about enrolling Tippy in this type of activity. I think she needs the company of other dogs during the day while I'm at work. But then again, I'd worry about her being in some stranger's care all day. I don't know. I guess I'll have to think on it."

She twiddled her thumbs. "Almost done, babe?"

"Ah-ha. Just two more. Now, here's one from a Nigerian prince. Says he's dying and wants to make me the sole heir of his substantial estate. But first, he needs my social security and bank account numbers so, upon his death, his lawyer can transfer the funds."

She looked at him with concern.

He burst out laughing. "It's a scam. I know it's a scam. I

know. I do. Come on. I'm not that much of a bumpkin. I'm going to delete it."

She shot him an agitated stare. "You shouldn't have even opened it. Just opening it probably put malware on your computer."

"I like to live dangerously."

"Uh-huh."

"Okay. Last one." She watched him scan the correspondence before he announced, "Oh. This one's from my old college chum, Clay Walton. Went to undergrad school with him at the University of Baltimore. We had an apartment together on Charles Street. Yeah, he became my roommate after they threw him out of his dorm for breeding *Midget Sharks* in the bathtub. They were little tiny devils, only about a foot long — a very, very rare breed of shark. But, you know, the powers that be weren't cool with it. Anyway, he has two tickets to the Orioles-Yankees game two weeks from tomorrow. Wants to know if I want to go."

She shook her head. "I don't like it. Sounds like a weirdo."

"Well, he's kind of okay. Not a bad guy, I guess. But I don't like hanging with him nowadays. He's really gotten into hunting over the last several years — big time. If I go to the ball game with him, I'm sure he'll be like — *only another six months until deer season.* He's always after me to go deer hunting with him. Has this place down near Crisfield where he likes to hunt. Every year he asks me to go. He calls me and says — *come on, Danny. Come deer hunting with me. It's great. You really connect with nature out there.* I just politely tell him — *thanks but no thanks.* I could never kill an animal, Grace. I don't even kill spiders. I just sweep them into the dustpan and take them outside. I know what it feels like to be *the hunted*. And it's not a good feeling. I would never want to inflict that feeling on another living thing. Not in the real world anyway."

"Tell him — *no.* Just say you have plans for that night. You don't need to be around someone who's going to dredge up bad memories. Or breeds *Midget Sharks* in bathtubs, for that matter. Tell him you can't go. You want me to reply for you? I'll be nice, I promise."

"No. I can do it. I'll do it tomorrow. I don't feel like coming up with a story right now."

"Okay. Fair enough." She paused, and thought for a moment before asking, "Danny, when you were overseas . . . did you ever . . . what I mean is, did you ever personally have to — you know? I mean — did you ever have to?"

"I guess you could say I did every single time I called in an airstrike or fire mission. But if you're talking about up close and personal — yes. Once. I fired an *AT4* rocket launcher at a Taliban vehicle. An old pickup truck that had a machine gun mounted on the rooftop — direct hit. There were four of them in that vehicle. There wasn't all that much left. They gave me four *certified kills.* LT gave me four Aces of Spades. That's the *death card.* Our calling card. And on the reverse side, the logo of the one-hundred-seventy-third was printed. They were customized playing cards, see? And we laid them on what was left of the bodies, with the emblem side up. So that when their buddies came along and found them, they'd know whose handiwork it was. We wanted them to know who did it. I might have killed more. You didn't always see the enemy. Sometimes you'd just shoot in their general direction. They'd do the same. Shooting, even if it was shooting blindly, gave you a sense that you had more control over the situation than you really did. Coping mechanism, I guess. Anyhow, maybe one of those times, I hit something. I'll never know. But I do know, for sure, those four."

"We're going to work on healing all of this stuff. Starting tonight. Okay?"

"Yeah. Okay. I'd like that, Grace."

She took his laptop from him and closed it. "Now, let's forget about cheap cigarettes from Eastern Europe and Doggie

Day Care—"

He interrupted and corrected her. "Doggie Day *Camp*."

"Sorry. Doggie Day *Camp*. Forget about Doggie Day Camp and dying princes and *blowout sales* on mulch and tractors. Okay?"

She rubbed his shoulders and noted, "You're tense. All tense. Just relax."

He snapped his fingers and pointed at her. "Oh, hey, I don't think I've shown you my coin collection yet. I just got some gorgeous Carson City Morgan Silver Dollars from the coin shop. They're worth, like, a lot of money, too. You want to see them?"

"Maybe tomorrow. But not now."

After a brief pause, he excitedly asked, "Say, did I ever tell you about the time I met the guy who played Lamont on *Sanford and Son?* Yeah, it's true. I did. He appeared last year at the Mid-Atlantic Nostalgia Convention in Baltimore. I got a picture and autograph. He even shook my hand and told me to *take it easy there, buddy*. That's exactly what he said — *take it easy there, buddy*. Just like that. His booth was right next to the one for the kid who played Urkel. I got his autograph, too."

"That's great. Just great. Hold on to those. I'm sure they'll be very valuable someday." She made a face.

After a few seconds, she told him, "I think you're stalling."

"Me? Stalling? No way, baby. Why would I stall?"

"Because you're nervous and scared."

"Well, you might be right about that. But just a little nervous and scared. Just a little."

"Okay. We'll say just a little. But you don't need to be. And once we get started, all your nerves will just melt away." She snapped her fingers. "Just like that. And the only thing that you'll feel is how deeply I care for you. That and a hell of a lot of physical pleasure. You believe me, don't you?"

"Yeah. It's just that this is so important. To you. To me. To us. That's why I'm nervous."

She got up off the sofa and held out her hand. "I'm going to be good to you. And you're going to be good to me. We're going to be good to each other. So, come on. Let's go. It's time. It's time to do this."

She took him by the hand and led him up the stairs. Once they got to the bedroom, she clapped on the light. *There's something very unsexy about clapping lights on and off.* She motioned towards the bed. "Go ahead and lie down for me, sweetie. On your back."

He lay flat on his back.

She climbed on top of him and placed her hand on his chest. "You're heart's racing like a freight train. Calm down, buddy. Remember, it's just Grace and Danny. That's all. Just Grace and Danny."

He fidgeted and moved his hips around.

"What are you doing?"

"I'm just trying to get comfortable. I need to find *the zone.*"

"Okay, but when we start, you'll need to be still. Very still. No fidgeting. You can't be a wiggle worm because I'm going to lower myself onto you, impale myself on you. And you don't want to be moving those hips while I'm doing that. Marshall Dillon could get hurt that way. It happens, believe it or not. This is actually the most dangerous sexual position for a man. I read in *Cosmopolitan* that nearly all penile fractures happen during cowgirl sex."

"Oh, dang. Penile fractures? That sounds extremely painful."

"Don't worry. As long as you give me a stationary target, it'll be fine. I'll go very slowly. You're going to feel a little pressure. But no pain. It'll feel so freaking good. Oh, and you'll hear the sounds of sex. Cowgirl sex has a sound all its own. You'll hear the sound of flesh pounding flesh. My flesh meeting your flesh. The harder I ride you, the louder it'll get.

It's such a sexy sound, babe. Seriously, you're going to love it. You're going to love the way I love you. Okay?"

"Yeah. Okay."

Next, she reached into her teddy and pulled out a folded piece of yellow legal paper from the top.

She unfolded it and held it up, explaining, "I had to put it in my boobs. There was no place else to put it."

"Gotcha," he said nervously.

"Before we start, I have something that I want to say to you," she told him.

"Something you want to say?"

"Yeah. Just humor me, okay?"

He nodded. "Yeah. Sure."

She cleared her voice and read from the paper. Her tiny hands trembled.

"Dearest Danny, well, tonight's our big night, isn't it? Tonight, I give myself to you – my whole self. I give to you – as a gift – not just my soul, but my body, too. I give to you everything I can possibly offer. And I take from you the gift of the Thorn Bird. For just as the Thorn Bird can only give the gift of its beautiful song once, the precious gift that you have to give can only be gifted once. And I'm honored that you're giving it to me. I know I don't deserve it."

She paused and looked up towards the ceiling, dabbed her eyes, and sniffled. Finally, she composed herself enough to continue.

"I know you haven't had an easy life. You've seen things that no one should ever have to see. And when you hurt, I hurt. I want to help you heal. I know I'm not perfect. I have lots of flaws. I curse, and I eavesdrop, and I'm probably too opinionated. Sometimes, I have a temper, too. And, yes, I can be bossy. I'm rough around the edges. I'm earthy. Too earthy, I know. And, no, I don't care for the hippies. Anyhow, I hope that my touch, my caress, can in some small

way, help you mend. I'm going to be very tender and gentle with you tonight, my love. You deserve that. Because you're the best guy I've ever known. God doesn't make them any better. Yours Always, Just Grace."

He had tears in his eyes. "That's the nicest thing anyone has ever said to me. May I have that paper? I'd like to keep it."

She sniffled. "Sure." She folded it up and handed it to him.

"Thank you." He reached over and placed it on the nightstand.

"You're welcome, baby. You know when I wrote that?"

"No. When?"

"Like, literally, a week after we met."

"Oh, God. Really?"

"Really. I knew. I knew the moment I laid eyes on you that first day inside of the church. Didn't you know, too?"

He nodded. "Yes. I suppose I did."

She wiped the tears from her eyes. "Oh, God. Here I am— trying to be all sexy and whatnot—and I'm bawling my eyes out like a little baby."

"Don't be ashamed of crying."

"I'm not. It's just that I don't want to cry right now."

He took her hand and held it. Then he interlocked their fingers and gently squeezed. "But it's a good thing when they're happy tears. So, let the tears flow. And let the love grow."

She started to cry harder. "Oh, God. *God.* Just stop it. Just hush." She held her thumb and forefinger close together. "I'm about this far away from an ugly cry. We'll never get through this if you keep saying sweet things to me."

"Sorry."

"It's okay. It's okay."

She took a deep breath, composed herself, and smiled down at him. "Okay. I'm good now. I'm good."

He reached up and took the hair clip out of her hair.

"You're better than just *good*."

She smiled down at him. "Look at you. Taking the initiative. That was good." She shook her head, and her hair fell down into her eyes. He brushed it to the side.

She dropped the straps of her teddy and pulled it over her head. Once she'd removed it, she tossed it to the floor. She was completely naked. He looked at her with big eyes, his mouth open.

She felt his erection underneath her. "God. I can't wait to get you inside of me. I feel you throbbing. I mean—I can literally *feel it*."

"You look very great tonight. And outstandingly beautiful. You know that?"

She laughed. "*Very great* and *outstandingly beautiful*, huh?"

"I guess I got a little tongue-tied—that kind of sounded awkward. My point is—you're gorgeous. The most gorgeous and the sexiest woman on the planet."

"So, you like my body?"

"I'm pretty sure you can tell that I do."

"Yeah, you're totally hard for me."

"Before we go any further, can I say something?"

"Say it, babe."

"Before I met you, I was lonely. Thank you for making me not lonely."

"Thank you for making *me* not lonely."

"This is going to heal, right? Because I need to heal."

"It's going to help heal, sweetie. I promise. It will help heal both of us."

"We're just Grace and Danny, right?"

"We're just Grace and Danny, honey," she repeated.

"Okay."

She whispered to him, "We're going to be angels to one another tonight. It's going to be just like *Some Have Entertained Angels* because God sent us to each other. As gifts for one another."

"Yeah. We're gifts to one another," he agreed.

He ran his hands along her legs, her smooth, silky legs, as she straddled him. "I love your legs. They're sexy as hell. Smooth, creamy. Oh my God. They feel so good."

"They're too short. And you're just saying that because I'm on top of you, getting ready to screw you."

"No, I'm not. Really, I'm not. I love your little set of wheels. I get a kick out of them, in fact. Get it? I get a *kick* out of your legs. I get a *kick* out of them."

She rolled her eyes. "Here we go with the cheese again. Not one of your better efforts, either."

"Seriously, I love them. I love everything about you. *Gorgeous woman.* Inside and out. I'm the luckiest guy on the planet. I mean that, Grace."

"Aw. And I'm the luckiest girl."

It got quiet.

She smiled down at him and whispered, "It's time, Danny. It's time. It's time for us to be angels to one another. Okay?"

He nodded. "Yeah. Okay. Let's do this."

She helped him get his shorts and shirt off. Then she rubbed his chest. "Here we go. I'm going to put you inside of me now. Don't be scared. And trust me. I'll never hurt you. Never."

He nodded.

She leaned forward, and her ample breasts pressed against his chest. He kneaded on them, gently squeezed them. A moan escaped her lips. They passionately kissed. Outside, the rain continued to fall. It was a steady but gentle soaking. They could hear the patter of rain on both the roof and windows.

When they momentarily stopped kissing, she again whispered to him, "Listen, Danny. Do you hear that? Do you hear the rain falling?"

"Yes. I hear it."

"Those are tears from Heaven. God's weeping down happy tears from Heaven for us."

They went back to kissing. As they did, she took hold of him and guided him inside her. "Oh, my God. That feels amazing. So tight. Like a velvety vice," he noted

And then they made love. And the tender rain kept falling all the while.

Chapter Twenty-Two: Harvey

Thursday morning. 2:00 AM. He held her. They were both awake. Tippy slept at the foot of the bed.

Grace rubbed his bare chest. "What did you think of that?" she asked.

"It was great. It was fun. It was passionate. Most of all, it was spiritual."

"Yes. That's what I say, too. Spiritual. At its best, lovemaking can be downright spiritual. You can actually sense God."

"Did I . . . did I do all right. I mean — did I satisfy you?"

She gently brushed his hair with her hand. "Most definitely. You're a good lover, especially for someone with no experience. I liked the fact that your odometer was at zero. You never picked up bad bedroom habits from other women. That means I can teach you how *I* like it. It's actually kind of thrilling to me. It's the ideal sexual scenario. I wouldn't trade places with any other woman in the world."

He nodded approvingly. "Wow. *Ideal,* huh? I'm glad you feel that way. I wanted to please you."

"And you did, babe." She held up her palm. "Here. Give me a high-five. That sex was high-five worthy." They laughed, and he gave her a high-five.

Tentatively, he asked, "How about my trip *down south?* Did that, ah, work out okay and all? I mean, did the *south* like my visit?"

She nodded her head emphatically. "Oh, yeah. Most definitely. You're welcome down in the *dirty south* anytime. Anytime." She giggled and winked at him. "Y'all come back now, ya hear?"

He chuckled. "I'm just glad that I didn't start any civil wars."

"I really like the fact that you're holding me now, too. That tells me a lot about you. You don't shy away from the post-sex cuddle session. And that's very important to us women. And it's a mandatory participation activity. For some guys, as soon as they come, they want to turn on *Sports Center* and just chill out. But I love the fact that my Danny Boy's a cuddle bear."

"I wouldn't have it any other way. How could anyone not want to cuddle after sex?"

"Do you like to go shopping?" she asked.

"What? Shopping? What does that have to do with anything?"

She repeated herself. "Do you like to go shopping? Simple question. Yes or no."

He shook his head. "Not really, no."

"Damn."

He laughed. "What are you talking about. I'm not following your train of thought."

"Well, it's like this — you're good looking, sweet, kind, generous, you put the damn seat down, you're a good lover, you regularly trim your finger and toenails, you don't send out dick pics, you take care of your appearance and dress nice, you don't put empty cartons back in the fridge, and you take off your socks when you have sex — oh, God. That's one of my pet peeves — men who leave their socks on. Orion did that. Men who leave their socks on during sex are freaking cavemen. Monsters even."

She continued. "Anyway, the only thing left is shopping. If you liked shopping, you would have gotten a perfect score. As it is, you would be highly sought after. You're basically a gay guy — only you're straight. You're a straight gay guy. Or would it be a gay straight guy?"

"I think they call it *metrosexual*," he offered.

"Whatever. Seriously, dude, you're like a freaking white tiger. You're on the endangered list. And that means poachers *will* be hunting your gorgeous ass—poachers like that Maria Gianelli. But I'm the game warden. And nobody hunts on my territory. You're not going to be anyone's trophy. Momma won't let that happen."

"Yeah. I wouldn't want my head hanging on the wall in someone's den or ski lodge."

She gleefully rubbed her hands together and announced, "Now—it's time for some pillow talk."

"Pillow talk?"

"Yeah. Pillow talk. That's a kind of post-sex activity. It comes after the cuddle session. Couples talk about things. Important things. There are no secrets during pillow talk, either. It's very important that you grasp the *No Secrets* concept. Important enough that we need to spend some time discussing it. So, as an example, let's say you have a friend. We'll even make him your best friend. And this friend tells you something in confidence. Let's give your friend a name. That'll make this little exercise more realistic. We'll call him *Harvey*. Let's say Harvey tells you that he won a thousand bucks on a lottery scratch-off. But he didn't tell his wife. Here. We'll give her a name, too. She's *Gladys*. So, we have Harvey and Gladys. You following me so far?"

He nodded. "Uh-huh."

She continued setting up the scenario. "Now, Harvey didn't want Gladys to know about his good fortune because he's selfish. He went out and bought himself a brand new set of golf clubs with that money. Even though his children are eating government cheese, and moths are eating away at all of Gladys' bras and panties. He tells you about buying the clubs with his winnings and swears you to secrecy. Well, during pillow talk, you'd not only have the right but the *obligation* to tell me about that because that's the rule that couples are bound by. They even have a name for it. They call it The Pillow Talk Rule. Still following me?"

He nodded. "Yeah. Sure."

"Good. So, I want us to roleplay this out a little bit, okay?"

"Roleplay? You want us to roleplay?"

"Sure. We're going to pretend that we're a married couple discussing this issue during a pillow talk session. And I want you to really emote, all right?"

"Emote? You want me to emote?"

"That's right. Emoting is important to good acting and roleplaying. When I did the guest appearance on that short-lived police drama, *Book 'Em Booker*—I played a battered wife who was also eight months pregnant—the director kept telling me—*Grace, you have to emote. You just have to.*"

"Well, I've never really emoted before. But I guess I could give it a try. I mean—if it's that important to you and all. I guess I could emote. I guess."

"Good. Thank you. And I don't expect an Academy Award winning performance or anything. Just do your best. You'll do fine."

"All right. I'll, ah, I'll do my best to emote. I do have one concern, however."

"Which is?"

"I just don't know how realistic this little scenario can be. I mean—the way you've painted him, I don't think I'd even be friends with this *Harvey* character."

"It's just a scenario, Danny. I mean—*damn*. It's not like I'm a witch who's going to say a spell and conjure him up, make him all real and whatnot. Plus, maybe you befriended him because you feel sorry for him. Or maybe you're trying to turn him around. Yeah—that's it. You're trying to put him on the straight and narrow. Be a good influence. That type of thing.

How's that? You like that better?"

"Yeah. I guess that's a little bit better. I'll ah . . . I'll just run with it."

"Yeah—yeah. Just run with it. So, I've laid out the scenario for you—we're in bed, we just had awesome sex. *Awe. Some.* We cuddled, and now, we're engaging in pillow talk. You know about Harvey's behavior. What are you going to do?"

"Well, I mean, Harvey swore me to secrecy and all."

"Right. But this is *pillow talk*. There are no secrets during pillow talk. That's the whole point of this exercise. You have to grasp that concept."

"So, I *have* to tell you about the thousand dollars and the golf clubs?"

"Absolutely. It's a basic, fundamental principle of couple-dom."

"Well, I'd tell you then. Yeah, I'd definitely tell you—no doubt about it. I mean—if that's the rule, that's the rule. So, here it goes." He cleared his voice. "Ah, say, babe, I just wanted to tell you that Harvey, well, Harvey—he won a thousand bucks on a scratch-off and bought a new set of golf clubs with it. And he hid that money from Gladys."

She reached over and patted him on the head. "Good. Good answer. That's exactly the answer that I was looking for."

"Now—question . . . do you know Gladys?"

"Yeah. Sure. She's *my* best friend."

"And are you going to tell her what I told you?"

She laughed. "Well, of course, I'm going to tell her, silly. She has every right to know that her husband's a self-centered asshole."

"But that means Harvey—my best friend—is going to get into trouble."

"He deserves it. He shouldn't have tried to hide money from his wife, especially when the family really needs that extra cash."

"Yeah, but now he's going to come at me and be, like, *hey, bro, I thought that was our little secret.* It'll put a major strain on our friendship. Might even wreck it."

"Sweetie, you don't need friends like Harvey. Let him go. You're better off with him out of your life. He's dragging you down. Face it, babe—Harvey's toxic."

"So, pillow talk cost me my best friend?"

They assumed their roles in earnest.

"It's a blessing, Danny. Gladys herself told me that the man's a total degenerate gambler and pisses their mortgage money away at the blackjack and craps tables. Plus, he likes to go to strip clubs and buy strippers hundred-dollar bottles of *champagne*, if you know what I mean. And you don't want to be mixed up with someone who frequents strip clubs—I know you don't. You're not a *strip club guy*. Strip club guys wear wife-beaters and lots of fake jewelry. They wear too much cologne, and for some reason, it's always some version of *Polo*. They don't take the tags off their clothing and wear their ballcaps turned around backward. They use money clips instead of wallets. Their pants droop down past their asses—looks ridiculous. They drive lowriders with wire rims and big woofers. Oh, and they have gold teeth, too. And speaking of teeth, Harvey's teeth are horrible. I hate it when he comes over here, tells one of his dirty, filthy jokes, and grins that shit-eating grin of his. Those hideous teeth! They're like little brown, baked beans in his mouth. Exhumed corpses have better teeth. God, he's so ugly that he could be a damn modern art masterpiece. Oh, and the way he gawks at my boobs! It creeps me out. And then there was that time we had him over for dinner. Remember that little fiasco? Hmm?"

Danny rolled his eyes and shook his head. "Oh, brother. Here we go. Again with the dinner story."

"*Yes.* Again with the dinner story. I went to a lot of trouble because you came to me at the last possible moment and told me — *hope you don't mind, babe, but I invited Harvey over for supper tonight.* And, naturally, Harvey's way too good to eat delivery pizza. Oh, no, no, no! Couldn't just order delivery. King Harvey had to have a fancy, homecooked meal. So, I made a real nice dinner. Took me all afternoon, but I did it. Sweated my ass off in that kitchen but, hey — what the hell? — it was for Harvey, right? Mister VIP himself. So, I made a Yankee pot roast with all the trimmings. And what did he do? He sat there at our table and passed gas the whole time. From the saying of the grace right up through dessert. And did he even bother to excuse himself? Hell no. He thought it was funny. *Here, pull my finger,* he said. *Was that you, Grace?* he said. *Don't nobody light a match,* he said. He made my home smell like the men's room at a damn truck stop. Oh, and then, he finally excused himself from the table to go to the bathroom. He was in there . . . like . . . forever. Long enough to read *War and Peace.* Twice. I knew he was up to something. So after he left, I went in, and what did I find? The first thing that hit me was the stench. The freaking stench. It smelled like death itself in there. And then I looked at the toilet. *Oh. My. God.* It was all clogged up. He splattered all over the seat. And, in the bowl, it looked like someone dumped a quart of motor oil down the john. It was just black — pitch black. And I'm not sure what the man ate, but when I mentioned it to Gladys, she promptly informed me that he tried to blame it on *my cooking.* Well, my food does not do that to people. My theory is that he had *Taco Bell* earlier in the day, and it was just starting to finally kick in on him. Oh, and who had to clean it up, huh? Did you clean up your friend's mess? Hell. No. You kicked up your feet, turned on *The Golf Channel,* and chilled. I'm the one who had to put the Hazmat suit on and clean up that filth. The man's a pig. I mean — Tippy has better potty habits than he does."

"Aw, come on, babe. Cut him some slack. He has *Crohn's.*

You know that. And it could have been worse. He could have pooped himself like he did when Tom and Helen Dittmeyer had him over to their place for Thai that one time. I saw Tom at the office watercooler the day after. He told me that the antique dining room chair that Harvey sat in that night had to be thrown out. It was *that* bad. But like I said—he has *Crohn's*, and I think even a touch of *IBD*. Maybe Gladys should diaper him before he goes out. And speaking of Gladys—she's no saint herself, you know. Harvey told me that she has a drinking problem. He said she goes through bottles of *Boone's Farm* the way Elizabeth Taylor went through husbands."

"Well, of course, she has a drinking problem. *Duh.* She's married to Harvey. That would drive any woman to drink."

"I think you're blowing things out of proportion just a little."

"Am not. I'm putting my foot down. He's not welcome here anymore. He's officially banned from this household."

"Wait a second—you're *banning* Harvey?"

She emphatically nodded. "I'm banning his ass."

"That seems a little drastic, babe. I mean—can't we just suspend him for two weeks? Kind of like a warning. And I'll have a talk with him about your concerns."

"The time for talk is over. I've tried to talk to the man—*Harvey, please don't light up those cheap, stinky cigars in my house. Harvey, please don't take food out of our fridge without asking first. Harvey, please don't take your shoes and socks off when you watch TV over here.*" She shuddered. "Oh, Jesus. I hate having to look at those long, razor-sharp, yellow toenails of his. And on top of that, he has those horrible hammertoes, too. It's what I imagine Dracula's feet must look like. It's disgusting."

"It's just that banning him is so final, babe."

"He should have been banned a long time ago. Like that time my cousin, Mary-Kate, came to stay with us for a few days when she was on her way down to Myrtle Beach for that conference. And Mary-Kate's a good Catholic girl, mind you. Graduated from Boston College, with a degree in social work. Summa Cum Laude, no less. Has an important administrative job with Catholic Charities. Goes to Mass every freaking Sunday. Says the Rosary every day. Hell, she's a freaking virgin, for God's sake. Saving herself for marriage. She doesn't even give her boyfriend blowjobs. She is a *good girl*. And *Harvey* was over. Supposedly, to watch some damn golf tournament with you. Does this ring a bell? Hmm? Because it should. Ah-ha, it really should. Mary-Kate and I walked into the living room with some snacks, and Harvey was sitting there watching porn on his phone. Porn. In my house. Just as nonchalant as he could have been, too. Didn't have a care in the world. *Oh, look at me, folks. I'm Harvey. I don't recognize or observe any social mores or taboos. I'm so freaking special that I can watch porn anytime I want, anywhere I want. Hell, I watch it in church sometimes.* He was looking at *TijuanaTwerkers.com.* I've never been so embarrassed in all my life. My cousin had to see that this is the kind of man who my husband pals around with. I was freaking *mortified.* I thought he was going to start jerking off right there in our living room. I really did."

"Listen, sweetie—I know that that wasn't too cool. It was a bad scene. It was. And I confronted him about it. I did. But it wasn't his fault. He got hacked. Russian hackers were controlling his phone. And they were typing in all those porn sites. He was the victim in this case. He doesn't even look at porn. Ever. That's what he told me anyway."

"Yeah. Right. You are so fucking naïve. Can I interest you in some oceanfront property in Arizona, too? And get this, mister—not only is he banned from our home—but I absolutely forbid you to hang out with him anymore. You need to sever all ties. Immediately." She feigned tears. "He's causing problems in our marriage, Danny. He is. He's a bad influence. And every time we fight, somehow, it always centers around him. It always seems to come down to Harvey. *Harvey.*

Harvey. Harvey. He's not worth our marriage, babe. And I don't care if he knows that I hate him. I really don't."

"He knows. He says you're a snob. And that you need to get off your *damn high horse.*"

"That snaggle toothed son of a bitch! I'll knee him in the balls if I ever see him again."

"Listen, we're not going to see eye-to-eye on this whole Harvey thing. I know the man has his problems, but I still say that he's not all bad. And making fun of his teeth is really hitting below the belt. He's very self-conscious about his teeth. But seeing how it's probably not worth getting into a big fight over my *imaginary* best friend and his slew of *imaginary* issues, let's move on, shall we? I'm officially breaking character now, and you should, too. At this point, I think we can both stop emoting. And . . . scene."

"Yeah. Okay. Scene. We can break character. That was good, babe. We really sounded like a married couple. I don't like the fact that you defended Harvey. We can work on that, though. But you did tell his secret. That's the most important thing." She smiled.

"Now, wait. Wait just a minute. Before we move on, I want to clarify something. The only reason I defended Harvey was because I thought that's what you wanted me to do — that that was my *role* in the exercise."

"Oh, no. No. That's not what I wanted. Ideally, you would have validated me. Don't you know about *validation?* Because that's another basic principle of coupledom."

He threw up his hands. "If I didn't know about pillow talk, what made you think that I'd know about validation?"

"Because validation is even more fundamental to a relationship than pillow talk. I guess I just figured you'd know."

"Well, I don't. I don't know anything about validation."

"Wow. You're even more clueless than I thought. You totally need remedial relationship classes. But that's okay.

There's plenty of time for that. I'll teach you. You'll be an expert in no time."

She caressed his cheek. "But, getting back to the principle of validation — you're supposed to validate — supposed to reinforce — my feelings, especially when I'm clearly in the right. So, in reference to Harvey, you should have chipped in with some of your own stories, which could have illustrated what a creep he is. For example, you could have chimed in about the time he borrowed a hundred bucks from you and never paid you back — that type of thing. And you should have been like — *yes, Grace, you're right. Now that we've talked it out, I can see your points. You've opened my eyes. I can now see that Harvey's no good for me. Thanks to your loving concern and guidance, I'm unfriending him, and my life will be better for it. And our marriage will be stronger for it.* And that would have validated me."

"Oh, shoot. I was supposed to say all that?"

"Uh-huh."

"I'm . . . I'm sorry. Next time, I'll know better."

"It's okay, honey. You did pretty good, all things considered. And, like I said, you did tell his secret. So you passed. You got the *gentleman's C* tonight for the pillow talk. Next time, you'll do much better. But don't feel bad because you got an *A* for the actual lovemaking. So, that still averages out to a *B*."

"I'm going to aim for the Dean's List."

She winked at him. "You'll get there, babe. With my help, you'll get there."

"So, ah, tell me, what else besides secrets gets talked about during pillow talk?"

"Momentous decisions are sometimes made."

"Really?"

"Yeah. Really. George Washington decided to start the American Revolution during a pillow talk session with Martha."

"Is that so?"

"Sure."

"Well, since I'm not contemplating starting a new country, what do you want to discuss?"

"For starters, I want to learn to play golf."

"Oh, yeah?"

"Yeah. I probably won't be good at it, mind you. But it's something that we could do together. That's all that's important."

"Right."

"Oh, and I was wondering — what's the real estate market like here?"

"Why?"

"I want to see about buying a house. Doesn't have to be a Beverly Hill-style mansion."

"Yeah, well, you're not going to find something like that here."

"I know. I do want something big, though. Something we can grow into. And something old. Something with character. I detest modernism when it comes to architecture. The older, the better."

"Is that right?"

"Uh-huh. And, I was thinking, maybe we should get another dog. I think it would be good for Tippy to have another dog to pal around with. We could pick one out at an animal shelter. I was actually on *Petfinder* yesterday afternoon, and there's a shelter in a place called Easton. Easton, Maryland. Where's that?"

"South of here. Probably about an hour and a half south of here. On the Eastern Shore."

"Okay, so not that far. Easily within driving distance. Anyway, they have this *adorable* little Min Pin named Shane. And that could be a good omen because wasn't there a famous Western called *Shane?*"

"Yeah. There was. I have it on DVD. Nineteen fifty-three.

Alan Ladd. One of the greatest Westerns of all-time."

"Yeah. So, maybe that's a sign. Maybe God's giving us a sign. I read his profile. He's a little older. Twelve. And he has epilepsy. Needs meds, like, every day. But we could do that. Easy. Oh, and he's missing some teeth, too. No biggie, though. When I was a little girl, I'd always bring home the ones that nobody else wanted. That was my thing. We had one dog with a heart condition, one with incontinence, and a cat who had hyperthyroidism. I think we should consider little Shane. He looked so scared and lonely in his profile photo. He needs out of that shelter."

"It's certainly something to think about. Maybe we can even take a run down there to see him sometime."

"Yeah. Definitely. Oh, and I want to tell you about my family."

"Sure. Tell me all about them."

"Well, like I said—I'm an only child. My dad and mom are David and Jennifer. Dave and Jen. My father sells cars, and my mother's an accountant. When I made it big, I gifted them more than enough for them to comfortably retire on. But they both say they want to work. So, what are you going to do? I can't make them quit working. They live at seven thirty-nine Mackinac Drive in Oyster Bay. Oh, and they have this huge black cat named Boris. That sucker has to be at least twenty pounds, probably more. He's very sweet but diabetic. He needs insulin sometimes. Fortunately, Mom's good at giving it."

"What are your folks like?"

"You'd like them. They're very devout Catholics. Go to Mass every Sunday. Mom says the Rosary. Dad serves on the Parish Council at Our Lady of Perpetual Sorrows. They've been to the Holy Land twice and even went to that one place . . . oh, what's it called? It's in Portugal. The place where the little kids saw the Virgin Mary."

"Fatima."

"Yeah. That's it. They've been to Fatima."

"Yeah, they definitely sound devout."

"Oh, and you and Dad have something in common. Before I was born, he was in the service, too. He never went to war, thank God. But he was in the Air Force for four years. He was a boom operator on a *KC-135*."

"Cool. The Air Force is a good outfit. And you have to be smart to even get into the Air Force."

"Yeah. They'd like you."

"You think? If they're as pious as you say, I'm not sure how they'd receive a Catholic priest who broke his vows. And did so with their daughter, no less."

"You're not still all hung up on that, are you?"

"I'm just stating the facts, that's all."

She dismissively waved her hand. "Whatever. Anyway, I was wanting to see my folks. To let them know I'm okay. Plus, I want you to meet them."

"Meet them?"

"Yeah. Sure. Meet them."

"But they live in Long Island."

"That's not that far. I'm guesstimating that it's no more than a three-hour drive."

"Probably closer to four."

"Okay. Fine. Four. Still, that's very doable for a day trip."

"What are you saying?"

"That I was hoping that tomorrow we could drive up there. Oh, and on the way back, maybe we could stop in Yonkers. My cousin, Mary Kathryn, lives there. Even though we're only cousins, we're very close on account of the fact that I never had any siblings."

"You want to stop to see your cousin, too?"

"Yeah. They're all worried sick about me, I'm sure."

"Grace, I can't just take off on the spur of the moment for

Long Island and Yonkers."

"Why not? Are you worried about leaving Tippy by herself all day? Because we can take her with us."

"No. It's not Tippy. It's just that tomorrow's a workday for me."

"Workday?"

"That's right."

"Aren't you resigning?"

"You mean resigning from the priesthood?"

"Yes. Of course. I thought we had that all worked out."

He stretched out his arms and yawned. "I don't recall us working anything out. And I haven't thought that far ahead."

"Well, you broke your vow of celibacy. You're tainted now. You have to quit. We made love. That's a game-changer, Danny. It totally changes everything. *Everything*. I always assumed that once we slept together, that you'd do the honorable thing and resign to be with me."

"Well, you know what they say about what happens when you *assume* things, don't you? When you *assume*, you make an *ass* out of *u* and *me*."

"But how can you continue to be a priest now that we've made love? How?"

"I . . . I don't know. They say that about fifty percent of all Roman Catholic priests break their vow of celibacy. In recent years, the Church seems to have adopted an unwritten and unofficial *don't ask, don't tell* policy."

"Are we supposed to sneak around? Keep everything on the down-low? Is that it? Because I won't do that. I won't tip-toe around like I'm someone's mistress. It's not right. It's just not. The mere thought of it sickens me."

"I'm just having a tough time with the reality of leaving the priesthood."

She shook her finger at him. "You made a choice. And we are our choices. Didn't some famous philosopher say that?"

"Sartre said it. Jean-Paul Sartre. He was a French Existentialist. He wrote novels and plays, and he thought that—"

She cut him off. "I don't give a flying fuck what he thought. The point is you were presented with a choice. You made a choice—end of story. You went all-in. Once you go all-in, you can't fold your hand."

"Just give me some time with this, okay?"

"Are you sorry we made love? Do you regret it?"

"No. Of course not. *Absolutely* not. These last several weeks with you have been wonderful. Idyllic even. I've never been happier. It's been the best time of my life. Literally. I don't regret anything we've done, including last night."

"So, what's the problem?"

"Being a priest is more than a job, Grace. It's a way of life. It's not like working at *McDonald's,* where you decide one day that you don't like it anymore and just go up to your boss and say *I quit.* The priesthood isn't like that. It's supposed to be a lifelong commitment."

"You feel guilty about last night?"

"No. I don't. It felt so right. Still does. I feel no guilt at all. And the fact that I feel no guilt is what's making me feel guilty."

"Are you going to resign or not."

"Yes . . . no . . . maybe. I don't know. I haven't gotten that far with it."

She wagged her finger at him. "You should have planned ahead—you know that? You should have planned ahead, pal."

"Let me make sure I understand you correctly. You want me to write a letter, today, no less, and send it off to the bishop of the diocese saying, in essence, that I met a woman and am hereby resigning from the priesthood. That's what you want?"

"Yes. That's exactly what I want. That's all I want. You do

that for me, and we'll be fine. Better than fine, in fact."

"That's all I want, she says. Aye yi yi."

"Danny, if it's money that you're worried about—don't. I told you that I'm worth three-hundred million. And I've invested my money wisely over the years. We'll never have to worry about finances, babe. And neither will our children. Or their children. Our family will be set for generations to come."

"It's not a money thing."

"What then?"

"It's just that this is a lot to take in."

"I gave myself to you. Don't you understand that? For a woman, that is so special. It's a precious gift. And you accepted what I offered. Gladly, you accepted it. No one held a gun to your head. We sealed the deal."

"I'm just trying to do right by both you and the Church, that's all."

"The only way to do that is to resign."

"I don't know. God, I don't know."

"Look at it this way—you used to live in the nation of Churchville. But as of last night, you moved across the border to a place called Graceland. And you're supposed to be in Graceland—not as a tourist—but as a permanent resident."

"Right now, I feel like a man without a country."

She got up and put on his terry cloth robe. "Oh, you have a country all right. Graceland is your country. But you're not loyal to it. You know what you are?"

"What's that?"

"A . . . a . . . a Benedict Arnold. You're a Benedict Arnold. That's what you are. A traitor!"

"Listen, I made a vow, a solemn vow, before Almighty God."

"You made a battlefield promise, Danny. You were young, and you were scared. You were half a world away, and people were trying to kill you. This is ridiculous. God understands these things."

"Does He?"

"*Yes.* Sometimes, I wonder if we believe in the same God. I think you see God as this kind of ultimate Catholic school teacher, with a little black book, giving people merits or demerits. I don't see Him that way. To me, He understands that we're only human."

"That doesn't mean He doesn't expect us to keep our promises to Him."

"And what about your promises to me? Huh? How about that?"

"I don't like ultimatums."

"*Ah-ha. Ah-ha.* Well, listen up, bub—I won't be used. I've been used by guys before. Never again."

"I just don't know if I'm ready to resign. There's so much finality in that."

"But there would be a new beginning. Don't you understand? Life is so damn hard. Alone, we don't have a chance. We're lost. But together, maybe—just maybe—we could have a life. This world is so *fucked-up*. It's fucked-up beyond repair. I don't know that even God Himself can save it. Maybe we have to save ourselves. Maybe that's it." She started to cry. "All I know is that there is something terribly wrong with a world where an eighteen-year-old kid dies half a world away before he even has a chance to get his own puppy. Alone, we're all lost souls. And the world will beat us down. But together, we can be happy. We can beat the world. Understand? Do you *get* what I'm saying?"

"Let me pray on it, okay? I need a sign from God. I need to know that He's willing to release me from our agreement. Everything hinges on that. I need to know that He's good with me leaving the priesthood. Can't you wait until He gives me a sign? Just be a little more patient? Please."

"No. I won't. I shouldn't have to. You knew what you were

doing. Now, either you can resign, or I'm out of here."

"God. This is insane." He paused and told her, "Look, I'll tell you what—I'll even stop seeing Harvey. How's that?" He laughed a nervous laugh.

"I guess my broken heart put you in a jovial mood, huh?"

"I'm just trying to break the tension, that's all."

"It's not the least bit funny."

"Oh, come on, Grace. This is ridiculous. It's nuts."

She yelled at him, "No! You come on. I thought you were different. I thought I could trust you, that you wouldn't disappoint me, that you wouldn't hurt me."

"I'm not trying to hurt you. I don't want to hurt you. You're the last person in the world that I'd want to hurt."

"Then resign. I'll help you write the letter. Danny, honey, write the letter and you can be free. Free of loneliness, free of fear. And we can live a beautiful life together."

"And what would I do?"

"I already told you—you can be the CEO of the *Benny Williams Foundation.*"

"Which, by the way, doesn't even exist."

"Not yet, it doesn't. But it will. I was totally serious when I talked about starting that. I have the money, and money does talk. One phone call to my lawyer and one to my accountant would get the ball rolling. It could be up and operational in about six months. You'd still be helping people."

"Yeah—yeah. I know."

"It's time to choose up sides, Danny. What's it going to be? Huh? Which team are you on? Are you on Team Grace or not?"

"I'm not ready to make this call right now. I think I should be able to play for both teams."

"You can't have it both ways. You made a choice. You made a commitment to me. And now, you're pulling back, and you're welching on it. That tells me that you don't want me. You never did. You just wanted to play house for a while."

"That's not true, and you know it. "

"What I know is that you're the biggest disappointment of my life. And I've had my fair share of disappointments."

"Calm down. Geez. We can work this out."

"Don't you patronize me."

He threw up his hands. "I'm not patronizing. Who's patronizing?"

"Jesus Christ! I can't believe I fell for you."

"I never knew things could get this complicated," he admitted.

"You didn't, huh?"

"No. I didn't. It's news to me."

"Well, here's some more news for you, mister — you're golf game sucks. You're stupid western outfits suck. Your silly magic tricks suck. You're dumb old coin collection sucks. *You suck!*"

"Now, come on. You've never even seen my coin collection." He laughed nervously.

She glared at him. "Again, I am not laughing. You're not funny. You're being a jerk by making light of this stuff. This is serious, Danny. As serious as it gets. To me, it is, anyway. I guess you never took our relationship as seriously as I did. Once again, the woman is the one with all the investment. And the woman's the one who gets burned. And all you do is make bad jokes about it."

"I'm sorry. That was another attempt to defuse the situation through humor."

"And a totally inappropriate one, at that. I put my *faith* in you. I gave my *heart* to you. I gave my *soul* to you. I gave my *body* to you. Well, you destroyed my faith. You broke my heart. And you ripped out my soul. How Christian is that? I hope you can live with yourself knowing that, padre."

"So, you're threatening to leave over this?"

"I will leave unless you resign. I'm nobody's whore. I *am*

not Marie Gianelli. Maybe that disappoints you. Maybe you secretly prefer those kinds of women. No messy entanglements. You just screw them and be done with them."

"Now you're just talking crazy talk, girl. You know me better than that. And you're the one who's obsessed with Marie Gianelli, not me. I haven't given her a second thought since that day she groped me over at her place."

"I think it's time for me to go. I've worn out my welcome here. This just isn't going to work out."

"Go? You don't have to go. I don't want you to go."

"Of course not. You've got a good deal. You figure you don't have to buy the cow because you're already getting the milk for free."

"That's not how I think, and you know it."

"What I know is that we had sex, and as far as I'm concerned, that's supposed to mean something."

"It *did* mean something. It meant everything."

"Obviously not enough. Because you've picked your career over me. What? Are you planning on running for Pope or something?"

"Now, you see, that comment right there shows how little you know. I'm an American. An American has never been Pope and never will be. It's, like, an unwritten rule."

"I don't want to argue this anymore. You are stressing me the hell out. I'll just get my things together and leave."

"And go where?"

"Back on tour."

"But you said you wanted out of show business. You said you wanted Mayberry. Remember?"

"I wanted love, Danny. I wanted to love and be loved. Just like every single person who has ever walked this planet. And I was crazy enough to think that I had found it with you. But you broke me. You fucking broke me. And, now, I just don't care anymore. I give up. I may as well go back to the only life that I know, even if I hate it. I don't think I'll ever be able to trust another guy ever again. Hope you're satisfied."

"Don't say stuff like that. You make me feel like a heel."

"Good. Because you are a heel. And I can't stand you. I can't fucking stand you! You make me sick!" She flipped him the double bird.

"Come on, Grace. I don't want you to leave. I can't stop you from leaving, but I don't want you to. Please stay. Give yourself time to cool down, at least. I mean — *damn*. How did things get so out of control so fast? Come on, Grace. You owe it to both of us to calm down so we can talk this out. Don't throw it all away so fast."

But she would have none of it.

She got dressed, picked up her purse, and headed for the door. She stopped and patted Tippy on the head. "I'm sorry I have to go, sweetie. You're such a good girl. I really thought that I might actually be your mommy one day. But your daddy doesn't want me."

"At least wait until morning. It's the middle of the damn night. Come on. In the morning, you might feel different. I don't want you to go, Grace. I don't. Please don't go. You're letting your temper get the best of you — yet again."

But she walked out the front door and slammed it. He followed her out.

He watched her back her *Mitsubishi* rental car out of the rectory garage. He walked over to the car, only wearing a pair of shorts. It was cold, probably no more than fifty degrees. But he didn't even feel it. His adrenalin was pumping.

She rolled down the window and called out, "I'll have my accountant send you your check for the expenses you incurred on my behalf. Matter of fact, I'll send you a check for twenty-five grand. How's that? That's a nice little profit margin for you, isn't it? That'll buy some new golf clubs, won't it? Now, *go to Hell!*" She flipped him off again. "Oh, and one more thing before I go—now I know why you and Harvey are such good friends. You all are two birds of a feather."

She peeled out of the driveway at a high rate of speed. The tires squealed.

And then she drove off.

As she did, he screamed at her, "I don't want your damn money! How many times do I have to say it? And I'm done with Harvey! He's the one who caused this problem. It's all his fault! We were doing just fine until he showed up at the party. Then everything went to hell. Screw him! Screw Harvey!"

CHAPTER TWENTY-THREE: WELCOME BACK TO SHOWBIZ, BABY

Two Days Later

Saturday. Grace sat in Kip Darby's office at *Starstruck Management LLC* in downtown Los Angeles. She was wearing jeans and a white t-shirt that read *I'm Just One Big Freaking Ray of Sunshine*.

Kip was seated at his expensive mahogany desk, directly across from her. He was in his 40s, overweight, and balding. What hair he had left was red, and his face was pockmarked. He wore expensive Italian suits, but the ties always hung down far too long. Grace thought the cologne he wore, some high-end French fragrance, smelled like a doctor's office. And he always wore way too much of it. It sometimes made her sneeze. He was a problem gambler who would bet on practically anything. Playing the ponies was his favorite. He was a regular at *Santa Anita*, but he also loved craps, blackjack, and roulette. Any game of chance, really. Despite the high six-figure salary that he made off of Grace's contract, he was in deep debt to the casinos. There was even speculation that he owed a sizeable amount to Tommy Gazzi, a Vegas loan shark. His other quirk was that he was severely asthmatic and had to take hits off an inhaler the way frat boys take hits off of a beer bong. Despite this, he was a chain smoker who regularly killed a pack of unfiltered *Camels* every day. On this particular afternoon, he read Grace the riot act.

"Listen, honey, I don't care where you were or what you were doing—none of my goddamn business. But the fact is that you dropped off the face of the earth for a month. A fucking month. You missed about twenty-five shows. You damaged your brand. Big time. And as I'm sure you know, there's all kinds of speculation about where you were. *Tattle Tales* is going to run with a story next week that you were on a month-long bender." He lit up a cigarette.

"I don't even drink. You know that," she replied indignantly.

"Oh, and that's not all. The TV show, *Hollywood Insider*, is saying Scientology has brainwashed you. And the *Star Gazer* website is reporting that you've been diagnosed with schizophrenia and have been in a mental hospital for the last month."

"None of that's true."

"It doesn't matter. People will believe it. That's why we have to act fast to rehabilitate your image. I personally don't care about the truth. All I care about is making sure that we all get paid. That's it. Now, the key is to get you back on tour as quickly as possible. And we have to be aggressive with it. The longer you stay out of the game, the tougher it'll be to recover. We have to prove to your public that your disappearance wasn't the result of some kind of breakdown."

"I don't care what *my public* thinks."

"You better start, kid, because you're losing money. Every day, you're losing money. I don't like losing money. Now, I think we should put out the narrative that you took a month off to care for your dad, who's recently been diagnosed with stage four lung cancer. People will understand that. When in doubt, always blame cancer. It's a guaranteed sympathy-getter."

"My dad's not sick. I just talked to him yesterday. That's a really fucked-up idea. You know that, Kip?"

"Talk to him again—get him on board with the story, honey. Tell him that your future success depends on him going along with it."

"I'm not going to do that. The only thing that's sick around here is your mind."

"You know my motto, honey—*whatever it takes*. And I mean that quite literally."

"Yeah. I'm well aware of that."

"Oh, and another thing—I talked to *Celebrity Centerfold Magazine*. And in case you don't know, that's a brand new nudie—or should I say—*gentlemen's* magazine that features female entertainers. They're aiming to get a lot of A-listers. And they want you to pose for them. Their premier issue hits the newsstand and internet in July. And they want you to have the honor of being the first gal to bare it all in their pages. How about that? They know that you taking your clothes off will cause their magazine to take off. Now, look—I already negotiated the deal. It's a great deal, a done deal. You'll make real good money on this. We all will. The shoot's going to be two days from now—on Monday—up at the *Celebrity Centerfold* building in the San Fernando Valley. Their facility has this brand new, state-of-the-art photography studio. It's gorgeous. You'll love it. I promise. Rehearsal will be in the morning that day. The shoot's scheduled for the afternoon. I just need you to sign the contract."

"I don't do nudity. You know that. Remember? Two years ago, I turned down *Playboy*."

"That was then. This is now. Circumstances are different. Back then, you didn't need *Playboy*, though I still think you should have done it, just gone for it. But now, you *do* need *Celebrity Centerfold*. You need something for the gossip rags to seize on and talk about. Something other than your unscheduled hiatus. This fits the bill. Not only that, but they're willing to pay a king's ransom for you. Plus, this is a brand new magazine. It's much bolder than *Playboy* or even *Penthouse*. It's edgy. It's exciting. It's happening. They're willing to push the limits, you know? Whereas *Playboy*, well, *Playboy's* just plain boring these days." He paused and stared at her. "Look, honey, you have a fantastic body and a beautiful face. Why not use it to your advantage? And everybody does nudity these days. Everybody. It's no big deal. It's not taboo like it used to be. Geez, freaking Debbie Gibson posed nude a while back. She was always little Miss Innocent. But even she took her clothes off for the camera when it benefited her career."

"I don't care what other people have done. I'm not comfortable taking my clothes off for the whole world to see. It's just not for me. And that's final."

"I can assure you—it'll be both classy and tasteful. Real artsy. I actually know the photographer a little. We have it all worked out. They're going to have you on this heart-shaped bed with red satin sheets. Very sexy. The bed's going to be covered with red rose petals, see? That was my idea. And you only have to show your tits and ass. No pink. We'll leave a little something to the imagination. That's where the rose petals come in. They're going to use them to cover your honeypot. Now, of course, if you *want* to show your honeypot, we can scrap the rose petals and you can just spread 'em—in which case, they'd be thrilled. If you'd be willing to do that, I could squeeze even more money out of them. It would also have a tremendous shock value. You might want to consider showing it all. It'd be really sexy," he told her as he flicked cigarette ash on his own desk.

"I'm not going to be showing *anything*. The shoot isn't going to happen."

"Yeah—yeah—yeah. We'll see about that." He thought for a moment, emphatically pointed at her from across his desk, and added, "You know what? You need to grow the fuck up. For Christ's sake, I'm just asking you to flash your tits and ass to the camera. I'm not asking you to do hardcore porn. Besides, they already put out the press release—*Grace Stevens To Bare All In The Pages Of Celebrity Centerfold*. So, we can't cancel now. It'll look bad."

She emphatically shook her head. "I'm not doing it. No way. Absolutely not."

"You'll do what I tell you to do. I am, after all, your manager. It's my job to *manage* you and your career. Don't be such a difficult bitch. After all, I *made* you. I plucked you from obscurity, from that little cesspool of a club in Schenectady. Everything you have, you owe to me. *Everything*."

She flipped him off. "Fuck you. I'm out of here." She got up and started to walk out of the office.

"Going to run away again? Is that it? Where are you going to go this time? You can get away with this shit once. But do it a second time and your career is over. Understand? *Over.* Then what are you going to do? Huh? Face it, Grace, you have nothing else. You don't know how to do anything except be a star."

She turned around. "I went to cosmetology school for a year before I made it big."

"Oh, excuse me. That's right—*cosmetology school*. A whole year of it, too, no less. Shit, you could probably get a job starting at, oh, I don't know, maybe thirty thousand dollars a year. And right from the get-go, too. Yeah, that's impressive, all right. Real fulfilling, too. You can spend the rest of your life dying grandma's hair blue-gray." He snapped his fingers. "But, oh, wait a second. You only went for one fucking year. You didn't even graduate, sweetheart. So, I guess you couldn't even do that, huh?" He pulled his inhaler out of his coat pocket and took two hits off of it.

She said nothing but sat back down.

Kip continued to detail his plan to rehabilitate her image.

"We're going to restart the *Amazing Grace* tour in two

weeks. Rehearsals begin tomorrow. And we're going to start right here in Los Angeles. That'll be your first show. Your comeback show. Very important to knock it out of the park with that performance. And we're going to do the backstage meet-and-greets for VIPs after the show. Five grand gets them backstage, a quick handshake with you, and one picture. Grace, we have to get you back into the public's good graces. Got it?"

She tentatively nodded.

"Now, we're looking at fifty-five shows over the course of fifty-seven days. You'll have two whole days off."

"It's too much. It's way too much," she protested.

He threw up his hands and smiled a sly smile. "Welcome back to showbiz, baby."

She changed the subject. "I want to talk about something else. I want to start a charitable foundation to benefit Gold Star families."

He shot her a confused look. "What the hell's a Gold Star family?"

"It's called *the honor that no one wants*. They're families who've lost a loved one in military service to the nation."

Kip nodded approvingly. "Yeah. That's good. Very good. Everyone loves it when celebrities get involved with shit like that. You'll get all kinds of kudos. After all, the public loves to *boo-hoo* over these stupid fools who go to the other side of the world just to die for people who don't even know how to speak English or use toilet paper. Hell, they pray to fucking goats over there, for Christ's sake. They think that a solar eclipse is the *moon eating the sun*. Ah, but I digress. We'll call it *The Grace Stevens Foundation*. See, now you're thinking. Stuff like this—this is how you get back on top. People are so sappy and sentimental. They eat this shit up."

"I don't want it named after me. I want to call it *The Benny Williams No Greater Love Foundation*."

"Who the hell's Benny Williams and how is he going to make our cash register ring? It only helps us if it's attributable to you. *You* have to get credit for it. Otherwise, it's a waste."

"To answer your question—Benny Williams is a hero, a real hero. Not a fake one. Look him up sometime. He won the Congressional Medal of Honor. You're not even one percent of the man that he was. The charity has to bear his name. People need to know who he was. I'm not doing this for PR. And one more thing, Kip—just because I'm sitting here listening to you doesn't mean that I respect you. You're a sleazy, slimy asshole. Danny would never let you talk to me this way."

"Danny? Who's Danny? First, we had Benny. Now, we have Danny. I'll bet they're both losers."

She pounded her fist on his desk, then shook her finger at him. "Okay. That's it. You know what? *You're! Fired!* I've been wanting to say those two words to you for a long time now."

He laughed. "Fired? We have a contract, pussycat. You're stuck with me for the next three years."

"Fine. I'll buy you out. What's your price?"

"You really want to know?"

"Yes. I'll pay anything."

"Fine. Eight mil. That's my price. I need eight million. Half of that would go to Tommy Gazzi because, you know, I owe him. And I just want to pay off the entire debt. Just get it off the books. Then, he'll let me start borrowing again. The other half would be to tide me over for a while. What do you say, Grace?" He took another puff from his inhaler.

"You're a fucking degenerate gambler, Kip! You've got it worse than Jordan. You know that? You owe Tommy Gazzi four million dollars? How does anyone get that deep in debt over gambling of all things?" She considered it for a moment. "But you know what? I don't care. Hell yeah, I'll pay the eight million to get you out of my hair. I can have my lawyer draw up the papers right away. You have a deal."

"Oh, there's just one other little thing that I want included in my severance package."

"What's that?"

"*Your body.*" He laughed an evil laugh.

"Beg your pardon?"

"I'll be blunt and crass about it. *I want to fuck you.* I've always wanted to fuck you. I've fucked a good many of my female clients over the years. At least the attractive ones. I consider it a perk of the job. You're one of the few that I haven't banged. Yet. Now, in my mind, I've already screwed you a thousand times. Give me the eight mil *and* that hot little body of yours for one night, and I'll be out of your life forever. Come on, make my fantasy come true, baby. Like I said before—I'm the one who made you into a superstar. How about showing a little gratitude?" He reached over and caressed her cheek.

She swatted his hand away and slapped him in the face. Hard. Hard enough to leave a red imprint of her little hand on his cheek. She screamed at him, "Go lick a dirty toilet seat, motherfucker! Because I wouldn't have sex with your ugly ass if the perpetuation of the human race depended on it. Literally."

He laughed. "Good. Good for you. You have standards. I respect that. But, if you don't want to play ball, or should I say, if you don't want to *play with my balls,* you better get used to having me around. Because I'm not going anywhere."

She cried, got up, walked out the door, and started walking down a hallway.

He followed her and walked down the corridor with her. "Don't forget—rehearsals start tomorrow at the *Staples Center.* Plus, you need to sign that contract for *Celebrity Centerfold,* pronto. And I'm going to have the publicist put out a statement on your *Twitter* feed that you had to take a sudden break to take care of your dad. Also—I see you dyed your hair blonde. It looks good, but your public is used to seeing you with brown hair. You need to go back to brown. Make sure you do it before the photo shoot. Oh, and one more thing — if you haven't had a Brazilian bikini wax lately, get that done before the shoot, too."

CHAPTER TWENTY-FOUR: MORE THAN A NAME ON A WALL

Grace arrived at the *Staples Center* the following day, Sunday, at 3 PM. She wore a pair of tight-fitting silver sequined pants and a matching top which showed her tight midriff. As she entered, flanked by Kip and her security detail, paparazzi took photos, and reporters shouted questions.

"Grace, how does it feel to be back performing again?"

"Grace, you put out a statement on *Twitter* to the effect that you took a break to take care of your sick father. We've been unable to confirm this. Are you sure that this is accurate?"

"Grace, do you have a drug problem? There are rumors that you're addicted to painkillers. Any comment?"

"Grace, there's a report that you've agreed to pose nude for *Celebrity Centerfold Magazine*. True? And, if true, why have you always shied away from nudity only to embrace it now?"

Kip stepped forward. "Folks — folks — folks. Grace is very happy to be rehearsing in preparation for her return to live performances. Her dad is holding his own, and we ask that you all keep him in your thoughts and prayers. I know I will. We have some press releases forthcoming that will answer all of your questions in detail. Now, if you'll excuse us, we have to get this show back on the road. Literally. And that means we've got to start rehearsing."

The rehearsal didn't go well. Her voice was flat. And, with the dance choreography, her timing was off.

Kip entered the dressing room afterward. Grace sat cross-legged on a black leather couch, drinking soda straight from the can. She had a new phone and was using it to listen to Rascal Flatts' *Mayberry*.

He shook his finger at her. "You'd better get your shit together, baby, because that kind of effort isn't going to cut it."

"My heart's not in this anymore."

"Where is your heart then? Huh?"

It's in the real-life Mayberry. "I don't know. But it's not here."

"Yeah, well, you were so rough this afternoon that we may have to have you lip-sync when the tour starts. That, and limit your dance routine."

"I don't lip-sync. And I don't respect performers who do. It's a rip-off. It's cheating the audience. I won't do it."

"Then you'd better find your A-game. And soon."

"Get out of here, Kip. Just get the fuck out."

He took a hit off his inhaler, lit up a *Camel,* and started to walk out, noting, "This goddamn asthma's getting worse every day."

Grace's Chief of Security, Cathy Wilton, entered. She wore a navy blue women's business pantsuit. Cathy was a kindly blonde in her mid-50s. There were still some traces of prettiness left on her face. After retiring young from her job as an FBI Special Agent, she'd gotten into the business of providing security to the rich and famous. Two years earlier, she'd dropped all of her other VIP clients to go to work full-time for Grace. And she was the only real friend that Grace had in her entourage.

Cathy passed Kip in the doorway as she entered. Sternly, she told him, "You can't smoke in here, Kip. You know that. You can't smoke in any building nowadays. It's not nineteen forty-three, for God's sake."

Kip turned back around, briefly reentered the room, and blew smoke in Cathy's face.

"Asshole," Cathy called him.

She sat down next to Grace on the couch.

"The first day back was kind of tough, huh?" Cathy asked.

"Yep. Real tough."

"You're just out of practice, that's all. You've been gone for a month. Just like anything else—you don't put a skill to use, and you start to get rusty. Tomorrow's rehearsal will be better. You'll see."

"I don't like this."

"Honey, nobody likes having a bad rehearsal. But it's not the end of the world."

"No. You don't understand. I don't like *this*. I don't like *this life*. I don't like show business anymore."

"Where were you when you disappeared? What happened? You can level with me. I won't say anything. That story about your dad being sick sounds like one of Kip's lies."

Grace nodded. "Yeah. It's a lie, all right."

"So, where were you?"

"Somewhere that's about as far from LA as you can get. And I fell in love."

"Really?"

"Really."

"That's wonderful. Congratulations. You know, Grace, you've never really had any luck in that area. Maybe this time, it's the real deal."

Grace closed her eyes and sighed. "Oh, it is. Or at least it was. But we had a big fight. And now, it's over. Done. Kaput. I doubt that I'll ever see him again."

"Aw, I'm sorry, honey. He was a good guy?"

"The best. He was the best I've ever had by far. But he just wouldn't put me first. And I won't play second fiddle to anyone, not even to God."

"To who? To *God*?"

Grace dismissively waved her hand. "Never mind. It's a long story."

Cathy nodded. "Must be."

"It hurts. It literally hurts. I get this queasy feeling in the pit of my stomach." She thought for a moment. "It's funny. I'm worth over three-hundred-million bucks. I could have anything. Anything except the one thing that I actually want."

Cathy looked Grace in the eye. "Listen, you've been honest with me. I'll be honest with you — get out, Grace. Get out of this business. It's eating you up. It almost always does. I've seen it more times than I'd care to remember. I've seen some very strong people destroyed by the demands of fame. Whitney Houston, Prince, George Michael. All of those people are dead. They're dead. And they all died young, way before their time. Don't be one of those stars that burn bright but only briefly. Get out. Let Kip find himself another meal ticket. Or better yet, just let him starve. Humanity would be better for it. You've got your money. You still have your sanity. And you still have your health. But, if you keep it up, you won't make it to forty, honey. That's my candid opinion. I don't mean any disrespect. I'm telling you as a friend."

"I know. No offense taken. It's just that I don't care anymore. I don't care enough to quit."

"You don't care anymore because of your guy trouble?"

Grace nodded. "Right. It has me down. Really down. More down than I can ever remember feeling in my life."

"Worse than when you found out Orion was cheating on you?"

"Yeah. That hurt, but not this bad. Not nearly this bad. In my heart of hearts, I think I always knew that Orion was a jerk. But with this latest one . . . well, he was everything I've always wanted. He was the real deal."

"Tell me about him."

"Oh, he was sweet and kind and gentle and decent. He was funny and adorably quirky, too. And in terms of looks — *ooh la la*! Baby blue eyes, black hair. Great smile, nice white teeth.

I swear—he looks like JFK Jr. A good lover, too. I mean—he doesn't have a lot of experience with women. His engine has low mileage, but that doesn't affect its performance, if you know what I mean." She giggled.

"Dang, woman. Sounds like you're describing the perfect man. What, specifically, was the trouble?"

"Like I said—he picked his job over me. Part of me thinks that I let my temper get the best of me when I stormed out. After all, I said some horrible things right before I left. I told him that I couldn't stand him, that he made me sick. *God.* I so regret saying that because now I'm lovesick. I *love* him. But another part of me thinks that I was right for taking a stand and forcing him to make a choice. I mean—I really do believe that I should come first, not second. I think every woman has a right to expect that from her man."

"It sounds like a tough situation all the way around, honey."

She threw up her hands. "I know. But it is what it is."

"Not for nothing—but what's his job?"

Grace took a deep breath and loudly exhaled. "His name's Danny, and he's a . . . a . . . a Roman Catholic priest."

"Oh, *shit.*"

"Seriously."

"That's a toughie."

"I know, right? Are you religious at all?"

"I used to be an atheist. But now I'm actually Catholic myself."

"Why'd you stop being an atheist?"

"Gave it up for Lent." They laughed.

"Seriously, though, I joined the Catholic Church about twenty-five years ago. I go to Mass every week, say the Rosary every day."

"Why? Why the complete turnabout?"

"I went to a girlfriend's wedding. She got married at this

Catholic church in Jersey. After the ceremony, I was taking some pictures around the alter. I looked up, and there was this statue of the Virgin Mary. And she was weeping. I saw it with my own eyes. God Almighty, she was weeping!" Cathy crossed herself.

"Oh, God. Really? I've heard about weeping Madonnas before. But I've never talked to anyone who's witnessed one."

"Yeah. I definitely saw one."

"Why do you think she was crying?"

"I don't know. I really don't. I just know that she was. Real tears, too. They tested them. I don't know. It's a mystery."

"Yeah. A mystery. I guess."

"Anyway, I guess it's tough for anyone to compete with God, huh."

"God won't keep him warm on a cold winter's night. And God won't hold him when he wakes up with flashbacks from his time in Afghanistan. He was in the Army."

"He saw combat over there?"

"Yes. A lot of combat. He's a hero, too. He won the Silver Star. And he was wounded in his left shoulder. But he has PTSD. Bad. Real bad. Horrible, in fact. Almost every night."

"Oh, God." Tears welled up in Cathy's eyes.

"What's wrong?"

"I never told you this, but I lost my nephew in Iraq. His name was Chris. Christopher Wayne Hill Jr. And he was a Marine. He died in two-thousand-three, at a place that nobody's ever heard of called Nasiriyah. I was *extremely* close to him since I never had any kids of my own. Me and Larry— we never made time for children. I was always too busy with my FBI career, and he was always too busy with his law practice. Anyway, when Chris died over there, part of me died with him."

"I don't know what to say, Cathy. I had no idea. And I have no words. So, I'll just say this—I am so very sorry."

Cathy dabbed her eyes with her fingers. "Thank you. He always wanted to be a Marine. As a little boy, he'd always say — *Aunt Cat, I want to be the best there is. I want to wear those Marine Corps dress blues. I want to be a man of honor.* Well, he *was* a man of honor, and we buried him in the most impeccable set of dress blues that you'd ever want to see. His name's on the wall, you know. There's a memorial wall for the Iraq and Afghan war dead in Chris's hometown, Irvine. He's on Panel F. I visited it. I saw it. I touched it. And it touched me back. Yes, it did. *My God, it did.* I got a rubbing of his name. I carry it with me, everywhere that I go. Here, I'll show you." She reached into her pocket and pulled out an aged piece of yellow-white paper, unfolded it, and held it up for Grace to see. Stapled to the sheet was a small, wallet-sized color photo of a good-looking young man wearing a set of Marine dress blues. It was a boot camp graduation photo. "See that?" Cathy asked. "The rubbing of his name and his boot camp picture." Cathy read the words from the sheet of paper aloud as her hands trembled. "*Christopher Wayne Hill, Jr, United States Marine Corps, Republic of Iraq.*" Cathy started to sob. She carefully refolded the paper and placed it back in her pocket. "It was like tracing a memory. But he's more than a name on a wall. So much more, Grace. Such a good boy. He wanted to do twenty years in the Marines, retire young, and start a second career. He said he was going to be a teacher. He wanted to eventually teach high school history. Because he had had teachers who inspired him, and he wanted to be that to other kids. In his last letter to me, he said that once he got back from Iraq, he was going to try to meet someone. He never had a serious girlfriend. And Chris wasn't one of these guys who wanted to screw anything wearing a skirt. He was sweet. He wanted to find true love — that special someone. And he never even had a chance to do that. I used to get angry with God over that. Sometimes . . . I still do. I mean — what kind of God would let a kid die like that, without ever knowing how it felt to be in love?" Cathy emphatically shook her head. "Not fair! And I can't help but wonder why pieces of shit like Kip Darby prosper while my nephew sleeps in the Garden of Stone at Arlington. But I still have faith. Faith that he's in a better place, a place where there is no war. Only peace. And every day, I pray that God will let him know that he's more than a name on some wall, you know?"

Grace started to cry. "Yeah. More than a name on a wall. I've heard that before. How old was your nephew?"

"Chris was nineteen. He had just turned nineteen. Now . . . he's nineteen forever."

"So young."

"War is a young man's game. What's the old saying — *war is old men talking and young men dying.*"

"Amen."

Cathy began to compose herself. "Anyway, it's something that you learn to live with, but you never get over it."

"I don't imagine you would. Not if you lived to be a hundred."

"I'm glad we're having this talk. I've always liked you, Grace. But I feel even closer to you now. We have something special in common. We've both been touched by war."

"Yeah. We sure have. You know, if I could take away all of his hurt and put in on myself, I would."

"You really love this guy, don't you?"

"I do. With all my heart. Is that wrong? To love a priest, that is. Tell me your honest opinion as a practicing Catholic."

"It's not wrong, sweetie. It's just a shame that the Church puts people in this position. The Pope could end this problem with one stroke of the pen. But don't hold your breath."

"I just think that love is love. How could God get angry over love? He couldn't. It's not God who has the hang-ups. It's humans. Maybe that's why Mary was weeping. Maybe she was crying because of the stupidity of humanity. Maybe she was thinking—*damn. I lost my only son over these idiots?"*

"Maybe that's it. Maybe you solved the mystery."

"But I haven't solved my problem. See, the thing is—I refuse to sneak around like he's married and I'm the other woman. And that's what it would feel like. That's what we'd have to do, sneak around. And I won't do that. Maybe I'm being conceited, but I think I deserve more than that. I want to be able to take walks on the beach and hold hands without worrying about who might see us, you know? Am I being unreasonable?"

Cathy shook her head. "No. Totally *not* unreasonable. You want a normal relationship. You're not *abnormal* for wanting to be *normal*. But I don't think you could ever have a normal relationship with a guy like this. Not unless he quits his job."

"I know. But I don't think he'll ever do that."

"Then move on. You could have any guy you want."

"But I want *this* one. I want Danny. I'm sitting here all worried about him. He's all by himself. Oh, he has a little dog, a Sheltie named Tippy. But that's it. And like I said, he has bad PTSD. He shouldn't be alone. Oh, God, he shouldn't. Maybe I should have been more patient with him. Maybe I demanded too much, too soon. Maybe, I let my temper get out of control. But I love him. I just love him. And I wanted him to love me back, that's all."

"I understand your feelings and concern, but he made a choice. And he managed to survive somehow before he met you. He'll probably be okay. Sometimes, you can't have what you want, sweetie."

"You don't have to tell me. I'm well aware."

"I'll pray for you, honey. I'll pray for you and Danny. Okay?"

"I tried praying for us. It didn't work. And I don't understand prayer anyway. If God already knows what we want and need, why do we have to pray for it? Huh? Ever thought of that?"

"Honestly, that's a fair question. I don't have the answer. All I know is that I saw a statue cry. So, I believe. If I hadn't seen that, I'd probably still be an atheist."

Grace nodded. "Yeah. Sometimes I think being an atheist is a lot easier than being a believer. You don't have to ask all these tough questions."

It was silent for a few seconds before Grace changed the subject. "Oh, did you hear the latest thing that Kip has lined up for me?"

"No. What's that?"

"He wants me to pose for *Celebrity Centerfold Magazine*. It's some brand new men's magazine. I'd never even heard of it before, but Kip says it's *bold* and *edgy*."

"Nude? He wants you to pose nude, I'll bet."

"Yeah. He says that I *only* have to show my tits and ass. But he thinks I should consider going all the way. Showing everything, including my *honeypot*, as he calls it. Because, of course, that's worth more money and would have more *shock value*."

"You're not going to do it, are you?"

"I don't want to. I've never done nudity before. I'm not comfortable with it. The whole idea weirds me out, even scares me. But the photo shoot is already set up. The press release is even out."

"It's not you, honey. It's not your style. At heart, you're an old-fashioned girl when it comes to stuff like this. Not only that, but I think posing in that kind of magazine is for desperate women."

"Well, according to Kip, I am desperate. And I'm definitely tired, just tired of fighting everything. It's easier to go with the flow. I'm so depressed that I just don't have the energy to argue it. I guess I don't care anymore."

"A word of advice—don't do something that you'll regret for the rest of your life. Once they take those pictures, that's it. They'll be all over the internet for all eternity. When you have kids, they'll eventually see them. Not only that, but just think—dirty old men will be jerking off to your photos. *Yuck.* That's just plain gross, right?" Cathy pretended to vomit.

"I know. I know. But like I said, I just don't care anymore. Besides, who knows if I'll ever have kids? I can't even find a guy. Kip Darby is the only man in my life at the moment. And I use the word *man* very loosely."

"Why don't you just fire Kip?"

"I tried. He has a contract. And you won't believe what he wants as a buyout."

"What's that?"

"Eight million bucks and . . . oh, God, I'm so embarrassed. I can't even say it."

"What? What else does he want?"

"He . . . he wants a night of . . . sex with me."

"Oh, *shit.* That can't be legal. That has to be some kind of crime, to bargain for sexual favors like that. You should report him."

"Yeah, but I have no proof. It would be my word against his. I'm just going to drop it. I told him that I'd never sleep with him. Ever. I think he got the message."

Cathy patted Grace's knee and got up, "Okay. If you say so, but I still think you should report him. I really do. Think about it. Because if he's propositioning you, he could be harassing other women, too."

She started to walk out of the room but stopped in the doorway. "Well, look, kiddo, I have to get going. I have to work on the security details for the tour. But I'll see you later, okay?"

Grace nodded. "Sure. Okay."

"And think about what I said. About not doing that photo

spread and getting out of this business altogether. Hell, I'm thinking about getting out."

"You are? Really?"

"Yeah. I'm tired of seeing my clients become prisoners of their own fame. I'm tired of all the tragic endings. If you've got even an ounce of humanity in you, it wears on you. And I absolutely hate LA."

"That makes two of us. I can't stand this town. But what would you do?"

"I still have my law enforcement credentials. I might go and find me a nice little small-town police department to join. Someplace where nothing ever really happens. Someplace where you can really get to know the people in the community. I'm originally from a tiny town in Iowa called Waterloo. Maybe I'll try to talk Larry into moving there. Small towns can be really nice places to settle down."

"Tell me about it."

Chapter Twenty-five: The Grace of God

Danny got home early on Sunday. After saying Mass, he'd taken Communion to the shut-ins and those in nursing homes, but he'd skipped his normal Sunday afternoon veteran's PTSD support group. He was tired and unmotivated.

He moped around the house, doing little chores along the way. The house seemed so quiet now, without Grace around. But reminders of her stay were everywhere. He'd find her clothes lying around. He found the book that he'd gotten for her. She never did finish it. The bookmark was still inside. *Wonder if she ever got to the part where the protagonists finally kissed?* The roses he ordered for her birthday were still wilting away in their vase. *I can't bring myself to get rid of any of this stuff.*

He finally settled in his bedroom, still wearing his black clerical shirt, black trousers, and Roman collar. He didn't feel like changing, didn't have the energy. Tippy lay at the foot of the bed while he sat in his black leather office chair and cleaned his golf clubs. After he cleaned his putter, he stopped and put the clubs aside. *What am I even doing? The hell with this. It's insignificant, meaningless.* He pulled out his wallet from his back pocket and took out the note Grace read to him before they'd made love. He read it again, and tears filled his eyes.

He talked to Tippy as his tears fell. "She's foul-mouthed — the language she uses would make my Army buddies blush. And too opinionated. And, naturally, *her* opinion is the only one that counts. She's prone to temper tantrums, especially when she doesn't get her way. She's bossy as hell. She has this weird, irrational obsession with hippies. She has a million flaws . . . but a million and one virtues. She's sensitive. Spiritual. And kind. She's kind, too. She looked out for me. Sometimes, she could be too protective. But I think that was only because . . . because . . . she loved me. I think she actually loved me. I think at one time she *did*. I swear — she has the sweetest soul of any woman I've ever known. She's a genuinely good person. Not to mention her looks. God, that woman is gorgeous. I love her, Tip. God, how I love her. I love her. And I can't do a damn thing about it. I made a promise to God, made a deal with Him. And that sucks. Right now, it sucks. It sucks to be me. But I'm never going to let this happen again. Never. It hurts too much. It's just like Afghanistan. You get close to people and then you lose them. And here's the kicker — I don't think God even cares. There. I said it. I don't think that He's all that concerned about my predicament." *God, have you forgotten about me?* He finally stopped crying and tried to shake it off. *Come on, man. Get a grip. It don't mean nothing. You hacked it in Afghanistan. You can hack this, too . . . can't you?*

He turned to his computer and went to Grace's official website. He read the various press releases. One stated she'd taken the sudden hiatus to care for her ill father. *Something her manager concocted as a cover story, no doubt. Grace would never lie like that, especially about her family.* There was another that announced the resumption of her tour in LA. *Hmm. Says that she's rehearsing at the Staples Center in preparation for her return to live performing. Good to know.* Finally, he read the one that announced her plans to pose nude for *Celebrity Centerfold* —

Grace is pleased to announce that she has reached an agreement with Celebrity Centerfold Magazine to pose for a revealing — but tasteful — pictorial that will be the publication's featured layout in its debut issue slated for release in July. The shoot will take place early next week, near Los Angeles. Grace looks forward to sharing more of herself with her fans and using this unique and exciting opportunity to push the envelope a bit. She relishes the chance to both explore and express her sexuality via the pages of an artistic publication like Celebrity Centerfold.

He was angry. Angry and jealous. He again talked to his dog. "Oh, *shit!* She's going to pose naked for some sleazy men's magazine. Can you believe that? *I hate that.* I hate the idea of other guys seeing things that only I should see. It pisses me off. I can't believe that she'd do that. That had to be someone else's idea. That just doesn't sound like Grace. Not even close. But what am I going to do? She's over twenty-five hundred miles away. Of course, it wouldn't matter if she was right next door."

He walked downstairs to get some dinner. There was a frozen pizza in the freezer. He got it out and was getting ready to cook it, but he changed his mind. *I'm not hungry. Food doesn't matter at a time like this. I'm trying to act like everything is normal. Like I'm okay. But things aren't normal, and I'm not okay.* He put the pizza back in the freezer, sat down on the living room sofa, and decided to embrace his misery. Tippy jumped up and sat next to him. He pulled out his phone, went to *YouTube,* and binged on sad songs. When Elvis's version of *Always On My Mind* played, he sang along. Tears again flowed. *This song hurts. Almost literally. She* is *always on my mind.*

After a half-hour, he put his phone away and again talked to Tippy. "You dogs are lucky. You don't have to deal with this stuff. Your life is a lot simpler. You eat. You drink. You poop. You pee. You sleep. You play. You do love, but not in a romantic way. And that's a good thing, too. Sometimes, I wish I could be more like you dogs."

At five o'clock, the doorbell rang. He loudly exhaled and

got up to answer it. Reverend Richard Mullins, the Methodist Church pastor, was standing there with a plastic bag in his hand and a somber look on his face. Reverend Mullins was in his 50s and wore a beard with a good bit of gray. Everyone said he looked like Kenny Rogers, so much so that that was his nickname around town.

"Hey, Reverend Mullins. How's it going?"

"May I come in for a few moments?"

"Yeah. Sure. Come on in."

Danny ushered him into the living room. Reverend Mullins sat on the sofa. Danny sat in the recliner.

"So, what's up? What's going on?" Danny asked.

Reverend Mullins took a deep breath and gave Danny a hard stare. "I'm afraid that I have some very bad news, Father O'Connor."

"Let's drop the formalities, Rich. Just call me Danny. Now, what's going on?"

"It's about Mike Jameson."

"What about him?"

"He passed away."

"*What?*"

"He died."

"When? How?"

"Early this afternoon. He was struck by a car on Main Street. They took him to the hospital. But he died about an hour and a half ago. I was with him when he passed."

The news took his breath away for a split second. A queasy feeling formed in the pit of his stomach. He felt almost as if he was outside of himself. "Oh my God. This is quite a shock, Rich. I was very fond of Mike."

"I know you were. That's one of the reasons I wanted to come over and tell you right away. He liked you very much. And he appreciated your kindness."

"It was truly my pleasure. Can you tell me, specifically,

what happened? How'd he get hit by a car?"

"That's the saddest part of it all. It didn't have to happen."

"What do you mean?"

"Well, I wasn't there, mind you. But the eyewitness reports say that he was preaching at the intersection of Main and Jethro Street when a group of four young men approached him. Early twenties or so. Outsiders, too. None of them were from North East. Evidently, they were on their way down to the river but stopped off in town to get some booze. They asked him what he was doing, and, naturally, he told them that he was Jesus Christ and was preaching The Good News. They started teasing him. One of them went to his car and brought out one of those paper crowns that *Burger King* gives to kids. They put it on his head and made fun of him—they told him—*look, it's Jesus Christ, The King of the Jews. Here, King—you need a crown.* They asked him to change their bottle of *Night Train Express* into *Dom Perignon*. Rubbish like that. Finally, they took his teddy bear, Max, away from him and threw him into the road. Mike didn't want Max to get run over because he's already in pretty rough shape. So, he ran out in front of traffic to grab the bear. And that's when he got hit by an SUV."

"*Good Lord.* I don't know what to say. I'm stunned. I'm at a loss for words right now, Rich. I'm sorry. So very sorry." Danny felt tears welling up in his eyes.

Reverend Mullins looked at Danny for a moment in silence. Finally, he added more to the story. "Everything about this story is messed-up, but do you know what's most messed-up about it?"

He shook his head.

"After Mike got struck and was lying in the middle of the road, basically dying, one of these assholes walked up to him and said, *he's Jesus Christ, but he can't even save himself. Come on, get up. Rise. How are you going to save the world if you can't even save yourself?* Reverend Mullins started to cry as he continued the story. "But Mike lay there and looked up at Heaven and said, *God, please forgive them. They don't know what they're doing.*"

Danny wiped tears away, shook his head in disgust, and told Reverend Mullins, "Never underestimate the cruelty and evil that lurks inside the human heart."

"Amen. Truer words have never been spoken. Unfortunately."

"Did the police arrest these SOBs?" Danny asked.

"Chief Hamilton responded to the scene and charged them with disturbing the peace and disorderly conduct. Plus, they had open containers, so they got cited for that, too. But they can't be charged with Mike's death. Legally speaking, they're not considered responsible."

"Sometimes, it seems like the law is on the side of the bad guys," Danny observed.

"I know. Tell me about it."

"What about his dog, Jake? Was Jake hurt?"

"No. Jake's safe and sound. I have him at my place."

"Good. That dog meant everything to him. Everything."

"I know. That's part of the reason I'm here. I was wondering if you might possibly be able to take Jake. That was Mike's desire. When I saw him in the hospital, as he lay dying, he told me that he wanted you to take care of Jake."

"Yes. Absolutely. I'll take Jake. I'll take good care of him. A very dear friend of mine recently told me that I should get a second dog to help keep Tippy company. But I didn't want to get a second one this way."

Reverend Mullins opened up the bag he was carrying and pulled out Mike's teddy bear. He presented it to Danny.

"He also wanted you to have this. Max. I'm not sure if Mike really comprehended that Max was just a teddy bear. He fussed over him like he was real. Always taping him up when his stuffing started to fall out. I told him that he should just get a new bear, but he said he couldn't do that to Max, that he couldn't turn his back on him and just discard him like trash."

Danny nodded. "Yup. That sounds like Mike, all right."

"Anyway, his memorial service is going to be at the Methodist Church on Friday morning at eleven. Do you think you can make it?"

"Sure. Definitely."

"The Church is picking up all the expenses since he didn't have any life insurance or savings. He only had seven bucks in his pocket when he died. That's all he had to his name. *Seven* dollars. So, we took care of everything in terms of costs."

"That's awfully kind of you."

"It's the least we can do. Oh, and the burial will be at the Methodist Cemetery, with full military honors, including a Marine Corps Honor Guard. I'm going to deliver the eulogy since he was living with me. But I was hoping that maybe you'd say a few words, too. He liked you very much, Danny. You were important to him. Extremely important, actually. He appreciated all you did for him and Jake. I know you helped with dog food and stuff like that."

"It was always my pleasure." Danny shook his head. "This tragedy just makes me sick. Almost literally. But I'd be honored to say a few words."

"Thank you. I appreciate that." Reverend Mullins paused and stared at him for several seconds. Finally, he said, "There is one more thing."

"Which is?"

"I think you should know that you were the last thing on Mike's mind before he left this world. Your name was the last word on his lips. Quite literally. He had a message for you."

"A message? For me? Really?"

"Yes, indeed. A message for *you*. A message for *little old Danny*, as he put it."

"*Little old Danny*? What was the message?"

"It was kind of cryptic. Very cryptic, in fact. He said he'd given you a gift, but you hadn't accepted it."

"But I did accept it. You see, he would drop off copies of that children's magazine, *The Little Shepherd*. I always took them. Okay—so maybe I didn't read the entire magazine cover-to-cover, but I did leaf through it. It's a nice little publication."

Reverend Mullins shook his head. "I don't think he was talking about some periodical. He told me that he'd given you the *Grace of God*—his exact words—so that you'd never be alone again. But he said that you hadn't accepted it yet. He was upset by that. Very upset, in fact. He said to tell you that he understands. That it's okay. You should accept his gift. And that you should accept it with great joy because it's a *good and perfect gift*—again, his exact words. He said that you would know what he meant by all of that. So there. I kept my word. I delivered the message. Take it for what it's worth. We all know that Mike wasn't all there. And that's putting it mildly. It's a shame that he never got the help he needed. I doubt his message means much to you, but I kept my promise to him. Even as he died, he was adamant that I had to tell you all of this right away. As in today." He paused for a moment, gave Danny a hard stare, and said, "I know that this is none of my business, and you can tell me as much—but does anything that I just told you make sense? Any sense at all?"

Danny stared at him in silence. For a good five seconds, it was just quiet as the two men looked at one another. Danny started to sweat and tremble.

Finally, Reverend Mullins asked, "Are you all right? You just turned white as a ghost."

Finally, he said, "Say, Rich, I have a favor to ask of you. Could you hold on to Jake for the next few days? And, if I give you a key, could you stop by and take care of Tippy for me?

Feed her and let her out to go potty and such?"

"Well, sure. I could do that. Are you going somewhere?"

"Yeah. I have to go to LA. And I have to go right away. Tonight. I have to go tonight. But I think I'll be back in time for Mike's service on Friday. At least I hope to be."

"LA? As in Los Angeles?"

"Yeah. Los Angeles."

"Again, none of my business—but why LA? And why on such short notice?"

"Because that's where the Grace of God is."

Chapter Twenty-six: Angel Eyes

He took the red-eye out of Baltimore/Washington International Airport to LAX. His flight landed at one o'clock in the morning, local time, on Monday. He took a cab to the *Residence Inn* on Olympic Boulevard and checked in. It was less than a half-mile from the *Staples Center*, where Grace's rehearsals were taking place.

When he left the previous night, he hadn't even bothered to change out of his clerical clothing. He still had his black clerical shirt, pants, and Roman collar on. He'd hastily packed a bag with toiletries and some fresh clothes. And he brought his laptop and his phone with him.

He'd never been to LA before. In fact, he'd only been to California once when he was in the Army. For training, he'd been to Fort Irwin in Barstow, California.

By three in the morning, he was trying to sleep. But it was pointless. His mind and his heart were racing. He wondered whether it was too late. All night, he stared at the ceiling and thought of Grace. And he prayed. He prayed that he'd be able to get to her. And that she'd still have him.

Finally, at ten o'clock in the morning, he fell asleep. For two hours, he slept. By noon, he was back up and in the shower. He shaved and sprayed on some *Green Irish Tweed*. He considered what clothes he should wear. After pondering it for a few minutes, he decided to wear his clerical clothing. He wasn't really sure why. It was just a gut feeling. He couldn't help but wonder if he was putting on his Roman collar for the last time. And if he was, that was okay. So long as he won back Grace's love.

He lay down in bed with his laptop sitting on his chest. He logged into his church email account and composed a short letter. It was to Bishop Kennedy, the head of his diocese and his immediate boss. It was an incredibly simple and, he thought, honest message. He skipped all the pleasantries and formalities—all the flowery language. He got right to the point—

Dear Bishop Kennedy,

I broke my vow of celibacy because I fell in love. And I can't live without her. I have to go all-in on this. I have to. Therefore, effective immediately, I resign from my position as pastor of Saint Mary's. I also resign from the priesthood itself. This decision is final and ir-revocable. I can send you a more formal, typewritten letter of resig-nation within the next few days. For now, I hope this will suffice. I'm sorry for any problems or embarrassment this may cause to you personally, the diocese, or the Roman Catholic Church itself. But I believe—no, I know—that God understands. And, in fact, that it is His Will for me to accept his Gift of Grace. The greatest gift He could have given to me. A good and perfect gift. One that I don't deserve but will accept with the greatest of joy. And treasure forever.

Sincerely,

Danny . . . Just Danny.

He looked at it, proofed it a few times. *He's not going to get the* Just Danny *thing. But it doesn't matter. God will. God will get it. That's all that matters anyway.* He positioned the cur-sor over *send* and clicked without hesitation. He felt relieved, glad that it was done. *She wanted me to go all-in. Well, this is all-in. This is the equivalent of an all-out frontal assault on an enemy stronghold. You're either going to break through and get the glory . . . or get massacred and people will talk about what a foolish charge it was, to begin with. I don't regret taking the chance, though. Because it's a chance on life's greatest reward and God's greatest Gift.*

By two in the afternoon, he was walking out the hotel's main door with a cup of black coffee that he'd gotten from a vending machine.

As he walked out into the southern California sunshine, he surveyed his new surroundings. The palm trees. The sky-scrapers. The traffic. The throngs of people on the sidewalk. The smog. *I'm sure as hell not in North East anymore.*

Since the *Staples Center* was so close to the hotel, he decided to walk over.

As he walked, he encountered some of the local flavor. There was a guy dressed as Batman casually strolling down the street. Then there was a Michael Jackson impersonator singing *Billie Jean* and moonwalking. A street performer did a ventriloquist bit. A man with dreadlocks and gold teeth was hawking fake Rolexes and Muslim oils. "What up, pimp?" he called to Danny as he walked by.

Danny nodded and casually waved. *Okay, but I'm not a pimp.*

Next, there was an old hippie/homeless man, decked out in tie-dye. But he also wore a vintage Marine Corps cover. The guy was holding a big boombox and loudly playing The Mike Curb Congregation's *Burning Bridges*. *How appropriate. I just burned a big one.* The hippie was a panhandler. He held up a homemade sign with his free hand, which read, *Vietnam Vet – USMC, Khe Sanh, '68. Just Hungry.* Danny pulled out his wallet and handed him a twenty. "God bless," the old hippie told him.

Danny nodded and replied, "God bless you, my friend. And thank you for your service."

Finally, he walked by a cute young woman standing on the street corner, fiddling with her cellphone. She was short, had shoulder-length black hair, and appeared to be in her mid-20s. The red hoodie she was wearing had a picture of a kitten on it. She wore tightfitting designer jeans and a pair of white *Gucci* sneakers that looked brand new. Around her neck hung a big, gaudy gold crucifix encrusted with diamonds. She made eye contact. He nodded and kept walking. She called back to him. "*Yo* – come back here, boy."

Danny looked back at her and pointed to himself. "Are you talking to *me*?"

"Most definitely. Now, get your cute little ass over here – yo."

He smiled, walked back towards her, but was careful not to get too close. "What can I do for you, ma'am?"

"It ain't what you can do for me. It's what I can do for you. And cut the *ma'am* shit. I ain't no *ma'am*. Don't be disrespectin' me like that. They call me The Wicked Witch of the West. Okay?"

"You're a witch?"

"Let's just say I have some potions for sale."

"Uh-huh. Say, I'm sorry if I dissed you. Didn't mean to. It's just that where I come from, calling a woman *ma'am* is actually a sign of respect, not disrespect. I learned that in the Army. Also learned how to make hospital corners in the Army. Yes, I did."

"It's all good, Bambi."

He threw up his hands. "So, what do you want to do for me?"

"A lot of things. But let's start with my business proposal."

"Business proposal?"

She looked him up and down. "That's right. You're perfect, too. That priest getup is wild. Way wild."

"Well, it's not a *getup*. And, what exactly would I be *perfect* for?" *She's got me curious.*

"A little road trip. How would you like to see this beautiful country of ours? Go coast-to-coast?"

"Say again?"

"I need you to take a package to Florida for me."

"Florida?"

"That's right. Deliver it to a Russian by the name of *The Fat Man*. Lives in Miami. I'll give you the address. Can you do that for me?"

"The Fat Man? I'm guessing there's a lot of fat men in Miami. I mean—when people retire, they tend to let themselves go a little and—"

She cut him off. "Yeah—yeah—yeah. Ain't his real name. It's his handle." She rolled her eyes. "Geez, dude."

"Oh, I see."

"Anyway, will you do it? I'll supply the car. A station wagon."

"Why me?" *Not that I'd ever do it, but I'm dying to know why she thinks I'm a good candidate.*

"Two reasons. One—the po-po would never in a million years suspect you. Pulling you over would be like pulling over Barry Manilow. And two—I have a special way that I'd like to pay you."

"Special way?"

She walked up close to him and grabbed his crotch, giggled, and noted, "Yeah. You're definitely a *mule,* all right."

He backed away. "I . . . I . . . I have to go. I'm looking for my girlfriend. I . . . I love my girlfriend."

"I won't tell. Or better yet—bring her to the party. I don't mind partying with chicks, too. But, seriously, babe—you just struck a match and lit my pilot light. Now, it's time to do some cooking. I'm into foreplay and shit, so we can start with a nice, long make-out sesh. I love to start off with a make-out sesh."

He nodded emphatically. "Right. Sure. Understandable. And, um, gee, thanks. Thanks for thinking of me. Very flattering. But, just the same, I think I'll pass on the whole deal. You know—the trip, The Fat Man, your payment. The pilot light.

The cooking. The make-out sesh. The whole nine yards." He turned and power-walked away.

She yelled out to him, "You don't even have to make the trip — yo. I'll just pay you and we'll pretend you made the trip. I only live two blocks from here. They say I look like the girl from *The Facts of Life*, you know — the tough one. What was her name? Jo. I think it was Jo — yo."

He stopped, turned around, and walked back to her. "Yeah. Jo. Jo Polniaczek. Played by the lovely Nancy McKeon. And you do look like her. And she was a major cutie. Had a huge crush on her back in the day, when I'd watch that show on cable, way back in the late nineties."

She continued to make her plea. "When I'm naked, you can even see my cute little freckles, just above my boobs. I'm serious. They're freaking adorable — yo. And my real name's Nicole. And . . . and . . . and *The Fault In Our Stars* makes me cry. *God*. That movie's so freaking sad. It rips your heart out, is what it does." She started crying. "And I'm just lonely as hell because it's tough being a woman in a profession dominated by men. Nobody respects me — yo. Maybe we can just get coffee. I think there might really be a spark there. I'm sorry I grabbed you. I'm just lonely. Don't go — yo. Don't go." She started with an ugly cry.

Tenderly, he took her hand and told her, "It would never work out." He pointed to her red hoodie and then to his own black clerical shirt. "We're reppin' different sets — yo. You're with the Bloods. And me? Well, I'm a dedicated, hardcore Crip." He closed his left hand into a fist, turned it sideways, and tapped his chest twice. "Thug life, *fo life*, yo."

She laughed through her tears. "That was a joke, wasn't it?"

"Yeah. It was. But what I'm about to say is serious — find yourself a better life, Nicole. You're better than this. And you'll never find any guy worth having when you're in the business of sending packages to The Fat Man. Understand?"

She nodded. "I want to go back to Kansas and become a veterinarian because I love animals."

He nodded approval. "Go back to Kansas and become a vet. Kansas is good. Very good, in fact."

She gave him a hard look, looked deep into those powder blue eyes of his for several seconds. Finally, she gasped and briefly covered her mouth with her hand. "You're . . . you're not even human, are you? *Oh, God.* You're not human. You're an angel. Those are angel eyes. I know they are. *Oh, Jesus.* I'm getting chill bumps—yo." She pulled her crucifix to her mouth, kissed it, and crossed herself.

"No. Listen, Nicole—I *am* human. Very human. *Too* human, in fact. But I do believe that there are angels among us. I think we can all be angels to one another."

She softly kissed him on the cheek. "Thank you," she told him. "Your girlfriend, whoever she is, is a lucky girl."

CHAPTER TWENTY-SEVEN: THANK YOU FOR YOUR SERVICE

By the time he arrived at the arena, he felt like he had run the gauntlet. Already, he hated LA. Now, there was only one problem. How would he get in? The *Staples Center* was a veritable fortress. Security was everywhere.

He decided the direct approach was best. He went to the main entrance and calmly walked up to the door. *Just act like you belong. Ninety percent of the battle is getting them to believe that you belong.*

As he pulled on the front door, he was met by a big, burly security guard. The guy looked to be in his early 20s, maybe twenty-two or twenty-three. He was taller than Danny by several inches. *Geez, he has to be at least six-six.* He was far more muscular and heavily tattooed. His most prominent pieces of body art were a tattoo of Jesus wearing the crown of thorns and one of the Marine Corps emblem—the eagle, globe, and anchor with the Marine motto, *Semper Fidelis*, etched below. The Jesus tattoo was on his left forearm, the Marine tattoo was on his right. His head was shaved. He wore a black t-shirt. In white lettering, it read *Grace Stevens Security*.

"Hi there. Good afternoon," Danny said with a casual smile as he pulled on the front door.

"You can't go in there, dude."

"I came to see Grace Stevens."

"Yeah. You and about fifty-thousand other people who I've turned away today."

"But I know Grace. I'm a good friend of hers. A very good friend."

"Right. I'm sure you are."

"No. Really, I am." He tugged on his Roman collar. "I'm her spiritual advisor."

"Uh-huh."

Danny pointed to the Jesus tattoo. "I like your ink, by the way. Isn't that the hip word for tattoo—*ink*?" He chuckled.

The guard said nothing, just stared at him with his arms folded.

Next, he pointed to the Marine Corps tat. "You were in the Marines, huh?"

The guard nodded. "That's right. The Marines."

"I actually tried to join the Marines. But they told me I scored too *high* on my ASVAB." Danny imitated a drum rim-shot and cymbal crash. "*Ba, dum, tss.*" He laughed a nervous laugh.

The guard flashed him a scowl.

"That was just a little military humor. I didn't mean anything by it. I have a million of them." He thought for a moment and asked, "Say, what do you call a Marine with an IQ of one-sixty?"

The guard just glared at him.

Finally, after a few seconds of awkward silence, Danny said, "Give up? Yeah, I guess you give up. Ah, anyway, a Marine with an IQ of one-hundred-sixty is known as a *platoon*. That would be a *platoon*."

Danny laughed and shook his head. "Seriously, though, it's all in good fun. The Marines are a good outfit. You know, I was actually in the service myself. So that kind of makes us bros, right? And bros help one another out, do special favors for each other, if you know what I mean." Danny winked at him.

"What branch, man? What branch were you in?"

"Army. Airborne. Afghanistan. Two-thousand-seven." He sang an Airborne running cadence for the guard. "*C-130 rollin' down the strip. Airborne Daddy gonna take a little trip. Stand up, hook up, shuffle to the door. Jump right out and count to four. And if my chute don't open wide. I have another one by my side. And if that chute don't open round. I'll be the first one on the ground.*" He smiled and nodded. "How about that, huh? That was our running cadence. Ran many a mile to that little ditty. Kind of catchy, huh?"

The guard chuckled. "*Sheeet.* Army. You know what Army stands for?"

"What's that?"

"Army—*A*in't *R*eady to be a *M*arine *Y*et."

Danny laughed and pointed at him. "Good one. I guess now we're even. Still, we are comrades-in-arms, right? I mean, we did play for the same team and all."

"Look, man, you're not going in. The rehearsal's closed to the public. Why would you think you had any chance at all of gaining access to this arena today?"

Danny grew impatient. He ignored the guard's question. Instead, he posed one of his own. "Listen up, Marine—have you ever been in The Shit? Hmm? I'm not talking about some damn live-fire exercise at Camp Pendleton. I'm talking about *The Shit.* When you're playing for keeps. When they're keeping score and whatnot. Have you ever been close enough to Mister T-Man himself that when he belched, you could tell what he'd had for dinner?"

The guard said nothing, just stared at Danny.

"I didn't think so. *I have.* Can't say I liked it much, either. It sucked. But I embraced the suck because it don't mean nothing. I hacked it. But I can't hack living without Grace. I'm not some crazed fan. I know her. I do. *I love her.* And I came all the way from Maryland to tell her that. I'm not lying to you, bro."

"Look, go save some souls, Father. Because you're wasting your time here."

"Listen, buddy—I traveled over twenty-five-hundred miles to be here today. I went coast-to-coast. And I am *not* leaving until I see Grace Stevens. Even if I only get to see her for ten seconds."

"Don't make me get physical with you, Father. I don't want to rough-up a priest. I have enough demerits on my account with God as it is."

"Don't we all. But, just the same, I'm going in." He pushed his way to the door and pulled on it. It was locked, so he started banging on it with his fist.

The guard got on his two-way radio and called for backup. "Vince to Mamma Bear."

A few seconds later, a female voice came over the radio. "Go for Mamma Bear."

The guard again talked into his radio. "Yeah, I have an unruly priest here at the main entrance. I need your assistance. He's getting very disagreeable. Not sure—but you might want to call the cops on him. You can make the call on that when you get here."

Again, a woman's voice came over the radio. "You have an unruly *what*?"

"A priest. An unruly, irate priest. I think he's some kind of nut case."

"Ten-four. I'm on my way to your location. Be there in a couple of minutes. Mamma Bear, out."

Danny continued to pull and pound on the door. He knew it was futile, but it was the only thing he could think to do. His mind was totally focused on gaining access to that building until he heard a female scream at him. "Hey! Hey! Hey! Stop that right now. *Right now.* Unless you want to go to jail."

Sweating bullets, he stopped pounding and looked at her. She was wearing an expensive cream-colored women's business pantsuit. On her hip, she wore her two-way radio on one side, and on the other side, a holstered 9mm pistol.

"Now that you've stopped acting like a child, we can have a civil conversation," the woman told him. "So, what's your issue?"

"I have to see Grace Stevens. Please. I have to see her. I'm not some obsessed fan. I know Grace. Very well, I know her. I have to see her. I just *have to.* That's all there is to it."

The woman scanned him from head to toe. "You look like JFK Jr. Anyone ever tell you that?"

"Yes. I get told that a lot, actually."

The woman turned to the security guard. "Vince, I'm going to take over this situation from here on. I'll handle all the paperwork, including the incident report. You won't have to do anything. Why don't you go ahead and go on break?"

"Are you sure you can handle this guy by yourself? He seems kind of unstable."

"Yes. I'm sure. Now — go."

Vince exited, leaving Danny and the woman alone together.

She began her interrogation.

"What's your name, hun?"

"Danny. Danny O'Connor."

"And you're a Catholic priest?"

"I was until this morning. I emailed my resignation to my bishop this morning."

"Were you ever in the military?"

"Yes. Army. Afghanistan.

"Were you wounded?"

"Yes."

"Where?"

"In the shoulder. The left shoulder."

"Why do you want to see Ms. Stevens?"

"To tell her that I love her. And that I want to be with her. And only her. Forever."

"Are you sure? I mean — are you *really* sure?"

"Yes."

"And you've resigned from the priesthood?"

"Yes. As of a few hours ago."

"Is that a final decision?"

"Yes."

"No chance whatsoever that you'd change your mind?"

"No. No chance. It's already done."

"My name's Cathy. Cathy Wilton. I'm the head of Grace's security detail. And she told me all about you."

Cathy extended her hand to Danny, and they shook.

"She did? She told you about me?"

"Yeah. We had a nice, long conversation about you, Danny. So, what changed your mind? Why did you resign from the priesthood? Grace told me that when she was still with you, you balked at that idea. She told me that she demanded that you resign for the sake of you all's relationship and that you wouldn't commit to it. So, what changed?"

"I was touched by the Grace of God."

"Yeah?"

"Yeah."

"Okay. Fair enough. I believe in miracles. I believe that God touches lives. After all, it's His universe. He can do whatever He pleases in it."

"Then can you help me? I just need, like, five minutes alone with her. That's all I ask for. Is she inside rehearsing?"

"No. She left about a half-hour ago. The building's still closed because they're breaking down her sound equipment. She went over to the *Celebrity Centerfold* building, up in the San Fernando Valley, to do that nude photo shoot."

"*Oh, God.* That's today?"

"Yep. It's today. And the area where they're shooting is a notorious hotspot for the porn industry. Seriously, they've filmed such classics as *Star Whores, King Dong,* and *Chitty Chitty Gangbang* up there. You know — real smut. That tells me that this rag is going to be pretty sleazy. I'm actually worried about it. The whole scene gives me a bad vibe, to be perfectly honest."

"Damnit! That makes my blood boil. It's not her. She wouldn't do that on her own. This had to be someone else's idea."

"It was Kip Darby's brainchild. He's her manager. And he's a piece of shit. It's all about the money and control. He doesn't care about what's best for her. I detest that man. And I would put nothing past him. And I mean *nothing*. Nada. He's a bad dude."

"Yeah. She told me all about this Kip character. *Damn*. I hate to see her do something that she'll regret for the rest of her life."

"That's exactly what I told her. Believe me, she doesn't want to do it. She just doesn't care anymore. You broke her heart. You know that, don't you? And, now, she's decided to let Kip steer the ship. The only problem is that the ship she's on is the *Titanic* and it's already hit the iceberg."

"Is there any way I could get over there to see her?"

"Are you positive—absolutely positive—that you love this girl?"

"I am."

"Okay then. I'm actually headed over there now. I can get you in. But after that, it's all on you, hun."

"Seriously? You'd do that for me?"

"Yeah. She loves you, Danny. I mean, that girl *really* loves you. Plus, I have a soft spot in my heart for military guys—a real soft spot for military guys. So, consider this favor my way of saying *thank you for your service*. Just don't hurt her. Don't you dare hurt her again. She can't take any more heartbreak. Grace likes to pretend that she's all rough and tumble, but the reality is that she's a fragile soul. She takes everything to heart. She gets hurt so easily and so deeply. And she's much better at taking up for others than she is at taking up for herself, you know? Minus her fame, she's just like the rest of us. She wants to love and be loved. That's all the woman wants. Seriously. And I don't know if you've ever been loved by a woman before—none of my business. But I can guarantee you that no woman ever has—or ever will—love you like this girl does. And if you don't claim that love, embrace it, and cherish it forever—well, you're a damn fool. Because she's a good one, a great one. But please don't play with her heart because she's not as strong as she pretends to be. So, just love her. Okay? Just love her. Deal?"

He smiled. "Okay. Deal. And, yes, I know how vulnerable she is. God bless you for helping me. I won't screw this up. I promise. I swear to God, I won't screw this up. You'll see."

She wagged her finger at him. "Now, look, when they grill you on how you got in, don't tell them that I let you in. Just tell them you got in through the door in the back that they use for deliveries."

He nodded. "Backdoor. Okay. Got it."

Cathy thought for a moment. "You know what? On second thought, when they ask you, tell them that I let you in. Yeah, go ahead and tell them. I don't care what they do. If Kip wants to fire me, he can. I'm taking a stand for what's right. I'm thinking of getting out of this line of work anyway." Cathy looked at her watch. "Okay, we have to get going. We're about a half-hour away from the Valley, and with this damn LA traffic, God knows how long it'll take us to get up there. If we're lucky, maybe we can catch her before she starts taking off her clothes."

CHAPTER TWENTY-EIGHT: GOODBYE YELLOW BRICK ROAD

Grace sat in her dressing room at the *Celebrity Centerfold* photography studio. She'd just had her makeup done. Lipstick, eyeliner, mascara, blush. The works. It was more makeup than she could ever remember wearing before. She didn't like it, thought it made her look cheap. Earlier, she'd had her hair done up and dyed brown, per Kip's orders. Her entire body had been freshly waxed, and her nails had just been done as well. She looked at herself in the mirror. She wore a very skimpy two-piece designer fire engine red bikini and a pair of red, four-inch spike heels. Her lipstick was red, as was her nail polish. So, red was the color of the day.

There was a knock on the door. It was Kip. "Hey, Grace, come on, babe. Time to go to work. The photographer's ready for you."

She looked down at her bikini top. The rim of a dark brown areola was visible on the left breast. She did her best to adjust the garment to cover herself. But the entire bikini was just way too small.

She put on a white satin robe that hung on the door hook and walked out of the dressing room and into the studio proper, nearly tripping on her heels. She could feel her breasts jiggle under the robe and looked down to verify that they hadn't popped out of her skimpy top. *Damn. I'm not used to heels this high.*

Kip clapped his hands and whistled a catcall. "You look

gorgeous, baby. Oh, this is going to be beautiful. *Bee-u-tee-ful,* I tell you."

She walked up to him and complained, "Um, Houston, we have a problem."

"And what's that, princess?"

"Well, it's just that the bikini is too small. The top is really tight. And the back is so thin that it looks like nothing more than a piece of dental floss going up my ass."

"Babe, what difference does it make? You're just going to be taking it all off anyway." He cackled, pulled out his inhaler, and took a puff. "Seriously, though, you look great. Sexier than you've ever looked in your life — and that's really saying something. I love it. This is the *new* Grace Stevens. You're going to shake up the world today, honey."

She shook her head. "Kip, I'm really starting to have reservations, and I don't think this is such a good —"

He laughed and interrupted. "*Reservations?* Listen, sweetie — reservations are for Indians, not for big stars like yourself. You have to be decisive. You signed the contract. Now, it's time to live up to your obligations."

"Yeah, I know, but like I was trying to tell you in your office the other day — my heart's not even in show business anymore." She looked around the studio and made a sweeping motion with her hand. "And it certainly isn't in . . . in . . . in *this* kind of thing."

"Princess, they don't need or want your heart. You can give your precious little heart to Jesus, for all I care. But, right now, that smokin' hot little body of yours belongs to *Celebrity Centerfold Magazine.* You're a big girl, and you signed up for this. And now that it's starting to get real — you want to bail. Well, it's not going to happen. You are *not* going to make a fool out of me. You read me, honey?"

She nodded and quietly responded, "Yeah. I read you. Loud and clear."

A few minutes later, a man walked in. He was in his 50s and tall. His gray hair was bound in a ponytail. And he wore a black silk shirt, which was unbuttoned to reveal a thick patch of silver fur-like chest hair. Several gold chains hung from his neck. And gold rings adorned his fingers.

Grace watched as he pulled a keyring from his pocket and locked the door from the inside.

The man walked up to Kip and shook hands with him. "Hey, what's up, Kip? How you doing, brother?"

As they shook, Kip looked around the studio and said, "I'm doin' all right, Tony, and it doesn't look like you're doin' too shabby, either, huh? Quite a gig you got for yourself here, right? I mean—am I right or am I right?"

"You're *right*. I'm *Celebrity Centerfold's* first-ever head photographer and pictorial editor. Nothing like getting paid to work around beautiful, naked women, right?"

Kip laughed. "I heard that. You still got that studio in Burbank?"

Tony nodded. "Oh, yeah, man. Most definitely. I still freelance. The name of my studio is *Tony's T and A Photography*. I tell all the girls when they first walk in that *T and A* stands for *talent* and *action*. But it really stands for *tits* and *asses*. They find that out soon enough."

Both Tony and Kip laughed evil laughs.

Grace shook her head in disgust.

Kip sat down on a white leather couch in the corner of the room, next to a watercooler. He took another hit from his inhaler and set it down on the seat of the couch, right next to him.

Kip casually asked Tony, "You got any coke up in this joint?"

"Um, yeah—matter of fact, I do. There's some in the little fridge, in the back room. But it's *Diet Coke*."

Kip laughed. "Well, of course, it is. Speed's a great appetite suppressant. I can lose twenty-five pounds when I go on one of my benders."

Tony laughed and told him, "Good one. I like your way of thinking. Yeah, the soda's in the fridge. And as for the other stuff . . . I have some in my desk." He paused and looked directly at Grace. "And who knows? Maybe when we're done, to celebrate the magazine's very first photo shoot, I'll put it out in a candy dish, and we can *all* partake." He winked at her.

I hope that was just a joke, but something tells me it wasn't.

Tony checked the settings on his camera and adjusted the lighting in the room. While he did, he and Kip made small talk.

"Another beautiful day up here in the Valley," Kip noted.

"Yep. Sure is," Tony replied as he continued to fiddle with his lights.

"Hey, Tony, how long you been doing this, man? Taking pictures of hot, naked women, that is? How many years?"

"Six."

"Six?"

"Six."

"Oh, I thought you had more experience than that. I'd think someone as old as you would have at least twenty or thirty years of experience in this stuff," Kip remarked.

"Nah, man. For a while, I was . . . I was . . . let's just say *away*. Okay? I was just *away*. Let's leave it at that. And no more questions."

Kip nodded. "Yeah. Right. No more questions. Sure, Tony. Didn't mean to touch on a sensitive subject or anything."

Tony shot him a dirty look and went back to checking his equipment.

Kip reached into his breast pocket, pulled out a *Camel,* and lit up.

Tony rebuked him. "Hey, man, you can't smoke in here."

Kip blew smoke out his nose. "Seriously? Can't I just finish this one? After all, these things are fucking expensive. Thirteen bucks a pack."

"No. Put it out, man. There's a cool mil in sophisticated equipment in here. And that equipment doesn't dig your nasty cigarette smoke."

Kip rolled his eyes but nonetheless got a cup of water from the watercooler and tossed the cigarette in it before sitting back down on the couch.

Tony smiled and nodded. "Thanks, bro. Now, if that had been some *Trainwreck*, I would have made an exception to the whole *no smoking* thing." Both men laughed.

Tony thought for a moment and turned serious. "You know, maybe I can call my candy man and get him to bring some *Trainwreck*—to go with the blow—for our little after-party. Pot and cocaine is an awesome combination. You can get really fucked-up off that wicked combo." Tony again looked directly at Grace, stared at her for a second, and smiled a devilish smile. "And when people get *fucked-up*, sometimes they just . . . *up and fuck*."

Tony and Kip laughed hysterically.

Grace, for her part, was getting more uncomfortable with each passing second.

Tony finished his equipment check and walked up to her. He took hold of her right hand, raised it to his mouth, and kissed it. "Hi, I'm Tony Tobias. And you're a fucking *goddess*. I'm going to be working with you this afternoon. And I'm going to make you look stunning. Okay? Not that you really need any help in that category." He chuckled. "Seriously, though, it's a pleasure to have you in the studio today. I'm a really big fan. My kids have all your albums. And my oldest, Paula, even saw you in concert, in Vegas, a few years back. We're going to have some fun today. And don't think of this as *porn*. It's not. I don't make *porn*. I make *art*. Okay?"

She looked him over for a few seconds. *Oh, geez. Cheesy. Very cheesy. And not in a cute, Danny-like way, either.*

Tony retrieved a clipboard from his desk and walked back over to her. "All right, angel. Before we start, I just have to ask a few questions. Okay?"

Graced nodded. "Yeah. Kay."

"What size are you, honey?"

She was confused. "Dress size? Shoes size?"

"Tit size. I have to know."

She hesitated but told him, "Thirty . . . thirty-four . . . double D."

He whistled. "Impressive." He wrote something down.

"Okay, now, moving right along—do you have any tattoos?"

"No. No tattoos."

He grinned a shit-eating grin and raised his eyebrows. "Not even a tramp stamp?"

Pointedly, she told him, "*No*. No tramp stamps."

"How about piercings? Got any?"

"My ears."

"Nah, I'm not talking about your ears, Pocahontas. I'm talking nipples and or genitals. Any of those?"

"No. Definitely not."

He frowned. "Aw, that's too bad. They're very, very sexy. You should consider having those done. Especially now that you're doing nude modeling and all."

"Well, this is just a one-time thing. I don't plan on ever posing nude again."

"Well, of course, it's a one-time thing. Still, you should consider having it done. Guys go wild for it. Your boyfriend will love it. And if you don't have a boyfriend, your fuck buddy will love it. And if you don't have a fuck buddy, the random strangers from the internet who you occasionally hookup with will love it." He laughed.

She ignored his lewd comment, cleared her voice, and asked, "Hey, Tony, why um . . . why did you lock the door?"

He smiled and pointed to her. "It's for *your* safety and security, sweetie. It's important that the set be quiet, safe, and secure while we're shooting. I'm the only one who has a key to this room. Even security doesn't have one. And that's all for you, darling. After all, you wouldn't want some pervert bursting in here during the shoot to get a cheap peek, would you?"

She tried to smile. "No. I definitely wouldn't want that. I guess that explains it . . . I guess. Thanks."

"You bet, honey. And if you have any other questions as we go along — please ask. I want you to be good with everything that goes on. I know you've never posed nude before, so I want to make you as comfortable as possible. If you embrace it, it can be very liberating."

Grace spoke up. "I do actually have another question." She pointed to Kip. "Does *he* have to be in here during the shoot? I'd really prefer if he wasn't."

Kip remained seated and matter-of-factly told her, "I have every right to be here, babe. It's in the contract." From the breast pocket of his *Armani* suit jacket, he pulled out several pieces of paper stapled together. He waved them in the air. "I refer you to section six, paragraph E, item number one of the contract. It clearly states that I'm entitled to be present at the shoot. If you'd read your goddamn paperwork, you'd have known that. You want to read it now? Before we start? So you can verify that I'm not shitting you?"

She waved him off. "No. No. Whatever. Let's just get on with it."

Kip told Tony, "Wait till you get a load of this girl's rack. Great tits! They're fuckin' amazing. All natural, too. No implants. The space between those tatas definitely ain't the Silicone Valley.

Tony nodded approvingly. "I know — I know. Thirty-four double D, for Christ's sake. I'm already drooling over here. I

344

can't wait to see them. It's going to be so groovy. And you know the policy of *Celebrity Centerfold* is to only showcase women with real breasts. And I'm the official Silicone Inspector. That means I have to personally verify that all of our models are natural before we begin the shoot. It should only take me a half-hour. *Per tit.* And sucking on them is the only foolproof way to tell if they're real."

Grace opened her mouth in shock and started to tremble.

After a few seconds of awkward silence, Tony burst out laughing. "What? I'm kidding, just kidding. Can't a guy kid around anymore? I mean, do we always have to be on our best behavior? Jesus, what's the world coming to? Grace, don't you worry your pretty little head over that comment. It was just a little studio humor. That's all." He lightly slapped his own wrist. "Bad, Tony. Bad, Tony."

He turned serious. "But all kidding aside—real tits are exactly what our readers are going to dig about this magazine. Big and natural is all the rage right now. Fake tits are a huge turnoff these days."

In her mind, she started making little jokes to help ease her fears and tensions. *What do you mean,* readers? *Nobody's going to read this magazine. You're going to have jerker-offers, not* readers.

Kip threw in his two cents worth. "Yep, guys love natural boobs. This spread's going to be so fucking hot."

Tony used Kip's comment as a segue. "Speaking of spread—is she going to spread her legs for us and show us that pretty little kitty of hers? And I am not talking about her pet cat." He again laughed at his own joke before composing himself. "Ah, I kill myself sometimes. I do. I really do. That was just more studio humor, Grace." He looked at her, smiled, and added, "I don't think cats are Grace's style anyway. I think dogs are her style. Yeah. That's it. I'll bet she's into *doggie style.*" He winked at her and laughed. Kip laughed, too. "Oh, shit. I am on a roll today," Tony declared.

Her heart raced. It felt like it was going to jump out of her chest. *I think he's only half-joking with all this sexual innuendo. Maybe not joking at all.*

Abruptly, he stopped laughing and asked, "Okay, seriously, is she going to show her pussy or not?"

Grace opened her mouth to speak, but Kip answered for her. "Oh, yeah. Definitely. She wants to show everything. Leave nothing to the imagination. This is the *New Grace Stevens*. She's not a little girl anymore. She's a woman. A wild, sexy woman."

Tony smiled. "Cool. I'm definitely down with that."

Grace finally spoke up. "Um, I am *not* going to show pink. Forget it. Not gunna happen."

Kip yelled at her, "You'll do whatever I tell you to do! Stop being so damn uppity!"

Tony intervened. "Hey, Kip, cool it. We'll play it by ear . . . okay?"

Tony looked at Grace and noted, "I think once she gets comfortable, Grace is going to *want* to spread em' for us. I don't think she'll even need to be talked into it." Tony winked at her.

She stuck her tongue out at him.

"Feisty little thing, aren't you?" Tony noted as he laughed at her.

He directed her to the bed. It was heart-shaped and had red satin sheets on it. He told her to stand next to it.

"All right, pussycat, let's start by losing the robe, okay?" He walked over to a sound system and turned on some music. The song that played was Roxette's *The Look*. "Just some mood music," he explained. "Some sexy mood music for our sexy lady. Because, you, my dear, most definitely have *The Look*." He positioned himself behind his camera.

Oh, God. Strip club music. He's playing strip club music. What a douchebag.

Grace spoke up over the music. "You know, this isn't such a good idea. I thought I could do it, but I just can't. It's not me. Not my style. I don't like this. This entire scene is kind of freaking me out, to be perfectly honest."

Tony stepped away from his camera and approached her. "Listen, Grace, I've photographed thousands of naked women in my career. *Thousands.* And the ones who make the best models are the ones who start out all shy and whatnot. The ones who are all like — *oh, but I could never take my clothes off for the camera* — those are the ones who turn out to be the best. Really. Those are the ones who almost literally set the pages on fire. You can do this. Be a big girl, huh?"

Grace nodded. "Yeah. Kay. I'll, ah, I'll be a big girl."

He walked back over to the camera and announced, "You know what? Let's start with something easy. Let's take a few pictures of you with the robe on. How's that sound? Easy, right?"

Grace nodded. "Kay. That's more comfortable for me."

Tony started snapping photos, complimenting her all the while. Each time he took a picture, the camera beeped, and a bright flash went off. "Hey, you're a natural at this. Really nice, Grace. Really nice. Fantabulous, baby. Now, give me that pouty look, angel. Pouty is sexy."

She put on her best pouty face.

Tony snapped away. "Great. Sexy. Very sexy. Now, make love to the camera, babe. The camera loves you. Love it back."

Seriously? Make love to the camera? This guy's a walking nineteen seventies porno flick. Why the hell am I even here? This is so wrong for me.

He took a couple more pictures, then directed her to take the robe off. "Just let it slide off your shoulder, okay?" Once she did, he started snapping away again. "That's it . . . beautiful. Just like that. Yeah — there you go! Let the robe fall to the floor now. That's right, just like that. *Ah. Ha.* Happy girl . . .

pretty girl. Big smile for the camera. Yeah. You've got the hang of this now, angel. You go, girl! Excellent. So freaking sexy. I am digging it."

She stood there in just her micro-bikini and heels.

Kip called out, "Damn. I'm getting a hard-on here. I can't wait for those tits to come out. I've been waiting almost ten years to see that rack." He winked at Tony.

Tony continued to direct. "Okay, Grace. I want you to lean forward so we can get a shot of your cleavage, just your cleavage. You don't have to remove your top yet. And I want you to give me a little bit of attitude, too. Like you're kind of pissed off. Pissed off but still sexy. That look that says *Damn. The guy from the gloryhole who I took home to screw is insisting on wearing a condom.* Yeah. *That* look is what we're going for here."

This guy has got to be the biggest pervert on the planet. Just get this over with so you can get out of here. She leaned forward, and her breasts almost sprung out of the bikini top. Tony took the pictures, telling her, "Oh, Jesus—you are so fucking hot. You are pure, raw sex, woman."

Kip again called out, "She has a body that's made for fucking. She really does."

Tony yelled at Kip, "Let me do the talking, man. Too many voices in the model's ear during the shoot isn't good. Okay? It's just not cool."

Kip put his hands up. "Sorry. I don't mean to be disruptive. I'll behave. I promise."

Tony spoke calmly and deliberately. "Okay, sweetie. What we've done so far is awesome. Really, really good stuff. But the camera wants to see a little more of you, okay?"

Grace said nothing but shyly nodded.

Tony continued. "So, first, we want to get some shots with your top off. So, I want you to go ahead and unhook the bikini top for me, okay? And then just hold it there. Don't drop it. Not just yet anyway."

She unhooked the top at the front and held it firmly against her chest.

He quickly snapped more pictures. "Great. Very nice. Are you sure you've never done this before? Because you're handling this like an old pro." He smiled and winked at her, but she just stood there silent.

"Okay. Now, I need you to let the top go. Just let it drop to the floor, okay? And once you do that, I want you to grab your nipples. Pull on them. Tug on them a little. Not too hard. Just enough to make the nipples pop. Big, erect nipples are very sexy. It's going to look really fucking hot. Hotter than the surface of the sun in July." *Yeah. Because I'm sure the surface of the sun is a lot hotter in July than it is in, say, October. God. It's like this guy's a caricature of himself. And he likes it that way.*

Grace just stood there, still holding the top firmly against her chest.

Tony called out from behind the camera. "Come on, honey. Drop the top so the camera can see your tits. We haven't got all day to do this."

Grace started to cry. "I can't do it. I just can't."

"Come on, now. No tears. Tears are not sexy, princess. We are not paying you for tears. We're paying you for tits, ass, and pussy. None of which you've shown yet. You can't stand there with an expression on your face that says — *my goldfish just died.* You need to be a happy girl. Happy that — of all the women in the world — *Celebrity Centerfold* picked *you* to be its first-ever centerfold girl. Now, that's a BFD. A. Big. Fucking. Deal. So, put on your big girl pants and get with it? Or should I say *take off* your big girl pants and get with it? Be a trooper. Be a professional. I'm a professional. I expect you to be one, too. Okay? Do you want a drink? Would a drink help you relax a little? I have some bourbon in the liquor cabinet. I even have this little white pill I could give you. It's like magic. I swear it is. It's guaranteed to make you feel *very relaxed.* And all of those silly inhibitions and hang-ups will just melt away.

A lot of the girls who I shoot like to take one before they pose nude. It liberates them. Allows them to freely explore and express their sexuality. Take just one of those tiny little white disks and the session will be over before you know it. And you'll be all done. Would you like one? I think it would help. I really do. How about if I grab one, or maybe even two, for you. Two might be even better. I mean — if one's good, two would have to be better, right? And I have a whole bottle of them right over in my desk." She could sense that Tony was becoming a bit frustrated.

"I don't use drugs," she said firmly.

"Well, of course, you don't, sweetie. I didn't mean to offend you. Just trying to make this thing as easy as possible. I like easy. Easy is always better than hard. Unless, of course, you're a cock. Then hard is better. In fact, the harder, the better. At least that's what *she said*." He again laughed at his own joke before explaining, "My humor's a little on the risqué side, I know. I hope you're not offended. I just enjoy kidding around with my models. Keep the mood light — that's what I say. I guess I have a silly side to me. I like to see people laugh. Laughter is a great way to deal with life, don't you agree?"

He paused for a moment, snapped his fingers, and made her an indecent proposal. "Hey — you know what? I just got a wild idea, a really wild, crazy, nutty idea. Let me lay it on you, Grace. I just kind of want to bounce it off you. See how you feel about it. I was thinking that maybe later after we finish with the photos, during our after-party, we could make a little movie. I have the ability to do that here in the studio, you know. I have some very sophisticated video equipment. The thing is — it's brand new, and I haven't had a chance to test it out yet. And I really need to test it. So, this would be a great chance to do that." He paused, looked over at Kip, winked at him, and continued. "Have you ever had two men at the same time before, angel? The French have a fancy word for it. They call it a *menage a trois*. Where I come from, which is Vegas, we just call it a threesome. Lots of fun. You could have two guys tending to your every sexual need and desire. It doesn't get much better than that . . . except, of course, during a gang-bang. And we could make a little movie of it for you to keep as a souvenir, just for you. We wouldn't sell the footage. Or upload it to the internet or anything sleazy like that. I promise we wouldn't." He held up three fingers. "Scout's honor. So, what do you say? Do you want to give it a try? If you don't like it after the first few minutes, we can stop. We can stop before any penetration takes place if you're not totally digging it. I promise. Now, on the other hand, if you *are* digging it, the building janitor, Clarence, is here today, cleaning toilets. He's seventy years old, bald, no teeth, and weighs four-hundred pounds. Naturally, a guy like that doesn't get much pussy. But, if you dig multiple men, maybe even Clare could get lucky today, huh? Hell, we could make you airtight." He cackled.

She was trembling but managed to shake her head and say, "Hell, no. You two are not running a train on me. No fucking way. I don't do that shit." She now knew that she was in the hands of two maniacs. She was even starting to fear for her physical safety. *Are these perverts going to try to drug and rape me? It's a legitimate question.* She started to pray. She prayed with all of her might. *Jesus Christ. Our Lady. Somebody. Anybody. Please! Please help me. Get me out of here!*

Tony tried to calm her down. "Okay — okay. No threesome for Grace. The threesome's out. Forget that I even mentioned it. A lot of women enjoy taking on two guys at once, but if it's not your cup of tea, hey, so be it. Different strokes for different folks, that's what I say. I don't pressure anyone into anything that they don't want to do. And I hope my suggestion didn't hurt your feelings or make you nervous. That wasn't my intention. But, hey, you can't blame two horny old guys for trying, can you? After all, it ain't illegal to ask." He chuckled as he fiddled with his camera lens. "Now, are you sure you don't want something to take the edge off? Who knows? Maybe if you loosen up, you'll feel more adventurous. Less repressed. Maybe we could even revisit the idea of the threesome at that point. What do you say? Just a couple of little white pills. You can't get addicted or die by taking just a couple. All you have to do is put them in your mouth and swallow. And I'll bet that you like to *swallow*. Yep, I'd bet my bottom dollar that you're a swallower." Tony and Kip both laughed hysterically.

Kip chimed in, "Oh, yeah. She'd swallow all right. She'd swallow it all. The entire load. Good to the last drop, huh, Grace?"

She shook her finger at them. "I told you, I don't do drugs. I don't even drink. And I will never, ever fuck either one of you, let alone both of you. So, just get that out of your demented minds, okay? You guys are a couple of sickos, is what you are."

Tony threw his hands up. "Fine. No pills and no booze. And you don't have to imply that I'm some kind of pervert. I'm just sexually adventurous and liberated. I don't have hang-ups about sex. It seems like you do. It's kind of sad because, with a body like yours, you could be having a lot of fun. But that's up to you . . . hey, let's just get off this whole topic. I asked about the threesome. You said *no*. And I respect your decision. I won't bring it up again. Okay? But we really do need to get these photos done. We're paying you a hell of a lot of money for this session, and so far, we've got a whole lot of nothing. Nada. I really need you to start cooperating. Understand?"

She sniffled, wiped away a tear, and nodded. "Yeah. I understand. I got you."

"Wonderful. I think we're getting somewhere. Now, Grace—show me your tits, honey. Please and pretty please. The camera will really dig them. They're gorgeous, even when they're covered, but they need to breathe a little. Sometimes, it's good to just let the puppies run free. You know what I mean? So, let's do this now." He clapped his hands together. "Come on now, Grace. *Gracie*. Can I call you Gracie? Anyone ever call you Gracie?"

She shrugged. "Well, my dad used to call me Gracie. I . . . I guess you can call me Gracie if you want. I guess." *This just keeps getting weirder.*

"You know, there was a famous Gracie. Gracie Allen, George Burns's wife. They had a routine where George would say, *say goodnight, Gracie*. And Gracie would say, *goodnight, Gracie*." He chuckled. "Funny stuff, right? But you wouldn't remember that. I do, but you wouldn't. You're *way* too young. How old are you again, sweetie? No. Wait. Let's test the old man's memory. I saw your age listed on the model's release. You're . . . twenty-seven. Twenty-seven, right?"

"I just turned twenty-eight."

"Wow. Twenty-eight. That's a wonderful age. What I wouldn't give to be twenty-eight again. Hell, I'd sell my soul to the Devil to be twenty-eight again. Oh, wait. I already *have* sold my soul to the Devil, so he'd let me have this cool job taking pictures of naked women. But enough about my dabbling into Satanism. You're in your prime, woman. Your sexual prime. Bet you want it all the time, huh? And I'll bet you get it all the time, too. A beautiful woman like you and all. Me? I'm fifty-six. Yes, ma'am, fifty-six. I'm an old man. Some might say a dirty old man even." He laughed. "But, hey, don't you know that I can still get it up? At a moment's notice, I can get it up. No problem. Don't even need *Viagra*. It's true. Hell, seeing your hot little body today might even get me up. That sometimes happens. I shit you not. I sometimes get hard-ons when I take pictures of hot women." He winked at Kip. "But I digress. Any-who, I'll call you Gracie. Because I'm very informal and I want you to be as relaxed as possible. Now, let's make some magic happen. Cool?"

She shrugged. "Yeah. I guess it's cool. It's just that . . . well, I honestly think that I'm not going to be good at this. Maybe you should think about getting someone else for your magazine's first issue."

Tony raised his voice. "Hey—hey—hey! Now, don't you even *think* of quitting on me, angel. We have a signed contract with your name on it. And we'll insist on *specific performance*. That's a legal term. It means you have to deliver the exact service that you've been contracted to provide. Nothing less will suffice. Nothing. I know that because I spent one semester in law school before I realized that taking pictures of women removing their bikini briefs is a lot more fun than filing legal ones. So—bottom line—you owe us nude photos. The law is on my side, princess."

Grace shook her head. "I'm no lawyer, but I don't believe that for one second. You can't make me take my clothes off if I don't want to."

Tony spoke sharply. "We can *sue* you, babe. And it wouldn't be nickel and dime shit, either. I'm talking about a multimillion-dollar lawsuit. Because that's what you would be costing us in lost revenue. We stand to make a fortune off this photo spread. Everyone's going to want to see Grace Stevens naked. If you walk out, you *will* be sued. That's not a threat. It's a promise. All I have to do is make one call to our legal department and it's on. Now, all I want to do is take some beautiful, classy pictures of your gorgeous body. They'll be very tasteful. I promise. You can trust me. I wouldn't lie to you. So, I'll ask one more time—please drop your top and let me see those nice big juicy tits of yours. Please."

Just do it. Do the pictures and get the hell out of here before they try to drug you. Because if they drug you, God knows what else they'll do to you. She nodded. "Okay. I'll . . . I'll drop my top."

Tony smiled at her. "That's my girl. I knew you had it in you. Come on. Let's have some fun. Forget about all those negative waves. Let's be positive. Because life's too short to be a Negative Nancy, right?"

Grace rolled her eyes. "Sure." *Yeah. Right. Whatever you say, Tony.*

Tony again started to direct. "So, what I want you to do is, rather than just dropping the top all at once, lower it very gradually. Ever so gradually. Each photo will show a little bit more of your tits until they're fully exposed. It'll be so fucking sexy. Once we get all of the tit shots, we'll get some ass shots. And then we'll have you lie down on the bed and spread your legs for the camera. I also want to get a couple of shots taken from behind, with you on the bed, on all fours. Ass in the air, like you're begging to be mounted. Sound like a plan?"

She hesitantly nodded.

Tony looked back into his camera. "All right. Let's get this done. And, Grace, I want you to give me your best wanton look. I want to see that look that says *I just screwed a room full of truck drivers and now I'm ready for them to bring on the bikers.* Yeah. *That* look. So, give me that and start lowering your top . . . now."

Slowly, she followed Tony's direction. But once again, she stopped and cried. She did her best not to, but she couldn't help it.

Tony became enraged. "Look, *bitch* — I've tried being nice to you, treating you with kid gloves and so forth. But you need to grow the fuck up. Big star or not, you're no different from any other whore who's spread her legs for my camera. So, stop with the goddamn tears! Because you are not going to get any sympathy from me or Kip."

Kip chimed in. "That's right, honey. No sympathy from me, that's for sure. I'm tired of this bullshit. I think you need something in that mouth of yours to shut you up, to keep you from whining." He laughed and grabbed his crotch. "And I got just the thing."

Tony continued with his tirade. "You're getting paid big

bucks to do something so fucking simple. I'm totally fed up with your baby antics. And it's getting to the point where Kip's going to have to hold you down while I pry your goddamn mouth open and shove a couple of those little white pills down your fucking throat. Do you want that? Do you?"

She sobbed. "I want to go home. I want to go back to Mayberry — *now*."

Kip laughed. "Mayberry, huh? You want to screw Andy and Barney, do you? Maybe even Otis the town drunk, too, just for good measure? Might as well do Gomer Pyle while you're at it." He howled.

Tony screamed at her, "Drop your goddamn top! Now, cunt!"

She cried even harder and just stood there.

Tony yelled, "Fuck this shit! No more games, slut!" He stormed away from the camera and into some back room, disappearing from her view.

While he was gone, Kip got up off the couch, shook his finger at her, and admonished, "You'd better start behaving, you little cock tease."

A minute later, Tony returned. He held up a small vial of liquid and a syringe. It was obvious to her that it was some kind of drug. He squinted as he attempted to measure out the correct dose. He told Kip, "Get ready to hold her down. I'm not fucking around with this little whore anymore. This stuff will make her very agreeable to basically anything and it kicks in very quickly — within seconds. It's much better than the little white pills. Stronger and faster."

She started to shake and hyperventilate. *God. They are going to drug and rape me. They are.*

Tony was having difficulty measuring out the medication. "*Damnit.* I forgot my glasses, and it's hard as fuck to see the lines on these syringes. They need to make this shit in large print."

He looked at Grace and smiled an evil smile. "Just give me

a sec to measure this out, angel. Then, I'll be right with you. Trust me. This will make you feel real good, real fast."

Kip laughed a sinister laugh. "Well—well—well. Looks like you're going to do that threesome, after all, honey. I mean—you're not going to be able to say *no*. And in my book, silence equals consent."

Tony was still trying to measure out the dose, but he laughed at Kip's comment and told him, "I like that. Can I use that line? *Silence equals consent.* Yep, that's exactly it. *No* means *no . . .* but silence means *help yourself, boys.*" They both laughed.

Tony looked at Grace and told her, "And this is why we'll need to make a movie of this, Grace, because you won't remember any of it. So, we'll make the film, and you'll have a little souvenir, a keepsake. Something to show your kids one day. So, your children can see what a fucking slut—what an absolute whore—their mom was back in the day."

Tony and Kip cackled.

"I almost have this measured out, bro. Get ready to hold her," Tony casually told Kip.

Grace decided she was going to resist for as long as she could. She knew she couldn't possibly win a fight against the two of them. But she was determined to make them pay the price, determined to go down fighting. *I'll kick them in the balls. When in doubt, go for the balls. That should buy a little bit of time. That and pray for a miracle.* She crossed herself and again prayed silently. *Hail Mary, full of grace. The Lord is with thee. Blessed art thou among women . . .*

Then came a loud pounding on the door.

Tony looked at the door and shouted at the top of his lungs, "Go away! We're working in here, man! There's a shoot in progress!"

The pounding continued. It got louder. Someone was trying to force their way into the studio. Tony again yelled, "Damnit! I said go away!" He looked at Kip. "Who the hell would be pounding on the door like that?"

Kip shrugged. "Fuck if I know."

But next came the sound of the door being battered with something from the outside.

Tony panicked. "Oh, *shit*. Someone's trying to break in. They're actually trying to break the fuck in."

"I'll call security," Kip said.

"Yeah. Get fucking security here ASAP. This shoot's going to shit," Tony lamented. He capped the syringe and placed both it and the vile of drugs in his pocket.

Grace hooked her bikini top back in place. She felt hopeful. The pounding sound continued.

Tony looked at Grace and shook his finger at her. "Stay right where you are, princess. Sit tight. Don't you dare move. Security's going to come and take care of this little distraction. Then we'll get back down to business."

Ten seconds later, there was one final, loud pounding noise. The door flew open.

Danny stood in the doorway, holding a large, silver fire extinguisher. He'd used it on the door like a battering ram. As he walked in, he dropped the extinguisher.

Grace yelled out, "Danny! Oh, God, Danny. *Danny — Danny — Danny. Thank God*! Oh, thank you, God!"

Kip said, "What the fuck's going on?"

Tony looked at Danny, threw up his hands, and said, "A priest? What the fuck's a priest doing at a porn shoot. Did someone call for a damn priest? Because I didn't call for no damn priest."

Danny casually told them, "I, ah, I came to, ah, bless your camera. Yes. That's it, my son. I need to bless that camera of yours. May I see it, please?" He grabbed Tony's camera from the tripod, threw it to the ground, and stomped on it.

Tony was enraged. "The fuck, dude? That camera cost fifty grand. Fitty grand, you dig?"

The expensive camera was in pieces on the floor. Danny looked at it, shrugged, and nonchalantly observed, "Geez, for a fifty-thousand-dollar camera, it sure turned out to be awfully flimsy, didn't it?"

Tony picked up the larger pieces. As he did, he muttered, "Speaking of flimsy, I knew those flimsy doors would end up biting me in the ass. They're paper-thin, for Christ's sake. I told them when they were setting things up. I said — *make sure the studio door is as strong as the door leading into the vault at fucking Fort Knox.* But the cheap-asses skimped. And now my brand new camera is ruined and so is this shoot."

Kip walked over to Danny, threw his hands in the air, and asked, "Who the fuck are you? And how'd you even get into the building?"

Grace yelled out, "His name is Father Daniel O'Connor, and he's a Roman Catholic priest."

Danny stared at her. Their eyes locked. After a few seconds of silence, he finally announced, "No. You're wrong, Grace. I'm not Father Daniel O'Connor. Not anymore." He took off his Roman collar and threw it on the floor, next to the pieces of Tony's busted camera. "I'm *just Danny.*"

Her lower lip quivered. Tears welled up in her eyes. "Well, then, I'm *just Grace.*"

Danny walked over to her. He picked her robe up off the floor and helped her put it on. "So, we're *just Grace and Danny?*" he asked.

"Uh-huh. We're *just Grace and Danny.*" She started to ugly cry. He put his arms around her and held her tight.

"I love you, Grace."

Through her tears, she managed to say, "I love you, Danny."

Cathy Wilton showed up. She looked at Kip. "You called for security, Kip?"

He pointed to Danny. "Yeah. Get that son of a bitch out of here. He ruined the entire photo session. She was finally getting ready to show her tits when this Jesus Freak broke into the studio. And he put the kibosh on everything. Everything."

Cathy just stood idly by with her hands in her pockets. She did nothing.

Tony yelled at her, "What the fuck are you waiting for? You heard Kip. You're the head of Grace's security. So, secure her, already."

Danny kissed Grace on the forehead and again told her, "I love you."

"She looks pretty secure as far as I can see. In fact, she looks more secure than I've ever seen her before," Cathy noted.

Kip screamed at Cathy, "You dumb bitch!" He told Tony, "See, this is what happens when you put women in positions of authority. They get all fucking sentimental. And they don't want to do their jobs anymore. They fuck everything up. Royally."

Danny broke off his embrace with Grace, walked over to Kip, got up in his face, and said, "You know, you should really be more respectful to women."

Kip threw up his hands. "What are you going to do about it, Billy Graham?"

Danny punched him in the stomach. Kip doubled over in pain. He had the wind knocked out of him and was sprawled out on the floor. After several seconds, he finally managed to speak again. He looked up at Danny as he held his stomach. "Goddamn you! You're a man of the cloth. You're not supposed to hit people. I'm reporting you to the Vatican."

"Well, as of this morning, I'm a former man of the cloth. You see, I resigned. I'm no longer a priest. So, it's not fair to hold me to such lofty standards."

Tony picked up his keys and put on a brown leather jacket. "Man, this whole session's a wrap as far as I'm concerned. No big loss, though." He pointed to Grace. "This broad was never really right for the job, anyway. Way too many hang-ups.

Plus, she's too fucking short to be a model. I mean—the chick's five foot nothing. If she were any shorter, she'd be living in Munchkin Land. Little tiny legs on her and whatnot. I mean, sure, she has a pretty face and a killer body and all, but models are supposed to be tall. And have nice, long, luscious legs. Plus, she's twenty-eight. *Twenty freaking eight,* man! She's ancient—way beyond her prime. I like them young. Real young. Young and nubile. I should really talk to the girl who plays the French maid on that TV sitcom, *The Butler Did It.* What the fuck's her name? Oh, yeah—Ginger Collins. She's, like, only twenty-one. Nice long legs on her, too. Yeah. She is *happening.* And she ain't no schizo prude like this one. She's wild and wanton. I heard at a Hollywood party that she's into gangbangs and loves little white pills and injections. Now, that's *my* kind of woman."

Tony walked out of the studio. As he exited, he shook his finger at Grace. "I'm sending you the bill for that camera, pussycat. Fifty freaking grand. You dig? You can pay for your boyfriend's temper tantrum. The whole scene was totally uncool. Very unprofessional on your part. And, I want that fifty grand, like, right away, baby doll. My camera's my life. I'm an *ar-teest,* and I have to get back in the game."

Grace walked to the door, stuck her head out, and yelled at him as he walked down the hall, "You're not getting shit from me. You can sue me for it as far as I'm concerned." She flipped him the bird. "Fuck you, asshole! Eat shit and die!" she screamed at him.

She then turned her attention to Kip, who was still on the floor. She walked over to him and pointed. "And as for you— you're fucking fired. And I'm getting a restraining order against your ugly ass. Because you tried to bargain for sexual favors."

Danny looked at her. "He did *what*?"

Grace walked back over to Danny and put her arm around

him. "He wanted me to sleep with him as part of his severance package. I told him to go lick a dirty toilet seat." She thought for a moment. "Hey, you know what would be really interesting? Talking to other female clients that he's had over the years. I wonder if they've had experiences similar to mine?"

Kip pointed at her. "Aw, fuck you." Then he pointed to Danny. "And fuck you, too." Then he addressed both of them. "And fuck both of you."

He stood up and told Danny, "You can have this silly little bitch as far as I'm concerned. Sluts like her are a dime a dozen. I'll find another protégé."

Danny walked over to Kip and stood toe-to-toe with him. "Nobody calls her a slut. *Nobody.* She's as far removed from a slut as any woman could possibly be."

"Oh, yeah? She's a *slut.* A fucking *slut.* A goddamn *slut.*"

Danny punched him in the mouth. Kip spit up blood and his two front teeth.

"Shit! I just had veneers put in, man." He gathered up his dislodged teeth and put them in his pocket.

Danny pointed to the door. "Get out of here."

Kip dismissively waved his hand at him. "Aw, fuck this shit, man. I'm going to the track. I have a hot tip for the eighth race at *Santa Anita.* It's a sure thing. A colt named *Panty Raid.* Love the name. He's a fifty-to-one shot. And a little birdie whispered in my ear this morning that he can't fucking lose. Of course, I am a little light on funding at the moment. Say, Grace, could you spot me a couple of G's? You know, just for old time sake."

Danny screamed at him, "Out! Get out! Out of this room! Out of her life! Or *I will* hurt you. Badly."

Danny grabbed him by the right arm. He twisted the arm so that it was around Kip's back. He applied pressure. Kip cried out in pain. "Oh, Jesus H. Christ! You're breaking my fucking arm, dude!"

He continued to apply pressure. Kip started to gasp for breath. He opened his mouth, but he wasn't getting any oxygen. "As . . . asthma . . . can't . . . ca . . . ca . . . can't bre—" He used his free hand to point to his inhaler, which was still sitting on the couch. He was trying to speak, but he couldn't even form words.

Danny looked over at the couch and saw the white inhaler but did nothing except slightly loosening his grip on Kip's arm.

Grace called out to Danny, "Do the whole world a favor. Let him just pass out and die. He wouldn't help you. Don't help him. Don't. This is exactly what he deserves. It's justice."

Kip was starting to turn blue.

Danny muttered, "Damnit. I don't know what to do."

Grace walked over to them. She looked Kip in the eye and spat in his face, telling Danny, "You don't need to do anything, babe. Let him go to Hell today."

After a few more seconds, Kip got a faraway look in his eyes.

Danny finally told her, "His inhaler. Go get his inhaler and toss it to me. He's got the *death look* going on. I've seen it before. In Afghanistan."

She stood there but did nothing. She dismissively waved her hand. "*Fuck him.*"

"Come on, Grace. He's turning blue. Give me his inhaler. Snap to it. Now, please."

She rolled her eyes. "Oh, all right. But I'm only doing it because you're asking. I'm not doing it for him." She started walking over to the couch but tripped on her heels. "God, I can't walk on these damn heels. I'm not used to four-inch heels. I'm more comfortable in sneakers."

"The inhaler, Grace. I need his inhaler. *Now.* He's getting ready to checkout. I'm serious. If we wait much longer, it'll be too late."

She took off her heels, threw them down, and walked over to the couch. She picked up the inhaler and tossed it to Danny. "Here you go."

He caught it, took the cap off, and held it up to Kip's mouth. "Open your damn mouth," he commanded.

Kip opened his mouth, and Danny pressed the nozzle thrice, giving him three doses of *Albuterol*.

Within a minute, Kip's breathing and his color returned to normal

"Better?" Danny asked.

Kip nodded. "Better."

"Good," Danny said, as he again tightened his grip on Kip's arm. "*Now*, you can get the fuck out."

"Okay. I'm going — I'm going. Careful now. You're breaking the suit, bro. And this suit cost more than your car."

Danny was walking Kip out the door when Grace stopped him. "No. Not yet. Not yet, babe. Here. Hold him still for me. I have a little something to give him as part of his severance package. A well-deserved bonus."

Danny turned him around and put him in a full nelson so that he was completely exposed and vulnerable.

She picked up her left high heel, put it back on, and walked over to Kip.

"Go for it, honey," Danny told her as he held Kip up for her.

"*Hi-yah!*" she cried out as she delivered a karate kick with her tiny left foot to Kip's groin region. She kicked him with all of her might, didn't hold anything back — nothing at all. After she'd delivered her punishment, she proudly proclaimed, "And *that's* what I do to men who get all obscene with me."

Kip dropped to the ground, assumed the fetal position, and clutched his groin. "Oh, shit. *Goddamn*. I'm never going to be able to have kids."

"And that's a good thing," she told him. "Your ass should

be neutered. No kid should have you for a father."

Danny pulled him to his feet. He twisted Kip's arm around his back and threw him out of the studio.

"Had to take out the trash," he casually noted as he dusted his hands off.

He closed the door and walked back over to Grace.

"Good job, sweetie," he told her. He held up his palm to her. "Here. Give me a high-five."

She took off her one high heel, threw it to the floor, and high-fived him. "That was my *Kung Fu Panda* impression."

He laughed. "That was a pretty good one, too. You definitely turned him into a soprano."

"Yeah. I just gave him a case of the blue balls. The black and blue balls."

They laughed and then embraced.

"Oh, God, Danny. It was awful. They wanted me to do a threesome with them. I told them I'd never do that. So, they were planning on drugging me so they could rape me. Seriously. They were. Those two are evil. They're pure evil."

"They *what*?"

"They were going to drug and rape me. It's true. That Tony character was getting the syringe ready when you busted the door down."

"Oh my God! Yeah — they're evil, all right. And there's a lot of that going around these days. But they're not going to get away with it. Now listen to me — before we go home, we have to see the police. And file a report on both of these pieces of shit. We have to. I know it's not an easy thing to do — but we have to. Okay?"

She shook her head. "I just want to go home. Please take me home. I want to go home now. I want to go back to Mayberry. Right this minute. I want to go back."

"Grace, we're going home. I'm going to take you back to Mayberry. But we have to see the police first. This is serious.

What they tried to do to you is as serious as it gets. We have to report it. We have to. They can't be allowed to get away with this. Okay? We cannot let this go. I'll hold your hand the entire time."

She nodded. "Kay. But then you'll take me back home? As soon as we do that — then you'll take me straight home?"

"I promise. We'll go back home the minute we're finished at the police station."

"Kay. I'll . . . I'll talk to the police because they're doing it to other women, too. They have to be."

He held her tight and nodded. "That's exactly right. They're doing it to other women, too. But you're safe now, baby. Nobody is going to harm you ever again. I won't let them. Never. Ever. This is all my fault. If I hadn't been so stupid and pigheaded, you'd have never been out here, to begin with."

"But I shouldn't have let my temper get the best of me, either. I shouldn't have stormed out the way I did. And I'm so, so sorry that I said I couldn't stand you and that you made me sick. God, I'm so sorry. Please forgive me."

"Let's not even talk about it anymore. The main thing is that you're safe. And we're together. And we'll be together forever. And I will never let anyone hurt you, Grace. *Never.*"

She looked up at him. "But how . . . how did you manage to find me? How did you know that I was here, and how did you get into the building? And you flew all the way out here . . . and —"

"It's a long story. Your friend, Cathy, was a huge help. She's the one who told me where you were and got me into the building. Without her, I don't think I would have found you. At least not in time. But the only thing that really matters is that I did."

"My hero. You were wonderful. That was gallant. Absolutely gallant."

"Just like the Old West. That's just what Marshall Dillon would have done if someone had pulled that shit on Miss Kitty."

"So, you got to live out your cowboy fantasy, huh?"

"Yeah. I guess. But loving you is my real fantasy. *I love you,* Grace Stevens. I love you with all of my heart. My friend, Mike, helped me realize that loving you wasn't against God's Will. It was part of it."

"I love you, too, Danny. *God, I love you.* I always have. From the moment I first laid eyes on you. I loved you at first sight. I did."

"I loved you at first sight, too. And I'm never going to stop loving you, either."

She laughed. "So, I guess we're just like . . . oh, what were their names? The president you were telling me about, the one who asked his future wife to marry him after only one date. Oh, damn. What were their names, Danny?"

"Lyndon and Lady Bird Johnson."

"Yeah. That's them. Lyndon and Lady Bird."

He laughed. "Yep. We're just like them."

They looked into each other's eyes. They both leaned forward, about to press their lips together. At the last second, he pulled back. She shot him an incredulous look.

"Just one moment," he told her.

He reached into his pocket, pulled out a piece of *Hubba Bubba,* and handed it to her. "Here. Chew this."

"Oh my God. You brought the *Hubba Bubba.* You remembered to bring the bubble gum. That's *so* freaking romantic."

"I figured I'd be optimistic," he told her as he winked at her. "And this might be the first time in history that bubble gum's been called *romantic,*" he added.

She unwrapped the gum, put it in her mouth, and chewed.

And once she worked it a bit, they kissed — a passionate but supremely tender kiss. And she passed the bubble gum to him.

When they broke off the kiss, he blew a huge bubble, and she popped it with her French manicured nail. They laughed.

He scooped her up and carried her, noting, "Boy, you really are just a tiny little thing, aren't you?"

In her baby talk voice, she agreed. "Uh-huh. I'm just a *tiny* little thing."

"By the way, we have another dog."

"We do? Is it Shane? Did you adopt little Shane? You know—that little Min Pin that I was talking about. The one who's at the shelter in Easton."

"Yes, I remember Shane. But it's not him. It's another dog. I'll tell you later. It's actually a long, sad story. Too much to go into right now."

"What about Shane? Can we still get him, too? If he's still there, that is."

"He's still there. I looked at *Petfinder* this morning. He's still there and still looking all lonely and scared."

"We have to get him, Danny. We have to. I mean—we can afford three dogs. Easy. So, can we? Can we get him, too?"

He nodded. "Yeah, we can get him, too. I'm sure he'll still be there when we get back. After all, who else besides us is going to want a twelve-year-old Min Pin with epilepsy and no teeth?"

"Exactly. And, I promise, after we get him—that'll be it. Three dogs are enough. I promise we'll draw the line at three . . . at least until the next needy one comes along."

He chuckled and shook his head. "I swear—you have the best heart. I'm a lucky guy. The luckiest guy on the face of the earth. Literally."

As he walked out of the studio with her in his arms, Cathy Wilton stood by and applauded.

"Way to go, Grace. Way to go, girl," she called out. "Godspeed to both of you." Cathy wiped tears from her eyes.

He walked towards the building's exit with her in his arms. She looked up at him. "This is *so An Officer and a Gentleman*. I swear I feel like Debra Winger at the end of that picture." She started singing *Up Where We Belong*.

When they walked out the building's front door, the publisher of *Celebrity Centerfold*, Stan Hicks, came running out after them. He was a man in his 60s. He wore an expensive black suit with white horizontal pinstripes. He had an unlit cigar jutting from his mouth. He'd invested a bundle into this new magazine and had clearly gotten the word that Grace had bailed without revealing anything.

He shook his fist at them. "Grace Stevens — you come back here. We had a deal. Where are you going? You welched on your end of the bargain. You have no idea how much money you just cost me. I'll sue you for breach of contract. You'll be hearing from my lawyers, you lousy bitch!"

Grace stopped singing, looked back at him, smiled, mockingly waved, and replied, "I don't know what to tell you. As of this moment, I'm retired from show business. I'm going back to Mayberry. *Bub-bye.*"

"Going back to *where*? To *Mayberry*?" He dismissively waved his hand at them. "Aw, to hell with you. To hell with both of you."

He carried Grace off the property. She looked at him, reached up, and tenderly caressed his cheek. "Why? Why did you help Kip? He's a piece of shit. He deserved to die. If you had been the one gasping for air, he would have let you die. Believe that. He would have. You're too good, Danny. Way too good."

"Yeah. I know. He did deserve to die. To die alone in a damn porn studio would have been a very fitting demise for him. I thought about it, too. I definitely thought about it. But that's where God's Grace comes in. The Grace of God is a gift. A good and perfect gift. One that I didn't even deserve. But

369

once you receive God's Grace, you have an obligation to pass it on. Even if the person you're passing it to is a complete and total piece of shit."

He changed the subject. Laughing, he told her, "But I'll tell you something, babe—I'm through with Harvey. He tried to swindle me with a Ponzi scheme while you were gone. Me. His best friend. You believe that? I broke up with him. Our bromance is over. You were totally right. So, I'm validating you."

They laughed.

"Oh, God—Harvey. We're really silly, aren't we?" she asked.

"Yeah, we are. But silly's good. Silly can be very good. Seriously, though, you're a good judge of character, Grace Stevens. And I know you're always looking out for me. Which is just one of the ten billion reasons that I love you. And want to be with you. You and only you. Forever."

"And I want to be with you forever, my Danny Boy." She started singing *Danny Boy* to him.

She didn't even get a chance to finish the first verse. He stopped and passionately kissed her.

When they stopped kissing, she told him, "Seriously, you might have actually saved my life today."

"Then we're even. Because you already saved mine."

Danny called the police. San Fernando PD showed up. They went to the precinct office, and Grace gave detectives a statement. Danny held her hand the entire time.

After they finished, arrangements were made for them to board her private jet at LAX.

When they got to the airport, they got out of her black chauffeured-driven limo. He scooped her up and carried her across the tarmac.

As he carried her up the plane's steps, she looked up at him, brushed his hair with her hand, and said, "I *love* you.

We're going to have a good life together. The world can't break us. It tried. It did its damnedest. We took its best shot. And we're still standing. It's the world that's lying flat on its ass, down for the count. And every day, our love will grow stronger." She started to cry as she continued. "The time will flow. And the love will grow. And that love is the only real anecdote for this insane thing we're going through called *life*. Okay. No more speeches. I'm off my soapbox. The only thing left to do is to get me out of this crazy, *phony*, screwed-up town. Take me back to Mayberry, babe. Please. I want to go home. Because I hate LA. I fucking hate it. So, goodbye yellow brick road. Hello, Mayberry. Take me home. Please take me home."

So, he took her home. To Mayberry. To the *real-life May-berry*.

EPILOGUE: NO OTHER MESSAGE, NO OTHER QUESTION

After Grace came forward, the floodgates opened. Numerous women came forward to claim that Kip Darby had sexually assaulted them or attempted to gain sexual favors in exchange for his representation. A subsequent investigation led to him being arrested and charged with various sex crimes, including first-degree sexual assault. The investigation also, incidentally, revealed that Darby had conspired to fix horse races at various southern California racetracks. For that activity, he was charged with racketeering. He was arrested and sent to the *Los Angeles Men's Central Jail* to await trial in lieu of posting bail. He faced the prospect of up to forty years in prison. But he died in jail before he ever went to trial. He had an asthma attack, and his cellmate had hidden his inhaler from him. All because Kip had allegedly stolen a pack of contraband cigarettes from the guy the previous day.

Police raided Tony Tobias's Burbank studio and found a stash of illegal narcotics, including *Rohypnol, GHB,* and *Ketamine*, all commonly used *date rape* drugs. They also found pornographic photographs of underage girls, some as young as twelve. Women gradually came forward to report that Tobias had drugged them during their photo sessions. Some reported that they'd been sexually assaulted or even raped during their encounters with him. He was arrested and charged with numerous drug and sex crimes, including rape and child pornography. He was also sent to the *Los Angeles Men's*

Central Jail to await trial. He was also held in lieu of bail and faced the prospect of up to seventy-five years in prison. When other inmates found out that he was a child pornographer, they severely beat him in his tier's common area. Numerous inmates repeatedly struck Tobias in the head with bars of soap wrapped in bath towels. He was left severely brain-damaged as a result—a vegetable.

Celebrity Centerfold Magazine ceased operations after the scandal broke. It went out of business without ever producing so much as a single issue. After the news got out that the magazine's head photographer had been arrested on an array of sex charges, no one was willing to pose for them, not even the C-listers. And Stan Hicks never even tried to sue Grace for breach of contract. After the scandal broke, he realized he had no case. He died of a heart attack while visiting a Nevada brothel shortly after the magazine folded.

On Friday, Danny and Grace attended Mike Jameson's viewing and funeral. They brought Jake with them. A small security detail accompanied them to keep the fans and curiosity seekers away. The entire town came out. It was a hero's funeral, with full military honors.

At The First Methodist Church, Mike was laid out for his viewing. He wore his t-shirt that said, *Smile, God Loves You*, and an old pair of blue jeans. In his hands, he clutched a copy of *The Little Shepherd* magazine. Pinned to his shirt were his various military medals.

Danny carried Jake up to the casket for him to see his daddy. Grace stood next to him with her arm around both of them. Danny peered into the coffin. He cried and whispered to him, "Thank you for everything. You showed me Grace. You showed me the Grace of God, buddy. I could never possibly repay you for that. Goodbye, my friend. Goodbye, Mike . . . or whoever you were."

Grace sang at the service. Beautifully, she sang *Mother's*

Pride, the song that meant so much to Danny. A violin and a piano accompanied her. A tear rolled down her cheek. But she held it together until after she finished the song.

And she sang not just for Mike Jameson but also for Benny Williams and for Steve Piatelli. For Christopher Wayne Hill Jr, for James *Willy Wonka* Balado, and Bobby Morgan. For Ricky Jarvis, Randy McClinton, and for Danny Michaels. And for her own Danny, too. She sang for all the kids who didn't come home and for all the ones who came home scarred, both literally and figuratively. She sang for those whose names were on memorial walls. And for all those who risked having their names on those walls. She sang for the heroes. The real heroes. The ones who didn't need a slick Hollywood PR machine. The ones who lived up to it. When she finished, for several seconds, there was silence in the Church. Deafening silence.

Over at the cemetery, the sun shone brightly, but it was windy. A Marine Corps Honor Guard carried Mike's flag-draped casket to his final resting place. They fired three volleys. A large, pristine American flag presented by one of the Honor Guard members snapped in the breeze. After a drum roll, the North East High School Band played a slow version of *The Star-Spangled Banner* and *The Marine Corps Hymn*. Danny smartly saluted during the playing of the Anthem and a tear rolled down his cheek. Bagpipers played *Amazing Grace*. And the Marine bugler played *Taps*. Then they put him in the ground and covered him with dirt. And that was that.

They started house hunting in North East. They found a nice, historic home that dated back to the Antebellum Era. It was just the kind of place that Grace had always wanted. Classy and old. It was big, too. The asking price was a mere six-hundred grand, and some change. It was perfect for them. It had a nice backyard for the dogs to play in. It was good for kids, too. Plenty of trees to climb, and it backed right up to the river, so they could still have their beach parties. Not a Malibu mansion, but that was okay. In fact, it was better than okay. It was Mayberry. It was a whole world away from smog, phonies, sleazy managers, and pornographers. Grace offered the full asking price. She didn't want to bother with dickering and negotiating. That stuff wasn't important to her. It had never been. In a month's time, they could move in.

Over the next several weeks, they mapped out their new life together. They made basic plans, via Grace's attorney, to start *The Benny Williams No Greater Love Foundation* to benefit Gold Star families. She named Danny as the CEO. It was to be up and running within six months. Also, a college fund worth two-hundred-thousand dollars was set up for a little girl named Kaitlyn Balado, twelve, of Akron, Ohio. It was all done quietly behind the scenes. No announcements were coming from publicists and so forth. Grace didn't want anyone to know that her money was bankrolling it. Because — *where your money is, there will your heart be, also.*

For her part, Grace took some time off to decide what she wanted to do — vocationally speaking — with the next fifty years or so of her life. The only thing she knew for sure was that she didn't want to be involved in show business ever again. She also vowed never again to set foot in LA. To her, the City of Angels was a Devil's Den. Too many bad memories.

She was leaning towards starting a program called *Pets For Vets*, a nonprofit that would seek to place pets residing in animal shelters with veterans who could benefit from a companion animal's friendship.

She was also interested in using her contacts in the entertainment industry to produce a documentary that would air on *PBS* during the holiday season. The inspiration for the film came from Danny's recounting of the death of Danny Michaels. The working title for the project was — *I Won't Be*

Home For Christmas. She envisioned it as an hour-long special, featuring Gold Star families' remembrances, recalling how their loved ones had celebrated the holidays. And it would detail the impact that their deaths had on the families themselves, specifically during the Christmas season.

Once they got settled, they visited the *Eastern Shore Animal Rescue League* and adopted Shane. The old, sick Min Pin. The one nobody else wanted. Grace doted over him, gave him his daily meds. She took him everywhere because, well, because that's the kind of woman Grace was.

Danny still had flashbacks. Nearly every night. Almost every night, he relived the horror that was the Korengal Valley. The Valley of Death. The difference now was that he had someone by his side, someone to hold him, someone to sing him to sleep. Someone to cry with him. Because every night, the Grace of God was with him. The Grace of God would be by his side forevermore. And the Grace of God was stronger than even the hell of war.

They had plans to get married later that summer. A wedding Saturday within the month of June. Their wedding song was to be *Can't Help Falling in Love.* "It's going to be more beautiful than freaking *Crazy Rich Asians*," she declared. Danny, for his part, wanted Toby Keith's *Should Have Been A Cowboy* played, too. Grace said, "We'll see."

So — Grace and Danny — well, they made out all right. She loved him. He loved her. And they both loved Tippy, Jake, and Shane. And Tippy, Jake, and Shane loved them. They all loved and were loved. And if there was a message in all of it, maybe that was it. And maybe it was the only message worth sharing. And maybe it was the answer to the only question worth asking. Because they weren't Grace Stevens, pop superstar, and Daniel O'Connor, Catholic priest anymore. They had become just Grace and Danny. They were finally — *just Grace and Danny.* And that was enough. More than enough.

About the Author

Arthur Archambeau lives in the United States. He is the author of *Her Innocent Marine* (2018), *Caged Lions Never Roar* (2019), *Sail Away* (2020), and *Purple Hearts* (2021).

www.ingramcontent.com/pod-product-compliance
Lightning Source LLC
Chambersburg PA
CBHW061305170626
46817CB00001B/63